L.A. CLAYTON

The Angel Project
Copyright © 2022 L.A. Clayton
Cover Art by Becky Monson

This book is a work of fiction. The names, characters, places, and incidents are the products of the author's imagination or are used fictitiously. Any resemblance to actual events, business establishments, locales, or persons, living or dead, is entirely coincidental.

All rights reserved. Without limiting the rights under the copyright reserved above, no part of this publication may be reproduced, stored in, or introduced into a retrieval system, or transmitted in any form or by any means (electronic, mechanical, photocopying, recording, or otherwise) without prior written permission of the copyright owner. The only exception is brief quotations in printed reviews. The scanning, uploading, and distribution of this book via the Internet or via any other means without the permission of the copyright owner is illegal and punishable by law.

Dedication

To my dad, the man who has filled my life with humor, love, and oregano oil.

ONE

I STOPPED COLD IN THE street the first time I saw an ad for my novel. It was a sign in a bookstore window: *The highly anticipated* Chipped *by Channing Walker coming soon!* I paused for a beat and tried to garner some excitement, like a normal person, but the only thing I felt was dread.

That said, the publisher was staying true to their word, organizing a massive ad campaign. I swallowed and started to walk away, but then turned back and forced myself to take a picture with my phone to post to the social media accounts my publisher had me signed up for. I'd never had a personal social media account—I didn't have enough friends to justify it. I had exactly two friends: Darcy, who I lived with, and Cole, who was over so often he could be considered a roommate by common law. And since those two always knew what was going on in my life, it seemed redundant to post about it.

I saw another ad on a taxi as I made my way home from the grocery store. Any normal person would have been overjoyed. But I wasn't normal—my parents had made certain of that. I never thought I'd see my family name in an advertisement that wasn't followed with: *Wanted—please contact police.*

The second ad had my heart speeding up, and not in the good way. My palms started to get sticky with sweat. I wished then, more than ever, I'd used a pen name; that I hadn't been so eager to get the book out there with my name attached; that I hadn't been so desperate to see if there was anyone else like me. It was more stressful than I could have imagined. Would anyone look me up? Would they see not only my sordid past but my family's as well? I swallowed and looked around, scared someone would recognize me, which was ridiculous considering I wasn't pictured on the poster. But if I'd learned anything in my relatively short existence, it was that fear wasn't rational.

I walked a few blocks down the street and hid in an alcove between buildings. I took my phone out of my bag and called Walton & Barker. When the cheerful receptionist answered, I replied, "This is Channing Walker, author of *Chipped.* I need to speak with Harris Green immediately." Harris was my contact within the publishing house. I hadn't had an agent when I was picked up, so they'd assigned me to the fifty-something, gray-haired man. He was kind and friendly and I liked him immediately. He was my advocate in the publishing process, and he really made me feel like he'd go to the mat for me. He probably wouldn't, considering his paycheck was signed by Walton & Barker and not me, but he was good at making me feel like he cared.

The receptionist's voice came over the line, "Oh, of course, Ms. Walker. Have you seen your advertisements popping up? We're so excited about the way they came out. I read your book last week, and I just want to say that it's the best thriller I have ever read. Like, seriously."

I swallowed and ducked farther into the alcove. My voice was small when I said, "Oh, thank you. That's"—I cleared my throat—"that's very nice."

She lowered her volume. "Like, seriously, though—it felt so real." She lowered her voice again, to little more than a whisper, "I've heard about this sort of thing in real life, ya know? Like, do you think it could be real? I mean, do you know someone in the FBI or something? Because, like, there are always conspiracy theories about this sort of thing, but the way you write about it . . . I'm just more convinced than ever that this is a thing." My palms got slicker, and my very expensive cell phone felt like it was going to drop to the sidewalk. I'd never cared that much for praise—it made me nervous. I was already anxious, and this conversation, if you could call it that, as I had barely murmured a word, ratcheted it up a few notches. I could hear her smacking her gum over the line, and the sound reverberated in my head. It was like nails on a chalkboard.

All I wanted to do was end this conversation. "It's pure fiction. Is Harris Green there?"

"Yeah, of course. But, for real, like, how did you come up with the idea? What inspired you? 'Cause that's crazy, you know what I mean?" Smack, smack, smack.

I almost hung up. But I really needed to talk to Harris before it was too late, even though it probably already was. "I got the idea from a dream. It's in my bio. I'm short on time—is Harris there?"

I must have sounded as annoyed as I was because the inept receptionist seemed audibly miffed. And with a professional voice suddenly loud and sweet as sugar, she responded with, "Of course, Ms. Walker. Hold one moment, please."

The phone blessedly switched to elevator music. But after about five minutes of being on hold, I cursed and hung up. Then called back.

"Thank you for calling Walton and Barker publishing, this is Ashley. How may I direct your call?"

"Yes, hi, Ashley. This is Channing Walker again. I've been on hold for Harris Green for several minutes. He never picked up." Nor had it gone to voice mail, which means Ashley had never really put me through to Harris—I knew how it worked.

"Oops. Let's try again, shall we?"

Elevator music, this time for a total of two minutes. I was about to lose it when the phone finally began to ring. "Harris Green."

"Harris, it's Channing Walker."

"Channing," his voice rang out, and I could hear the smile in it. "Our rising star! How may I be of service?"

It took me a second to respond; after all the fuss of getting Harris on the line, I'd momentarily forgotten my purpose in calling. But it hit hard when I saw yet another cab drive by with my book cover blaring from the digital taxi topper. "I'm going to get right to the point. I've seen my ads starting to pop up, and they look great. Better than great, really." I tucked a strand of my dark-brown hair behind my ear and cleared my throat. "That said, I'm hoping that it's not too late to use a pen name."

THE ANGEL PROJECT

I couldn't see his face, but his tone betrayed his surprise when he said, "Why in the world would you want to do that?"

"I'm just uncomfortable using my real name, and I didn't realize how uncomfortable until I saw it in print." You know, that and the fact that I came from a long line of murderous criminals. And I may not have disclosed that when I signed my contract. No big deal. In my defense, they didn't specifically ask, and no one just offers that kind of information.

Harris cleared his throat. "Channing, I'd love to help you here, but I'm afraid it's much too late. It's in your contract that you may only use a pen name if you choose to write in another genre. Add to that the fact that we have taken out ads and billboards and sent the posters to every bookstore in the country, as well as bookstores in some of the bigger cities around the world. I'm afraid the train has left the station, so to speak."

I blew out a breath. I knew he was going to say that, but I had to try. I nodded, even though he couldn't see me.

"What is this all about, Channing?" I could hear the genuine concern in his voice. "Are you concerned that the paparazzi is going to start chasing you down? We did tell you you'd be famous, after all. Rest assured that authors' names become famous, but hardly anyone ever recognizes them on the street. Your life will likely stay as anonymous as it is now. Even if you become a number one *New York Times* bestselling author overnight, you'll still be able to go to restaurants and malls without any kind of fanfare at all."

I knew that authors in general rarely got recognized; that wasn't what I was afraid of. I was afraid of being looked into, of my past coming back to haunt me. This was probably the last chance I'd get to set the record straight with Walton & Barker, but there was a part of me that was terrified that if they knew who I really was, they would drop my contract. I needed that money, and more than that, I needed the book to be out there on the wind, where no one could call it back. I sighed, "It's okay, Harris. I think I'm just freaking out a little. I figured it was too late to change to a pen name, but I thought I'd try on the off chance that it might still be possible."

"If it's any consolation, pen names rarely hide an author's real identity. They always get found out."

That made sense, and did relieve some of my stress, but also added some in a different way. When I'd decided to use my name on the book, it had been with full knowledge of the possibilities, but I had been reckless then. Now that I had some money in my bank account from my signing bonus, and the very real possibility of making a lot more, I realized that maybe I wanted that life. The life that was easy. Once that book hit the shelves, the easy life would be a thing of the past for me. Unless it totally bombed and no one actually read it. But that had never been the point of publishing *Chipped*. I sighed. "That actually is helpful. Thanks, Harris. The ads really do look great. I think I'm just nervous."

We said our goodbyes and I hung up. I leaned back against the cool brick of the building and closed my eyes for a moment. This was it. People were going to know who I was. They would know who my father was. I'd known when I wrote that stupid book that it would be a hit—I could feel it in my bones. There was one other thing I could feel in my bones: its release would change my life forever.

TWO

I DROPPED MY GROCERIES OFF at my apartment and instead of signing back on to my very exciting job at the call center, I threw on some leggings and sneakers and walked in the crisp early-autumn day to my favorite place—the gym.

I wasn't one of those LA people who lived to sweat and ate only organic vegetables with the occasional side of activated almonds. This gym was something different entirely. It was where I learned to fight my demons. Where I learned to defend myself, and where I learned that I was worth defending.

I walked in the door and shouted, "Anton!"

Mike, the owner, squinting to see me clearly, shouted back from the ring, "Anton's not here, Walker. You weren't due in for a couple of hours." He looked at me, assessing my need for some stress relief, lifted his eyebrows, and said, "If you need to blow off some steam, I'd suggest one of the punching bags. Or you could always hop in here with Beef." He used his thumb to point behind him to Brady "the Beef" Caper. At 6'3" and weighing in at

THE ANGEL PROJECT

a whopping 295 pounds, he wasn't the biggest UFC fighter in history, but he was up there. And the guy was agile. I'd never seen someone his size with that kind of thick-roped muscle move like he did. His abs, which were always purposely on display, were the defined in the extreme; that was no small feat when one was just shy of 300 pounds. Beef was in a category of his own, and he was Mike's prizefighter. He was also far too gentlemanly to give me a good fight. Not that I could take a punch from him—I'd probably die. It didn't matter, though; if I got in the ring to fight him, he'd turn and leave. He wouldn't even humor me.

"Ha. I'll take the punching bag." Mike and Beef both smiled at me and went back to training. The gym was pretty quiet this time of day, and I had my pick of equipment. I threw my bag down on the bench that lined the back wall. There were no lockers here, and the only bathroom was unisex, which, in a gym that trained far more men than women, made for a ripe-smelling space I used only when it was an absolute emergency. The gym was far from fancy; it didn't look like one of those nice, glossy MMA gyms that were rustically beautiful. This place was just rustic. But it was also cheap, and that was the only reason I could afford to train here. Mike could've churched it up a bit—with more than a few prizefighters training here, they could most definitely afford it. But I think that the guys liked it on the gritty side; it was real, rugged, and uncultured.

I pulled my hand wraps and a hair band out of my bag, threw my long dark hair up into a top knot, and then began the process of wrapping up my knuckles and wrists.

Over the three years I'd been training here, I'd become a much more skilled fighter, but I still wrapped my wrists like a novice—for which I was teased endlessly. But my hands were small, so I could get a good wrap on both my knuckles and wrists with a classic 180-inch wrap. Frankly, there was a life outside mixed martial arts, and I wanted to make sure that I maintained the use of my hands.

My first interval of hits was like coming home. Most of the time it washed my mind clean of all the horror I'd seen in my short life. But after seeing my name in lights, there was no washing away the past today. Instead, the training allowed me to channel my anger, which was something I desperately needed. My twenty-five years of life felt like three times that many years. There were certainly moments where I thought I would never escape my past, that I could never amount to more than the terrible cards I'd been dealt. Writing a book and getting said book published proved that false. I still felt like an impostor. There's nothing like watching your father murder your mother, right in front of your eyes, to scar you for life.

I was only eight when it happened. My life changed forever, and not just in the obvious ways, like the fact I no longer had a mother. My father went directly to jail to await trial and eventually received a life sentence. I went directly to foster care. No child can be prepared for that kind of assault on their security. No child of eight quite understands the magnitude of the statement, "No family member is willing to take you, so you will have to go into the system." No child raised by two parents who seemed to love each other up until the day her world went black, can fully understand that once she entered the foster care system, no other parents would want to take on a little girl whose father killed her mother. No couple wants a child with that kind of baggage, even if she's pretty—or so I was told. But then, because of the abandonment, the shame, the utter loss and despair, out of necessity and the base need to survive, that child becomes the exact thing everyone feared.

I sucked in a breath at the ache in my knuckles and stepped back from the bag, using my forearm to push my sweaty bangs back from my forehead. I'd gotten lost in my thoughts and had gone too long that round. If Anton were here, he'd be yelling at me. He'd also be trying to get me to talk about my feelings. Anton believed in the power of a good punch, but he also believed in therapy and thought I should get some. He knew more about me than most. Many of the things he taught me required trust. But I was little more than a scared and scarred alley cat when we met—skittish, scrappy, and mean. It had taken years, but he traded me secret for secret to get me to talk. He knew quite a bit about me now; there were some things he knew that even my roommate, Darcy, didn't know.

I heard a throat clear behind me. I'd have recognized that sound in my sleep. I didn't even turn around. "Mike called you, didn't he?"

"He said you looked ready for a fight."

I turned then and looked into Anton's stunning blue eyes and smiled. "You shouldn't have come in early for me. I'm cool with hitting the bag; I know it's not my scheduled time with you." I used my forearm to wipe the sweat from my forehead once again. "I just needed to blow off some steam."

One side of Anton's mouth curved up. "It wouldn't have to do with your name and book cover taking up the biggest window in the biggest bookstore in Los Angeles, would it?" I cringed. "That's what I thought." He stepped a little closer, and I could smell the familiar spicy notes of his cologne. "Am I going to have to read your book with the masses, Walker? Are you seriously not going to give me an advanced copy? After all we've been through?"

I smiled almost shyly, a feeling only Anton brought out in me—it annoyed me as much as it endeared me to him. I wasn't interested in romance of any kind; my life was a big enough mess without the added drama. And one thing was certain: if I was interested in a relationship, it wouldn't be with Anton—a self-described womanizer. And yet the feelings of attraction plagued me at times. I hypothesized the reason for that was the safety in it. Neither of us wanted a relationship—we could be friendly, flirt on occasion, and it would never go further than that. We both ultimately wanted the same thing: to stay single. I tipped my head to the side and said, "I wasn't lying when I told you that no one has read it aside from me and my publisher. Not even Darcy. I'm not giving out advanced copies." I held up a hand to thwart his objection. "I'm not even sure I legally can at this point." I paused, the image swimming through my mind of Anton reading my book. It made my nerves fire off. "Anton, if you read it after it comes out, I don't want to know what you think. Especially if you hate it." I rethought that last statement.

THE ANGEL PROJECT

"You know what, don't even tell me if you've read it. I don't want to know."

Anton's smile widened, and I finally got a view of his straight, ultra-white teeth. He had a beautiful mouth, a beautiful face—not that it mattered. He got up real nice and close and enunciated slowly, "I'm going to tell you what page I'm on every single day you come in for training. Then I'm going to pepper you with nonstop questions about the ending." His smile widened and he brought his face closer to mine. "Nonstop." His lips popped on the *p*.

I punched him in the stomach. He laughed because his stomach was the equivalent of a brick wall—he probably didn't even feel the hit. He put his hands on my shoulders and spun me around. "Take it out on the bag, Walker."

And so I did. After several intervals, mostly to the sound of Anton's jeering, I was dripping with sweat. After a particularly hard set, he held out my water and quipped, "Nice work, C. Ready for the ring?"

I nodded while breathing heavily and drank deeply while we walked over. "Hope you're not too tired, Walker, because we're just getting started today." He flicked my shoulder. "You don't give me any special treatment with your book, I won't give you any in the gym."

"Ha! I'll pass on your 'special treatment,' thank you, very much." Anton's idea of special treatment was to make you work harder and get stronger. The man never let up, no matter how much he liked you.

He shot me a wolfish grin, and I knew I'd stepped in

it. "Oh, sweet Channing, you've never had my special treatment. But I guarantee, if you had, you would *never* pass it up."

I laughed and rolled my eyes at the same time. "Still a hard pass, A."

"Wasn't an offer, C. I just wanted to make sure you knew what you're missing out on, that's all. But if it's an offer you're looking for—"

I looked at him pointedly and made a show of touching my finger to the ring. Anton cut off his speech immediately. He shook his head and gave me a smile that said, *I'll get you back for that.*

There was a hard and fast rule at Mike's Punching Bag: the ring was sacred. Once one entered the ring, all joking—or in Anton's and my case, flirting—stopped abruptly. Everyone here joked around and laughed a lot, and we also razzed like there was no tomorrow, but once you entered the ring, the games were over. The ring was where the real learning happened, and it was serious business.

I entered over the ropes because I'm a female in America, and Anton jumped over after me. "All right, Walker, we're hitting it hard today. We'll start out with a few classics, but after that, I'm coming at you in all different ways, and you need to use your training to figure out how to stop me."

I nodded, trying to plan for every possible attack but knowing it wasn't possible. I couldn't plan for Anton's attacks any more than I could a stranger's on the street, which was exactly the point. He stepped forward at lightning speed, and before I could decide where he was going with it, his hands were around my neck, squeezing hard. I would bruise from this, but this was the type of training I had asked for. It was what I craved. Anton knew I hated this maneuver—it was why he did it every time, though he didn't often start with it. I hated it, but it was also the first thing I had wanted to learn. I'd witnessed my father choke the life out of my mother, and every night that I had relived that nightmare, I'd woken with a greater desire to never let anyone do the same to me. I didn't have that nightmare anymore, and it was in large part due to the education I'd received from Anton. I could stop someone from choking me from the front, behind, or the side in less than a couple of seconds.

While I struggled for breath, I put my hands up, palms open, on the outside of his elbows. There were several different maneuvers that could get me out of this, and they all depended on Anton's defense of my offense. With my hands up and open, I could ram my palm into his nose or gouge his eyes with my fingers and nails. If he blocked me on one side, I could knee him in the groin and then finish with my assault on his face. I decided to start with the groin because it was important to switch things up. He wore protection with me because he didn't want me to hold back, so I didn't. I rammed my knee up, and then when he doubled over, as an attacker who wasn't wearing protection would do, I brought my hand up to strike him in the nose; this I didn't do with full force, just enough to get him to break his hold on my neck.

He stepped away from me. "Good." Then without a second's rest, he grabbed the top knot I'd thrown my hair in earlier and pulled. It hurt my neck, and my head. I put one hand over the other and used the double palm strike to snap his head back, then finished with a knee to the groin.

When a woman was defending herself against a man, the groin was always the endgame. It held the highest potential for pain with the lowest amount of required force. I'd learned early on that my strength against a man like Anton was practically nonexistent. My strongest punch would do nothing to stop, or even slow him, unless it was just the right way to just the right place. I was 5'7", and regardless of how much I worked out, I was often described as willowy. I was muscular, but long and lean, far from bulky. Anton was 6'2" and a powerhouse of muscle. I had to be smarter and faster, because stronger wasn't an option.

We worked on my defensive moves until I was so tired I thought I might pass out. Only when I was starting to fail did Anton finally end our session. That was another rule here: it wasn't over until your trainer said it was. When the schedule allowed, Anton liked to work past the point of tired; he opined the importance of being able to fight well even when you weren't at your peak. Although I didn't like it much in the moment, it was undeniable that my stamina increased with each training session. Anton was a veteran, and he often used the phrase "Pain is weakness leaving the body." At first, I thought the quip was rather motivational, but I now hated it. Partly because he overused it, but also because it was only true with regard to building strength through exercise. In all other ways, pain was not weakness—pain was part of the human experience, and it didn't necessarily make you stronger. Sometimes it just hurt.

Out of the ring, Anton held up his hand for a high five. "Good work today, Walker. That double palm strike was masterful."

I smiled. Still trying to catch my breath, I gasped, "You should have worn your training mask; your face is covered in smeared half-dried blood. It's making me feel like a real winner, and I know how much you hate that."

Anton laughed and rubbed at his face. There really wasn't that much dried blood, but there was some, and I enjoyed the fact that I was the one who had put it there. Not in a sick, sadistic way, but in a self-satisfied way. Anton only wore a training mask with me when we were working specifically on face moves—otherwise he deemed it unnecessary. I had proved him wrong; I was a worthy opponent. "Yeah, yeah, Channing. I'll admit, you got me pretty good there." He winked. "Bet it won't happen next time."

I laughed, sat down, and began unwrapping my wrists while looking up at him. "Challenge accepted."

I grabbed my bag and shoved my things inside—no need to make it pretty. It all needed to be washed; I was literally soaked with sweat. But all my worries had taken a back seat for the last two and a half hours, and that was exactly what I'd come for in the first place. Mike's Punching Bag never disappointed.

I waved at Mike and Anton as I walked to the door. "Thanks for the beating, Anton. See ya, Mike."

THREE

I WALKED OUT INTO THE welcoming cool of the late-evening air. Instead of walking home I decided to grab a rideshare back to my apartment—a thing I almost never did. But I was tired, and I had some money in my bank account for a change.

The silver Honda Civic approached Mike's, and I waved, letting the driver know I was the one he was looking for. He tried to speak to me in Spanish, but I only knew just enough to get by. I told him so, and we were pretty quiet the rest of the ride.

Due to the infamous Los Angeles traffic, the drive to my apartment from Mike's took longer than the walk. The driver took the shortest route, though I would have paid extra for a different one. The short route took us through Skid Row, an area of LA that I was more familiar with than I'd like to have been.

The high from my workout dimmed substantially during the drive through the dirty, rat-infested streets. The driver cursed when he had to stop short because a completely naked man, high as a kite, ambled out into the road. Only a few seconds later, when a child darted onto the street, he hit the brakes hard enough for my seat belt to catch and constrict my torso firmly against the seat. "*Lo siento.* This place is loco."

I nodded. "It's no problem." I didn't see this area of town so much as crazy as I did sad. Though it was really both crazy *and* sad, as well as dirty, desperate, and scary as hell. My gut churned at the memories that plagued me every time I made my way through these streets. I knew that if I rolled down the window, I would hear babies crying, adults screaming, the almost constant assault of car horns, and likely a siren or two blaring somewhere in the area. And among the noise would be the mumbling of the psychotic and intoxicated. Always the mumbling. That was the noise I hated the most. The sound that haunted my dreams. The sound that the woman in my neighboring tent made for the eighteen wretched months I lived there.

Eighteen months of hell on earth. Before Skid Row, I thought being in the foster care system was the worst thing that could happen to a person. I was wrong. After I'd aged out, I'd been basically let loose. Turning eighteen and moving out on your own was supposed to be like a bird being freed from the nest, flying on spread wings, the wind in its face, having been taught all of the things necessary to sustain life and flourish in the great unknown.

Turning eighteen and aging out of the system was a lot more like someone taking out the trash. That trash was never meant to thrive or survive, to become a meaningful part of society. It was meant to go to the landfill and be buried by more trash, so the world would no longer be forced to see it and be guilted into feeling something. On the rare occasion a piece of that trash jumped from the pile and made something of itself, and when it did, the state was lauded, the reformed trash held up as an example of what was possible, probable even, with a little elbow grease and hard work.

The foster system had the decency to make sure I'd had a place to live after aging out. And by make sure, I mean the only thing I had to show them was a legitimate address. I had one—I was going to rent a room with Trish, another girl from the system, a person I thought was my friend. I didn't know what real friendship was at the time, so the bar was low. In any case, the house was dilapidated and in a terrible area of Los Angeles, but beggars couldn't be choosers. Trish and I were going to be sharing a tiny room—more like a large walk-in closet, as it had no windows and no door, just a dirty little curtain hung in the opening that separated us from the hall. We had no money and no jobs, but the guy who owned the house didn't mind. He said we could move in and start looking for jobs—he was giving us the first month of rent for free, and he'd told Trish he might even have some work for us.

Things had seemed like they were falling into place. I was going to be free of the foster care system and able to live my life. I had no idea what I wanted to do with my life, but having a roof over my head seemed like a good place to start. What I didn't know at the time was that almost any other roof, and perhaps no roof at all, would have been better than the house we were moving into.

On moving day, when we'd been dropped off by a cab, paid for by the state, I smelled it before we even walked in the house. That telltale cat urine—that wasn't actually cat urine—smell, mixed with a healthy dose of rotten egg. The windows were covered, and there were fans blowing air out of the basement egress windows, which were the only brand-new part of the run-down and neglected property. They had several ADT signs and stickers arranged around the porch, and there were a couple of cameras placed on the front of the house as well as one around the side. I knew the signs; I'd lived for six months with a foster family whose next-door neighbor's house smelled just like this. I sucked in a deep breath of the acrid air and stopped and glared at Trish, my mouth in a tight line. To her credit, she looked a little sheepish when she eked out, "It was the only place I could find." I continued to glare, and she went on, her cheeks pinked. "Look, Channing, we're foster kids with no jobs. It's either this or the streets. We'll make enough money here to get on our feet, and then we can move into a real place."

I knew I should have chosen the streets; I chanted it to myself like a mantra, over and over as we walked toward the door, and I vowed to stay there only long enough to find another place—one week. A month tops.

Turns out that places to live were hard to come by when you had no family, no job, no credit history, and no money. The only place to live was a meth lab, which counted on the freeloading residents to make deliveries. That was the work the owner had for us: we were dealing meth.

Jeremiah, the owner of the house, was a tall, skinny, fair-skinned man in his early thirties who had only half a mouthful of blackening teeth. Every day he wore a dirty white tank top with equally dirty jeans, a brown weaved belt holding his oversize pants at his waist. He had a few poorly done tattoos running down his arms as well as what I could see of his back, and his hair was a mousy-brown buzz. He was mean, at times viciously so, and one of the least attractive people I'd ever come across. Trish was smitten with him. She had the classically low self-esteem of an unwanted foster kid, and in her tainted world vision, a man who ran his own business and owned his own house in LA was quite the catch.

The upside of their quick coupling was that I got my own room, at least for a little bit. The downside was that within a few short months, I watched Trish, an already damaged and sad girl, diminish to little more than a husk of a person. She started getting high regularly and retreated into herself, barely talking to me, or anyone else for that matter. Originally, I'd wanted to stay for her, so that she wouldn't be alone in that horrible house, but my patience was running thin. Even still, I continued to hold out hope that maybe I could help her. But one day when I ran into her in the hall with her sunken eyes, thick with dark circles, and graying front teeth, and she didn't even recognize me, I knew that ship had sailed. It was time to leave.

Unfortunately, the very next day, before I had my stuff together, the Sheriff's Proactive Methamphetamine Laboratory Investigative Team decided that it was time to take down Jeremiah, and the rest of the household with him.

I ended up with an overworked public defender who didn't do any defending at all in my case. Obviously, the

THE ANGEL PROJECT

evidence was stacked against me, but a good attorney would have listened to what had really happened. Was I making drug deliveries? Yes. Yes, I was. But it was because I was literally forced to if I wanted to have a place to live and food to eat. I was young and had no friends and no home, and my only known relative was serving a life sentence. It was a flaw in the justice system that a person like me was held to the same standard as a person who had every opportunity at success and chose a life of crime. I didn't choose that life; I had no other options. Fortunately, my attorney, who never so much as listened to my story, did get my charge reduced from a felony to a misdemeanor. It was a class A misdemeanor, but again, beggars can't be choosers.

I was grateful I wasn't a felon—that was a stain that almost never came out in the wash. Once a person was charged with a felony and subsequently paid their debt to society, the job opportunities were slim to none. Which, of course, required them to find an illegal way to make money, because everybody's got to eat, and the cycle just kept repeating itself forever. Unless that person started a business or something in that vein that didn't require an application stating that, in fact, they were a felon. Then they just might go on to succeed, at which point the state could parade them around and say what a wonderful job their correctional institution did; they'd proven that rehabilitation was possible. Insert eye roll.

I was sentenced to 364 days in prison and a $1000 fine. The fine had to be paid when I got out, because it was clear I had no money. Jeremiah didn't pay us in cash, ever. That might have given us a chance to leave.

L.A. CLAYTON

When I got out—only five months into my sentence due to the overcrowding in the prison system—I lived in a halfway house for the better part of six months, until I got a real job and found a subsidized apartment. I had my own place; it was tiny, shabby, and run down, but I'd never felt more accomplished. It took me months to gather the money I needed to buy a few secondhand furniture items and kitchen supplies, but once I did, I was so happy I couldn't stop a few tears from flowing. My life was looking up. Which I should have recognized was a bad sign. Almost as soon as the apartment was set up, I was evicted. I'd been swindled. My landlord was a man maned Markus, one of the managers of the halfway house. He'd told me that he'd had a subsidized apartment available and he could speed up the process so I could bypass the wait list and move in quickly, within the week. All I had to do was fill out the HACLA form and he'd turn it in to the authorities, and once I was approved, I was good to go.

It turned out there was an eleven-year wait list for low-income housing in LA, and there was no such thing as bypassing the line. That apartment had never belonged to Markus—I think it may have belonged to a family member or a friend of his, because when they were ready to sell the apartment and found me squatting there, they recognized his name. The woman was nice, she didn't call the police, though she had every right to. She looked at me with pity and maintained, "This apartment doesn't belong to Markus, he never had the authority to rent it to you." She blew out a breath on a sigh. "I'm sure that you're in a hard way; I can give you a couple of hours to pack up your things, but you have to leave today. It's been sold. There's nothing I can do."

I called Markus, trying to explain what had happened, and he swore and said something about how they "weren't supposed to be selling it for a few more months." Then he hung up on me and blocked my number. I didn't even cry as I packed up what I could carry and left the apartment. It just seemed it was par for the course of my life.

Anyone who'd lived in Los Angeles for any period of time knew about Skid Row. In that moment, I knew it was the only place I could go. I was homeless, and that was where the homeless lived. I went to the big box store that I worked in and picked up a tent and some supplies, including a wheeled cart to more easily carry everything I owned, and took the bus to Alameda Street. Once I entered Skid Row, I randomly decided to turn onto Fifth Street, since five was a number I'd always liked, in hopes that I'd find a place to set up my tent. Ironically, the main reason I hadn't left Jeremiah's meth house sooner was because I knew I would eventually end up there. Turns out you can't escape fate.

It felt like a turn for the better when I found a cheap hotel, rather than a street corner, that had a vacancy I could afford. I rented the room for $500 a month. It took every dime I had to pay that first month's rent—in fact I only had $494.67, but the person working the desk said they could let me move in for that, and they would tack on the remaining money owed to next month's rent. I would have to wait four days until I got paid again to eat a real meal and make the snacks I'd purchased at work stretch. But I had a roof over my head, and that was a huge improvement from where I'd thought I'd be.

The room didn't have a private bathroom—there was one in the hall, which was almost always in use. I discovered the first night the bed was infested with bedbugs. I had to wait until my next paycheck to purchase the things I needed to get rid of them, but they were so bad that a new mattress was likely required, and I knew without asking the hotel management wouldn't provide one. That was the thing about renting a low-budget place: it was unsanitary and likely well below code, but it didn't matter. If I'd complained to the city, they would have either ignored it or decided to do an investigation, which would have required them to shut the whole place down, and that was the last thing I or anybody else living in that hotel needed.

After six months of living in the hotel, I moved out to find a place on the streets. The hotel was a complete dump and living on the street was free. I was never going to get off Skid Row if I couldn't save some money. I only made $11.00 an hour, and after taxes my paychecks were meager, to say the least. I couldn't keep paying $500 a month to the hotel and ever expect to get out of Skid Row permanently. The hotel's power and water were turned off so regularly I wasn't getting my money's worth anyway.

I found a space on Fifth Street and set up my new home. It wasn't as depressing as it sounds: I was excited about the prospect of saving money so that I could get out of there. I had a plan, so living on the street was a temporary means to an end. I wasn't one of the drug addicts or severely mentally ill residents of Skid Row. I had a working head on my shoulders, and I was determined to use it.

The next year and a half almost broke me of any hope I had for a better life. But before I had time to travel down that dark road of memories, I was abruptly pulled out of my reverie as the rideshare car stopped. The driver said something to me in Spanish. I shook myself out of my own head, thanked him, and let myself out of the car.

Driving through or walking past Skid Row always did that to me. Like I was in a trance, remembering the past. I rubbed the goose bumps down my arms and reminded myself that I'd worked my way out of that horrific place. I hadn't even recalled the worst of it yet. I felt myself tremble at the memories that were pushing at my consciousness, clawing at my mind like a crooked finger motioning for me to enter.

I rubbed my eyes, wishing I could turn around and go back to the gym to work off the aggravation I'd just stirred up, but I needed to eat, and while exercising until I almost passed out certainly worked to clear my mind, I was trying to employ other coping mechanisms.

FOUR

I WALKED UP TO THE door of the apartment I shared with Darcy, and could hear her moving around inside. Darcy was my oldest and closest friend, which wasn't saying much; we'd only known each other for three years. Fate stepped in the day I'd answered her ad for a roommate. The minute we met, we snapped together like long-lost puzzle pieces.

Being around Darcy was the best way to get my mind out of the dark space where my memories existed. I reminded myself again that I had a nice place to live and a clean, bug-free mattress. Not only that, but I had a decent-paying job and a book that was about to be released. I was out of the nightmare of my younger years—dark clouds no longer followed me around, intermittently pouring rain down on my life.

I opened the door and smiled as soon as I saw Darcy standing in the kitchen, stirring something that smelled atrocious on the cooktop. She wasn't the best cook, and by that, I mean that she was a terrible cook, but she tried. She claimed that pre-prepared foods were bad for you, which was probably true, but you know what else was bad for you? Wasting money on food you were never going to eat. And yet, she did it on the regular. I automatically looked around for Cole—and wasn't surprised to find him absent. He never would have allowed this culinary massacre.

"What're you making?" I asked, keeping my voice bright while simultaneously cringing at the fumes coming from the kitchen.

She growled. "It started out as shrimp stir-fry, but apparently if you cook it too long, it turns into a kind of vegetable mush, soupy, burnt thing."

I avoided breathing through my nose while I walked over to peek. The shrimp was beyond rubber, and the vegetables were indeed all mushed together and cooked so long they'd lost all color and were devolving into soup. I couldn't help the noise I made in the back of my throat when I saw some cheese in there. Cheese had no place in stir-fry. I kind of wished I had been here to film Darcy making this monstrosity so that I could send it to Uncle Roger, my favorite YouTuber. I looked at the pot next to the soupy stir-fry and saw steam mixed with smoke. "I don't think the stir fry is what's burning." I pointed. "I think it's the rice."

She swore and took it off the burner. "Gah! How hard can this be?"

"Well, using a recipe would probably be a good place to start." I shrugged unapologetically. She snarled at me, and I laughed. "Want to order a pizza?"

Her eyebrows shot up. "Well, look at you, big spender."

I smirked. "Whatever. It's a pizza, not a thirty-course meal from Urasawa." Darcy was right, though. I never ordered food; I could never afford it. I could make a pizza for a few bucks—why spend twenty plus tip to have it delivered to my door?

She looked from me to the stovetop and back. "I'll halve it with ya."

"Deal. I'm going to shower, and if you could have that"—I gestured with my hand at the pots and pans on the burners—"toxic nightmare discarded by the time I get out, I'd really appreciate it." I said it with a smile to let her know that I was mostly kidding. But honestly, the burned smell was searing my nostrils. "And light a candle!" I yelled on my way back to the bathroom. I laughed when a throw pillow hit me in the back of the head.

One hour later we were sitting side by side, our feet up on the coffee table, stomachs deliciously full of pepperoni pizza. "That was so good," I practically moaned.

"Well, it was no fancy steak, but you won't hear me complaining." She looked over and smiled at me. A few months ago, I'd taken Darcy and Cole to a fancy steak dinner to celebrate my signing with Walton & Barker.

"Ha ha. That was embarrassing. That server hated me."

She laughed. "Rightfully so. You changed your mind like ten times."

I threw a pillow at her. "I'd never been to a restaurant like that before!" I remembered my leg shaking under the table; I'd put my hand on my leg to steady it, but it left the rest of me feeling restless. I'd never had steak at a fancy restaurant before—not in my adult life anyway—and I hadn't had a lot of fancy steak period, so I had no preference on how I wanted it cooked. I'd once heard that if you cooked a steak any more than medium, it was ruined. I kept looking at the menu and changing my mind. Without words, the server had made it quite clear that he had more important things to do than stand there and wait for me to order. But it was important to me; that night of all nights, I deserved to have the best meal I'd ever had. And logic dictated that the best meal started with the right order.

The minute he'd left our table, Darcy, no stranger to the finer things in life but knowing very well that I was, had looked at me with deep suspicion. "Out with it. What in the *what* are we doing at one of the nicest steak houses in the Los Angeles?"

Cole nodded. "Yeah—what's the big news? I mean, I'm assuming that there's big news"—he lifted his arms—"with all this pomp."

I looked down at the table and smiled. I did have big news. Huge news, really. I wasn't at all sure how to tell my friends, as I'd never had anything of this caliber to share. But I could feel the tentative smile curving my lips just thinking about it. Darcy moaned, "I'm dying here, Channing! Get on with it already!"

I looked up at them, the only two people in the world that I had to share this with, and my smile grew so big, I knew I looked a little crazy. I took a deep breath and blurted, "I got a book deal." Darcy gasped, and Cole's mouth grew into a wide, surprised smile. "A real book deal with an advance and everything."

Darcy jumped out of her tufted, red velvet seat and

pulled me out of mine, taking the breath out of me with a very tight hug, pieces of her meticulously curled blonde hair getting stuck to my Chapstick. When Darcy pulled back, her eyes had misted over, and her face was covered in big red blotches—it was the reason she tried not to cry. She was an emotional being, though, and despite the insane facial redness, she teared up far more than the average person. I loved it. She was the yin to my yang when it came to open displays of emotion. I had grown up with vulnerability as a constant companion and now hated the feeling. She held my face and exclaimed, "I'm so proud of you, Chan. Seriously, so proud."

"Thanks, Darce. I've been dying to tell you; I've been in negotiations with the publisher for the last week." I smiled. "It was worth the wait."

Darcy's mouth dropped open, her eyes wide, the hurt in them apparent. "A week? Channing!"

I smiled and threw as much love into it as I could. I'd known she'd be upset, but there were some things a girl just had to do by herself. She sat back down, not quite as happy as she'd been a minute earlier. I felt Cole's hand on my shoulder. I turned, and he was standing, holding his arms out for a hug and smiling like a proud parent. "Congratulations, Channing. This is huge. I'm so happy for you."

Cole and I sat back down and immediately Darcy started in, "Channing, I could have helped you! You know I have resources for this sort of thing. How can you be sure you got the best deal? Why in the world didn't you so much as mention it to me?"

"I did a lot of research, Darce; I got a good deal.

THE ANGEL PROJECT

Better than most first-time fiction authors. You know I would never ask you to go to your dad for help." Cole stiffened at the mention of Darcy's father.

She gave me a look that indicated that she was both irritated and appreciative. She said softly, though no less sincerely, "I would have gone to him for you, Channing."

"I know you would have, which is why I didn't ask." Cole must have heard the resoluteness of my tone, because he relaxed back in his chair. I wasn't about to ask Darcy to face her demons for anything so simple as a book deal. Having terrible fathers was one thing we had in common and one of the things that bonded us so tightly. On occasion, we argued over whose dad was worse, but it always ended in a stalemate. Mine may have been spending the bulk of his good-for-nothing life in prison, but if Darcy's dad hadn't had so much money, and therefore power, he'd probably have been my dad's cellie.

Cole turned his deep-green eyes on me, his darkblond hair shining gold in the low lighting. I loved that I could see his genuine excitement when he turned to me and asked, "So what kind of deal did you get? Do you have a release date yet?"

I smiled, still amazed that I'd had this kind of success with my first book. "I got a twenty-thousand-dollar advance." Both Darcy's and Cole's eyebrows shot up in surprise. "Normally they split those up in thirds: one-third upon signing, one-third upon completed work, and the last third upon publication. But in this case, they split it in half for because my book was completed when I signed. I got half yesterday and I'll get the other half in a few months when the book goes live."

Cole's eyes bugged out. "A few months?"

"Yeah, they want to fast-track it. They think it's going to be a huge hit." I tried to smile in excitement about the book, but I was filled with misgivings concerning the release. However, what I could smile easily about was the fresh money in my bank account—far more money than that account had ever seen.

The thought of the book brought me out of my reverie and back to the present moment. Darcy rolled her head over to look at me, as if she were so full of pizza that it was the most movement she was capable of. "What's wrong, Chan?"

Was I that transparent? I supposed when it came to Darcy, I was. I sighed, and instead of telling her about my concerns regarding the book, I took the easier, though no less disturbing, route. "I took a rideshare home and we drove through Skid Row." That was all the explanation needed. Darcy was aware of my history.

"Channing—I thought we'd agreed that you wouldn't go there anymore."

I blew out a breath. "I know, I know. The thing is, I feel like I can direct a cab to take the long way home because I'm paying them by the tenth of the mile. It seems wrong to ask that of a rideshare."

She looked at me for a second, her mouth pursed. I was expecting something of a lecture, but instead she asked, "Did you see her?"

I shook my head. "I wasn't really looking this time. I was lost in my thoughts, and before I knew it, I was home."

She blew out a breath. "It's probably better that way."

I nodded in agreement, but in my head, I wasn't so sure. There was a time that I'd spent every spare minute that I had looking for Jenna Freeman, my only friend from my time in Skid Row. I had wronged her, and I'd regretted it since the day it happened. I pushed Jenna from my mind—as much as I could—and turned back to Darcy, ready for a change of subject. "So, what's going on with Ranger?" I singsonged.

She let the subject change slide and smiled widely. "You mean the hot hunk of man I work with? He's still hot, and I'm still trying to seduce him with no luck."

"Darcy, if you really are trying to seduce him and he's not biting, then he's either gay or in a committed relationship." Darcy was stunning. She was tall and lithe with big gray eyes and long blonde hair. Her skin was tanned, and she had a few of the cutest freckles known to man, dotting her nose and cheekbones. Her teeth were large and white, and the front two just barely overlapped the teeth on either side of them, making her smile unique. Where I was skinny, Darcy was shapely. There wasn't a straight man within ten feet of her that wasn't staring and practically drooling. She was just that kind of girl. On top of that, she was one of the few people I could honestly say was as beautiful on the inside as she was on the outside.

She laughed. "It's probably because he's my boss. At least, I think that's why he's keeping his distance." She shrugged. It wasn't that Darcy was oblivious to her charms; it was that she was terrified of men. She was attracted to them, but if they got too close, she backed off about a thousand feet.

I cocked an eyebrow. "Boss shmoss. You work retail,

Darce. There is no rule in the retail business about intraoffice dating. And if there is, no one follows it. Shawell's especially—that place is the *Grey's Anatomy* of department stores." It was true—the stories she came home with would make members of a frat house blush.

"Don't I know it; Shawell's is insane. But Ranger keeps his distance. My flirty looks get me nowhere." She smiled psychotically and waggled her eyebrows at me, and we both laughed.

"If that's what your flirty looks are like, he's probably keeping his distance because he's afraid you're gonna shank him." We laughed but I was inwardly sad. I had my doubts that Darcy ever gave real flirty looks. I'd never seen her offer any male one in the three years I'd known her. Except for Cole, who she naively thought was safe. He was, in a way, because Cole was well aware of Darcy's issues with the male species. He was smart and always kept their friendship easy. He was clearly in love with her, but he would never make a move—he'd seen the consequences too many times.

I humored her, though, because that's what friends did. "Darce, if you're really interested in him, then you probably need to spell it out. Inference is not a male strong suit."

She rubbed her hand on her full belly. "Meh, I'm not really that interested in him." She sighed. "I just want to make out with him in the backroom on occasion. Is that asking so much?"

I laughed. "He'd probably love to be the no-strings-attached guy you make out with hidden among all those backroom racks of clothes."

She shrugged. "Maybe." Then she paused and her eyes narrowed. "What's the latest with you and Anton? Still acting like neither of you are interested?"

That is the thing about good friends: they know too much about each other. The truth was that both Darcy and I needed serious therapy, and neither of us could afford it. So we were both stuck slogging through the mud of our pasts. The good news was we rarely called each other out on it, because the issues went both ways. "Ha. No, nothing is happening between me and Anton, and it never will. We tease each other, and I really enjoy our banter, but that's it. Besides, the guy's a player with a capitol *P*."

"I'm not saying that you should be in a long-term relationship with the guy—I'm just saying that maybe there should be a little Mike's Punching Bag locker room romance going on."

"First of all, Mike's doesn't have a locker room. It has one unisex bathroom that always stinks like sweat and ... bathroom. Second ..." Good excuses were evading me, and Darcy was fighting a smile. "I'm not interested." We both laughed, but the sad truths of our reality lay just under the surface.

Darcy, her eyes bright, said, "How is the book release coming along?"

I shrugged. "Good, I guess."

Her eyes widened, and she heaved herself up to turn her body toward mine. "You guess? Chan! This is huge! Why in the world are you so ho-hum about it?" She mimicked me in a much lower pitch than I had actually used: "*Good, I guess.*"

I hugged a throw pillow to my chest. "I've been a little nervous about it today. I called Walton and Barker to see if I could use a pen name. They told me it was too late."

She balked, "Um . . . yeah . . . I'd say so. I saw a pretty big poster in the corner bookstore prepping people for the release. That train has left the station."

I laughed humorlessly. "That was the exact same phrase Harris used today."

Our doorbell rang. Then through the door we heard, "Is that pizza I smell?" Darcy let Cole in. He was still in his scrubs, and delight was written all over his face that, for once, our apartment was filled with the smell of good food.

Darcy chuckled and motioned to the coffee table. "There are a couple of slices left. Have at it."

Never one to turn down an offer for food, Cole was seated next to me on the couch, grabbing for the pizza box within seconds. He turned to me, eyebrows raised. "Pizza and breadsticks?" He whistled. "That advance is burning a hole in your pocket, eh?"

Darcy smirked. "I know, right? That's what I said. She's acting all rich these days."

I rolled my eyes. "Spending a few dollars on pizza isn't going to break me."

Cole pointed a greasy finger at me. "Over time it will."

The three of us were the picture of frugality. We hardly ever spent money, because we had little money to spend. Each of us was just barely scraping by. My job as a health care customer service representative paid okay. It was a lot more than I made working for Walmart, but in LA it was still really quite little. My goal was to be able to pay my bills, eat, and save a measly twenty dollars a pay period. And even that didn't always happen. But I was content with my life. It was the best it had ever been, and I didn't take that for granted.

I smirked at him. "Yeah, yeah. I know." Cole was the best with money among the three of us, but I always pointed out that was because he made the most out of the group. He always countered with the fact that as a surgical resident he made less per hour than Darcy and I did—it was just that he worked an average of a hundred hours a week. Regardless, Cole was smart with his money. Every extra dime he had, he paid toward his student loans. He was always talking about compounding interest, and how paying just a little extra made a huge difference over time. Debt was something I'd managed to avoid, probably thanks to both Cole's many financial lessons and the fact that I had no credit.

Darcy turned back to me, narrowing her eyes. "Don't think you're going to get out of the conversation we started before Cole walked in." She looked at him. "We were discussing Channing's book."

Cole held out his hand for a high five; I obliged. "Dude! I saw your ad on a taxi. You've hit the big time. Congrats!" I cringed. He looked confused. "Aren't you excited? Walton and Barker must love your book. That's a lot of advertising dollars they are throwing your way."

I nodded awkwardly. "I'm excited, but now I feel a whole different kind of stress. What if it doesn't perform like they expect it to?" Or the scarier question that I wouldn't voice: *What if it does?*

He shrugged. "No skin off your back. They're investing their money in you—if you don't make any, then it's their loss." I nodded, acting like my concerns were that simple. Better to have them think that than the truth.

"I'm still salty about this whole thing." Darcy looked at me pointedly.

I sighed. "I know, Darce. I honestly think I made a good decision with Walton and Barker. They couldn't wait to get their hands on the book. *They* were trying to convince *me* to sign with them, not the other way around. When I got there, they had this fancy spread of food and drinks. They also had a presentation of how they planned on doing the release. They shared cover ideas for the book with me. And they convened a team whose soul purpose was to persuade me to sign with them. I think they thought I had other offers on the table or something."

Darcy's look became even more pointed. "That's because you *could have* had other offers on the table. You could have used that leverage to get a better deal."

Having someone care about me at all was still a new feeling at times. One I cherished, even when that care came across as irritation. I held up my hands to stop her from continuing down that road. "I know, and I agree. But then they handed me a check for ten thousand dollars and . . ."—I shook my head—"that's a lot of money, too much for me to say no to." I shrugged, and my expression pled with Darcy to understand. Twenty thousand dollars was a huge advance for an unknown author. There was always the possibility that I could have gotten more, but it was just an advance—money that would have to be paid back with my first earnings. I took a breath and covered Darcy's hand with mine and gave a gentle squeeze. "I know this is a whirlwind, but it's legit. I promise."

Darcy pursed her lips. "I'm happy for you, Channing, I promise I am. But I would've felt so much better about this if you'd let someone at my father's firm look at the contract."

Darcy's dad was a well-known, perhaps the *most* well-known, entertainment lawyer in Los Angeles. He had a large firm in town and represented almost all of Hollywood's elite, which also meant that he represented a truckload of Hollywood's most vile. The creeps who were known for requiring sex in trade for fame, the pedophiles, the rapists, the blackmailers—the dregs of our society who appeared as the beautiful and sophisticated. There were good people in Hollywood, of course, but the dark side was vast, and most of us laymen were blind to the difference. Darcy was not a layman. No one knew the dark side of Hollywood like Darcy—her father was part of it—and I would *not* subject her to that for my personal gain. It would have made me just as awful as them.

I shook my head. "No, Darce. I told you before—absolutely not. Not on my behalf. If I've made the biggest mistake of my life by signing with Walton and Barker, then so be it. It's my decision and it's already been made."

Darcy harrumphed and then told Cole about me trying to switch to a pen name. "Why'd you want to use a pen name anyway?"

I stretched my neck to the side, buying me some time before I had to answer. I was trying to decide which way to play this. While at this point in my life, I firmly believed that honesty was the best policy, sometimes I just didn't want to deal with the fallout. A half-truth seemed appropriate. "I'm just worried about my past coming back to haunt me."

She shook her head. "I think you're looking at this the wrong way. You've come from the hardest of circumstances and made something of yourself. You're a classic rags to riches—America loves that trope. Your past will be a huge part of your future success. I guarantee Walton and Barker feel that same way."

"I actually agree with Darcy on this one." Cole paused to swallow his mouthful of food. "Even if you use a pen name, your past would eventually be found out. You should own it, be proud of it, even. You've had it rough, and you've come out on top. That's no small thing."

I filled up my cheeks with air and avoided eye contact with both Darcy and Cole. Darcy's eyes grew several sizes. "Channing . . ."

I blew the air out of my cheeks and cringed.

Darcy's eyes went wild. "Channing . . . tell me they know about your past?"

Still cringing, I asserted, "If they do, it's not because I told them . . ." I sank farther down into the couch.

Cole's mouth dropped open, revealing a mouth full of half-masticated breadsticks.

Darcy's head reared back. "Are you insane? Like, seriously, Channing . . . You *can't* do that. You signed contracts!"

I rubbed my eyes. "I did sign contracts, and I read each one. They asked me questions about my past, and I gave them short and honest answers. 'Did you grow up in Los Angeles? 'Yes. 'Are you a convicted felon? 'No. No one asked if my father murdered my mother. No one asked if I spent any time in the slammer. All of my answers were honest."

She slapped her palm to her forehead. "Channing . . . you can't do that; it's so wrong. They're investing in you. They think you're something you're not. I'm no lawyer, but I'm pretty sure you can get sued for deceptive business practices—or something like that. You need to schedule a meeting and tell them before it's too late."

Could I be sued? "I can't imagine why my past is any of their business. My book is their business. Regardless of my level of omission, I answered all of their questions honestly. Isn't it their job to vet me? It wouldn't be hard to find my history. All it takes is a simple search." I shrugged, hoping to look casual, even though my insides were twisting uncomfortably. Darcy was still looking at me, at a complete loss for words. I sighed. "Darcy, what if they knew where I'd come from and decided that I wasn't worth the drama? Worse, what if they liked the drama, and wanted to play it up? I already had to live through the horror; I would prefer to leave it in my past. I feel like the best way to do that is to not talk about it."

Darcy shook her head. "Channing, I understand why you feel that way. But you need to tell Walton and Barker. If what you really wanted was to conceal your past, that's what contracts are for. You could disclose your history and have it written into the contract that they can't exploit it."

Cole piped up, "It's a bit too late for that now, isn't it?"

She sighed. "Right, it probably is too late. They may have already done that simple search to find you and already know all the things you didn't disclose." Her face looked a little pained, like she didn't want to say what she was thinking but thought she should anyway. "That may have been part of why they wanted to sign you. Your life would make a story. How many more people will want to read your book when they find out that you watched your dad kill your mom as a child? That you grew up in the foster system? Spent time in prison? Lived on Skid Row? You suddenly become incredibly interesting."

Cole nodded. "For better or for worse, Chan, it makes you very marketable to the general public."

My stomach dropped. She was right—they probably did already know about me. Why work so hard to sign an unknown author? I knew the saying "If things seem too good to be true, they probably are" all too well. And things seemed too good to be true. I remembered the way Darcy looked at me that night at dinner with Cole when I'd told them about my book deal. She was concerned. I thought she was worried I'd been given a bad deal. But now, it seemed she was concerned about much more. I blew out a breath. "I guess it is what it is at this point."

She nodded. "I wasn't trying to be harsh, Chan. I haven't read your book"—she looked at me pointedly—"but I have seen snippets of your writing, and you're good. There's a chance Walton and Barker don't know anything about your past and signed you purely on the book itself. I just want you to be prepared if things aren't the way they seem. The entertainment industry is the definition of shady." She looked down at her hands. "If there is one thing I've learned, it's that they'll do anything for money and notoriety." She shook her head. "You may not be able to outrun your past. But you *can* let it motivate you to be something different." Suddenly, I didn't think we were talking about me anymore.

I looked at Cole and could tell he was thinking the same thing I was. "Darce?"

Her eyes got a little sad, and she twisted her pursed mouth. She took a deep breath and said, "My dad called today."

Cole flexed his jaw, a vein popping out in his neck. And I gasped, "Darcy! I've been home for two hours! Why didn't you say anything earlier?"

She looked down and shook her head. "I was trying to forget about it."

That, I could understand. "What did he want?" The question came out with all of the suspicion I was feeling. That man did nothing that didn't benefit himself.

She huffed out a humorless laugh. "He wanted to set me up with someone."

Cole exploded, "What?!" Darcy flinched.

I shook my head. "Is that what that scumbag is calling it these days?"

She swallowed and her cheeks went blotchy, and I knew she was on the verge of tears. "It's not that I actually think he'll change. He's proven himself to be evil through and through. But there is always this stupid small bit of hope somewhere deep inside me that it's all a misunderstanding and he's not the evil man I'd always thought him to be." Darcy's dad, Jack Grant, was the worst kind of human being—a disgusting pig who sold his daughter to the highest bidder, and still continued to try, even after she'd grown old enough to say no. He hadn't called her in months, and this was why he'd decided to pick up the phone? There weren't enough bad words in the Urban Dictionary to describe Jack Grant, and yet Darcy still held out some weird hope that there was some good deep down inside him. I supposed that most children who come from horrible, awful people felt that way to some extent. You never want to believe that one or both of your parents are truly evil; after all, you were part of them. But it was plain as day the bulk of Darcy's issues stemmed from the emotional and sexual abuse she endured as a child and teenager. Instead of being the key witness in a case to put her father behind bars forever, Darcy was always half *hoping* that the next call would be an apology from a changed man. Hence the need for therapy.

I nodded my head. "I'm sorry, Darce." There was really nothing more I could say. I'd tried before to tell her she had other options—you know, like testifying in court against the man who'd arranged her abuse for the bulk of her life. But those conversations never ended well, and I avoided them now.

Cole couldn't take it, though. I could see his clenched fists and practically hear his heart racing. Even his breathing had gotten harder and louder. He wasn't going to be able to keep it together for much longer. The man was gonna blow. He stood abruptly. "I better go."

Darcy nodded, well aware that he was angry, and

said, "I'll call you later." Which was the equivalent of *Keep your feelings to yourself.*

He blinked a few times, his jaw so tight that I thought the vein in his neck might burst. Then he nodded and walked out the door without looking back. Cole knew talking sense to Darcy on this subject went downhill fast, but he just couldn't take being an enabler. I'd text him later and finish the story and he could rant to me. It was how any conversation about Darcy's father usually went.

How we felt about our equally evil fathers was where Darcy and I differed the most. I hated mine: he had killed my mother and ruined my life. There was nothing that could redeem him in my mind. Not that it mattered. He was in prison for life, with a minimum of thirty years. It was hard to believe his sentence was already more than halfway over. The possibility of him getting out when I was thirty-eight used to seem so distant. Now it was only thirteen years away, and it seemed far too soon.

After the door closed, Darcy looked at me, her face continuing to blotch up in her telltale red patches. She never liked to make Cole angry, but when it came to her father, the two of them were at an impasse. She cleared her throat. "He also said that he wants to see me."

My eyes widened. "You told him he could shove that request right up his—" Her expression turned one part ashamed and one part embarrassed. My eyes practically bulged out of my head. "Darcy! No!"

She had an anguished look on her face. "Come with me?"

I was so glad Cole had left—he would have lost his mind. There were so many things I wanted to say. All of them leading up to the fact that this was the stupidest thing she could ever do. Ever. But instead of blurting out the words that were practically begging to roll off my tongue, I bit them back and sighed. "Of course." Grateful that at the very least she had the sense not to go alone.

FIVE

I WOKE FEELING LIKE AN ominous cloud had blown in, and then I remembered I'd agreed to join Darcy for a meeting with the devil himself. I knew some advance coping was in order, and I'd never been so grateful for my Saturday-morning commitment at Mike's. I rolled out of bed, threw on workout clothes, tied my hair up, and jogged to the gym. Mike's Punching Bag was packed, as was typical on Saturdays. There were loads of grunting, groaning, and sweaty men working their bodies in several different capacities, their muscles bunching and flexing. Darcy would have loved it, but no matter how much I tried, I never got her to come to Mike's with me. She did barre regularly and claimed she couldn't afford anything more.

Over the years she'd heard me talk about a lot of the guys from Mike's, but she'd only ever met Anton, over a year ago when we randomly ran into him at the grocery store. She'd witnessed our flirty banter, an activity she'd never before seen me engage in, and she'd been obsessed with the idea of him and me ever since.

My time at Mike's and my time at home with Darcy

and Cole were so separated that sometimes it felt like I lived two lives. In one I was strong, confident, and tough. In the other I was private, scarred, and scared—always worried that the next thing around the corner would ruin the comfort and consistency I had only recently allowed myself to become accustomed to.

"Channing!" Anton yelled from the back of the gym by the weights. "You gonna stand there staring all day? Get a move on. You're late." I looked down at my watch: 9:00 a.m. The exact time my session with him was scheduled to begin.

I rolled my eyes. Anton often repeated the obnoxious saying, "Early is on time, on time is late, and late is unacceptable." I made my way to the back of the gym, giving out some high fives and encouragement to those working hard along the way. Anton made a show of yawning and looking at his watch repeatedly, as if it took me twenty minutes to get to the back instead of one. I did stop for a second to encourage Jon James, a welterweight, who was holding his own in the ring against Beef. He wouldn't last long, but just going up against the behemoth showed some real guts.

Anton flashed me a look that said he was onto me and his humor was wearing thin. I hurried to his side, knowing that if I took too great of an advantage of his good nature, I'd pay the price. He'd work me so hard I wouldn't be able to get out of bed the next day. Regardless of the consequences, my snarky nature always seemed to take over when I was in his presence. I stopped a foot away and saluted him. "Reporting for duty, sir." He tried for an annoyed smirk, but I could see a smile breaking through.

THE ANGEL PROJECT

He cocked an eyebrow. "You've done it now, Walker."

"Yeah, yeah. I'm going to have to crawl out of here, blah, blah. I've heard it all before."

He smiled, and smoldered; it was a smoldering smile. I didn't know that was a thing before this moment. "Heard it before? I've seen you *do it* before."

"Oh, geez." I threw up my hands. "One time! One time, and I'll never live it down." About a year ago, I was having a particularly bad day and I told Anton that he needed to train me so hard that I'd forget about my problems. He said he would and stayed true to his word. An hour and a half in I threw up—not an uncommon thing in this gym, but it was a first for me—and when I tried to walk to the bathroom after we'd finished, my legs were so wobbly I fell to my knees . . . and crawled the rest of the way. At the time, everyone in the gym had cheered, that kind of all-in effort was celebrated at Mike's. Anton had preened; he was so proud of himself that he never let me forget it.

He waggled his eyebrows. "There's not one person in this gym who wouldn't like a repeat of that performance, Channing. Watching from behind as you crawled into the bathroom was a sight not many would be quick to forget. Myself included"—wink.

I laughed and shook my head. "Too bad that was a one-time thing, then, eh?"

"That sounds a lot like a challenge." He stepped a little closer, and I could smell his spicy cologne. I really wanted to take in a deep breath of it, but I knew he'd notice and give me crap about it for the rest of forever. "I really like challenges."

"Yeah, well, I really like being able to walk. And I'm going to need that ability when I leave here. I'm going with Darcy to have dinner with her dad tonight."

His brows lifted in surprise, and all humor fled his face. "You're going to have dinner with Jack Grant?"

I winced. I hated that man's name. I hated that man, period. I blew out a breath. "Yep. Unfortunately. We're going to his house, no less."

His eyes filled with unease—only for a flash, but I caught it. "You don't seem concerned enough about this. I feel like you need to go home and watch *The Devil's Advocate* before you go. You know, to remind yourself of the kind of man you're dealing with." Jack Grant was a name pretty much everyone in LA knew. He was more infamous than famous, with his A-list clientele always in some kind of trouble. Everyone knew he was the man to go to if you were beautiful on the outside and ugly as sin on the inside. Over the years, I'd told Anton a lot about my life, and Darcy was a big part of it, so naturally he knew a lot about Darcy, including the bulk of what she'd gone through growing up. Without even really knowing Darcy personally, it was clear that he wanted to beat the ever-loving life out of Jack Grant, which I took as a good sign regarding Anton's character.

"No reminder needed. I've known enough Jack Grants in my life. My eyes are wide open." I stretched my neck; the tension of the impending meeting was making me tight. "I could really use some stress relief, though. I'm not looking forward to tonight at all."

THE ANGEL PROJECT

The glint was back in Anton's eye. "You know, there are a lot of ways to relieve stress . . ."

I smiled, glad to be back in familiar territory. "None that interest me. Not with present company, at any rate."

"You wound me." He clasped a hand over his heart. The wound must have been pretty shallow, though, because half a second later he clapped his hands and pronounced, "All right, let's get to work."

Anton started me with some cardio on the treadmill and then moved to weights. Saturdays were conditioning days; I had a love-hate relationship with conditioning. I liked to see how far I could push myself physically, and I was always amazed that each week I was able to go a little farther, a little faster, and a little heavier. Progress was a real motivator, as was seeing Anton excited about said progress. But conditioning was still conditioning, and I preferred fighting and self-defense.

While I worked out, Anton peppered me with questions, as was his way. I liked it; he was one of the few people I really talked to. Since our lives weren't otherwise connected, I felt like I could say what was on my mind and none of it would come back to bite me later. Also, it kept my mind off my burning muscles.

"How's the book coming along? When's release day?"

I grunted out my answer, while pushing up the bar in a bench press. "Just over three weeks away now."

Looking down at me from his spotting position, he whistled. "Coming up fast. You were pretty stressed about it yesterday. Feeling better?"

"Yes." I pushed up again. "Kind of." He helped me

move the bar back to the rack for my between-set break, and I wiggled my arms while trying to catch my breath. "I don't know, really. I've been having second thoughts lately. Wondering if I should have kept the book just for me. The idea of having it out there in the world is stressing me out."

Anton nodded. "Fear of rejection? Or is it more than that?"

Way more than that, but I wasn't going to go down that road, not with Anton or anyone else, for that matter. I told Anton the truth, just not all of it. "Fear of rejection is definitely part of it. But I'm also concerned my past will come back to haunt me. My past isn't something I want broadcast." My conversation with Cole and Darcy flittered through my mind, reminding me that my past may be the very reason for my generous book deal. The thought was a rain cloud that wouldn't go away.

His eyebrows furrowed. "What does your past have to do with your book? I thought it was sci-fi."

I shook my head slightly as I brought the bar down again. "It's a thriller, a sci-fi thriller." Though it would sell as science fiction, there was a whole lot more truth to it than anyone would ever believe.

Anton's forehead smoothed back out, and he nodded in what he thought was understanding. "Afraid your dad will see it?"

I was terrified my dad would see it, but not only for the reasons he probably assumed. In an attempt to keep the conversation in a vein I was comfortable with, I acted like it wasn't that big a deal to me. I shrugged and felt sweat pool in the center of my back from the movement.

THE ANGEL PROJECT

Anton nodded for me to pick up the bar for my next set. I waited until I was pushing back up to answer his question. I wouldn't lie to Anton, but I didn't have to tell him the whole truth either. I had to be careful not to show my hand, though. If Anton knew that there was more there than I was letting on, he would stop at nothing for the withheld information—the busybody. "Maybe. I don't want my dad to think my success has anything to do with him. Every difficulty I've suffered in life has everything to do with my parents, or lack thereof." I took a break to inhale. "I've had to fight tooth and nail to get where I am—I don't want him, or even less, the state, to take a victory lap."

Anton cocked an eyebrow. "Prideful much?"

I would have smirked, but all my effort was being used at the moment. I grunted out my response. "Yes, very." We stopped talking while I pushed through the last few reps.

When the bar was back in place, Anton declared, "You know none of that matters, right?" I looked up at him, eyebrows raised in silent question. "What others think of your success? Who they credit? You know how hard you've worked to get where you are. *You* know. That's all that matters. People will think what they think. You have no power to change that."

"Yeah, yeah. I know all that. It still gets to me, though. Being a ward of the state is one of the worst fates in life. Not *the* worst—I know that. But it's an extremely damaging thing, going from home to home, having no one you can really count on, no one who loves you. There were a couple of good families I was placed with, but neither of them lasted long. The first one, the dad ended up getting a job transfer out of state. The second was just a husband and wife. They got a puppy and decided that a puppy and a foster child were too much to deal with at one time. They kept the puppy."

Anton flinched. It's hard to hear the realities of what kids without parents go through. As a species, humans tend to brush over painful things, giving as little attention as possible to the darker sides of life. I certainly didn't want to be a mouthpiece for the forgotten, but those kids need good people to know their plight. How many good families out there would take children who needed homes if they really understood what the wards of the state were going through?

Growing up, Child Services employees would often say things like "Life is hard" and "Be grateful for a roof over your head and food to eat." Since I'd aged out of the system, I'd heard many of the same platitudes. They all basically meant, "Buck up—things could be worse." There was truth in that, obviously, but those kinds of banalities completely skipped over the things that made life worth living: security, love, family, a place to call home. When all of that is stripped away, children become merely shadows of what could have been. Human beings are born with endless potential. And when raised properly, one can realize that potential and become the amazing person and contributor to society they were meant to be. Raised like I was, the opposite is more likely true. There were exceptions, though, and I reminded myself daily I had worked hard to make myself one.

THE ANGEL PROJECT

There was a time, when I was in jail, that I felt the worth of freedom slipping away. Not only the worth of freedom, but also my own worth. I got used to the way things were. The regularity of my meals, my daily time in the yard, a bed to sleep in, even the bars on my cell. The rules were clear cut, it was safe, and there was security and comfort in the repetitiveness of it all. I'd heard of people getting out of prison and intentionally committing a crime to earn their way back. Before my time there, that was something that I could never understand. But once there, I not only understood it, I spent many nights imagining what kind of crime I could commit to get myself back in once my time was up.

The real world is scary. A place where only the strong survive. When I'd gotten out of county lockup at a little over nineteen, I didn't feel strong. I was terrified of living life on my own. I knew I didn't want to be that frightened person anymore. I wanted more, a normal life. A place to live that I paid for with money I earned from a job. But I had no idea how to change my circumstances.

The halfway house helped me get started by setting me up with my first job. After which I got completely screwed over in the housing department thanks to Markus, but I was determined to learn from my experiences. One of the social workers at the halfway house, Regina, a woman with whom I met regularly, once told me that my success in life would be inevitable if I stopped seeing myself as a victim. I was offended by that statement. I didn't *see* myself as a victim—I *was* a victim. I was a victim of failed parenting, a child brought up without a place to call home, without a mother and father who loved her. It had turned my life inside out, and it was the cause of all my very substantial hardships.

Even though it made me angry, I couldn't stop thinking about what she'd said. I kept turning it over and over in my mind. After several days, the penny finally dropped: my past didn't have to shape who I became, not unless I allowed it. My future was still a blank slate. Hardships and difficulties were a side effect of living. I could learn and grow, or I could shrivel and die. Those were my only two options. I knew going back to jail was most definitely choosing the latter. I had a chance at life, a real life, and I decided then that I was going to take it.

When I was eleven, a family whom I'd done everything in my power to please, whom I'd wanted to stay with more than anything, chose a dog over me. It hurt; my little-girl heart ached in a way that had only been rivaled by the death of my mother. Looking back on that moment now, it still hurt. I felt sad for the little girl inside me who had to endure that kind of rejection, but I knew now that situation wasn't really about me. Those young parents weren't ready to take on an eleven-year-old girl with a complicated past. They likely didn't feel equipped to meet my needs. If I could have gotten past the rejection back then, I would have told them that the only need I really had was to be loved. But I couldn't. Instead, I rolled around in that rejection like a pig in mud, until I was completely covered in it, until the mud was so thick that my little heart could no longer be penetrated.

Now, years later, I didn't want anyone to feel sorry

for me, Anton included. Nor did I want my father or the state to receive any glory in what I had and would accomplish. Was it prideful? Yep. I felt pride in the life I'd created, and I didn't feel bad about that. Yet, if I were truly honest with myself, I knew what Anton said was true—it didn't really matter who the world credited for my success. But the thought of the credit going to my father or the nightmare that was the foster system really chafed.

Anton knew better than to show me any pity. It wasn't his way anyway. He looked down. "Remember what I said about other forms of stress relief? I've got one ready for you right now." I cocked an eyebrow, and he smiled slowly. "You've got twenty minutes of hard rowing ahead of you." I groaned.

Anton, for his part, acted like what I'd revealed about my past just rolled off his back, but I could see in his clenched jaw and tight expression that he was anything but unaffected. He didn't say a word on the walk to the rowing machine. His nostrils flared and his fists clenched. I was grateful he didn't make a big deal about it, and that it made him angry. Until today, I'd never told anyone about the time I'd been passed over for a dog. But Anton was my friend, he was trustworthy, but most importantly, he was always in my corner, and he never had to say it out loud.

I was so grateful in that moment for his constant support that when we arrived at the rowing machine, without thinking it through, I grabbed his hand and gave it one long squeeze before letting it drop. I wasn't sure I'd ever made voluntary contact with him outside the ring. I'd touched him plenty before but touching his hand like that felt different. The gesture wasn't lost on him. For just a second, we looked at each other, having a silent conversation. His big blue eyes, openly angry and depthlessly sad, bored into mine. The intensity of emotion swirling in his expression caught me by surprise. My breath stuttered, and I turned abruptly and sat on the seat before he saw the moisture gathering in the corners of my eyes, a rare thing for me. Anton squatted down behind me, the heat of his body warming my back, and whispered in my ear, "I want to hunt down those foster parents, Channing. I want them to know what an amazing person they passed over. And then I want to punch them both in the face."

I could often tell the things I told Anton about my past affected him, angered him, and sometimes surprised him. But this was the first time he'd expressed how he really felt. It made me feel seen in a way I wasn't comfortable with—it made me feel raw. I closed my eyes and took in a shuddering breath. Anton didn't touch me, but I could still feel him close at my back, his warm breath on my bare shoulder, as the first tear escaped my eye and rolled down my cheek. More tears joined that one, and my shoulders began to shake. If he said another kind word to me, I was going to start full on bawling, right there in the middle of Mike's. That was a level of humiliation I didn't think I'd ever live down.

It was proof of how well Anton knew me when he laid a hand on my shoulder and said, "Row it out, C." And so I did.

SIX

WE STOOD IN FRONT OF the Grant residence and looked up at the hulking mansion by the sea. Darcy's dad lived in a classic Santa Monica Spanish Colonial Revival–style beach home. It had over eight thousand square feet inside with an additional four thousand square feet dedicated to outdoor-living grandeur. I'd been here one other time a little over two years ago and was absolutely blown away by the way Darcy grew up. I'd thought our apartment was a nice place, and it was. We had two bedrooms and one large bathroom complete with both a shower and a tub. We also had granite countertops in the kitchen. I'd never lived anywhere with granite countertops that I could remember. It was the nicest place I'd lived since I was eight years old and still lived with my parents. My rent share cost half of what I made at the call center, but it was worth it. I lived in a safe area, with a roommate who always paid her share of the rent and also turned out to be my closest friend.

But the first time I'd come here, when I'd seen the way Darcy grew up, I was overwhelmed, and concerned that she would never be happy in our little apartment, not when she grew up in this kind of opulence. I'd voiced my worry to her the first time we pulled up to the house, while staring up at the monstrosity in awe.

She'd merely shaken her head and in a voice that was oddly hollow, said, "This house is a prison to me. I can't think of a single good memory I made here."

Up until that time, I had only gotten glimpses into Darcy's past. I knew that her father was a high-powered attorney and that her mother had left them before Darcy had turned two. I knew Darcy had grown up with money, not only because she let things slip, like how beautiful the Maldives were in the winter, but also because people with money had an air about them. They were well taken care of—very different from the people I'd known most of my life. But Darcy said little of her childhood or her father, and when she did, it was with a huge helping of disdain. She generally worked hard to ignore the fact that he was a living, breathing person. I was surprised she'd asked me to come with her that first time to have dinner with him. She and I were still just getting to know each other, and I wasn't even aware they ever spoke.

It wasn't until after that first visit Darcy started to really open up to me. It was impossible not to notice the way her dad treated her, the false kindness and warmth. The near-constant manipulation. He acted as if he owned her. Darcy, for her part, seemed to become a person I'd never met around him. She was passive, quiet, and obedient. It wasn't that she was wholly ignorant to the way her father was treating her—it was that she didn't know another way to behave in his presence.

THE ANGEL PROJECT

And the man had a presence. One that was larger than life. Jack Grant was one of those people whom one *felt* before they even saw him. And when you saw him, you immediately understood what you'd felt. He was tall, athletic, and very handsome. His hair was slate gray with a little white at the temples. He had Darcy's gray eyes, with laugh lines that cracked the tan skin of his face. It made him look almost genial, but when he smiled, there was nothing genial about it. It was an adder's smile, so much so that I almost expected a forked tongue to slide between his perfectly formed lips.

After that first dinner, the most uncomfortable meal of my life, Darcy didn't say a word as we got in the car and began to drive away. We drove in silence, until she pulled into the closest public beach access, just a few miles down the road. Then she rested her forehead against the steering wheel and cried. A novice to friendship, I had no idea what to do or say. I awkwardly put my hand on her back and began to rub—a thing I remembered my mother doing for me when I was upset as a child. She looked over at me, her skin blotchy and red, and whispered, "I'm so sorry for asking you to come with me. That was awful."

I nodded; "awful" was the understatement of the century. "Why do you let him treat you like that?" Darcy and I were twenty-three years old, adults by any standard. I couldn't understand why she stood for that.

Then she blew out a breath and set her head back against the headrest, and without looking at me, she told me all about her past and the things he'd made her do. The awful things he'd guilted, coaxed, and often tricked her into and then showered her with gifts as penance.

I didn't understand the ins and outs of child abuse, but I understood enough to know the way she behaved around him stemmed from fear. Even at twenty-three she was powerless against him. I couldn't imagine what life had been like for her when she was living under his roof, at his mercy. I'd suffered mild abuse and moderate neglect in some of my foster homes, but none of it compared to what Darcy had endured.

The thoughts and memories of my first time at Darcy's dad's house plagued me as she pulled the car into the driveway. This time there was no awe at the sight of the incredible home, only discomfort and disgust, mixed with a healthy dose of fear. She parked the car, and we sat there in silence for a minute. One look at Darcy told me all I needed to know. She looked downright sick. "Darcy, why are we here?" I could hear the pleading in my voice. I turned toward her in my seat, looking at her profile. "We can just drive away right now, splurge on some Taco Bell. Just because he asked you to come for dinner does not mean that you have to respect his wishes."

She took a couple of deep breaths. "I'm saying goodbye tonight." She looked at me briefly. When she looked forward again, her nostrils flared slightly. "After the last call, when he tried to use me again, I'd decided to take him up on his offer for dinner so I can tell him once and for all what a terrible person he is and that I never want to see or hear from him again."

I sucked in a breath. "That's a tall order, Darce. It might be better to do that over the phone or email." I'd witnessed the way she behaved in his presence; he had a weird power over her. My feelings of foreboding grew.

THE ANGEL PROJECT

Darcy swallowed, then shook her head. "I need to do this in person. This time I am finally going to be strong."

I scratched my neck, my anxiety level requiring me to do something with my hands. I wanted to tell her life wasn't a movie, where the main character developed the guts she needed to overcome her demons with one epiphany. This sort of strength required time, and growth. But I also wanted to be a supportive friend, the kind she deserved. I would be by her side regardless of whether she said what she came to say or not. "Okay, Darcy. I'm here if you need me."

She nodded her head once and unbuckled her seat belt. I followed suit, and we left the relative safety of Darcy's car and walked up to the house that was equal parts beautiful and terrifying.

The housekeeper let us in, and Darcy said tersely, "Hello, Consuela."

With wide eyes that were full of concern, Consuela quietly said, "Darcy. I'll show you to the dining room."

Clearly annoyed, Darcy said, "Consuela, I lived in this house for twenty years. I can show myself to the dining room."

I could tell Consuela wasn't being rude or aloof—between the tone of her voice and the look on her face, it was clear that she was giving us a warning. Something was taking place of which we were unaware. The foreboding I'd felt earlier zinged through me again, and I turned to Darcy to tell her with my eyes that something wasn't right here.

But Darcy wasn't looking at me; she was looking at Consuela with the cold eyes of the betrayed. Apparently, she wasn't here to tell only her father how she felt about him—she was ready to let them all have it. She'd told me once how hurt she was by Consuela's complacency in all of the abuse she'd endured. The housekeeper had been with the Grant family prior to Darcy's birth, and there was little doubt she was fully aware of the things Darcy was forced to do. Consuela was the one Darcy had gone to when she felt sad and worthless. During those conversations with me, Darcy often asked, "What kind of monster allows that to happen? Why didn't she alert the police?"

While I agreed that Consuela's refusal to act on her behalf was despicable, I also felt that the depth of Darcy's dad's reach played a role. I'd bet money Consuela had been blackmailed, manipulated, and more or less forced into keeping her silence. Jack Grant was not a person who left loose ends. I was sure that through whatever means necessary, he made certain his household staff kept quiet.

Darcy leaned toward the housekeeper, and in a voice that was as cold as ice and little more than a whisper, she said, "You're a monster." Consuela closed her eyes and nodded once, but Darcy wasn't done. "Only a monster would allow a child to suffer for years." Her voice cracked on that last word, and I could see the redness crawling up the fair skin of Darcy's neck, but she persevered: "Only a monster would comfort a sad, hurt, and desperate child and then send her back to the wolves." A tear slipped down Consuela's cheek at the exact moment one slipped down Darcy's, and my heart broke. There were no winners here.

I took Darcy's hand and pumped it twice, begging her to look my way. When she finally did, her eyes were haunted and sad. She'd told Consuela how she felt, but it didn't heal her wounds the way she imagined it would. I think she knew deep down Consuela was trying to help her the only way she could—by giving comfort. Consuela was acknowledging Darcy's words with acceptance, even relief. It was clear, to me at least, that her guilt had consumed her for years.

Interestingly enough, Darcy's words seemed to snap Consuela into action. She grabbed Darcy by the shoulder, leaned in close, and whispered, "Don't stay. I don't know what your father's up to, but it's not good." She looked into the corner of the room, where a camera was focused on us. She was taking a risk, talking to us in this manner. She then looked to me, and her expression implored me to help.

I pumped her hand again. "Darce, something doesn't feel right. I think maybe you should see this out a different time."

Darcy's face flitted between mine and Consuela's, both of us silently pleading that we leave now. But Darcy just shook her head and pulled herself away, her hand sliding out of mine. "No. This ends now. Tonight. Channing, if you don't want to come, I totally understand. You can wait for me in the car." She took a resolute breath and said, "Which dining room, Consuela?"

The housekeeper hung her head, closed her eyes, and sighed. "Lanai, west side."

Darcy gave her a curt nod, turned on her heel, and began walking. She was intent on having her say tonight, and regardless of how I felt about it, I wouldn't let her go into the lion's den alone. I blew out a breath and thought of the pepper spray tucked away in my purse, knowing that if worst came to worst, I had a backup plan. Anton always taught me to have several layers of defense. I blew out one more breath, then caught up with Darcy's quick steps.

As we got closer to the outdoor dining area, the first thing I saw was the presence of two additional men seated with Darcy's dad. It looked like one was roughly the same age as Darcy's father, and the other was a decade or two younger. Darcy took a sharp breath when she, too, saw that her dad wasn't alone. She stopped short, swore under her breath, and then turned to me and said, "Chan, you really don't have to come with me. I have no idea what we're walking into."

I shook my head. "I'm not letting you do this alone." She nodded once and then gave my arm a squeeze.

"Okay, then. Let's go." Her pace increased. Maybe I'd underestimated Darcy earlier. Perhaps she really was ready to call her father out and end this thing.

We walked to the empty seats, opposite the men as they stood to greet us. Darcy's dad smiled—that poisonous snake smile—and drawled, "Darcy, so glad you could join us." He looked at me and, still talking to Darcy, murmured, "And that you brought the friend I requested." My eyes grew wide, and I felt Darcy stiffen beside me.

"You didn't request that Channing join us."

He smiled. "I did." And his smile grew. He had manipulated her into bringing me and she hadn't realized it. One look at her and I could see the embarrassment written clearly on her face. He rolled right over it and motioned to his right and left. "These are friends of mine."

THE ANGEL PROJECT

He pointed to the man near his age on his left. He had a head full of salt-and-pepper hair and wasn't an inch over 5'7", with a paunch and a sheen of sweat on his upper lip. "This is Roger Mets, an executive producer with Silver Screen. And this man here"—he motioned to his right—"needs no introduction."

He certainly did not. It was Alec Stone. He'd been in at least thirty major motion pictures, and I'd seen every single one of them. Under any other circumstance, I'd have been completely starstruck and probably have made a fool out of myself fumbling over my words and asking for a selfie. But seeing him here, in the company of Jack Grant, of his own free will, made me certain of one thing: I'd seen my last Alec Stone movie.

Jack motioned to our seats and said, "Sit." No *Please have a seat* or *We'd be honored if you'd join us*. Just *Sit*—like we were dogs to command. My eyebrows hit my hairline, and I looked over to Darcy to see if she was ready to say what she had come to say so we could hightail it out of there. No time like the present to tell this man where to shove it. To my frustration, she pulled out her chair and sat, like a good pet.

It was in that moment that a few things dawned on me. Darcy was dressed to impress. She had on a beautiful, one-shoulder, red silk dress that flared slightly at the waist and hit just below her knees. She'd paired the dress with strappy gold heeled sandals, and her blonde mass of hair was slick straight with the help of a flat iron. Her makeup was flawless and included false eyelashes—a lot of time had been put into her appearance. She'd lent me a dress, a black number that was fitted to my knees. She'd helped me with my hair, which was in large, soft curls that fell down my back. My makeup was understated compared to Darcy's, but still much more than I regularly wore. We were dressed up for this dinner. Why would Darcy have dressed up to tell her dad that she was done with him?

Dressing smartly did give a person a certain kind of confidence. But she and I both knew nothing would make Jack Grant angrier than having his daughter disrespect him with sweatpants and a T-shirt. One of two things was happening: either we'd gone into this dinner like a normal one and Darcy had only decided to stick it to him on the way over, or the little girl inside of her still hoped her father would suddenly show her the love he should have for all those years. I wanted to heave a sigh of frustration; neither of those situations was a good one, but this wasn't about me. So I swallowed my pride and sat as I'd been commanded.

Darcy's dad gave me a half smile, as if he understood my inner turmoil and enjoyed it. But other than that, he proceeded to ignore me, much like the first time we were here.

He turned to Darcy and said, "You look lovely tonight, Darcy." Beside him, Roger nodded and practically salivated. "Have you decided to dip into your trust fund and move out of that dump you call an apartment?" Darcy's very sizable trust fund came with about a million strings. She hadn't touched it; it was one area in which she had managed to stand strong.

She shook her head demurely. I wanted to scream, *Tell him that you don't want his dirty money! Tell him that he's evil and that you never want to see him or hear from him again. Something—anything!* But she remained silent, looking at her hands on her lap. Again, the urge to get up and walk out hit so hard that I almost did it in the hopes that it would wake Darcy up and maybe get her to leave as well. But what if it didn't spur her into action? What if she stayed in this pit of vipers by herself? It was a likely possibility, and one I couldn't bear. I wouldn't leave her alone with this manipulative snake.

Jack's smile grew broader as he watched Darcy shrink back into the obedient daughter. "Darcy, get Mr. Mets here a drink. Whiskey neat." When she didn't move right away, he tutted, calm as ever—a shark circling his prey. "Darcy, don't be rude. You want our guests to have a good time, don't you? Mr. Mets is a very important and very well-connected individual." Roger, for his part, seemed to enjoy this exchange. But Alec Stone, to his credit, seemed slightly weirded out by the way Jack was speaking to his daughter. I still wouldn't be watching any of his movies.

She stood, and I stood with her, because maybe she was leaving; but if she really was going to get that disgusting man a drink, perhaps I could talk her out of it and steer her toward the door. But before we took a step, Consuela came out on the lanai with a whiskey neat for the sweaty Mr. Mets. Darcy immediately sat back down, relieved. I wasn't sure why she was relieved, but I figured it was probably because she didn't have to decide whether or not to follow her father's orders.

This time I did heave out an irritated sigh as I sat back down. Darcy's eyes cut to me, full of guilt and shame. The last thing I wanted was to cause *more* guilt and shame for Darcy—she'd had enough of that to last a lifetime. But I didn't want to sit here and watch her allow her dad to treat her like this either.

I was caught up in my thoughts when Jack pronounced, "Darcy, did you know Roger and Alec here just bought Shawell's?" My head whipped to look at Darcy—her eyes had grown two sizes. She loved her job at Shawell's, and she knew what this meant: she was going to have to find a new job. "I've told them what a wonderful place it is and what a good investment a company like Shawell's could be." He turned to his companions and said, "Darcy is in lower management at the store in Santa Monica Place."

Alec smiled and remarked, "That's great—a real live employee. I'm sure you could tell us a lot about how things work from day to day" at the same time Roger said, "Perhaps we could work out a promotion?" Alec looked at Roger like he was crazy, but Roger only had eyes for Darcy. I was about to toss my sparkling water in Roger's face.

A ghost of a smile crossed Darcy's lips, and she looked at Alec and then at Roger and shook her head. "I've just quit actually." She looked down at her lap, took a breath, and then looked back up. "It was a really great place to work, though. Congratulations on the new investment." I was proud of her for taking a stand.

Her dad laughed, not affected in the slightest by Darcy's lie. "Darcy loves a good joke. I happened to talk to her boss, Ranger, yesterday. He said she was the best employee they have."

THE ANGEL PROJECT

Her eyes narrowed. "Why would you talk to my boss?"

That's when the adder's smile made a reappearance. "Because, darling, I invested in Shawell's along with these two gentlemen." And with that comment, what was left of Darcy's composure burst like a bubble. Was there anything she could do that was out of her father's reach?

"Roger here would love to meet with you privately regarding your work at the store. He's going to be over HR, he's excited about the career change." Irony at its best.

Darcy's skin gave her away, and I saw her chin give the tiniest of quivers. I felt deep anger grow in my blood. How dare he? Why wouldn't he just leave her alone? Hadn't he done enough damage to his daughter? But I knew better. He was the kind of man that craved and loved control; he'd never stop. That anger in me sharpened and turned into something tangible, something I could touch, mold ... *turn on*. I was in dangerous territory. I'd had this feeling twice before, this electricity, this power. Once was when I was a child and the other was with Jenna Freeman from Skid Row. I'd done something to her that fateful day. I'd promised myself that under no circumstances would I ever do that again. But there are times in life that promises are meant to be broken.

I looked at Jack Grant, my eyes boring into the side of his face, willing him to look at me. His head turned, and I locked my eyes to his. I could feel that he was trying to look away, but he couldn't—the connection had been made.

The whole thing took less than a minute.

SEVEN

HE KNOCKED ON THE APARTMENT door, even though the lights were off and he'd watched Channing and Darcy drive away earlier. But there was always the chance their friend Cole was over. He gave it about thirty seconds before the silence on the other side of the door convinced him that the place was indeed empty. He made quick use of his lock pick kit and let himself in.

It was the first time that he'd been in Channing's apartment. He'd found her three years ago, but there was no way he could approach her without hurting her, possibly permanently. It was a thing he wouldn't risk.

Without turning on any lights, he walked down the hall and into the room he knew was hers. It was pretty plain; white walls, white bedding, and an old—and very used—nightstand and dresser set were all that adorned the room. It was so clean, he wondered if she white-glove tested it daily. Not a speck of dust to be found. It made his job both harder and easier. A person with a dirty room didn't notice little things out of place. But on the flip side, with a room this clean, there was no dust to leave prints in. He wasn't all that worried about leaving a sign that he'd been there; he was mostly concerned with what he needed to get.

He'd seen the ads all over town and had no doubt what her book was about. The real question was: What did she know? What did she remember? He walked over to her computer and sat down in front of it. He turned it on and began to download the book. From what he could see already, she knew too much and too little. Just enough to be a danger to herself, and not enough to protect herself. He shook his head.

He wasn't quite sure how to feel about what he was reading. He wasn't quite sure how to feel about her.

He'd barely gotten through the first chapter when his phone rang. He didn't have to look to know who it was. It was Harlow, and she was going to want answers that he didn't have yet. He hit the answer button without looking at the screen. Irritated to be interrupted, he brusquely asked, "What?"

A rough voice came through the line. It wasn't Harlow's. "She's used the chip again."

He used several colorful words. "I'll be done here in a few minutes." How could she be so unbelievably stupid? So reckless? He knew, in the back of his mind, she had absolutely no idea the trouble she was getting herself into, but it didn't do anything to quell his anger.

After hanging up, he took a minute to finish downloading Channing's manuscript and a few of the other files he'd found on her computer. It was a violation for sure, but he was desperate to know her, and he'd take any avenue he could to find out more about who she was.

EIGHT

SILENTLY WE WALKED OUT THE door of Darcy's childhood home and got in her car. Instead of starting it, she just stared out the windshield and asked, "Channing . . . ? Are you going to explain what the hell happened back there?"

My stomach twisted. I doubled over and groaned out, "Nope."

She looked at me then, ignoring the fact that I was clearly suffering physically. "How do you know my father? Like, outside of me?" Her suspicion was turning to anger. "The way you looked at him, the two of you were communicating without words." She shook her head, her hands clenched so tightly to the steering wheel it was turning her knuckles white.

After I'd done what I'd done, Darcy's dad stood, followed by his two companions, both of whom looked thoroughly confused after he declared, "Thank you both for coming. I'm sure you can see yourselves out."

Darcy's expression quickly went from disoriented to suspicious. I ignored it. I took her arm and gave it a gentle tug. My stomach was cramping uncomfortably; I had to get out of there. She looked between me and her father a couple of times and finally stood.

As we walked past the table to go back into the house, Jack stopped us. "Darcy." She looked back. "I am an abhorrent human being for what I've done to you." He all but spit the words out of his mouth.

Darcy looked shocked. "Is that supposed to be an apology?"

"I'm Jack Grant. I don't apologize."

Darcy shook her head, the suspicion and confusion confounding her speech.

My stomach cramped again, violently, and I gave her arm another tug. She turned toward me, her face a mask of distrust. I wasn't yet sure how I was going to explain what had just occurred, but that was a hill I would climb later.

Now sitting in the silent car, I knew there was an easy fix to this situation: I could do to her what I had just done to her father. But I wouldn't, not to Darcy. Once, when we'd met, before I'd gotten to know her, I was so desperate for a place to live that I'd considered it. But I'd made a promise to myself after Jenna, and until tonight I'd managed to keep that promise.

She wasn't going to start the car without some answers. "Darcy, I promise you I have only met your father when in your presence. I realize what just happened was ... unusual." I couldn't think of a better way to describe it. The acute pain in my abdomen was still there, but it was playing second fiddle to my fear of the talk Darcy and I were going to have to have. "Let's go; we can talk about it at home." I needed to buy myself a little time.

Still angry and wholly distrusting, she started the car, and under her breath, in a half mumble, she said, "Oh, you're going to talk about it, all right. You are going to tell me what happened back there, Channing. Every single bit of it."

One thing was for sure: whatever Darcy thought had happened at her dad's, she was wrong. There is no way she knew what I'd done to her dad. And no way she was prepared for the truth. That said, she would likely know enough to piece it together when she read my book, which would be out soon.

I felt sick. Just like I did every time I used the chip. I assumed that the thick, muddy swirling in my stomach was psychosomatic, for doing something I knew was wrong and downright dangerous, but I couldn't be sure. This technology was something I knew very little about; I had only my experiences and the memories from my childhood to go on. Psychosomatic or biologic, my stomach churned uncomfortably.

I closed my eyes and rested back against the headrest, grateful for the Los Angeles traffic for the first time in my life. What in the world had I been I thinking? Had I thought it would all just blow over? That Darcy would assume her dad had very suddenly come to his senses? I suppose I knew what I had been thinking in the moment: Jack Grant was lower than the scum of the earth and he deserved what was coming to him. But using it right in front of Darcy and her dad's two dinner companions? Reckless. So incredibly reckless.

Even more than that, I had a book coming out. And if things went as well as the publisher thought they would, then it was possible that the whole world might discover what my parents had done to me. My ill-advised and brash decisions just continued to pile up, and the higher the pile grew, the greater the impending fall. Writing the book had been cathartic, a way to release my feelings. But sending the manuscript to Walton & Barker? Allowing it to be published? Signing contracts and cashing checks? That was the point of no return. I was headed over that waterfall, and survival seemed very unlikely. Not that fretting about it mattered at this point. Walton & Barker would sue me if I tried to pull out now. Probably for the money they'd already spent, as well as the potential loss of income. I was in this and there was no getting out of it. Which I welcomed, in a way, masochistic as it was.

My life was a mess. I suppose I have my parents to thank for that.

Even though the silence in the car was densely thick, my mind wandered back to that fateful day. The day my dad killed my mom.

They were fighting, yelling at each other about me. They had moved from directly in front of me to behind the large, stately, walnut desk in our home office. I was fewer than ten feet from them, but they argued like I was no longer in the room. My mom insisted that they needed to report me to the Angel Project right away. That it was great news—amazing, really. My dad disagreed, vehemently. He kept telling her that they would use me and that I would never have a normal life, that I'd be hunted, and he would not let that happen to me.

I could see my mother in my mind's eye, so thrilled after I showed her and my dad what I could do. The way I could enter their minds. My mom's hair was dark brown, like mine, cut into a chin-length bob that swung around as her hands cupped her mouth in shock and utter happiness at my newfound abilities. But my dad's words were a wet blanket to her joy. Her elation had been replaced with incredulity as she shook her head. With her hands in the air, she looked at him like he'd lost his mind and exclaimed, "Charles, her life will never be normal regardless."

My dad scoffed, his big blue eyes bulging, "So just take every possibility of normalcy away from her? Evelyn, she's eight years old. She's just a child. TAP doesn't need to know about her just yet. Give her some time to grow, for crying out loud!"

My mom took a few steps toward my dad, her voice a little louder now, her expression stern. "Charles, we've been working toward this for years. This is the culmination of our work. Our baby"—she looked at me then with fondness and excitement, and something akin to reverence—"is the *one*. It worked. You were right."

My dad swallowed and shook his head. "I was never right, Evelyn. Neither of us were. Can't you see that now?" He pointed to me. "We've turned our daughter into an experiment. They will hunt her, from all sides. How can you look at her and think this was ever a good idea?"

My mom stepped even closer and put her hands on his cheeks; her voice was softer now, imploring. "Darling, how can you look at her and see this as anything less than a huge success? TAP will take care of her, protect her. They, more than any of us, know what's at stake."

It was so strange to see my parents arguing, even

more strange to witness them all-out fighting. They were scientists—logic dictated all their choices. They never raised their voices, believing that any good argument stood on its merits. But their voices were raised now, my father's especially. I felt sick to my stomach. When I'd shown them what I could do, I was so excited—I thought I was giving them what they'd wanted. But now I wished I'd kept it to myself. My mom was elated, but I'd never seen my dad more upset.

My father put his hands over my mother's cheeks, and in a voice that was thick, said, "Don't do this, Evelyn. It's *wrong*. Give her a chance at a normal life."

My mom started shaking her head. "I'm calling in for my nightly check-in in a few minutes. I'm going to tell them then." She smiled, somewhat sadly, her eyes imploring my dad to understand. "You'll see that it's the right thing to do."

My father dropped his hands to her shoulders and cajoled, "Is there anything I can do to convince you otherwise, Evelyn?"

She smiled serenely and shook her head. "It will be great, Charles. You'll see." With a tear rolling down his cheek, my father moved his large hands from her shoulders to her neck and began to squeeze. My mom didn't stand a chance against my father's strength. Her eyes bulged when she realized what was happening. The only noise she could manage was a choking sound. She couldn't scream, so I did it for her—at the top of my lungs. My dad looked at me, recognition dawning on him that I was in the room, watching him choke the life out of my mother. The look he gave me was pure sorrow. But he didn't stop until my mother quit the fight, not until her lips were blue and her hands fell lifelessly at her sides, her body still.

Darcy pulled to a stop in front of our apartment building, dragging me from my dark memories. My stomach still ached, but the acute pain had subsided a bit. "Channing?" I realized then I was staring straight ahead; I probably looked like I was in a trance.

I roughly blew out a breath and looked at Darcy. "I'm okay. Let's go." I motioned with my head toward the door. "We can talk upstairs."

The entire way up to our apartment, I racked my brain, trying to decide what to say. There were no good explanations for what had happened earlier, and no way to show her. I'd only ever told my parents, and that went about as badly as anything possibly could have.

Darcy opened the door ahead of me, then shut and locked it after I'd walked in. I was still at a loss for an explanation. I sat on the couch and Darcy sat next to me, looking at me pointedly. My leg bounced while my eyes roved all over the room. Finally, she put her hand on my leg to stop the movement and said, slowly and pointedly, "Channing, what happened between you and my dad?"

I sat there, a deer in the headlights. I'd never had a friend like Darcy. Until I'd met her, I'd never had a real friend at all. Her friendship was something I never wanted to risk. But I supposed the minute I used the chip on her dad, I'd compromised the normalcy between us. I'd had so little normalcy in my life, I was desperate to keep this. I wasn't desperate enough to manipulate Darcy's brain, though. That wasn't real friendship—that would make everything that came after a lie. I'd rather ruin it now with the truth and have something real to remember than taint our friendship for the rest of forever.

I would only use the chip on her if this went *really* poorly.

Darcy squeezed my hand. "Channing, I'm not mad, but I *am* seriously confused . . . and maybe a little mad. Have you had a relationship with my dad behind my back? Did he blackmail you into something?" My eyes widened and I shook my head fiercely. Is that what she thought? The idea of my having any kind of relationship with her father made my already-sensitive stomach turn. The idea of having a romantic one made me taste bile. She let out a deep breath. "Okay, I'm glad we at least got that out of the way."

She ran a hand through her hair and looked at me again. "Does he know you from somewhere? Is he afraid of you? Why in the world would one look from you have him behaving so completely out of character?" She took a shaky breath and continued," Channing, I love you, and to be honest, I'm grateful for whatever it is you have on him that made him have such an abrupt turnaround. I just want an explanation. I *need* an explanation."

I worried my lip. I wanted to lie. I wanted to lie so badly. She'd inadvertently given me a good opening too. I could simply tell her that I'd had a talk with her dad after our first dinner at his house and threatened to go to the authorities with what he'd done to her. That I was willing to act as a witness against him in court. She would be hurt, and probably angry that I would do that behind her back, but I think she'd get over it. But that story certainly left some pretty large holes, like how he'd seemed genuinely pleased that she'd brought me along tonight—though we both knew he was only pleased because he thought he could use me the same way he used his daughter. But if I had threatened him in such a way, not only would he not have wanted me there, but he probably would also have had me killed a long time ago. No, that lie wasn't going to work, and I'd given up lying three years ago. But the truth sounded like the most elaborate lie in the world. It would sound like I was a total nutter, better suited for a straitjacket than this little black dress. I chewed my lip while I tried to figure out the gentlest way of telling Darcy what I'd done back at her dad's house. I swallowed. "The explanation is the problem."

Part of me wanted to print out a copy of my book and have her read it first, so that she had at least a little bit of an idea before I laid all my crazy at her feet. But I knew Darcy wouldn't be willing to wait that long. "Any chance you'd be willing to accept it as a favor and move on?"

She narrowed her eyes and shook her head.

I swallowed again; my mouth was bone dry. "Darcy, in order for you to understand, I have to go back to the beginning." She nodded. And I rubbed my sweaty palms down my dress. "My parents were scientists—neuroscientists, to be exact. Everything I know about them, I learned in my first eight years of life, and while those may be very formative years, a mind that young couldn't possibly understand the complexities of their work." She nodded slowly, disoriented by the turn of our conversation. I looked past Darcy, almost through her, as I uttered the next words aloud for the first time in my life.

THE ANGEL PROJECT

"They worked for a group, on something called the Angel Project—that may have been the group name or the name of the project they worked on, I'm not really sure—they called it TAP. When I was a young, I was a test subject for them." Darcy gasped. I looked directly into her eyes. "They gave me a shot that had a nanotechnology chip in it that attached itself to my brain."

Darcy's eyes widened, and then almost as quickly, her eyebrows slammed down. She put her finger up. "Hang on. Are you for real right now? Like for real, for real? Because if you are lying—"

"I am unfortunately for real, and I'm not trying to change the subject. I'm trying to explain. It will all connect."

She nodded but couldn't stop herself from asking again, "So are you claiming to have a chip in your brain? Like right now? This moment?"

I nodded and took a deep breath. "My memory of that time is a little fuzzy. I think I blocked out a lot. But I remember some things very clearly. I remember the day I was chipped like it was yesterday."

Darcy reared her head back. "You remember them giving that to you?" Her face contorted with shock and disgust. "How do you know it attached to your brain? What type of people would do that to a child?"

I nodded. I tried hard to keep eye contact with her, but all I wanted to do was look away. "It's easy to see *now* that my parents weren't the best of people. I was five when they injected me with the chip. My mom explained what they were doing and what the technology was for. I was not the first person to be injected, but I was the first child of such a young age. They were hopeful it would work differently for me. Over the next few years, my parents would ask me questions. Things like 'Have you been able to turn on your chip yet?' and 'When you do, try to send Mommy and Daddy a message. Tell us that you've figured it out, exactly those words—*I've figured it out.*'

"I worked on it for a long time, and finally, when I was seven, I learned how to turn it on. I had been told that I couldn't go to a friend's house that day, and I was talking to my parents angrily in my mind. Suddenly it felt like there was the slightest of vibrations in my head—a little bit of a giddy feeling." I took a deep breath; the story was strange enough up to this point, but this was when things got really weird. Darcy seemed like she wasn't even breathing. "After that day, I could turn it on with just a little bit of concentration. One day, shortly after I turned eight, I turned on the chip, locked eyes with my mom, and felt it—the tether between my chip and hers. I willed it to open up, and just like that, it did. It was like a portal that I could mentally speak into, and I knew, intuitively that whatever I said would travel directly to my mother's mind. I sent her the message, 'I've figured it out.' In my mind's eye, I could see the message land directly into her chip. I knew then that the chip would deliver the message to the three parts of her brain that would make the memory permanent. I could see it happen—the message working its way through the portal and into her brain, seamlessly, and settling there, as if she'd had the thought on her own."

Darcy was looking at me like I was crazy, or at least that's how I felt. That's how I would have reacted if I'd

THE ANGEL PROJECT

been in her place. But all she said was, "What happened after that?"

I blinked, keeping my eyes closed a bit too long. "My parents had the chip too, and they had theirs programmed for the exact message I'd sent. That message did something to my mom's chip—whatever it was, she'd understood what I'd done. She knew that I'd managed to send her a message. She was overjoyed. She picked me up, spun me around, and was laughing and cheering. She called my dad into the room, but he had the exact opposite reaction. He looked terrified and had me do it to him. He freaked out." I told her the rest of the story, up to the point of my mom's death.

Darcy sat there in silence for a few minutes, just staring at me, her eyes wild. When she finally spoke, she said, "This is really hard to wrap my head around, Channing." She hesitated. "I'm sorry about your mom. But I have to ask, can you do that to me?"

"Use the chip on you?" She nodded. "Um . . . yes, I think so. Maybe. I've never tried to use it on you, Darcy—I wouldn't. I don't use it on anyone. I just kind of lost control tonight with your dad. In all honesty, I have no idea how it all works. It's something I'm trying to figure out."

"But you used it on my dad tonight—that's what you're trying to tell me, right?" She looked at me, her expression guarded. I'd be lying if I said I was comfortable with her reaction. It was exactly what I had been afraid of: disbelief mixed with a healthy dose of fear. "So you can use it on anyone? How does it work? Can you make anyone do your bidding? Compel us? Use us all like puppets?" She leaned back in her seat, farther away from me. It was just a tiny bit, but it told me everything I needed to know.

I closed my eyes. I was scaring her, and if I wasn't really careful, I'd lose her for good. "It's not like that, no."

Suspicion made a home deep in her features. "You just told me that you don't really know how it works. So you don't really know what you're capable of with this chip, do you?"

My leg bounced restlessly. I couldn't have stopped it if I'd tried. "You're right; I have no idea what I'm really capable of. But I do know myself, and I would never use or abuse people like that, even if I could. I've only used the chip three times in my entire life: once with my parents, once on Jenna, and once tonight, on your father. I'm attempting to find answers."

Understanding dawned in that moment and she realized aloud, "So that's what happened with Jenna. I never really understood." Then an instant later, something else seemed to click, and she mouthed a word I'd used earlier. *Chipped.* She gasped, "Your book!" I closed my eyes tightly for a split second and nodded. "Is that why you've never let any of us read it?"

"Part of it. When I started writing *Chipped*, I wasn't planning on ever doing anything with it. I had this newfound desire to write. It started out as a journal of sorts, a way to put my thoughts and life to paper. I'd done some research into therapeutic activities, and journaling was a common theme. So I wrote my life in the form of a story. But when I was finished, the only thing in the world I wanted was to find out how the story ended. I needed answers about the chip and the science experiment my life had become." I swallowed and looked Darcy in the eye. "I figured that the only way I was going to get answers at this point was to have people read it and see if there was anyone else out there like me. So, with the click of my mouse, I sent it to Walton and Barker." Almost everyone within the publishing house who'd read my book seemed to love it. And a few asked me privately if I thought it could really happen, if there was a thread of truth to it. The idea of mind control has been around for a long time. The deep conspiracy theorists of the world believe our minds were chipped at birth, either immediately or later through vaccines—which, frankly, would be a poor delivery method as only eighty-five percent of the world receives regular vaccinations. Even though I was young when I went into foster care, my mind was already geared toward the sciences, taking after my parents. I didn't get a lot of time to explore that part of me growing up, but once I lived with Darcy, I began to frequent the local library and delve into neuroscience as I tried to learn more about what had happened to me and if there was a way to remove the chip. I spent a lot of time trying to convince a few of the employees of Walton & Barker, particularly the ones who didn't trust the government, that I'd made the whole thing up. That the book was merely a figment of my overactive imagination. But, with the exception of a handful of embellishments and a whole lot of name changes, the entire book was true. It ends on a cliff-hanger because . . . so does my life. It ends with what happened to Jenna. What I did to Jenna. And the rest is as much a mystery to me as the future. I was contracted to write two follow-up books for Walton & Barker, but once *Chipped* was out there, I had no idea what turns my life would take. If I would live long enough to write any more of my story.

Darcy ran her hands through her hair. "Channing, that's so reckless. Reckless for you, and for *me*, and everyone else who knows you. Did you even think about that before you *clicked your mouse?*"

Had I thought about Darcy, or Cole, or even Anton before I sent that book? It wasn't like the thought of danger never crossed my mind. It crossed my mind all the time. But in all honesty, I thought it was only dangerous for me. All of a sudden I could see how utterly short-sighted and selfish that was. I swallowed the growing lump in my throat.

Before my dad had been taken by the police that fateful day, he told me several things—one of which, arguably the most important, was that I was *never* to use the chip again, under *any* circumstances. That by using it, I could be tracked and they would find me. If I ever used it again, I would never be safe, and no one could protect me. When I'd accidentally used it on Jenna, I was terrified. I went back to my tent and stayed there for days. I called in sick to work and lay in the fetal position, waiting for TAP or some other government entity to find me and do whatever it was they were going to do to me. Over those days, I imagined all of the things I could say to them, ways that I could plead my case. I'd had no guidance in my life regarding the chip. I'd had no one to teach me or explain to me how it really worked. I would promise never to use it again and beg for the only thing I really wanted: to have it removed. To give me a chance at a real life. Hadn't I suffered enough? But I never got to ask if that was a possibility, because no one ever came for me. I was expecting handcuffs if I was lucky, a bullet to the head if I wasn't. Instead, I was fully and wholly ignored. Eventually, I crawled out from my tent and cautiously got back to my life. And the more time that passed, the more confident I became that, somehow, what I'd done to Jenna had flown under the radar and that no one was coming for me.

It wasn't long after Jenna that I vowed never to use the chip again. I'd gotten lucky that time, but why tempt fate?

I looked at Darcy, completely defeated. "I'm so sorry. I was selfish, and I didn't think of what this might do to you. Of how you might be affected. If I'm being honest, I never had any intention of telling you any of this at all. But I see now that when the book is released, people are going to come looking for me, and I live with you." I closed my eyes and sighed heavily. I would never have allowed the book to be released if I'd thought for one second that it could hurt Darcy. But we lived together—if someone came for me, they might find her instead.

Darcy was angry and scared. I knew—because I knew her—that she wasn't just scared for herself; she was scared for me too. "Channing, who exactly is going to come looking for you?"

"I have no idea. The government group that was assigned the Angel Project? The FBI or the CIA? It could be anybody. But if my father is to be believed, someone will come, and when they do, my life will never be the same. He said that I would be hunted. Probably by more entities than one."

With her mouth gaped, Darcy sat back against the couch as if her body weighed a thousand pounds. "Channing, what have you done?" Big red blotches bloomed on her neck and chest, making me feel even worse. Having a friend, someone who cared about me, was harder than I'd imagined. I wanted to ease her pain, to erase everything that had transpired tonight from her mind.

She sat straight up in her seat, hand up in the universal *stop* position. "Wait! Channing, wait. The book isn't out yet. You can call it back. Break your contracts! Thank goodness." She blew out a breath, almost laughing, and ran her hand through her beautiful blonde hair. "Good grief, I was scared to death for a minute there."

I wished it were that easy. I swallowed. "Darce, it's too late."

She shook her head vehemently. "It's not too late. If it had been released, it would be too late. You can break your contract. Yes, they would sue you. Yes, it would be expensive. But your best friend happens to have an untouched trust fund the size of Texas"—she put her hand up to stop me from responding—"and there is nothing I would like to do more with that dirty money than help you out of this mess."

I smiled; I was touched by her offer and told her as much. I hated that I was going to have to say what I was about to say, but she deserved my honesty as much as I deserved answers. "Darcy, I'm not going to break my contract. And not just because of the money and potential lawsuits." Her mouth dropped open, and her blotches deepened right along with my guilt. I'd been so scared of having the book out in the world, but it wasn't until that moment that I realized how much I *wanted* it to be released. "I need this book out there. I need answers. I understand the risks. I've been training in self-defense for years. I've had gun training, fight training, and I suppose if all else fails, I can break into people's minds." I paused for a minute. "I need answers; I need to do this."

She shook her head. "No. Absolutely not. You have no idea what the risks are. You are blindfolded, jumping into a fight you're not prepared for. You don't even know who you're fighting! Not to mention the small fact that you're willing to drag me into the fight with you." She closed her eyes and took a deep breath, as if my naïveté was more than she could stand. "Channing, your life is more important than *any* answers you might find from the release of that book. Once it's out there, it really will be too late. You won't be able to call it back. Call Walton and Barker now." She looked at her watch, just then realizing that it was close to midnight on a Saturday. "Tomorrow. Do it tomorrow, first thing. You need to call Harris and tell him it's an emergency. The sooner they stop production, the better."

I bit my lip and gave my head a small shake. "I'm not breaking my contract, Darcy. Not because I feel some strange sense of loyalty to Walton and Barker, but because regardless of the cost, I need answers. I can plant ideas in people's minds. I can tell them what to think, what to do. It's not normal. This chip has ruined my life. My father killed my mother over it. I was tossed from foster house to foster house because of it. I have never had a romantic relationship because of it. You are the very first real friend that I've ever had, and I've had to lie to you about this." I waved my hand around my head. "I have to work from home because being in an office surrounded by people I'm expected to get to know makes my anxiety skyrocket. Darce, my life isn't what it should be, not even close. And since I've lived with you and gotten to know you and Cole so well, I've realized what I have isn't a life at all." My voice thickened on the last few words, and I felt tears well up behind my eyes.

She threw up her arms and yelled, "Can't you just forget that the chip is there? Just move on and live your life? For the last three years, you've managed to make close friendships, and even have a pseudo-romantic relationship with Anton. Why not give it some more time?"

I shook my head. "I've tried, and it doesn't work. It's ruled my life. I have to walk on eggshells around my own brain. Ever since Jenna, I never know when I might accidentally use it again. I have to work so hard to keep my emotions in check, because I know what can happen. I hate my parents for doing this to me. I always claim the reason I haven't visited my dad in prison is because he killed my mom. But that's not really it, or at least that's not all of it. He also told me to never come see him, and that if I ever attempted to write him, he would refuse the mail. I know he was cutting all ties with me. That he was trying to protect me—save me. He killed my mom *for* me, regardless of how messed up that is. But it doesn't erase the fact that they both did this *to* me. They put this chip in my head to begin with, and it's messed me up so thoroughly that there is no normal for me anymore. There are only answers, and I'm willing to risk the life I have to get them."

Darcy growled. "So, what? You're just going to give up? Throw in the towel? You know that whatever group your parents were working with, they clearly don't value human life. They implanted a *child's* brain with an experimental chip. They have already taken so much life from you, and you are just going to hand them the rest? Just so you can die with answers, if you even *get* any?"

"Well, I'm hoping I don't have to die."

She huffed and shook her head. "You believe your dad was saving you?" I nodded. "He killed your mother because she was going to turn you over to them?" I nodded again. "He sacrificed your mother and subsequently spent the rest of his life in prison just so you could avoid whatever it is that was going to happen to you. And now you've decided to throw all that away and just bring it on yourself anyway?"

My voice was quiet. "Darcy." I motioned to myself. "This isn't a life worth saving. I'm always scared—I never know when I'll be found out. The other shoe needs to drop; I can't live like this anymore."

A tear ran down Darcy's perfect face. "Is life with me so bad? I know we both have issues, but we can be spinsters and grow old together." I let out an awkward laugh, as that was most certainly our current path. "Channing, I don't want to lose you; you're the best friend I've ever had."

With a choked voice, I managed, "Darcy, your friendship means the world to me. I love you more than words can express."

"Then why won't you call the book back? I understand your desire for answers, but some things are better left unknown. Let it lie, Chan. Move on with your life. Your dad, for all of his many, many faults, gave you a chance at life. Don't let that be in vain."

I bit my lip as a rare tear welled in my eye. "I'll give it some thought, Darce."

She hugged me. "That's all I ask." Then, with an almost instant shift in her mood, she rubbed her hands together, smiling. "I want you to tell me a few more things." I nodded, slightly suspicious. "What exactly did you say to my dad?"

I laughed. "'You are a piece of human filth. You will recognize what a vile human being you are and the extreme harm you have caused your daughter. You will leave her alone and let her live out her life in peace, no longer trying to insert your influence upon her in any way.'"

Her eyes lit up and her mouth dropped open. She froze like that for at least thirty seconds. Then she laughed so hard she had to clutch her stomach. "He *is* a vile piece of human filth. That is the perfect description. I wish I could have been a fly on the wall of his brain when he heard that." She laughed harder, then almost as quickly, she sobered up. "Do you really think it worked? I mean, I know it worked—I saw it with my own eyes. What I mean is, how long will that be in effect? Is it, like, forever?" She blew out a breath. "This is so weird, Channing. Like

THE ANGEL PROJECT

Fringe weird." She shook her head, trying to wrap her head around this new reality she'd been catapulted into. "If I hadn't seen it with my own eyes, you could've never convinced me you have a chip in your brain."

I laughed humorlessly. "I wish that I were just crazy. I'm sure it's hard for you to make sense of all of this, but it's been my reality for almost my entire life." I shrugged. "As for the long-term effects, I honestly don't know. I only have what I learned as a child to go on, which was that these messages land permanently in one's memory, supposedly deep and immovable." I was desperate to know more about it, really—particularly the long-term effects. It's part of why I'd looked so hard for Jenna. I wanted to know how she was doing after what happened. After I stole her free will . . . and more. I had been obsessed with finding her for so long, it had only been in the past six months that I convinced myself that she was either dead or purposefully lost. I shrugged again. "Maybe a person with a strong mind could work around it? Or in your dad's case, if a person is evil to the core and intent on abuse, how long until they override the message for their own desires? It's one of the many things I'd like to find out."

Darcy nodded thoughtfully. "Okay, one other question." She stopped for a second. "Actually, I have roughly a million questions. I'll try not to throw them all at you in one night. But, have you thought about sharing this all with Cole? He is training to be a neurosurgeon, after all. Maybe he could find the chip in your brain and remove it?"

"The thought has crossed my mind, at least a

thousand times, but there are several reasons I haven't gone to him. First, I'd have to convince him that I'm not a total loon. But more importantly, he's still young in his career and he couldn't do it on his own. I doubt he'd even be able to find it. The chip is a nanotechnology, and I'm not even sure where to tell him to look. The biggest reason, though, is because I don't want to endanger him. The fewer people who know, the safer we all are."

She gave me a deadpan look. "You're releasing a book about it, Channing. To the entire world."

"Well, yeah, but the world will think it's fiction. Only the people who *know* will know."

Her expression remained unchanged. "That makes no logical sense. Of course only the people who *know* will know. But if it's safety you're concerned with, why not let Cole take a look before you release the book? If he can find it and remove it, then you can cancel the release, and this can all be over before it even starts."

I could see that she thought this was the best idea in the world, as if I'd never in my life thought to find a doctor who could remove the chip and be done with it. I used to dream of walking into a neurosurgeon's office and using mind control to have him remove the chip.

But getting rid of the chip was a dream that would probably never be a reality, for a variety of reasons. The biggest one being the chip had been attached to my brain at the age of five—removing it would be complicated at best, but it was likely impossible. Regardless, if I were really honest with myself, I wanted answers even more than I wanted the chip removed. I wanted to know why they did this to me. If others had been chipped as well.

THE ANGEL PROJECT

How many others? What was the goal of the chip? Mind control? And if so, what kind of danger was the general public in with all of these chipped people running around?

I knew there was a possibility there had been no subsequent chipping after me. Due to my mother's death and the imprisonment of my father, TAP was never informed my implantation had been a success. It was possible that the Angel Project had considered itself a failed experiment and shut down. But there was something deep inside of me that knew it wasn't true. They wouldn't just give up—they would adjust and try again. That's what science was all about. And if there was even a small chance that there were more people like me out there, I was in the unique position to make the world aware. I'd never seen myself as a person who was capable of big things. But publishing my story was huge. It felt like my duty. A thing I had to do.

For that reason alone, I swallowed down the shame and utter disgust I had with myself and looked Darcy in the eye.

Even as tears welled in my eyes and my stomach cramped and spun, I willed my chip to turn on. As soon as I felt the connection, I mentally spoke the words that made me hate myself more than I'd thought possible: *Darcy, tonight during dinner your dad seemed to awaken to the fact that he is a miserable human being. You were relieved and delighted at this change of events. You have decided to have nothing to do with him in the future. A decision you will stick with, come what may. We came home and laughed and cried in relief.*

I worked my way back to myself and turned off the chip. Darcy's countenance immediately lightened. She smiled and laughed. "I still can't believe all of that happened tonight." She waggled her eyebrows. "I still can't believe we met Alec Stone."

I did my best to smile while my stomach cramped and roiled, and my self-disgust grew to a degree that made even my bones ache.

Darcy shook her head in disbelief. "I feel so free! Like I can do anything without my father's noose around my neck. I'm quitting my job, obviously—what am I going to do with all my time?" She threw herself back against the couch. Then her eyes lit up, and she sat up excitedly. "Let's spend some of my blood money and go on a trip! We could go anywhere." She gasped, "We could go *everywhere*. Spend years traveling the world. See everything we've ever wanted to see and places we've never even heard of." She grabbed onto my shoulders and shook them just slightly. "Channing, we can do anything!" One of the tears I was holding back dropped down my cheek. Darcy pulled back a bit. "What's wrong, Chan? We don't have to travel the world; it was just an idea."

"It's the best idea I've ever heard, Darce. I hope we can make it a reality someday."

"Someday? We don't have to wait." She threw out her arms. "We're free!"

Unable to get my emotions under control, I pulled her in for a hug and said, "I'm so happy for you, Darcy. Let's get some sleep and talk about everything we can do with your blood money in the morning." Then I quickly got up from the couch and made my way to my room.

NINE

I LAY IN BED AFTER quietly packing half my stuff, my stomach spinning and twisting from using the chip. I couldn't stay here and possibly bring trouble to Darcy's doorstep. I knew that didn't mean trouble wouldn't still find her, but now, after what I'd done, it would be clear to anyone who bothered looking into her that she knew nothing about the chip.

My memory fluttered back to Jenna. The week after I'd used the chip on her, I was still scared to death of it, but there was suddenly a reason to believe that my dad had been wrong. I'd used it and no one came for me—the world didn't stop turning. The world hadn't even stuttered. Literally nothing happened. And so for the first time in my life I'd been tempted to use the chip for my own benefit.

I felt emboldened, like I could do anything. I could force someone to let me live in their rental for free—a property on the beach, perhaps. I could take food from grocery stores to feed my almost always hungry belly—scratch that—I could eat for free at five-star restaurants. I could get accepted to a top university. Get hired for jobs that paid a living wage. Convince a judge to wipe my record clean. Endless. The possibilities were absolutely endless. That hunger for things, things that I hadn't earned, things of comfort, things that would drastically improve my life, it consumed me for months. So many months of dreaming, wanting, *coveting*. It was easy to justify why I should have those things. I hadn't picked this life; I'd never asked for the chip. If there were no direct consequences to utilizing it, why shouldn't I take advantage of it?

I almost did. A place had just come up for rent on Craigslist that was far out of my price range, so far it was in another stratosphere. My plan was to get a meeting with the owner and use the chip to get it for free. After the hand I'd been dealt, I felt I deserved a roof over my head, and if that roof happened to have a view of the ocean—all the better. I spoke with the owner over the phone, an older woman named Sherry. She sounded like she was perhaps in her sixties, and I could tell by her voice that she would be an easy target. Not that I'd had any experience in taking advantage of people, but for whatever reason, she just sounded easy to swindle.

The day of the meeting, I'd rented a few hours at a seedy hotel near Skid Row so I could take a full shower instead of a sponge bath. I applied the little makeup I had in my possession, put on my nicest clothes, wore my sunglasses on the top of my head, and tried to look the part of a person who could afford to rent the little cottage on the beach. We'd planned to meet at a Starbucks in Santa Monica. When I walked in, she was the only person

THE ANGEL PROJECT

in her age range in the coffee shop. I walked toward her and extended my hand. "Sherry?" She took it and smiled warmly at me, offering me the seat across from her. She introduced the man next to her as her son, Harold. He was in a wheelchair, capable of neither speech nor, it seemed, voluntary movement. His body jerked around in his chair, and every few seconds his head lurched from side to side, straining his neck in a way that looked uncomfortable.

Within a few short minutes, I learned that Sherry's husband had passed away and she was the sole caretaker of Harold. She was renting out their beach home and moving somewhere less expensive so that she could afford better care for him.

I was rendered speechless at the thought of what I had come here to do. I was going to steal from this kind and humble woman. My life may have been a disaster of epic proportions, but it was only then that I realized that very few people in this world had life handed to them on a silver platter. Sherry was the perfect example of that. We all had our own challenges. In my naïve mind, I had thought that I was going to rent a place from a person who had several properties and wouldn't miss the rent on one little beach cottage. I couldn't have been more wrong.

I felt like I was going to throw up. I took one more look at Sherry and her son and blurted out, "I'm sorry to have wasted your time; I'm no longer interested in your rental." Then I hastily got up and practically ran out of the coffee shop.

I made it down the block and around the corner before I broke down. I sat on the dirty sidewalk, against an equally dirty building, and buried my head in my hands, breathing heavily. Tears hit the ground. I was upset both at myself and at my circumstances. I couldn't believe I had been planning to steal from Sherry—or anyone, for that matter. This wasn't the person I wanted to be.

After what had happened with Jenna, you'd think that I would have learned my lesson. But the pull of the chip was strong. What had happened with Jenna was atrocious, but there was no denying it was a success. And the pull of that kind of power, particularly when living on the streets without any friends or family, was almost too much to withstand.

One thing that always niggled at my mind was I had no knowledge of the chip's long-term effects. I had no idea how it would effect either me or the people I used it on. I could potentially hurt so many people in the short and long term. If I used it at a restaurant, making the server believe I'd already paid for my food, what happens to that server when the till is short at the end of the night? There would always be consequences, for others and myself. Though I might benefit in the short run, what would become of me in the long run? I'd be a thief; my life would be a lie. I would eventually hate myself.

Up until Sherry, I'd been a pretty good person who'd suffered through a lot of difficult things. If I'd gone through with my plan, how could I have ever lived with myself? I refused to travel down that dark path. That was the moment I decided I'd never use the chip again, for fear it would propel me down a dark rabbit hole from which I may never climb out.

I couldn't help but remember the words from my counselor in the halfway house: your success would be inevitable if you'd stop seeing yourself as a victim. I had to set myself free. I had the power to escape from homelessness. I was smart, young, mentally and physically capable, and I was addiction-free. I knew that I was one of the few inhabitants on the streets who could say that. I determined then that I would climb out of that hole and make something of myself, and I didn't need the chip to do it.

Now, years later, as I lay in bed, I almost wished that I'd never left the streets. I wasn't sure Alfred Lord Tennyson was correct when he penned, "'Tis better to have loved and lost than never to have loved at all." I would have to do something in the morning that would haunt me forever. Two things, actually. I couldn't help but wonder if it would have been better to never have met Darcy or Cole. I eventually fell into a fitful sleep and woke foggy and depressed.

I walked out into the living room, and Darcy's smile beamed up at me from the couch. I would miss that smile and her friendship more than anything, but because I loved her so much, I refused to put it off any longer.

My heart broke as I looked her in the eye. Instead of meeting her smile with one of my own, **I turned on the chip**. As soon as I felt the connection, I sent the message. *Channing has been your roommate for the last three years. She paid her rent on time and kept things tidy. She was a good roommate, but never really a friend. You never really knew her; she was quiet and kept to herself. She is moving out next month.* My body trembled, and my heart ached as I felt the message sear into her brain, right where her memories were permanently stored.

When she looked at me then, it was with a kind of vacancy I'd never seen on her face. "Hi, Channing." The pain in my abdomen from using the chip had nothing on the pain of the lost friendship I faced in that empty stare.

"Hey, Darcy." I swallowed back my tears. I knew Darcy, and whether she was a friend or not, she would always comfort someone who was hurting. And in that moment, I just couldn't take any comfort—I would break down. "I wanted to let you know that the apartment I'm renting has become available earlier than expected. I should be fully out of here by Tuesday. I can pay next month's rent so I don't leave you in a lurch." I couldn't offer her more money than that; I just hoped that she'd be able to find a roommate by then.

She looked at me and smiled kindly. "Don't worry about next month's rent. Cole has been talking about moving in here; I'm sure he'd be happy to take your place." Cole owned his apartment; he had no intention of moving in with Darcy. I knew she was just being nice.

I smiled. "Okay. Well, thank you." I pointed back to my room with my thumb. "I'm just going to get back to packing, then. I'll be out of your hair before you know it." I don't know why I threw in that last line. I think I was feeling sorry for myself more than anything.

"You were never in my hair, Channing. You've been a great roommate; I'm sad to see you go." The words were sincere, but there was no depth to them.

I swallowed, nodded my head, and went back to my room. Not two minutes later, I got a text from Cole. *You're moving out?*

THE ANGEL PROJECT

Ah, the second thing I had to do that day. Yes. Do you have a minute that I can see you today? Like ASAP?

Of course. I can take a break in an hour. What's going on? Did you and Darcy fight? Her message to me was weird and kind of cryptic. Channing, arguments happen, you two will work it out. Don't move out. Darce can't live without you. Not to mention me—when will I see you?

A tear rolled down my cheek. I'll explain everything when I get there.

I packed a little longer but quit with enough time to throw on some clothes and call an Uber to take me to West Hollywood Presbyterian Medical Center. I cried the entire twenty-five-minute drive. My best friend was lost to me. It had to be done for her safety—I knew that—but that did little to stanch the pain. And I was about to lose the only other real friend I had.

I texted to let Cole know I'd arrived and let myself out of the car. I walked into the lobby, and he was there waiting for me, looking handsome in his scrubs. He saw my puffy eyes and puffy face right away and came over to give me a hug, rubbing my back in comforting circles. "Channing, what happened? Nothing could possibly be this bad." Gently, he corralled me down a hallway and toward a door marked *Staff Only*. "Come in here; we can get a little more privacy."

We walked into an empty supply closet. "The hospital is transitioning this room, so no one should bother us." He put an arm around me and said, "What is going on, Channing?"

I pulled away and stood in front of him. I didn't want

to drag this out any longer. It was painful enough. I looked into Cole's deep-green eyes and willed my chip to turn on. As soon as I felt the slight buzz in my head and the portal open, I sent the message. *Cole, Channing is nothing more to you than Darcy's roommate. You've talked to her on occasion, when you've been by to visit Darcy, but you don't know much about her. She keeps to herself.*

My heart snapped in two when I felt the message travel down the portal to Cole's brain. I'd never been so sad about anything in my adult life as I was at the loss of Darcy and Cole's friendship. The pain felt acute, like I'd been stabbed.

Cole just stared at me, his expression unchanged. I had to extricate myself from this closet and get some air. I gave him a wobbly smile. "Sorry to pull you in here like this, Cole. I know you hardly know me—I just had to get that mole checked out. Thanks for your help."

I turned the handle on the door, and just as I started to pull it open, his hand came up and slammed the door back shut. "Channing, what in the hell is going on with you?" His eyebrows were slanted down in anger and disbelief. "You tell Darcy you're moving out, come here in tears to explain it to me, stare at me for an entire minute, and then thank me for checking out your *mole*?"

TEN

Time stood still. Surprise and fear bolted into me at the same time.

It didn't work. The chip didn't work on Cole.

"What are you taking about, Channing? What chip didn't work on me?"

It was only then that I realized that I'd been speaking my thoughts aloud. I shook my head in shock, then stopped, then shook my head some more.

"Channing, you're freaking me out." He paused. "Actually, I'm way past freaked out. What is going on here?"

"I didn't know this could happen. I thought the chip worked on everyone."

Cole grabbed my shoulders. "Channing! What chip? What are you talking about?"

I didn't know what to say. How could it not have worked? Who else didn't the chip work on? And more importantly, *why*? Were some people too mentally strong to be manipulated by it? Had I just been lucky with Jenna, Darcy, and her dad? Regardless, I was in a situation I hadn't foreseen, and didn't know how to deal with. The chip hadn't worked on Cole. How do you tell a friend—a neurosurgeon, no less—that you've been trying to use mind control on them? That you have a nanochip in your brain you can use to control people? How do you say that without ending up in the psych ward in a straitjacket?

I was at a complete loss for words. But I had to say something. I had to try to explain. "Cole, how much time do you have right now?"

He looked at his watch. "I could squeeze out an hour."

It wouldn't be enough, but then, no amount of time really would be. I cleared my throat. Then swallowed. Then worried my lip. Finally, I blurted, "I have a nanochip in my brain."

His expression went from concerned to incredulous in an instant. "You know what? Fine, Channing." He shook his head and motioned his hand toward the door. "Just leave, then. If this has all been a joke to you, if my and Darcy's friendship means nothing to you, then just go."

I closed my eyes for a long blink, unsure of what path to take. I could've taken Cole up on his offer made in anger and left. And maybe I should've. But there would've been so many loose ends. Cole would've been utterly confused when he talked to Darcy about what had happened between her and me. She would be so nonchalant about my moving out, acting like she and I were never friends. No, she wouldn't *act* like it, she would *believe* it. Cole would never just let that go. He would search and push for answers to what had happened to me, and why I'd ghosted them, and why Darcy seemed totally fine with it. What would happen if Cole reminded her about our friendship? Could it override the message I'd sent? Would she remember everything? Would she be in danger again?

"Cole, I swear to you *none* of this is a joke." I folded my arms across my chest. I was scared to tell him what I'd told Darcy the night before. I had no power to take it back with Cole. For reasons unknown to me, the chip didn't work on him. Whatever I told him, he'd remember. "My parents were neuroscientists." His eyes widened slightly at that—I'd never really talked about my parents with him, and he'd had no idea that they were in the same field of work that he was. "They worked for a company who contracted with the government. Or it was a government entity they worked for." I blew out a hard breath, irritated I didn't know more about them. "I'm not really sure who they worked for. But I do know there was a government connection. In any case, I was used as a test subject for them beginning at age five. I was given a shot containing a nanochip that attached to my brain." His eyes widened for a fraction of a second, but then a wary and very suspicious expression quickly took over. He would not make this easy on me. "I know what you're thinking. Let me explain further before you decide whether you believe me or not." I swallowed. "I learned how to use the chip when I was eight. I could turn it on and send messages to people's minds."

He leaned back against the wall, folded his arms, and gave me a look that was pure irritated frustration. "So you're telling me that you're telepathic? Like an X-Man?"

"No, that's not what I'm saying at all. It's not

telepathy, or any other made-up science fiction. It's a technology. I don't know if there's a name for it. The group or experiment was called the Angel Project. I think it was a little tongue-in-cheek, like the angel on your shoulder. It's a chip that messages can be sent through. The messages go directly to the part of your brain where permanent memory is stored. Once the message is implanted, it becomes part of what you believe. From what I remember, the messages from the chip supersede reality or history. Your brain believes them so thoroughly that anything contradicting the message is shifted to fit within the parameters of the message, and the message becomes the person's reality. I think. Honestly, I don't really know how it works, but I know they implanted me at a young age in hopes that it would work differently for me. That I could use it, which I can. The people who created it don't know that, though, because my father killed my mother to keep my abilities secret."

"Oh, good grief. So your father's a saint now? The man that you've hated the entire time I've known you?"

"Did you hear anything that I just said? My parents had my brain implanted with a chip, Cole. They used me as a lab rat. My father is far from a saint."

He shook his head in surrender. "I don't have to listen to this garbage. I'm skipping my lunch for this, Channing. Which I was happy to do when I thought you needed someone to talk to. But I get one break today, and I'm not wasting it on this. For whatever reason, you don't want to be friends with me or Darcy. Fine. That's fine. No need to make up fantastic stories to get rid of me. For the record, that's pretty low to stoop for a friend of three years." He shook his head in disgust. "Did you tell Darcy these weird lies too? Because, I gotta tell you, from Darcy's last text, it would appear she's already written you off. I'll do the same, okay? Just stop with the crazy already."

I felt anger surge through my blood, but almost just as quickly, I quelled it. How could I be mad at Cole for his reaction? I would have felt the same if the tables were turned. "Did you not think it was weird that Darcy wrote me off so quickly?"

He threw up his hands. "Well, I did! But now I think I'm starting to get it."

"I told her. I told her everything, after I used the chip on her dad at dinner last night."

"Used the chip on her dad?" The skeptical tone of his voice told me just how deeply he disbelieved me.

"Yes. I told him that he was a horrible, awful person and that he would never abuse Darcy again. I also compelled him to let her live her life out in peace."

He rubbed a hand down his face in exasperation. "As much as I now wish what you are saying is true—" He shook his head. "Channing, you don't really believe this. I know you don't. You've always been so levelheaded. What's the deal? Are you a closet drug addict and just started using again?"

I really, really wanted to get defensive. But I knew Cole, and it wouldn't help the situation. He reminded me of my parents in that way—logic was the only way to understanding. He was baiting me right now, and if I got angry and yelled back, he could walk out of this closet with a clear conscience. I was not going to let that happen.

"Cole, I *am* levelheaded. I've never lied to you before, and I'm not lying to you now. Every word I've spoken has been the truth. I came here to say goodbye to you. To send you the same message I sent Darcy. But for some reason, the chip doesn't work on you. I thought it worked on everyone. But as I've told you before, I don't really know how it works."

His eyes narrowed. "Exactly what message did you send Darcy?"

"I told her: Channing has been your roommate for the last three years. She paid her rent on time and kept things tidy. She was a good roommate, but never really a friend. You never really knew her; she was quiet and kept to herself. She is moving out next month."

He looked at me differently then. "Those were your exact words?"

I nodded. "I'd worked on them all night."

He pulled out his phone and tapped and scrolled until he found what he was looking for, then held the phone up to me. It was the texts between him and Darcy that morning.

Darcy: Channing is moving out on Tuesday. Maybe you should sell that dump you live in and move in with me.

Cole: What??! Why? What happened?

Darcy: . . .

Cole: Seriously Darcy, what happened? Where is she moving to? Is she staying in LA?

Darcy: Why should I know where she's going? She almost never talks to me. I hardly know her.

THE ANGEL PROJECT

Cole: What am I missing here? What in the world is going on?

Darcy: Nothing but you being weird. I'd like to find a new roommate. I was mostly joking when I offered the spot to you. I know you won't sell your place. But if you hear of anyone who needs a roommate, like at the hospital, can you send them my way? No big rush, I have money, but I don't like living alone.

Cole: You have money? Since when? Are you talking about your "blood money"?

Darcy: Yeah. Crazy thing happened last night. I'll tell you about it later. Suffice it to say that things are done for good with my father. Why not use the money? I earned it after all.

Cole: What the hell Darcy?

Darcy: Not funny, then? Too soon? Seriously, though, I'm ready to take a dip in that fund. I'm going to use if for something fun. Adventurous. You should join me. I vaguely remember trying to get Channing to join me last night. I'm sure she thought that was awkward. Ha ha. Maybe that's why she's moving out early. I think maybe I drank too much in celebration.

Cole: You drank? I've never seen you take more than a few sips of alcohol. Look, I'm coming over tonight. Tell Channing to be home so that we can all talk about this.

Darcy: Um . . . no, that would be super weird. Let's go get some dinner—on me. <winky face>

Cole: What?! No—the three of us are going to talk tonight. I'll tell Channing to be there, since you're clearly refusing. I'll see you tonight.

I handed the phone back to Cole. It hurt to see Darcy

so flippant about me, but it was also a comfort. Her disregard for me meant that she was safe. I handed the phone back to Cole. He just looked at me, for what felt like forever, his jaw working tightly.

When he finally spoke, his worlds gave me whiplash. "Prove it. Prove it to me." Then he opened the closet door and grabbed the first person he saw—which happened to be a nurse—and hauled her into the closet. She looked excited at first, until she saw me, and then she looked a little crestfallen. She was clearly hoping this closet encounter was for something a little more one-on-one. I got it; Cole was a good-looking guy. Unfortunately for her, this was most definitely not that kind of encounter.

He looked at me expectantly. When I didn't respond, he insisted, "Do it. Prove it."

First of all, I was morally opposed to using the chip. Particularly on people who did nothing to deserve it. Second, it didn't work on Cole—how was I supposed to know if it would work on this girl? So far, I was three for four. The odds were in my favor, but if it didn't work, where would that leave Cole and me? Where would that leave Darcy?

I decided I was going to have to give it a try and whatever happened, happened. It made me feel slimy. I looked into the very wary nurse's eyes and turned on the chip. My stomach cramped, though the cramping wasn't as violent as it had been previously. Maybe my body was getting used to using the chip. I wasn't sure what that revealed about me. I felt the connection and didn't hesitate. *You were looking for a mouse that you saw run down the hallway and slip under this doorway. You were surprised to find us in here. We caught the mouse and disposed of it.* Then I backed out of the connection and turned the chip off.

The nurse immediately gave us a relieved smiled. "Oh, thank goodness! We have a JTC inspection later today. I don't think they would have approved of that mouse." She laughed nervously. "Well, I'll let you get back to whatever it was you were doing." She let out another nervous laugh, her cheeks pinking a little as she scurried out of the closet.

Silence. Utter silence. Cole was staring at the door, mouth slightly agape. When he finally spoke, I could tell the words were hard to get out. "Even with that kind of evidence, this is all way too much to believe." He shook his head. "I could probably watch you do that to a hundred different people, and I don't know that I'd believe it. Humans don't want to believe this kind of technology is possible. I'd rather you just had some kind of supernatural capability than a nanochip. A thing that could do so much damage." He roughly ran a hand through his hair, mussing the dark-blond strands.

Cole dragged a hand down his face. "Channing, this is insane. This is all so insane. Do you have any idea of the implications? The possibilities? I mean, how many of you are out there?"

My irritation flared. "There is only *one* of me out there, Cole. I am an individual, regardless of the fact that scientists used me as a lab rat. As far as how many people have the chip? I have no idea. Was it just an experiment? Was I the only child to get it? I don't know. And for the record, I may not be a doctor, but I'm not an idiot, Cole.

Neither am I entirely selfish. Of course I've thought about the implications. The way a thing like this could be misused." I bit my lip to stop myself from calling him a name I couldn't take back. "It's pretty much all I've thought about. I need to know more about the chip. I'm trying to get those answers now. It's why I wrote my book, actually." His eyes widened a fraction as he finally put it together. "I'm looking for answers, and hoping to educate the public in the only way I can."

He guffawed. "You're hoping to educate the public about all of this"—he motioned around the room—"with a *novel?*"

I sighed. "I'm doing what I can, Cole. The truth is that I know very little. I'm hoping the book will bring out other people like me, if there are any others, without getting me killed. So one way or another, I need to let the world know. As for finding a better way to spread the word?" I shrugged. "Right now, the best I have is a book contract—it's better than nothing, and I'm going to use it."

His eyebrows shot skyward. "The people who did this are going to want to kill you?"

I shrugged again. "According to my dad, they will. But ultimately, I don't really know. I was a terrified eight-year-old girl the last time my father spoke to me. I can't really be certain of anything." The funny thing was that there were certain memories that were so strong and sharp they felt like they'd taken place yesterday. Those few minutes after my dad killed my mom most definitely fell into that category. I sighed. "There's too much to explain in one hour, Cole. Probably too much for ten hours. You have to go back to work, and I need to find a place to stay. Why don't we meet at your place when you're off and we can talk some more?"

"Where are you going to stay?"

I shrugged. "Probably an Airbnb."

He shook his head. "You're staying with me." My eyes widened to saucers. That was the last thing I thought he would say. His gaze became somewhat scrutinizing. "Channing, I care about you, supernatural or not." My mouth dropped open, ready to explain why me staying with him was a bad idea. But he smirked and grabbed my hand, giving it a squeeze. "We have a lot to talk about." He pulled his keys out of the pocket of his scrubs and held them out for me.

That was the understatement of the year. We had a *ton* to talk about. I'd only told my parents and Darcy about my abilities with the chip. The first had resulted in my mother's death and my father's incarceration; the second, in the loss of my closest friend. So far, this was the best outcome I'd had, and I wanted to tell Cole the whole story. It was therapeutic to talk about, but also, I needed someone in my corner, someone I could throw ideas at. With the chip not working on Cole, I knew that he was my best chance at having some help and comfort. I really wanted to say yes, but ultimately, I shook my head. "It's too dangerous for you. I don't know what's going to happen after the book comes out."

He gave me a look indicating he wasn't all that concerned with the danger. "Channing, *at least* stay with me until the book release. We'll figure out what to do after that. We can talk it all out, come up with a plan. You need a plan." He wasn't wrong about that. My plan A admittedly wasn't great, and I'd yet to come up with plans B through Z, which I'd surely need. He jiggled his keys. "Go finish packing up the five things you own and let yourself in. I'll be done here by five or six o'clock."

I was grateful for the offer of a friend for the next few days. It was a luxury I wasn't expecting nor would I turn it down. "Okay." I took the key and went in for a hug. His familiar fresh soap scent enveloped me. "Thanks, Cole."

I opened the closet door, and to my complete surprise and utter confusion, Anton was there, arm up, poised to knock. I had to do a double take, and then a triple take. I'd hardly ever seen him outside the gym. And here he was at West Hollywood Presbyterian Medical Center, I could only assume he was looking for me. I stared at him dumbfounded for at least ten seconds.

It took far too long for me to register that he was in a suit, and in the hand not poised to knock, he was holding up an FBI badge.

ELEVEN

"Anton?" My confusion was a thick fog.

In my peripheral vision, I could see Cole's face turned toward me, his eyebrows slammed down, but I couldn't take my eyes off Anton. "Anton? Your trainer from the gym, Anton?" I nodded yes without looking his way.

Anton's eyes were trained only on me when he ground out, "Special Agent Antonio Garcia. Channing, you're coming with me." His face was void of emotion—it was like he didn't even know me.

I fought through the sting of his stolid expression and put my hand up. "Hold on a second." My heart was beating hard as I studied his face, looking for anything. His eyes softened just a fraction, just enough for me to know he had acknowledged he knew who he was speaking to – he knew me. Regardless, I couldn't process what I was seeing. How could Anton be an FBI agent? He spent all of his time at Mike's. And he was here to take me somewhere? Where were we going? Was I being arrested by *Anton*? How did he know that I was here, in this hospital closet? I would have been less shocked to see an elephant walking down the hallway. I managed to sputter out a few of my internal questions. "What's going on, Anton? Where are you taking me? Am I under arrest?"

Anton's face was back to stone cold. "Not yet. You're required for questioning."

"Are you serious right now? What do you mean *not yet*? What law have I broken?" The longer he stood there, showing no remorse for lying to me for the past several years, the angrier I became. This was Anton, one of the very few people I called a friend. Yesterday morning when I was training with him, his kindness had made me cry. Now he was here to arrest me? Or question me? Or whatever this was? Had anything he'd ever said to me been true? I felt like I'd been zapped into an alternate reality.

Cole spoke up, "Channing isn't answering a single question without an attorney present."

Anton laughed humorlessly. "That won't be necessary, Mr. Miller. There's not a single question I'm going to ask her that an attorney can help her with." He followed that enigmatic sentence with a condescending smile. I could feel Cole bristle at the implication that neither he nor anyone else could do anything to help me. I saw Cole take a step toward Anton out of the corner of my eye. Anton stood taller and squared his shoulders. They were pretty close to the same height, with Anton beating Cole by only an inch. But that was where the similarities ended. Anton had a dark olive complexion with hair so dark it was nearly black and the most striking blue eyes. Cole was blond with green eyes and fair skin.

THE ANGEL PROJECT

Anton was built—his shoulders and neck broad and powerful, biceps and forearms corded in muscle. I could see the definition of his quads and calves through his suit pants, almost as if it was hard for the fabric to contain the breadth of him. Cole was not out of shape by any standard, but it was clear he didn't spend all of his free time working out. With barely a glance at Cole, Anton deemed him no threat, and he turned back to me. "You know what this is about, Channing."

I swallowed. It could only be about one thing. The chip. It had to be. I'd used it, and they were finally here for me. Before the book even came out, before I had any hope of finding others like me. If Anton was indeed a federal agent, then they'd been following me, and gathering intel on me, for a considerable amount of time. All of Anton's incessant questions . . . He was always so good at getting me to open up, better than any other person I knew. Which now made sense, considering that's what he was trained to do. I was a job to him, and that thought made me so incredibly sad; as well as left me feeling more than a little violated.

Anton could clearly see the hurt in my expression. And for just a second his eyes showed a modicum of remorse. But it was gone in a flash. I looked at Cole, who was quietly freaking out, trying to find a way to help me. Because that's what Cole did. He was a good guy, and I didn't want to be even more of a burden to him. I wished I could send a message to his mind. I'd tell him I was going to be okay, and that I had to go. This had all been a long time coming. I tried the best I could to convey that with my eyes. But Cole wasn't buying it.

His nostrils flared, and his jaw was clenched tight. He turned to Anton and said, "Can we have one minute? Before she goes with you?"

Anton looked at me then, the question, *Is that what you want?* written on his face.

I nodded. His face turned to stone. He glanced at his watch, then looked down the hallway in both directions. "One minute. We're in a hurry."

Cole pulled me into the closet and shut the door. "Channing, don't say a word without an attorney present. I have a friend who practices criminal defense. He's good. I'll text you his contact info."

I put my hand on his bicep attempting to ratchet down his panic. My voice came out much calmer than I was feeling. "I haven't committed a crime, Cole. I don't know what a defense attorney could do for me. This is about the chip—it has to be." I blew out a breath. "I used it a little over three years ago, by accident, just before I met Anton at Mike's. I didn't use it again until last night. And I've used it several times since then. I'm certain if people knew mind control was possible, it would be a crime, but I doubt it's on the books. No attorney can defend me for this. I'm not even sure it requires a defense. I'm just going to have go with Anton and see where this takes me. Who knows? Maybe the FBI can help me." I had to admit now that I'd had a minute to think it through, I was actually relieved that this might be about the chip. What did they know that I didn't? What could I learn about it? About me?

He looked to the closed door and then back to me,

and his jaw tightened a fraction. "I'm not sure that guy wants to help you as much as he wants to sleep with you."

I reared my head back. "We're not like that, Cole. At all. Nothing has ever happened between me and Anton, and I can guarantee that it never will. Especially now." I'd just found out he's been lying to me for the last three years, all the while pretending to be my friend. Nothing could have been further from my mind. What kind of person did Cole think I was?

He cocked an eyebrow. "The waves of jealousy coming off that guy could drown a city, Channing. He thinks that there's something going on between us; that's why he's being so cold to you." Cole knew how inexperienced I was in regard to these situations—maybe not the extent of my inexperience, but he knew enough to know that he had to spell it out for me. "He would've loved nothing more than for me to throw the first punch so that he could grind me into the ground. Pretty unprofessional for a United States federal agent."

I had nothing to say to that. I didn't think it was true, but what did I know? I shrugged, indicating as much.

"My point is I don't trust this guy. He seems far too invested in you to do his job correctly. Maybe that will work out well for you, but it's hard to know right now." He put his hands on my shoulders and asked, "Channing, are you sure you're okay leaving with this guy?"

I huffed out a laugh. "Cole, I have to be okay with it. He's a federal agent. A well-trained one. What am I going to do? Beat him into submission? Outrun him? And to what end?"

"I can take off early, tell my boss I'm sick—which at

this point wouldn't be a lie—and come with you." He gave my shoulders a gentle squeeze. "You don't have to be alone."

A wobbly smile stretched across my face. I'd always been alone; it was still hard to believe I had friends who would drop everything to help me. "That's a really nice offer, Cole. I can't tell you how much I appreciate it. Right now, though, I need to face the music. Besides, if things get really ugly—I have an out." I winked and tapped the side of my head.

Cole's mouth dropped open. "Wow. I never even considered that. Suddenly this supernatural thing you've got going on doesn't sound so bad."

"It's not supernatural, it's a—"

"Technology. I know." He smiled at me, but worry was still etched deeply in his face.

I stood on my tiptoes to give him a hug. "Thank you, Cole. You're a good friend. And thank you for the offer to stay with you." I pulled back and handed him his keys, then motioned my head toward the door. "In light of the recent developments, I think staying at your place would be a bad idea. If they even let me go. But I'll call you when I get out of questioning."

He hugged me tighter. "I want to be the first call you make when you get out of there."

I laughed. "Cole, you are literally the only friend I have at the moment. You'll be the first, and only call I make if they put me in jail."

He pulled back. "Not funny."

I laughed and pulled the door open and was again

face-to-face with Anton, who was even more stoic than before. "Is this funny to you, Channing?"

I wiped the grin off my face and replaced it with the emotion I was really feeling toward Anton: anger. "Let's go."

He gripped my bicep with a little more force than was necessary and spun me toward the direction of the parking lot. I shot a wide-eyed glance back at Cole, who tapped the side of his head and mouthed, "Use it when you need to." I gave an imperceptible nod and turned back to begin walking with Anton.

"Geez, Anton." I yanked my arm out of his grip.

He looked over at me, a little surprised. "I didn't realize I was holding you so tightly." It was only then I noticed that he wasn't really focused on me at all. His eyes were scanning the hallway around us, his menacing gaze telling anyone within sight to stay far away.

"What are you looking for?"

He looked at me again, his expression somewhat haunted. I could tell that he was debating what to say. "There are other people looking for you at the moment. They try to get their people before we do."

Too many things to unpack in that sentence. There were people looking for me? More than that, whoever they were, they thought I was one of *their* people? What else did Anton know? I was so taken aback, I wasn't sure where to start. I went with my first thought: "Are you talking about TAP?"

His pace stuttered, and he blinked at me in disbelief. "You know about the Angel Project?" It seemed like all the air had left his lungs; the shock was evident on his face.

But the utter surprise in his expression was mixed with a healthy dose of consternation. "What else do you remember?"

This time I grabbed his bicep, even harder than he'd held mine earlier. I pulled him to a stop right in the middle of the lobby and looked him square in the eyes. "What else do I *remember*? Anton, I was five when they did this to me—I remember that. Eight when I was basically orphaned; I remember that very clearly. Beyond that, I've got practically nothing."

He blinked slowly a few times, as if he were trying to register everything I was saying, while at the same time trying to measure his words carefully. "I've been Investigating TAP for the last several years."

I balked. "How long have you been with the FBI?"

Again with the shifty eyes, he replied, "Several years."

"You've been investigating TAP, the people who did this to me?"—I pointed to my head—"for *several years*? I've seen you three times a week for the last three years, and you've never said a word?" I huffed out a breath. "I've been so lost, Anton, trying to find out more about them. More about *me*." I paused while Anton's eyes scanned the room again. I wanted his full attention. I wanted him to know how serious I was. When he finally looked at me, I demanded, "I want to know everything you know about them. Everything."

"I know. It's part of why I'm here. But if we don't leave now, they'll get you first, and you'll never get to hear the truth." With that, he grabbed my hand at the wrist and pulled, urging me to move.

THE ANGEL PROJECT

I wasn't naïve. I knew he could be lying, baiting me with the answers I so badly wanted to accomplish whatever ends he desired. He had failed to tell me anything about TAP or the chip in the years that I'd known him, after all. But there was something about Anton; there always had been. His eyes practically shouted that he was honest and good. Setting aside my mixed emotions for a minute, I asked the question I'd put on the back burner, but probably should have been at the forefront. "Anton, why are they looking for me? Do they want to kill me for using the chip?"

His head reared back. "Kill you?" He shook his head. "No. They want to use you. They've been looking for you for a long time, Channing." Chills ran down my spine, and my thoughts became cloudy. Anton looked at his watch and pulled me along a little faster. "We've got to get out of here, right now. We're running out of time. We can talk later."

My stomach felt infested by a swarm of murder hornets, and my heart was liable to beat right out of my chest. My mind felt muddled and foggy with confusion. I was certain about one thing, I had to know more. "How would they use me? And if they've been trying to find me for so long, how come they haven't yet? I haven't exactly been in hiding."

"You've been hiding better than you think, actually." We walked at a quick pace, just shy of a run. We were quiet, our breaths quickening.

I guess homelessness was a form of hiding. I had no address for years. "If they haven't been able to find me yet, how could they find me now?"

"They can track the place that the chip is used. Just like we can."

Fear slammed into me so hard I stumbled. "Anton, I used the chip on Darcy, at our apartment."

He didn't look over at me. Instead, he worried his bottom lip, stalling. "They've already been there."

This time my knees really did buckle. He hefted me back to standing and pushed my lower back, forcing me to move forward. "Darcy's fine, Channing. The apartment, not so much. I'll fill you in once we get to the Federal Building."

Darcy's fine. I repeated it in my head like a mantra. Finally, the gravity of the situation seemed to break through my mental fog and hit me with force, and I picked up my pace. The Angel Project was after me. I was an asset they had been trying to acquire for quite some time. They would use me in all the ways my dad had feared. That same fear and some adrenaline surged through my veins, and I started walking as fast as my legs would carry me. I could pick Anton's brain later.

We exited the hospital, and just as we entered the parking garage, Anton swirled me around, backing me into a small cement alcove, and slanted his mouth over mine. I gasped and tried to pull back, but my head was against the wall and his mouth was relentless. As were his hands. His arms wrapped around me, rubbing down my back, my sides, my hips. I felt one of his hands graze my backside, and then in an instant he pulled my leg up around his waist and he leaned in. Pressed so tightly against him, my body was completely enveloped by his.

This wasn't my first kiss, but I'd *never* been kissed

like this. Even my inexperienced self could recognize the need and want in it—the desperation. It took a minute, but eventually I began kissing him back, in earnest. He growled and the kiss intensified. His hands were on my face, tangled in my hair. Adrenaline surged through me again, but this time for a completely different reason. I was too caught up in the moment, too caught up in Anton. Years of skirting around my physical attraction to him had made this moment something more than it was meant to be.

I may have been green in regard to relationships, but I wasn't insensible. Even through the fog of desire, which was thick and deep, I could hear the screech of tires in the parking garage, the slamming doors. The hushed but urgent voices and the quick steps toward the hospital. I knew Anton was kissing me in an attempt to conceal me, to keep me out sight from those searching for me. Probably also to shut me up. It was all so unbelievably cliché, but regardless of why he'd kissed me, I couldn't stop the physical response I had to him. Couldn't stop the desire swimming through my veins, the sparks shocking me everywhere we touched.

As soon as the last rushed footstep left the parking garage, Anton wrenched his mouth from mine. His red, swollen lips parted as he breathed hard, his eyes swimming with a want that was so heated his gaze practically burned me. He swore under his breath and quietly said, "That was unexpected." Then just as quickly, he turned around, his back to my front, still pressing me into the back of the alcove, while he searched the parking lot for any trace of danger.

What was unexpected? That he had kissed me and felt something? That I had kissed him back? That he'd kissed me at all? All of my questions were inane at the moment, but they floated through my mind nonetheless. I did my best to concentrate on my breathing to get my mind back where it needed to be, the imminent threat against me. It wasn't easy.

Anton stepped forward and grabbed my hand. "Let's go. We only have minutes before they realize you're no longer in the building. We need to be long gone by then." He turned back to look at me. "Are you ready?"

I nodded my head only once, and we were off. We ran as quickly as one could through a parking garage. Between the parked and moving cars, it was a challenge. Near the back of the structure, Anton slowed down as we came up on a black sedan. He yanked open the back driver's-side door, and with his hand on my lower back, he propelled me into the back seat and shouted, "Stay down."

He jumped into the driver's seat, and to my surprise, that's where the urgency ended. I'd figured he would pull out, tires screeching, and speed out of there like he'd stolen something. Fortunately, he was smarter than that, because when we pulled out of the garage, I lifted my head just enough to see a small group of angry people leave the hospital in a hurry. If Anton had rushed out, it would've put a target on our backs.

I started to breathe a little easier when Anton pulled onto the 101. The traffic was, of course, moving as slow as molasses, but we were now one car in a sea of them, as hard to find as the proverbial needle in a haystack. I started to sit up, but Anton pushed me back down. "We can't afford even the smallest of slip-ups right now, Channing."

"Don't you think this is a little overkill? We're on the highway with a million other vehicles."

"You have no idea who we're dealing with." He took the next exit and began turning down side streets, getting lost in the labyrinth that was Los Angeles. "Every precaution is necessary. I guarantee they took off in many different directions and are looking for you as we speak."

I grumbled; my back was beginning to ache from being hunched over. But I could hear in Anton's tone that this was an argument I wasn't going to win. I decided to lay the upper half of my body down, with my head on the seat kitty-corner to Anton's. I had a clear view of his profile.

"Yeah—but you're FBI. Isn't there someone who can watch the traffic and guide you through this?"

"Well, there would be," he said uneasily, "if I were on official business right now."

My body tensed and my heart rate took off. "What? What are you saying, Anton?" I could barely force the words from my lips.

He scrubbed a hand down his face. "That I'm currently doing the most reckless thing I've ever done."

"What does that mean?" My mind spun with the possibilities. Had I been kidnapped? Should I be trying to get the attention of the drivers around me? Anton knew about the chip and TAP, but that didn't mean he was ultimately on my side. In my quest for information, had I jumped into the arms of the first person who'd offered me a bread crumb, only to be lured into some new kind of unknown nightmare? And yet, there was something about Anton. Something I trusted. But that didn't change the fact that this whole thing scared me on a level I'd never felt before.

"The FBI doesn't know that I have you yet, and I'm not answering my handler's calls. They're likely also out looking for you. And me."

"Why? Anton, what is going on? You're seriously freaking me out!"

"Channing, there are some things I want to explain to you. Just the two of us, before the FBI or TAP get involved."

"Well then, you better start explaining. Because, I'm not gonna lie, I'm about to jump out of this car and run in the opposite direction as fast as I can." My breaths were coming out in pants, my body having a reaction that I had no control over.

"Channing, *please* don't. That would be bad. Really bad." He checked to make sure the doors were locked, as if that would keep me in. "They want to use you."

"You already told me that. How does TAP want to use me?"

"No, that's what you don't understand. They both want to use you. The FBI and TAP, just in different ways. Frankly, neither is all that good."

How could being used in any way be good? I shook my head, trying to shake it free from the fog that kept seeming to cloud my mind. "Why? In what way?"

"I'm going to have to go back to the beginning." His jaw was so tight, it looked like it was carved from stone.

THE ANGEL PROJECT

"The government began chipping the population decades ago." Fog hit my brain so hard I could barely register what he was saying. "Those who weren't chipped at birth were chipped later, through other means. Science had shown that there were some people who had the capacity to use their chip on others. They could use it on any chipped person, being able to turn their chip on voluntarily and connect to the chip in another person's mind. There are people who can do even more than that. Finding these people is how TAP began."

My head began to throb. Pound, even. Then I felt shooting pain, like an electric charge, rack my brain. I groaned and grabbed onto it, squeezing it tightly, trying to alleviate the agony, even if momentarily. "I'm sorry, Channing. I know the truth is hurting you, but I have to tell you. You have to know."

I couldn't make sense of his words. I could do nothing but hold my head and pray it didn't explode.

"Your brain is overriding your chip. It feels like a brain fog as thick as a blanket at first, and then it can feel like shooting nerve pain. Just hang on. It comes and goes in waves. It will pass. It's not good to work through the pain for too long, but it's okay for a little bit." He gave me a minute for the pain to subside, and then he continued. "At first TAP attempted to find out why the chip worked that way in a small part of the population. What did those people's brains do that was so unique? As scientists within the group, your parents discovered certain rare genetic components that were common in those who could utilize their own chips. Your genetic testing came back positive."

I shook my head, trying to physically clear the fog yet

again. Some of that made sense, but some of it didn't. I didn't know they had been chipping the entire population, and for so long. "If there were people already able to use the chip, why did they test it on me?"

He swallowed, choosing his words carefully. "At first they killed anyone they suspected could use the chip. They didn't have the technology to see who had used the chip outside their network then like they do now, but the outliers were few and far between and fairly easy to find. It took a while, but the idea finally took hold that these outliers could offer a massive boon to our country and ultimately our world. They needed to be studied instead of killed outright. So TAP was born."

"Why wasn't I chipped at birth?"

"How do you know you weren't?"

"Because I remember; being chipped at the age of five is the clearest memory I have."

He squinted his eyes, seemingly trying to figure out how to respond. "Well, there could be a lot of reasons for the delay. If I were to guess, I would say because your parents were scientists for the government entity making the chips, they were probably allowed to wait until you were older. There are other reasons that babies don't get chipped at birth, but those are mostly due to health." It kind of felt like he was placating me.

"I guess my dad would be the only one able to answer those questions." The idea of visiting him in jail crossed my mind, and not for the first time, but the very thought had me recoiling. Visiting him was not an option—I'd have to get answers another way. "Regardless of how it happened, the experiment was a success, but my dad killed my mom to keep it secret. So how does everyone know about me?"

He shook his head. "You got on everyone's radar the night you used the chip on Jenna. We assumed it was a fluke. It's not uncommon for a person who can use the chip to do so under great duress. But our research has shown that just because a person uses it once, it doesn't mean they can do so at will. It rarely works like that, actually. At first, TAP tried to train anyone who used the chip once to control it, but those training sessions were almost never successful. The FBI put a stop to the practice. You used the chip for the first time at almost twenty-two years old—that kind of one-time activity would normally be ignored. But I was put on the case for reasons unknown to me. It was a cake job . . . at first." He looked back at me, one eyebrow raised. "TAP didn't come after you that first time for the same reason the government usually doesn't. Chip use one time in twenty years is meaningless."

I shook my head. "So everyone's after me now because I used the chip . . ." I tried to take a mental tally, but my brain hurt, and Anton beat me to it.

"Five times in twenty-four hours. That's why everyone is after you. You're officially an asset now."

I took a few seconds to let that sink in. I was an asset. I couldn't for the life of me figure out why they needed me. Surely there were plenty of people who could do what I could by now. What was one extra?

"So what now? Are we going to be on the run forever?"

He shook his head. "I'm turning you over to the FBI very soon. But there are things you need to know before I do. The first thing you need to know is that the chip can and has been used on you." Pain shot through my head like fire. It reverberated like a bell's toll. My head lolled, and my eyes began to roll back in my head from the onslaught.

Anton's arm shot through the front seats; his huge hand palmed the back of my head and roughly pushed it between my knees. I took deep gulps of air and tried to focus on staying conscious through the pain. Anton had the information I'd wanted my whole life. Our time was limited. There was no way I was going to miss one thing he had to say to me.

The pain began to subside, and I lifted my head. "I'm susceptible to the chip? Anyone can use it on me?"

He nodded. "You are. You can use your chip on others, an incredibly rare thing, but the chip can still be successfully used on you. At least until you learn what it feels like. You can learn to block it, and the messages can be overridden, but it takes time and practice. It's part of what we train people to do." The fog in my brain became thicker, and the throbbing began again, though not as bad as the last time. I held my head, knowing that the electric pains would come eventually. Anton turned back to look at me, the look on his face as serious as I'd ever seen it. "A lot of what you understand about your life has been implanted." He took a deep breath and said, "Your name is not Channing Walker."

I had only half a second to let what Anton said sink in before I shrieked in a pain so intense I thought my head was going to literally explode. I couldn't make sense of what was in my mind, or the world around me.

THE ANGEL PROJECT

Everything was spinning. It wasn't until the car came to a stop that I realized we'd been hit. The shocking pains were still reverberating in my head, and the mental fog was so thick that my brain felt like mush. The car door opened, and hands and arms were inside the vehicle, grabbing at me, calling my name. I was pulled out of the car, and all I could do was moan and groan in pian. The last thing I saw was Anton, unconscious, blood running down his face and dripping onto his suit. He was slumped over the steering wheel, the car horn blaring.

TWELVE

I PUSHED AND PULLED MY sore body against the hands holding me, trying to get back to Anton. To see if he was okay, to get more information. I had to talk to him. I knew in my gut he was the only one who would tell me the truth about who I was. My head continued to pound when I thought of his last words to me. *A lot of what you understand about your life has been implanted. Your name is not Channing Walker.* If Anton had been accurate concerning the mental fog and shooting pain caused by the brain's attempt to override the chip, then the way my head hurt now indicated what he'd said must be true. How could that be? Channing Walker wasn't my name? What was it? Who was I? The shocks wracking my head felt like direct strikes of lightning, one after the other.

My mental fog was so thick I was having a hard time fighting the people who now had their hands on me. I had to stop trying to override the chip. I needed to feel like myself, or at least whatever version of myself I'd been told was true. I thought back to my parents, to the fight they'd had over me when I was eight. They'd called me

THE ANGEL PROJECT

Channing in that memory. I thought of my father's sentencing. I thought of the foster care system, the meth house with Crystal, Skid Row. I let the memories wash over my mind like a hot shower, warm and comforting. Finally, my mind began to clear, and I was able to begin to gather information about what was going on around me.

I was being pulled backward, an arm through each elbow. My feet were dragging along the pavement at a fast clip. We were in an alley between buildings. I could tell the buildings' bottom floors housed restaurants as the mixture of savory and rotten smells assaulted my senses as they wafted from the dumpsters.

I was about twenty feet from Anton's car, and I heard a door from another vehicle open behind me. I could make out enough in the conversation to know that I was about to be put into their car. A memory of my training with Anton flashed through my mind: never go to the second place with a captor. Because you rarely escaped the second place. I needed to fight like my life depended on it not to go with them, because it probably did.

With that thought, I twisted my wrists and yanked them from the grasp of whoever was pulling me across the asphalt. She yelled for assistance, but I was too fast for that. I jumped to my feet and used the momentum to push her back, so she landed on her backside several feet away from me. I turned around just in time to spin away from a dark-haired man, my female captor's accomplice. She had recovered and was back on her feet and charging toward me. I kicked her to the ground. The thud of her fall was muted against the asphalt. She rolled on the ground, desperately trying to catch her breath. I had knocked the wind out of her, and she likely had a broken rib or two.

The dark-haired man then took a good look at me, the surprise evident on his face. He held up his hands and said in a placating voice, "Channing, we're here to help you."

I crouched into my fighting stance: feet apart, rooted to the ground, my legs bent slightly at the knees. I pulled my loose fists close to my face, my elbows close to my sides, and my chin down. "I don't want your help."

"We're here to teach you more about yourself. That's all."

"Likely story." Suddenly everyone wanted to tell me about the chip.

His hands were still up in the universal sign of surrender. "Like I said, we're here to help you." When he finished his speech, his icy blue eyes connected with mine. It was only then I noticed a metal device fitted to the side his head. With a tap from his finger, a tiny light on the device flashed from red to green, and I felt the light buzzing in my brain; my whole body went on alert. If I hadn't used the chip so many times in the last eighteen hours, I wouldn't have even recognized it. It would have been like the time with Jenna, when in my anger, I didn't feel the chip turn on, didn't realize what I'd done until it was too late. But this time, I felt when the connection was made, the tether between our minds. My stomach clenched, and a level of fear that I'd never known wreaked havoc on my body. He was going to use the chip on me. He was going to make me want to go with them, to trust them. I would lose all the knowledge I'd just gained from Anton. I had reasons to trust Anton, and many reasons not to, the least of which was the fact that our relationship, as I'd understood it, had been a lie. But so far everything he'd told me had checked out, and I couldn't deny that something deep inside me trusted him. And this man, this stranger who'd hit Anton's car and dragged me out of it, was going to try to take it all away.

And just like that, the fear surging through my veins turned to anger.

No. He would not manipulate me like this. I would not allow it. I turned off my chip, just like I normally did when I was done using it. I shut it down as fast as he'd turned it on. The buzzing in my head stopped in an instant, and the man gasped in surprise. Then almost just as quickly, his expression turned suspicious. "Who taught you to do that?"

Anton had said I could control it with training; having never received any such training, I'd done the only thing that made sense and got seriously lucky. But I wasn't about to tell the dark-haired man that. I used his surprise to give him a roundhouse kick to the face. I didn't so much as wait for him to fall to the ground before I turned and ran back to Anton.

The horn continued to blare, indicating he was still passed out on the steering wheel. I wrenched open his door and was relieved to find him breathing. I shook his shoulder, hard. "Anton. Anton, you need to wake up. We've been hit and people are after me. I think it's the TAP people." I didn't think that was how the FBI operated.

As hard as I tried to stay calm, panic began to seize me. I only gave him about five seconds to come around, and when he didn't, I started to push him over to the passenger seat. But with Anton being well over two hundred pounds of solid muscle, I could barely get his dead weight to budge. "Anton. Please." The alarm in my voice was rising, and I didn't know if that was what did the trick or not, but Anton finally started to stir.

He moaned. "Channing." Then in an instant, like a man possessed, he shot up in his seat, his head turning every direction until he saw me. His relief was evident for only a moment before he looked over my shoulder and yelled, "Get down!"

I didn't hesitate. But it was too late. I felt the darts hit and a surge go through my body. It felt like hundreds of bees swarmed under my skin, stingers out, dragging them along my nerve endings. It made every muscle in my body cramp like a full-body charley horse. I heard Anton grunt as he was struck as well, felt his body tense behind me. The woman kept her Taser trained on Anton, while the dark-haired man, with what appeared to be a broken and bloody nose, picked me up and walked me the twenty feet to his car. I was helpless to stop him. He dumped me in the back seat unceremoniously, then delivered another electrical shock, probably payback for the broken nose. I grunted as my body spasmed, cramping worse than the first time.

He got in the driver's seat and drove over to pick up the woman. He went so fast that I rolled into the space between the front and back seats, and I could do nothing to stop myself. I felt almost paralyzed from the muscle contractions. The woman opened the door, then shot Anton with the Taser again, presumably to buy them some time, and gingerly jumped in the passenger-side door, all the while holding her ribs.

I heard Anton yell my name as we peeled out of the alley, but there was nothing for it. I was in the hands of the Angel Project.

THIRTEEN

My muscles screamed for relief. I tried to separate myself from the pain so I could think logically. I knew a shot from a Taser gun lasted anywhere from five to thirty seconds, and I could tell that this was the thirty-second variety. That said, regardless of how long the shock lasted, full recovery typically took about fifteen minutes. Getting shot twice in a row was a new experience for me and one that I'd rather not repeat. I could tell my body was going to take its sweet time to get me to a place where I could fight back. Even though I could feel that the effects were wearing off, my body felt weak and sore, while it trembled with the trauma I'd just experienced.

"Make the call," the man instructed the woman.

She nodded and pulled a phone out of the console. She held it up to her ear and said, "We have her." There were a couple of "nos" and "yeses" followed by her hanging up the phone. She looked at the man and on a shallow breath hissed, "This better be worth it."

In my less-than-ideal state, I tried to take stock of my

surroundings. There wasn't much to note. I was in a sedan with the man and woman who'd taken me captive. The car moved as quickly as the crowded side streets of LA permitted, which wasn't very fast. If I could just regain composure of my body, I could jump out of the car at a stoplight. But I knew I wouldn't get very far in my current condition. Every minute was crucial to my body's healing. But every minute I was stuck in their car meant I was that much farther from Anton.

The woman and the man were a little worse for the wear, but they were alert and seemed to be functioning on a much higher level than I was at the moment. They were both wearing those devices on the sides of their heads, which were about the size of the external portion of a cochlear implant but made of metal. The woman's was covered by her hair making it more difficult to see, however, the metal reflected off her dark hair and skin when it came in direct contact with sunlight. I couldn't tell if they were implants or something that could be removed and replaced at will. They weren't talking but looked at one another every so often with raised eyebrows. Like they wanted to talk about what had just occurred but felt like they shouldn't in my presence.

From the passenger seat, the woman looked back at me every few seconds, a Taser gun firmly planted in her lap, her expression pained and suspicious. She continued to hold her arm across her rib cage, and every time the car hit a dip, her gasp was audible. The man kept his eyes on the road, and a wad of tissues held to his still-bleeding nose, the bruising around which was beginning to color deep and purple.

I needed to get away from these people, but I had to wait until I was sure I could truly get away before I even attempted it. Too early and I'd just end up Tasered again but possibly tied up. The fact that I wasn't tied up now attested to something that was becoming clearer to me by the second. These two had never dealt with a target who fought back. They didn't seem particularly well trained in combat, nor in the use of Tasers, which they had wielded like novices. They probably just used mind control and therefore only dealt with willing victims. No combat training necessary.

It was possible that all of TAP was the same, relying on the chip to do the work for them. But they'd never met someone like me. I would fight tooth and nail to keep them out of my brain.

What scared me the most was the unknown. I had no idea what I would be facing when we got to our destination. Did they have some kind of supercomputer that could override my attempts at shutting them out of my mind? Would I turn into some kind of mind-controlled drone?

Though I was in incredible pain and struggling with immense confusion and brain fog, I didn't want to forget a single thing Anton had said. Not one single thing. I needed to see him again; I needed more answers. Forgetting what Anton had told me—forgetting Anton— that was the biggest fear I had at the moment. I wanted to know who I really was. And Anton was the only one willing to tell me. *Your name is not Channing Walker.* Just that little thought thickened the fog in my brain into impenetrable clouds. I desperately wanted to know what that fog was hiding. But I didn't have time to think about it.

Getting back to Anton was my priority. In order to do that, I needed out of this car.

As the minutes passed, I felt the trembling in my limbs begin to calm, and little by little I could feel my strength returning. I heaved myself back up onto the seat, still lying down, causing the woman to turn back, Taser up. She pointed it at me. "Don't move."

I held up my hand and spoke in the most pained voice I could muster: "Don't shoot. I just needed to get off the car floor." I needed a plan. A better one than jump and run. Then again, maybe that was good enough. I could outrun the man and the woman, and I could definitely outlast them. They had office job written all over their physiques. They didn't have my training. Anton had taught me so many valuable skills and worked me to the brink. I hoped I'd get to thank him for that someday. Even better if that day happened to be today.

It took several minutes for me to inch toward the door on the driver's side, ever so slowly. Then a few things happened at once, and I got my lucky break. A phone rang and the woman answered it, effectively distracting her from me and the Taser in her lap. Simultaneously, the car stopped at what I assumed was a traffic light. This was my chance.

Still lying down, I scooted quickly toward the door. I reached between my feet, staying low, and silently pulled the handle. Then I took a chance and grabbed the Taser out of the woman's lap, kicked the door open, and jumped feet first into the street. The man yelled for me, fumbling to put the car in park and open his door, but he was no match for me. I ran with abandon.

My goal was to get as far away as fast as possible. It took me a bit to take in my surroundings. We were at the entrance to the Bob Hope Airport. They were going to take me somewhere that required a *plane*? Where were their headquarters? My parents had worked for TAP out of Los Angeles. Anton's words rang in my mind: *A lot of what you understand about your past has been implanted.* Did I know anything that was true? For all I knew, I'd grown up in Ohio. Would I ever get the truth?

I ran down the street using the shoulder. There were no cars coming my way or I would have flagged one down and begged for ride. But I could hear a car behind me and I pushed harder.

At the sound of screeching tires, I looked back to see how much space was between me and the incoming car, and my heart nearly stopped. It wasn't the same man and woman coming for me this time.

I felt like I was about to breathe fire with how hard my lungs were burning. But adrenaline pumped through my veins and I took off again. I hated the concrete jungle that was Los Angeles. There were no forests of trees to hide in, no big lake to jump into. I was out there running like a maniac for everyone to see. There was nowhere to hide. At least nowhere obvious. I couldn't keep up this pace forever, and I couldn't outrun a car. All they had to do was keep an eye on me and I was as good as theirs. I would have to slow down eventually. If I was going to get away, I was going to have to get creative.

"Channing!" The voice made me stop in my tracks. I

turned on my heel and saw Anton in the back seat of the second sedan. I could have crumpled in relief. But the feeling didn't last long—the man and woman who'd originally taken me hostage were speeding up behind Anton's car, trying to force a collision. Anton saw the panicked look on my face and turned around just in time to pull his gun up and start shooting.

A bullet went straight through the windshield and right into the middle of the man's forehead. The shot was so perfect it almost seemed fake, like we were in a movie. But it didn't stop the car from barreling forward. The driver, though dead, must have kept his foot on the gas pedal. Anton's car lurched forward but didn't have time to move completely out of the way. It was rear-ended. Thankfully, the collision wasn't nearly as devastating as it could have been.

I ran for the black sedan as soon as I was close enough. Anton pulled me inside next to him and shut the door, and not a second passed before the car took off. I was seated right beside him, our bodies touching from shoulder to ankle. He looked back at the car behind us, and his mouth nearly touched my ear as he whispered, "They got to the hospital before I did and took you. I pursued their vehicle, and that's when the collision happened in the alley." I nodded while I tried to work the new story out in my mind. Anton was trying to keep his cover, and I was more than happy to assist. I wanted a lot of things, but nothing more than to finish the conversation we'd started earlier.

Anton turned back toward the front of the car and scooted over a few inches. I immediately wished he'd move back—being so near to someone who knew me was a comfort I really craved in that moment. I'd grown soft in the last few years. Having friends I could count on made me want conversation and human contact in a way that made me weak. But I couldn't help it, and I didn't want to go back to being alone. Right now, I only really had two people left in this world, and Anton was one of them. Being in the car with him, so close my senses were filled with his spicy scent, made me want to lean into his reassuring touch.

The two men in the front of the car looked like textbook FBI agents. The one in the passenger seat appeared to be in his mid-forties; his medium-brown hair was cut short with a side part, and he was wearing a dark-blue suit with a white shirt and dark skinny tie. His look was topped off with dark sunglasses. He turned back to me. "Channing. I'm Agent Reid Baldric, FBI. Glad to see you in one piece." He pointed to the man next to him, whose curly hair was shiny, jet black, and also cut short. He was wearing the same dark suit. He was younger, though, in his thirties perhaps, and his skin was a rich brown. "This here is Agent Krithvik Diaz. We call him Vik." Vik made eye contact with me in the review mirror and greeted me with a somewhat flirtatious eyebrow raise. His smiling eyes had the bright appearance of good humor. He seemed to be quite curious how this whole thing would play out, and he didn't hide that fact. I liked him immediately.

I nodded but kept my eyes wild, looking around the car. I shot Anton a questioning glance and looked back at Baldric. "I guess I can assume that it wasn't just fortuitous timing that the FBI showed up in the exact moment I needed them?"

Agent Baldric's expression gave me nothing. "Why do you think we picked you up?"

That was the most annoying law enforcement question ever. Either you got it right, all but admitting guilt, or you got it wrong and further incriminated yourself with another infraction. He was waiting for me to respond. But I had no idea what to say. This was a potential minefield. I didn't know the ins and outs of the version of the story Anton had told them. If TAP picked me up at the hospital and Anton failed to extricate me from their clutches, did I know that Anton was with the FBI? Should I be surprised that I'd been picked up by the FBI? Should I be angry at Anton for the years of deceit? That much I wouldn't have to fake. I may have craved his familiarity, but I was still beyond angry that everything I had experienced with him had been fabricated.

Unsure of what to say, and still breathless from all the running, I huffed out the safest response I could imagine on such short notice. "Am I under arrest?"

Baldric looked me over for a solid minute like he was trying to read my face and body language. I couldn't tell if he liked what he saw or not. I was pretty good at reading people, as one had to be on Skid Row, but Baldric gave nothing away. Fortunately for both me and Anton, if there was one thing growing up in foster care and living on the streets had taught me, it was how to lie. I could be innocent, guilty, experienced, cunning, virtuous, or any number of things to get what I wanted. I'd sworn off lying when I'd decided to change my life and leave the streets behind, but at this point all bets were off. I was right back in Survival 101—the stakes were just higher now. I looked at Anton and then back to Agent Baldric and schooled myself to appear downright cagey. "Are *we* under arrest? I don't know what's going on here, but Anton was just trying to help me." I pointed behind us. "Those people kidnapped me."

He studied me again. This time his eyes narrowed a fraction in disbelief. I could only assume this was the handler Anton was talking about. The one whose calls he had ignored. Baldric was definitely suspicious. Not to be deterred, I forged ahead. Grabbing Anton's hand, I gave him a guilty look and then looked back at Baldric, letting him see I did in fact know exactly why the FBI was after me. "He has nothing to do with this; he was only trying to help." I swallowed and looked Agent Baldric in the eye. "I'll tell you whatever you want to know."

Anton stiffened a bit beside me. Baldric, not missing a thing, said, "We know who you are, Ms. Walker. We know just about everything there is to know about you." He looked pointedly at Anton. "Anton here is the one who fed us the information."

"What?" I looked at Baldric and then Anton in utter confusion. When Anton had nothing to say, I made a show of dropping his hand. "Anton, what is he talking about?"

Anton looked guilty, and to his credit, it didn't seem feigned. Then he shot Baldric the dirtiest look I'd ever seen him give. "I'm an FBI agent, Channing."

THE ANGEL PROJECT

The air left my lungs in a sharp hiss of disbelief. "What . . . ?" I channeled all the hurt and shock that was still very real and very fresh and looked at him like he was completely foreign to me. The shock may have been an act, but the hurt, that was 100 percent real. "What?" The question came out breathy, almost a whisper. "Since the beginning?"

He nodded once, succinctly, and couldn't quite make eye contact with me. The guilt on his face was real; it was eating him up. That fact didn't make me feel bad in the slightest.

I scooted as far over as I could in the small space, until my body was pressed against the door. My chin trembled, and a tear fell down my cheek. My emotions on this subject were raw and unprocessed—the whole thing still had me reeling. Rehashing it made the hurt I'd suppressed, in favor of survival, surface anew. I still couldn't believe Anton had done this to me, *spied* on me. The pain I felt was like a knife to the chest—or back. He'd probably been in my apartment, probably bugged it, probably heard every private word I'd said to Darcy. Another tear rolled down my cheek. My body began to shake with the suppressed pain, rage, and downright embarrassment that accompanied that kind of violation. I sunk even closer to the door.

"I was trying to protect you," Anton's husky voice rang through the silent car.

It was all too much, the thought of him picking my brain for information while training at Mike's and him rifling through my things at night. I lashed out and yelled, "You were lying to me!" His eyes widened, and he reared back like I'd punched him. Quietly, I professed through my tears, "I thought you were my friend." That was a much harder blow than any punch. He knew that I had very few friends, that my existence had been a lonely one, fraught with heartache and pain. He *knew* how hard it was for me to put my faith in another human being. And I had given that to him: my friendship, my loyalty, my trust. All of it. I'd put all of my trust in Anton; not in a million years would I have thought that he could've done this to me. That's what hurt the most. Quietly, so quietly, I said, "I trusted you."

Anton closed his eyes, bowed his head, and rubbed a hand down his face. He looked at me and nodded, his eyes heavy and desperate with apology. Then he turned to face the window, giving me as much space as the car would allow for. There was no acting here—this was a conversation that needed to happen. I'd been able to set aside my feelings during the chase, but they came back with abandon now. Hurt and betrayal flooded my body until I was drowning in them. I'd lost Darcy this morning, and now I was losing Anton. Aside from Cole, whom I didn't know if I'd ever see again, I had no one. After all of that work, after all of the effort it took to put myself out there, to love and trust the few people I had, to love and trust Anton—it had all been stomped on. This beautiful part of my life, the only beautiful part of my life, had become bitter.

Agent Baldric cleared his throat. He appeared to be somewhat taken aback by the intensity of Anton's and my argument. "I'm sorry you had to find out like this,

Channing. The relationship between an agent and his charge has always been a difficult one."

I scoffed. "I'm not anyone's charge. I never asked for a babysitter."

"No, you didn't. But we were kind enough to assign you one anyway."

My head snapped up. "So you're saying I should be thanking you?" Baldric looked back at me like I was a teenaged girl having a tantrum. But I continued on, turning to Anton, "Thank you so much for lying to me for the last three years, Anton. For gaining my trust and then stomping on it." I turned back to Baldric. "Thank you for assigning him to me, for forcing him to violate our friendship for whatever information you desired. Thank you also for—"

"Stop." Baldric cut me off. "You have no idea what you're capable of, nor what you're up against. Believe it or not, Anton was assigned to you not only to protect you, but to allow you to have a normal life. And believe it or not, agents often become friends with their assigned charges, real friends. They often develop feelings for them that are outside the bureau's standard guidelines for appropriate behavior." He gave Anton a pointed look. "We overlook that as much as possible, because we understand that when you invest that much time and effort getting to know someone, nature has a way of overtaking professionalism."

I snuck a glance at Anton; he was stonefaced staring straight at Baldric, his expression one I couldn't fully read, like too many emotions were whirling through his mind. The only one I could pick out was anger—that one was loud and clear. For my part, I didn't know how to process Baldric's words. I winced every time he said *assigned*. The idea that I'd been assigned to Anton really chaffed. More than that, it hurt. It was embarrassing. I trusted him, confided in him. And I'd been his *assignment*. That was the crux of it: I felt like a joke. Like a clueless loser who couldn't see the forest for the trees.

If I could've seen past my embarrassment, I would have supposed that Baldric was trying to tell me that the relationship between Anton and me was real, in the sense that he believed that Anton's friendly feelings for me were real. But honestly, what did Baldric know about Anton's real feelings? I forced all that down and moved ahead with the most important issue: "Why don't you tell me what I'm up against, and what I am capable of? Because if I'm valuable enough to be *assigned* a federal agent for three years, then it has nothing to do with allowing me to have a normal life. Last I checked, the Feds don't waste time playing therapist."

He again looked at me like I was little more than a petulant child and attempted to placate me with, "You'll get the answers to that once we get to the bureau." Then he faced forward, effectively indicating the time for explanations was over.

I turned to look at Anton. He gave me a look that was half unease, half sorrow. I gave him a small upturn of my lips, a look I hoped conveyed that I understood that he was just doing his job. I hated that I had been said job, but I knew enough to understand that one probably didn't say no to an assignment in the FBI.

As I sat there, though, a few things dawned on me.

THE ANGEL PROJECT

First, Anton had picked me up at the hospital, outside the FBI's knowledge. Then he'd driven me around and given me information—he had things he wanted to tell me, things that the FBI apparently wouldn't. That proved he was loyal to me, at least in some regard. I looked at him again, this time with different feelings, warmer ones. He could see the softening in my expression, and he let out a deep breath, closing his eyes, his shoulders sagging a fraction in relief.

One thing I wanted to know was, Why hadn't he come forward sooner? Why hadn't he talked to me about what was going on? Why wait until the bottom had dropped out and everything went crazy?

This was a conversation we needed to have, but it was obviously going to be put on hold. I dropped back in my seat and allowed my head to lean back against the headrest. I hadn't gotten much sleep the night before, and my day thus far had been more than a little exhausting. My head lopped toward the window, and I looked at the car next to us. There was a man in the driver's seat. He was young, younger than me at any rate, with fair skin and longish, dark, curly hair. He was keeping speed with our car, his window aligned with mine, and he kept looking over at me. We made eye contact, and he held it, intensely, for several seconds, until he had to look at the road. As soon as he could, he looked back at me again, just staring with that intense, almost imploring, look.

I looked back at him confused, unsure of what he wanted from me. He continued looking at me, almost as if I should know who he was. Like I should trust him.

We continued our staring contest until Agent Diaz—Vik—peeled off the road onto the on-ramp for LAX. The strange game lasted for at least a few minutes. When Vik made the move to leave the highway, my staring stranger appeared to panic. He slammed on his brakes and attempted to get over—to follow us? Me? I didn't know, and it didn't matter, because behind us, I could see that he never made it onto the off-ramp.

FOURTEEN

I LOOKED OVER AT ANTON to see if he'd seen the strange exchange between me and the guy in the car next to ours. He was still shooting daggers into the back of Baldric's head, so it was safe to assume he'd missed it. I couldn't stop thinking about it. As if Anton could sense my discomfort, he looked over at me imploringly. I could tell him and the rest of the car about it, and probably should have, but there was something about the exchange that had me staying quiet. The man's intent hadn't felt malicious, and in fact felt quite the opposite—he looked like he wanted to help me. Like he might be worried about me. I wasn't sure what to make of it.

I was so caught up in the stranger that I didn't even notice the car had stopped until Agent Baldric was opening his door and getting out. I tried to do the same, but it appeared my door was child locked—Anton's as well. He sighed and waited for Vik to open his door. In the few precious seconds we had alone in the car together, he asked, "Everything okay?"

He immediately cringed. I let out a short puff of air,

a mix between a laugh and a sigh—everything was most definitely not okay, and he knew it. Before I had a chance to respond, our doors opened. As I was exiting the car, I heard Vik say, "Come on out, Blue Eyes." I turned back, and Anton was rolling those very same blue eyes at Vik.

"Don't hate 'cause the ladies love me." Then he winked. I was half annoyed and half surprised they could make jokes at a time like this. Regardless, I couldn't hold in my snort. They both looked over at me and smiled.

I got out of the car, and Baldric's hand clamped around my arm only slightly looser than a vise. I looked at him, clearly annoyed, and tried to shake his hand off. His grip tightened. "I can all but guarantee enemies are closing in on us. We're not going to take any chances."

He could only be talking about TAP. Being in FBI custody was comforting by comparison. I didn't care much for Baldric, but his intentions toward me didn't seem pernicious. If I was going to pick one entity to be in the custody of, it was the FBI, hands down. I sighed heavily to let him know I was not happy about the strength of his grip, but I stopped trying to fight it.

Anton took my other arm, and Vik came around the front, staying a few feet ahead of us. I may not have been handcuffed, but I felt, and certainly looked, like a prisoner. "Does the FBI typically fly commercial?" I asked no one in particular.

It was Baldric who answered. "We only use government aviation transport when we're on a mission."

My eyebrows rose in question. "Is this not a mission?"

Baldric looked down at me from his height of at least

an inch or two above six feet. "It is, but not the caliber requiring excessively expensive transport."

"Huh ... even when the 'charge' has the power of mind control?"

His grip on my arm tightened. "For the record, Ms. Walker, using the chip on anyone is a crime. Using it on a federal agent is a serious felony."

I laughed. "Are those laws on the books, Agent Baldric?"

"They are where you're going. We have a whole set of special laws for Chip Utilizers, and we do enforce them." He looked at me for a fraction of a second. "Just be sure you don't get any ideas, all three of us are well trained in deflecting the chip. It's why we're the ones who have the pleasure of picking you up."

I remembered then that Anton was the one who'd told me I could block messages from other people's chips. That it was something they train people to do. "Is that what you're going to teach me? To deflect chip infiltration?"

Baldric looked at me then, really looked at me. His expression was hard to read. "It appears you already know how to do that, Ms. Walker."

I cocked my head in question. "Are you talking about when I was with TAP?"

Anton cleared his throat. "I saw that they were wearing transmitters."

I shook my head. "The things attached to their heads? Do they work like the chip?"

Baldric nodded. "They're computers made to infiltrate chips. How did you get around them?"

I shrugged. "That was a fluke. The man tried to send me a message; I felt the connection and my chip turn on. All I did was turn it off. The man was so shocked that he make another attempt."

"You turned what off? Your chip?" He looked at me, his eyebrows practically touching his hairline.

Vik looked back at me too, and I shrugged and nodded. He whistled under his breath.

Baldric stared for another second. "Huh," was all he said before facing forward again.

"What?"

"Maybe we should have used government aviation after all."

We got to bypass the security line, which was a serious perk, because the line snaked for what seemed like a half a mile. We still had to go through security, but it was a much shorter version. I'd flown before, but it had been a long time ago . It was back when I was still living with my parents. We went on vacation, usually once a year. Those trips were almost always to the beach—my mom said it was her "happy place." For the first time, that particular memory struck me as weird. If I'd grown up in Los Angeles, why would we have taken a plane to the beach? My mind began to fog up when I tried to recall the location of the beach. The fog blurred my memories and made it impossible to recall them. It was incredibly frustrating. I could see us at the beach, the palm trees swaying, my parents holding hands and laughing from their lounge chairs, watching me build a sandcastle. I could almost feel the grains of sand between my fingers.

But when I tried to remember where we were, there was nothing.

Who was I? Who were my parents? Why had they done this to me? *What was my real name*? That last question had my head pounding. The mental fog was thick, and I could feel the shooting pains gearing up. I moaned, and all of the agents turned at once. I winced. "I have a sudden headache." Anton pumped my arm as the other two looked away.

I looked up at him, and he looked down at me with the sternest expression he could muster.

I shook my head, trying to clear the fog. "It's just that I haven't flown since I was a kid. I was trying to remember where I'd traveled to." I shrugged. "All I remember is the beach. We could have been in Hawaii, Tahiti, or Florida—it's unbelievably frustrating that I can't remember where I've been."

Baldric casually replied, "All of our memories from childhood are fuzzy. Wait until you get to be my age." The man wasn't sixty-five—he was forty-five, maybe fifty if he had aged really well.

Anton pumped my arm again. This time he mouthed, "Stop trying to remember. It's dangerous."

It was only then that I noticed a person keeping pace with us. He was just a few feet to the right of Anton. With a jolt I realized it was the guy from the car. I gasped, and Anton looked at me and more resolutely mouthed, "Stop!" He thought I was still trying to get my old memories to resurface. He couldn't have been more wrong. I looked over at the guy from the car again, and this time he was looking at me with that same concerned expression from our earlier staring contest. Anton caught me looking, but he must have quickly deemed the man a non-threat, because he instantly moved on. Who was he? How had he caught up with us? How had he made it through security so fast? And the most obvious and frightening question of all: Was he with TAP? I was about to alert the agents to his presence when one thought stopped me. If he was with TAP, wouldn't he have tried to run our car off the road earlier? Wouldn't he be grabbing at me now, trying to separate me from the FBI? But more than anything, he wasn't wearing a transmitter I could see.

Adrenaline pumped through my whole body. My heart was beating so fast I thought Anton and Baldric must have felt the blood rushing through my arms where they were holding me. I didn't know what to make of this guy. I needed time to think—time I didn't have. I knew nothing about the stranger, which scared me, but a gut feeling, deep down, made me keep my silence. I looked over again. The man had walked a few paces ahead of us, so I was looking at his back. With his arm resting at his side, I could see that he had a hot-pink Post-it Note in his hand. It was folded in half, and he toyed with it between his fingers for a few seconds, then slipped it into his pocket and picked up his pace.

I watched him walk away from us in the hallway, seeming for all the world like he was just another person about to board a plane. My eyes didn't leave the back of his head. He eventually turned into a restroom, which we passed by without incident. I almost craned my head back, to see if he was going to follow, but I didn't want to attract any more attention from the federal agents.

There was something about him, though, something different altogether from the FBI or TAP agents. Something safer. It was just him, one person. He was on the skinny side, and he didn't look particularly trained in self-defense, though I knew better than to judge a book by its cover. He just didn't seem threatening; he seemed the opposite. Not that it mattered. I was being held tightly by two large agents. I wasn't going anywhere they didn't plan on taking me.

We arrived at our gate and sat down. After a quick and disappointing search for the guy from the car, I fell back against my seat exhausted. This felt like the longest day in history, and it was only a little past lunchtime. Unfortunately, time didn't fly when you were scared for your life. It inched by, every tick of the clock dragging out longer than the one before.

Vik looked at Baldric. "Things seem pretty chill here, boss. All right if I run to the bathroom before we take off?" Baldric nodded and Vik got up from his seat.

Baldric's phone rang. He took it out of his jacket pocket and looked at the screen with a sigh. He stepped just a couple of feet away to answer it. I heard him quietly say, "Hi, honey. Things okay? How are the kids?"

Anton sighed, "Finally. I thought we'd never get a moment alone."

I gave a half-suppressed laugh and nodded, when something caught my eye. I turned to Baldric's empty seat, and there was a half-folded hot-pink Post-it Note sitting right there in the middle of his chair. My pulse sped up, but I worked hard not to show any outward sign. Instead, I acted like I was looking over at Baldric and said, "Yeah, well, we have way too much to discuss for just a moment." As Anton looked away, I nonchalantly picked up the note and slipped it into my pocket.

Anton blew out a breath. "Channing, we've got so much to discuss a month wouldn't be enough time." He picked up my hand and gently squeezed it a couple of times. "How are you holding up?"

I looked at him. "I'm not, really. I think I'm running on adrenaline and fumes." I worried my lip. "Where are you guys taking me, Anton?"

"Quantico."

I cocked my head. "Not the FBI Headquarters?"

He shook his head. "No, the BAU. The Behavioral Analysis Unit."

My mouth dropped open. "Like *Criminal Minds*? Am I considered a violent criminal? Am I going to the Violent Criminal Apprehension Program?"

He laughed heartily. "First of all, the ViCAP isn't a place. It's a database—a tool available to all law enforcement agencies nationwide. Secondly, *Criminal Minds* is a television drama. The BAU is not the same as the one you've seen on the show. The real BAU is split into two halves, one for typical criminal investigation and the other for atypical criminal investigation. In more recent years it's where we deal with crimes regarding the chip."

"So I'm under investigation, then?"

He blew out a breath. "You've used the chip five

THE ANGEL PROJECT

times in the last twenty-four hours, Channing. Each one of those incidents is a crime in and of itself." He held up his hand to stave off my objection. "It's clear you didn't use it maliciously. And at the moment, the FBI has no interest in pursuing criminal charges. But, for obvious reasons, people who can utilize their chips, can't go around controlling other people." He paused, not sure whether he should tell me the rest. "You are going to have to go through our training program." I scrunched up my face in confusion. "Not FBI training, but CU training. Chip Utilizers. In order to live in society, all CUs must be trained and agree to follow the laws governing Chip Utilizers. Above all else, you will be trained and taught how to use the chip, and you will be properly warned of the criminal liability of unauthorized usage. There's work at the BAU and FBI Headquarters for people who can utilize their chips. They'll want you to work for them." I reared my head back. "That aside, you have proven excellent at controlling your chip on your own I know of no individual who is able to exhibit such skill with regard to controlling their chip. The FBI is going to want to know how you do it." He clicked his tongue. "So, are you under investigation? No. Could they threaten you with criminal charges if you don't play ball? Yep." He looked directly at me. "So, my advice? Play ball." He shrugged and looked away. "Who knows, you might enjoy the work we do there and want to be a part of it."

I had so many follow-up questions, I didn't know where to start. More than anything, his words from earlier plagued my mind. I lowered my voice to a whisper. "Earlier, you said both TAP and the FBI want to use me."

He snuck a look at Baldric, who was still on the phone six feet away from us. Anton nodded, just once. "What did you mean? How does the FBI want to use me?"

He let that question stew for a moment—a moment we didn't have. "I was just referring to the work you would do there." He shrugged. "It's not 'using*'* you if you agree to it."

That was cryptic. "What if I don't want to work there?"

"I would recommend waiting until you are fully informed before making a decision."

"Are there a lot of people like me there?"

His eyes softened. "There's no one like you, anywhere."

I smiled slightly and shot him half an eye roll. Suddenly, I felt like we were back in familiar Channing-Anton territory. I really wished that were the case. That we were hitting the bag, or in the ring at Mike's, bantering back and forth.

He chuckled. "If you mean, are there other people there who can utilize their chips? Yes. There are quite a few, actually. We estimate about two-point five people per million." I did some quick math—that was almost one thousand people in the United States alone. Suddenly I couldn't wait to get there. I wanted to talk to other people who could use their chips—I wanted to pick their brains, to know how they dealt with life. Was TAP after them too? How did the FBI guard those CUs against TAP? Anton cut my thoughts short by tipping my chin up as he locked eyes with mine. "Channing, I don't think you realize how different you really are. And I know you have no idea what the chip does to people. People who can use their chips can't stop themselves. It's like a drug—but worse. So much worse. We usually have no issue locating a person who has discovered they can use their chip because they leave a trail a mile wide. They suddenly have a host of power that they're either unable or unwilling to control. We have Chip Utilizers who literally go insane over having to stop. We often catch them as children, and children don't have the capacity to fully understand the moral obligations that kind of power holds." He paused, seemingly lost in a memory for a brief moment. He shook his head and let go of my chin. "The chip is dangerous; the people who can use it are dangerous. But you ... you're something different altogether. You've known you can use your chip for the bulk of your life—your difficult, miserable life—and yet you didn't. That family—those parents who chose the dog over you—you could have compelled them to keep you. To love you. Why didn't you? Literally everyone else in the world would have."

"You can't compel someone to love you, Anton. That's not real love."

"Not real love, no. But they would have believed they loved you and treated you accordingly. You went from foster home to foster home, some of them abusive, and never took advantage of the chip once. You lived in a meth lab, in a condemned hotel, and on the streets of Skid Row, and you never once took advantage of the easiest way out. When I told you that a twenty-two-year-old using the chip for the first time was a nonevent, it's because it's absolutely true. It happens on occasion, and it's always an accident, and the chip user is always none the wiser. They just think whomever the were arguing with suddenly had a change of heart. But you knew. You knew what you did, and you knew it worked, and then you didn't use it again over the course of the next three years." He shook his head; I couldn't tell if it was in wonder or irritation. "You're unheard of. We have never come across someone like you. Not one single person."

He abruptly sat back in his seat and stopped talking to me. I turned behind me to see both Baldric and Vik coming toward us.

I felt my eyes prick. Anton thought I was special, a good person against all odds. I knew better. The reason I hadn't utilized my chip had nothing to do with being altruistic, but everything to do with abject fear. There were times when I'd turned down using the chip because I knew it was wrong, like with Sherry and the beach cottage, but the temptation to use it almost constantly gnawed at me. There were moments in my teenage years I lay in bed at night and dreamed of using it. There was a time I wanted to compel one man in particular—a foster dad—to bang his head against a brick wall for all of eternity. The real reason I didn't use the chip was because I was terrified of it. My father made sure of that with his parting words to me.

My father called the police after killing my mom. While we waited for them to arrive, my father knelt in front of me, taking me by the shoulders, with tears streaming down his face. He pulled me in and held my shaking body. He told me over and over again that he loved me, and how sorry he was, while he rubbed my back. I bathed his shirt in my tears. He pulled back from the

THE ANGEL PROJECT

embrace. With a broken but insistent voice, he said, "I know you're upset about your mother; I am too. But I need you to listen to me. You need to hear what I am about to say." I nodded, tears dripping off my chin and onto the collar of my dress. My dad had killed my mother right in front of my eyes. I'd just experienced the worst trauma a child could imagine. I should have been pushing him away, but I couldn't. My instincts were to pull closer, to hold onto him like lifeline. I think I knew, even at my younge age, I was going to lose him too. I had a weird sense I was losing everything in that moment. Like everything I loved had been or was about to be taken away, and my soul felt empty, so unbelievably empty. I could sense he was saying goodbye, and I couldn't let it happen. I needed him.

    I pulled him close and burrowed my head into his shoulder. He smoothed my hair and hugged me close, but too quickly, he pulled back again. With his forehead resting on mine, he said gently, "Channing, I know you're scared. I am too, but there is something important that I need to tell you. Are you listening?" He wiped the tears from my eyes and waited for me to nod. "The chip is used to control people. You can send messages into someone's brain that they won't be able to detect. Messages they will believe to be true. It's wrong. It's wrong to steal a person's free will. But more importantly, it's dangerous. More dangerous than you can imagine. Channing,"—his grip on my shoulders tightened—"you can never use the chip again. Ever. Do you understand what I'm saying? You can never use it again, not for any reason throughout the entirety of your life. Don't turn it on, don't send any messages, no matter how tempting. Not ever, no matter what happens. Not for any reason. If you use it, they will find you. I've done everything I can to protect you, but if you use the chip again, they will hunt you down. You will never know peace again. Your life, as you know it, will be over." The sirens got louder. His fingers bit into my shoulders. He was pleading when he said, "Channing, promise me. Please promise me you'll never use the chip as long as you live."

I nodded. "I promise."

He pulled me back into his arms. "If you do, they'll find you, Channing. Don't ever let them find you."

The boarding agent knocked me out of my reverie. "Flight 2334 to Washington, DC, Ronald Reagan Airport will begin boarding shortly."

I wasn't sure how to feel about my current predicament. If I was being honest with myself, I knew a large part of me had wanted this for a while, otherwise I never would have submitted my book for publication. The very act of writing it had been dangerous. Yet, I now felt like the rebellious teenager who always chose to learn life lessons the hard way. Ironically, I had hoped by publishing my book, I would find others like me, find answers to this thing haunting me. But the book wasn't set to be published for another three weeks, and here I was, not under arrest—but very much under arrest—with the FBI, about to meet people like me. I was getting my wish, just not in the way I imagined. At least I wasn't with TAP, the people my dad had warned me so desperately against. The other positive point was Anton's companionship and support since revealing his FBI status. He seemed willing to give me answers no one else would. Perhaps this was the best outcome I could've hoped for.

Even so, the pink Post-it in my pocket practically screamed to be read. Every time I adjusted my body, I could feel the telltale crinkle in my pocket. Car Guy had gone to a lot of trouble to get it to me, and I was desperate to be alone so I could read it. What could it possibly say? What could he possibly want me to know? Who was he with? One thing was for sure—it wasn't the FBI. But he was remarkably good at staying under their radar. Trained. No one was naturally that stealthy.

We boarded the plane, and as soon as the *Fasten Seat Belt* sign went off, I stood. "I need to use the restroom."

Baldric sighed and stood along with me.

"Are you joining me?" I raised an eyebrow. "That's gonna be a pretty tight squeeze . . ."

He all but rolled his eyes. "I'm going to guard you, Channing."

"Why? Do you think TAP is on the plane? And if they are, where exactly do you think they're going to take me?" I gestured around our metal box in the sky.

"I'm not worried about them taking you; I'm worried about them killing you. They would prefer you dead to working with us. They can shoot you in the head in plain sight, and in a matter of minutes convince the rest of the passengers they witnessed your suicide by using their transmitters."

Well, that painted a pretty picture.

He gestured to the front of the plane with a pained smile. "Now that that's settled, can we get on with it?"

I nodded. I almost thanked him for his protection,

but he was kind of a jerk about it. Honestly, Baldric was kind of a jerk, period.

As soon as I was in the tiny bathroom with the door locked, I pulled the note out of my pocket. The sticky side was holding the note closed. I carefully peeled it open. At the top of the Post-it was a phone number. The rest of the note read: *When you're questioning your existence, call me. Pax.*

FIFTEEN

I SPENT THE REMAINDER OF the plane ride thinking about his words and his name: Pax. He seemed so familiar. I had a classmate named Paxton while living with one of my foster families, but he was Korean. I was ten at the time. It wasn't so much Pax looked familiar—it was he *felt* familiar. I couldn't help but wonder if I *did* know him, but thanks to the chip, my brain had been rewired.

When you're questioning your existence, call me. Well, that ship had sailed years ago. I'd been questioning my existence after becoming an unwanted eight-year-old. Assuming Pax knew who I was and therefore my history, I wasn't sure what he meant by the statement, nor was I sure I really wanted to find out.

I was quiet on the flight to DC—so quiet Anton continually sent me questioning glances. I would just lift my hands as if to say, *Look where I am at the moment. Not feeling all that talkative.* He got the message, but I could see it concerned him that I wasn't my usual snarky self. Honestly, I didn't know if the snark was the real me or just something Anton brought out in me. I felt like my entire life I had played a series of roles. For a short time I was the keen daughter, then I morphed into whatever necessary for whichever family I was assigned. I could be kind and innocently sweet, or cold and indifferent. The time I spent behind bars and living on the streets only amplified my acting skills. I was always in survival mode. I could adjust my personality for whatever situation I found myself. When I moved in with Darcy things began to change. I would joke around with her and tease her. It made us both laugh, and I enjoyed it. But I was always careful to hide my past, to hide who I really was. No one wanted a roommate who could implant thoughts in their head. With Anton, I was different still. We joked around, for sure, but I was flirty. It was a side I enjoyed, but he was the only person who brought it out in me.

There was one boy on Skid Row—Ty—who never showed any romantic interest in me, but he was a friend of sorts. His whole family lived on the streets. They had for years. His parents were both addicts. His mom had overdosed and died, and his dad was too high to care for his kids. Addiction was a crazy thing. One was either high or doing whatever they had to do in order to get high again—it was the only thing that mattered. Ty's dad talked a big talk—he was always "just one high away from getting his life together and taking care of his family." He always needed just one more fix, and it would do the trick; it was the professed key to him getting straight. And so the cycle went.

Ty could have easily followed suit, but instead, he'd taken on the responsibility of raising his four younger siblings. They had all managed to stay clean. Ty was nineteen when we met. He and his sixteen-year-old sister both worked, but they couldn't make enough money to get their family off the streets. Especially with their dad finding their cash and stealing their meager earnings. They suffered, for sure, but Ty always had a smile on his face. I had no idea how he did it. He was one of those people who chose to be happy. I didn't know how to do that. At the time I didn't understand that happiness was a choice, but after knowing Ty, there was no denying it. He was the only one who could lift my spirits. If it weren't for Ty's influence, I don't think I would have smiled the whole time I lived on Skid Row.

Ty's skin was the beautiful warm color bred from having parents of different ethnic backgrounds. His smile was wide and full of shockingly straight white teeth despite never having braces. He kept his hair short and his clothes clean. The latter was thanks his job at a Laundromat. An added perk was the opportunity he and his siblings had to sort through the plethora of abandoned clothes to supplement their wardrobes. I couldn't understand how poor people forget their clothes, it always baffled me. From time to time he would gift me something too. Usually a hoodie, because he knew I loved them. They were one piece of clothing that did the job of two. It was a sweatshirt and a hat. I almost always slept in a hoodie.

He would come and visit me in my tent, just to chat. He made it clear he was not going to end up on the streets with children of his own, so our visits were only of the friendly variety. That didn't stop me from having a huge crush on him. It was impossible not to. And I wasn't the only girl around his age who felt that way. While he didn't appear romantically interested in me, I was on the receiving end of the majority of his attention, a thing that never failed to make me feel good.

As we got to be better friends, Ty would stop by my tent, after caring for his siblings, to see me every night we were both off. Those nights were far and few between. Sometimes there were two to three weeks between visits, but I always looked forward to seeing him. There weren't many people I could turn to for help. If he was home, he always came to my defense when I was harassed by someone on the street. He even helped me the evening I returned from work to find a belligerent squatter in my tent. One of the unspoken rules of Skid Row was no squatting. Ironic, given we were all squatters.

Ty was so different from the people I typically met, and I was different in his company. I laughed. I teased. I didn't flirt, because I knew it wasn't what he wanted; and I didn't really know how, for that matter. Looking back, I could now see that flirting is a two-person game; if the other isn't into it, it doesn't work. But regardless of the nonromantic status of our relationship, I loved hanging out with Ty. He made me smile. And he brought feelings out in me I had never experienced.

Now, thinking about the relationship I had with Ty, I could objectively see that I liked to tease people and give them a hard time, particularly if it made them smile. It was clearly a personality trait of mine. I was sure everyone liked to make other people smile, but that was something I could pinpoint about myself. I wanted to find out who I really was, but I was certain I wouldn't be able to do that under duress. I didn't know when I *wouldn't* be under duress in the near future, but that one trait was something I had to hold on to. Something that seemed to be me—the real me.

I knew Anton was searching for the authentic part of me he knew better than most. He wanted to banter with me. He was worried, and this one thing would make him relax. It would be a signal to him I was okay. But I couldn't bring myself to act like everything was okay at the moment. Everything was far from it.

I did feel safe, at least physically. But in fewer than twenty-four hours my life had been turned on its head. I'd lost my best friend. TAP, the group my father had killed my mother to keep me from, was now after me—either to use me or kill me, and neither option was appealing. The FBI was taking me to Quantico. To train me? To question me? To use me? I had no idea. Aside from Anton, these agents had told me nothing, and even what Anton had told me was puzzling. I had no clue what I was about to face. Then there was Pax. Who was he? What did he want with me? It seemed like he wanted to help me, but in what way? And how could I trust him? What if he worked for TAP, and this was all just a sly way to get me to go with them?

Regardless, having his number in my pocket felt like a safety net. If things got ugly, I could use it. If nothing else, he'd proven himself resourceful: getting into the airport and past security, finding me, and fooling the FBI were no small feats. Pax was an option I hadn't had even just two hours earlier. But aside from the instinctual feeling I had that he was safe, I had no reason to trust him. I do have good instincts. That is one benefit I can attribute to the horror show my life had become. You couldn't get through foster care and meth houses and jail and homelessness without trusting your instincts. I knew who to show respect to, who to befriend, who to lead on, who to placate, and who to steer clear of. I had previously managed it all with ease, and I knew I could do it again. I just didn't want to. If I were smarter, I would've acted respectfully toward Agent Baldric. Of the three agents I was with, he clearly had the power. They deferred to him in all things, even when they needed to use the bathroom. And one thing was for sure: no one appreciated respect more than a cop. Particularly the head of the group. He wasn't the top dog at the FBI, but he was certainly someone of position and considerable power.

He didn't like me; that much was clear. I didn't know if it was due to his position of power, or if it was because I knew he wanted to be treated with respect that I just couldn't bring myself to show. I'd always been able to put survival first, but at the moment, I was sick of it. Regardless, they had me in their clutches, and there wasn't anything I could do about it. I was stuck, and he could deal with my obstinate behavior.

At an ear piercing volume, the pilot announced that he was starting the descent into Washington, DC, and all four members of our group flinched at the aural assault. Anton rubbed his ears. "I hate it when they do that."

We disembarked and walked straight out of the airport to the curb and into a waiting black SUV. Baldric took the front passenger seat, and I sat between Vik and Anton in the back. Baldric made quick introductions. "Channing, this is Agent Ashti Ahmadi." I barely looked at her, I was so lost in my own thoughts. "Ashti, this is Channing Walker. I have a feeling she needs no introduction."

Ashti turned around and smiled at me, holding out her hand for me to shake. She was Middle Eastern and had thick, long, black hair and rich, golden brown skin. Her dark-brown eyes were huge; they reminded me of an animated Disney princess. I wasn't great at assessing ages, but she looked fairly young. Maybe in her late twenties or early thirties. "Welcome, Channing. I've heard a lot about you. It's always fun to meet new fellow Chip Utilizers."

My eyes snapped up to meet hers, and I shook her hand. Another person like me.

She looked so normal—not that I thought people who could use their chips would look different, but I thought maybe I'd recognize another CU when I saw one. Yet there was no connection. I wouldn't have known she was a Chip Utilizer if I'd seen her on the street. She had a pretty thick British accent I found surprising. My shock must have been written all over my face because she looked at me questioningly.

I shook my head, as if to clear it. "I'm sorry. I guess I didn't realize people outside the United States could be chipped."

She looked incredulous, even as she continued to smile. "Huh. So strange. They told me you knew nothing, but I didn't really believe them. In any case, I moved to the States as a teenager."

I shrugged. "I don't even know what there is to know." She laughed heartily. I shrugged again, a little embarrassed. I'd always assumed there were others like me, but there was a small part of me that honestly thought I might be the only one. This whole exchange made me feel stupid. "Regardless, you have no idea how nice it is to meet you, Ashti. I've never met another person who could use their chip."

"Uh . . ." She looked to Baldric, who just shook his head, then slowly said, "It's very nice to meet you too, Channing." She looked at me and laughed again. "An adult CU who doesn't utilize her chip." She shook her head, still smiling. "Unheard of. I'm still not sure I believe it."

I grinned awkwardly. "Believe it." I was still trying to piece together the exchange between her and Baldric. She knew something about me I didn't, and it made me feel more insecure than I already was.

Anton, sensing my discomfort, grabbed my hand and squeezed it once lightly. Ashti eyed our joined hands and smiled again, lifting an eyebrow. "Been mixing business with pleasure, Antonio?"

"Zip it, Ahmadi." Anton didn't return her smile, but he did let go of my hand. "Let's get on the road already."

She giggled, then trolled, "Whatever you say, Garcia." She pulled off the curb, and we were on our way to Quantico.

I wasn't sure what to make of Ashti. She laughed a lot and smiled even more, but I couldn't tell if she was sincere or sincerely laughing at us. I shrugged it off, because she could use her chip, and she was right here, in the same car with me. I kept staring at her; I couldn't take my eyes off her pretty face in the rearview mirror. I wanted to pick her brain at the earliest moment possible.

THE ANGEL PROJECT

Roughly an hour and a half later, Ashti pulled into the Marine Corps Base in Quantico. It was both surreal and terrifying. It was late evening, and the base was bathed in twilight. It was light enough for me to see the beautiful grounds, the trees and bushes starting to change with the season to rich yellows, reds, and oranges. There was still a lot of green, as it was only the end of September, but the change into fall had begun. Southern California did have a fall, but we didn't have the trees found in Virginia, and it was clear this would be the kind of autumn I'd only seen in pictures and movies. I asked everyone and no one, "Why are we at the Marine Corps Base?"

Baldric was typing away on his phone and answered my question under his breath in his typical I-have-no-time-for-you manner. "The academy is on the base."

I turned to Anton. "I thought we were going to the BAU."

It was Baldric who answered. "We're not going to the BAU tonight."

Anton sighed. "The base houses the FBI Academy, the BAU, and the Operational Technology Division."

We drove into a set of large beige buildings. They were separated by well-kept sidewalks lined with pretty landscaping. It looked a lot like a college campus. Vik noticed me craning my neck to see everything outside his window. "Pretty cool, huh?" I nodded. "The academy sits on five hundred forty-seven acres. It's a full-service national training facility. It has conference rooms, classrooms, dorms, a gym, a pool, firing ranges, a library, dining hall, and even a mock town."

My eyes got wider with every new area of the facility

he mentioned. It was impossible not to be impressed. "Am I being trained?"

Vik smiled widely. "If you want to."

I furrowed my brow. "If I want to, I can become an FBI agent?"

Vik shrugged. "Of a sort. We do more than train future FBI agents here. We also train special agents, intelligence analysts, professional staff, law enforcement officers, foreign partners, and even the private sector."

"Where do I fall in?"

"Right now?" I nodded. "Nowhere." My brow furrowed further. "Right now, we have to test you. See what kind of voodoo"—he held up his hands and wiggled his fingers around—"you're capable of. Only then can we assess your value—"

Baldric cut him off. "That's enough, Vik."

Vik looked at me and winked.

I looked over at Anton to get his reaction, but he was looking out the window, oblivious to Vik's and my conversation. I wasn't sure how it was possible, considering that the entire side of my body was pressed against his. He must have been really tied up in his thoughts.

I sat back, no longer enamored with the scenery. They wanted to *see what kind of voodoo I was capable of*? That's why I was here? To test the level at which I could use my chip? There was a part of me wanting to know that as well. I knew, from my experience with Jenna, that I could do more than should ever be possible. More than I wanted to show to anyone anytime soon, *if ever*. It was dangerous and terrifying and wrong, so very wrong. And having never found Jenna after the incident, I didn't know the long-term effects of that kind of chip use. The feelings of guilt plagued me. Did she know what I'd done? Where was she? Where had she gone? She had all but disappeared. I searched for her for so long, trying to right my wrong—I so badly wanted to find out what had become of her.

If what these agents had told me was to be believed, then one thing was certain: I had a lot to learn. Maybe every chip user could do what I did that night with Jenna. Maybe that was something normal I could learn to control. Perhaps through the education I received here, I could hone my skills. Or maybe I could learn to turn the chip off and have a normal life. Someone could replace Darcy's memory, and I could go back to being her roommate and best friend. I ached for my former life, for the consistency it had provided. I ached to be the poor girl who couldn't afford a pizza or a rideshare. If I could go back, I would have avoided Jenna like the plague. If I could take back one thing, it would have been those few detrimental moments with her. I never would have used the chip, or written the book, or any of it. I could be living a simple life with my two friends.

But everything had changed that night with Jenna, and I couldn't go back. It set my life on a course I never wanted to be on, and I was seemingly powerless to escape it.

SIXTEEN

MY HEART HAMMERED AS WE pulled up to one of the beige buildings. This was the moment of truth. The moment I would discover for the reason for my being here. What did the FBI want with me? It was the question coursing through my mind from the very minute they'd picked me up and taken me to the airport. My trepidation only grew as I looked at Anton's grim facial expression. I couldn't tell if he wasn't happy to be here, or if he wasn't happy I was here. It seemed like it was the former, considering he was barely looking at me. What was this place to Anton?

Baldric finally put away his phone and motioned us all forward, toward the building marked *Special Agents.* Was Baldric a special agent? I had no idea what it meant, nor their purpose. But the title sounded legit.

I felt very out of place in my street clothes walking into an FBI facility. The rest of our group were all dressed professionally in their suits. Even with the dried blood on Anton's suit from the car accident, he still managed to look more professional than me. In even bigger contrast to my T-shirt and jeans, was the way the group walked through the door with confidence; it was clear that one of these things was not like the others.

The building was nice and recently renovated, with marble floors and dark wood trim. Along the walls were professional photos of what I could only assume were agents. We walked right past the receptionist. Baldric acknowledged her by name, "Terri," and with a single nod of his head as we passed by.

The group of agents walked quickly, but I was distracted by surroundings causing me to lag behind. There really wasn't all that much to see. It was just a bunch of hallways and offices. But I peeked inside each of them anyway. All the offices seemed to be empty at the late hour.

We walked down several hallways until we got to an unmarked door with a keypad to the right side. Baldric punched in a long code, the keypad beeped, and then he punched in another one. The door clicked, and Baldric pulled it open to reveal a set of four elevators, each with their own keypads. Baldric picked the first elevator on the left and punched in a code.

The elevator went down what felt like a couple of floors, and we walked out to a hallway resembling the ones we'd just left. The difference was the deafening quiet. We eventually made it to a boardroom equipped with a twenty-five-foot boat-shaped dark wood table. All but five of the tall, white chairs were full of what I could only assume were special agents. We walked in and I stopped short, uncomfortable with so many eyes on me. I heard the heavy door close and lock automatically with a soft chime. Anton was behind me and put his warm hand on my lower back. His touch soothed me for an instant, until he pushed me forward.

The agent seated at the head of the table stood and smiled. He was easily in his late fifties, with striking blue eyes and short gray hair a side part. "Ms. Walker, welcome. We're all anxious to meet you. Please, take a seat." He motioned to the five open chairs on the far side of the table. As soon as we sat down, he started in. "I'm Special Agent Davis." He motioned around the table. "I won't bog you down with names on your first day." The group gave a courtesy laugh. I was relatively certain my only expression was one of obvious panic. *My first day?* How long was I expected to be here? Not that I had anywhere else to go. That thought made me sad. I was homeless, yet again. At least this time I had some money, and I had Cole.

I looked around the table at all the new faces. There were at least fifteen others, men and women of various ages and ethnic backgrounds, all clean cut, and all wearing suits. It was a lot to take in. I audibly swallowed.

Special Agent Davis spoke again," We are all gathered here this evening to meet our newest Chip Utilizer." He turned to me. "As you may have heard, it's been a very long time since we've come across an adult who can manipulate their own chip at will. CUs are typically found as children and, on occasion, teenagers." Anton perceptibly stiffened beside me. Agent Davis carried on. "We have some questions for you, and all we ask is that you answer them in detail as honestly and wholly as possible."

I cleared my throat. "Is this the part where I ask for

an attorney?" They all laughed. I wasn't trying to be funny. I wanted someone here, in my corner. I needed someone to tell me what to say and what not to say. There was no way I could be fully honest with these people. But I wasn't sure exactly what to omit either. I'd never felt so absolutely clueless. I had no idea if I could or should trust these people. Anton had been so secretive earlier. And it couldn't be denied that if he fully trusted them, he would have never intercepted me when I was with Cole to provide me information these agents would not.

"No attorneys in this division, I'm afraid. We work on a different level here. We're part of the Domestic Counterterrorist Agency."

My eyes felt like they were going to bug out of their sockets. "You think I'm a terrorist?"

Agent Davis laughed loudly at my reaction. "Not at all. But I'm sure you can understand why we have to treat all CUs as potential terrorists. The power you hold is significant, to say the least." He held up a hand. "Before you get upset about this, please know the bulk of people in this room are also considered possible domestic terror threats." This generated several chuckles. Anton stiffened again. This time I glanced over at him, and he looked nervous.

I didn't have time to ponder why Anton was acting shifty. I was too caught up in Agent Davis's announcement that most of the people at this table were Chip Utilizers. I looked around with new eyes and saw several smiling faces, as well as some with varying degrees of sympathy. So many people like me at this one table. I kind of wished that I could just meet with them each personally. I wanted to hear their stories and see how their experiences with the chip lined up with mine.

Davis went on, "Channing, we know this is probably uncomfortable for you. But we assure you we are here to help. You will be with us for some time. You will need to go through specific testing so we can better assist you. The more up-front you are with us, the more we can do that. Among other things, we'll need to know how using the chip feels and works for you. It might surprise you, but it's a bit different for each of us. As are our capabilities." He winked. Davis was a CU.

I could take comfort in one thing: I'd been here for several minutes with all of these Chip Utilizers, and no one had tried to control me. It had only taken seconds with TAP for that to happen. That actually went a long way toward putting me at ease. The people here really did all seem earnest in wanting to hear my story. Whether it was because of my status as a CU or if it had to do with being an anomaly as a newfound adult CU, I wasn't sure. Everyone was quietly looking at me. I cleared my throat. "I'm sorry. I'm not really sure what to say."

Davis's smile was warm this time. "I understand. Perhaps it would be helpful if we told you some of what we already know about you?"

My brow furrowed. "What you know about me?"

He nodded, then gestured to a slightly older man seated a few seats down from him. The man gave a questioning glance back at Davis, and Davis nodded. The man gave me a grim smile and introduced himself. "Ch ... anning" He seemed to have a hard time getting my name out. "I'm Dr. Theodore Rucker. I worked with your parents on the Angel Project."

My heart stuttered, and all the air left my lungs. My dad had warned me against the people he worked with above all others. Had I just walked right into their hands? I was locked in this room, locked in this basement. The desire to escape was overwhelming. I felt my breath coming faster and faster. Then I felt Anton take my hand. With one look, I could see that he was in my corner. He whispered in my ear, "You're okay, Chan. Give him time to explain." His words soothed me, but only slightly. It was nice not to be on my own for a change, but it was also harder, relying on someone else. I wasn't good at trusting, and frankly, humankind, as a whole, wasn't all that trustworthy. Most people were out for themselves. I didn't necessarily fault them for that—it was human nature. Even Anton had not been completely truthful with me. But I couldn't deny that he cared for me. I'd felt it time and time again. I nodded back to Dr. Rucker to go on.

"I'm sure that comes as a shock to you. Finding you was certainly a great shock to me." He rubbed a hand over his face and chuckled. "It appears I'm not sure where to start either."

Davis interjected," Start at the beginning."

Dr. Rucker nodded. "Our government began chipping people decades ago. At first, they were rather rudimentary. The chips have increased exponentially in technological advancements over the years, becoming smaller and more powerful. I'm a computer engineer, specifically hardware, with a specialty in functional systems at the molecular scale. I wasn't on the original team of creators; I was brought in thirty some-odd years ago, before your parents were recruited. The group had begun as a study into the application of microchipping—at the time nanochips were still just an abstract concept. And microchips seemed like the obvious wave of the future. They were designed to make life safer and more convenient. Microchipping could have several applications, but under the skin is far and away the easiest and most useful form for the human race. There are massive benefits to microchipping, but it's always been a hard sell to the public, for the obvious reason of autonomy.

"Microchipping in the wrist could do amazing things for society. It would hold your identification, such as your driver's license and passport. It could house your credit cards and bank accounts. No need to carry a wallet, nor risk having your wallet stolen. It could house memberships to clubs, libraries, and gyms, and hotel and restaurant reservations. No unidentified bodies. It would be incredible for infant and elder safety. We could eliminate kidnappings by GPS tracking. And the same technology would help us find lost hikers or injured mountain climbers.

"It can carry your health metadata. With a scan of a wrist, your doctor or hospital can know what your allergies, any prescribed medications you're on, as well as your medical history. One could be brought into the hospital unconscious, and the treating physicians could glean lifesaving information from scanning the chip. Criminal management would be huge, both in and out of prisons. Smith and Wesson have already embraced an

THE ANGEL PROJECT

implant-firearm system requiring weapons to be in close proximity to their owner when fired. Whether your arsenal is stolen from your home or an officer's gun is wrestled from their hands in a struggle, no one but the registered owner would be able to fire the gun. The possibilities and safeguards are endless.

"Of course, it would come at the price of privacy and autonomy, and that price is still too steep for the bulk of Americans." He took a break to wink at me. "And yet those same Americans are smartphone and social media users, with homes full of audio and video security systems." He waved a hand, as if to say how dumb the average American was. Then while laughing he continued, "Not to mention the Patriot Act or even more recently Israel's Pegasus spyware, which the United States has already purchased." He laughed and slapped his knee, as if Americans not knowing they were constantly spied on was so unbelievably hilarious.

"But I digress. We realized quickly that regardless of how life changing the microchip implantation would be for the world, it was just too dystopian for society. So we pivoted into nanochips. Even if society couldn't see how convenient microchipping was, the government couldn't deny the benefits, if only for the fight against crime alone. And if we could chip people in a way they never knew about—then we wouldn't have any pushback. The obvious choice was chipping the brain, and BCIs—Brain-Computer Interfaces—were born. At first our experiments yielded little result, but as the technology advanced and the nanochip was created, the capabilities grew faster and wider than we could have ever imagined.

"In the beginning, we had to implant an electrode in the skin of the brain and then connect it to the chip. But quickly, through my research, we were able to engrave the chip into the electrodes themselves. At that point, we knew we'd hit on something huge. The chip could enter the body anywhere and be programed to arrive at just the right spot in the brain. The chip was so small we colloquially named it Smart Powder. Conspiracy theorists believe that the nanochips enter the body via vaccines, and to be sure, they can and do. But it's so much more than that, so much easier than that. They can be delivered in hundreds of different ways. Smart Powder is so small it can be absorbed by the skin. The chips could and have been effectively dumped in the water supply from time to time."

Davis interjected. "If you're quite done with your glory lap, Theodore, let's move on to the realities of the chip, please."

Dr. Rucker knowingly smiled, his cheeks pinking the tiniest bit. "Yes, well, I suppose Ms. Walker doesn't need all the details." He looked back to me. "In any case, we believed we could not only make society better, but we could improve diseases of the brain like Parkinson's, multiple sclerosis, and even Alzheimer's. We also found nanochips could help the disabled to walk, talk, and use their hands. We have technology allowing the chipped to drive a car with their mind and type one hundred words per minute without tapping a single key. It's remarkable, really." Agent Davis pointedly cleared his throat. "Yes, well anyway, it turns out there were unforeseen complications. We, the group of scientists working on the technology, were all implanted and were more than delighted to find the chip was performing perfectly and was completely undetectable. After a time, and several more successful studies, we began to systematically chip the population. Soon we discovered some anomalies. The foremost being that, very rarely, there were people who could use their own chips. They could turn them on and connect to another person's chip, sending mind-altering messages.

"At first we were terrified. The damage these people could do was absolutely tremendous. And even though there were relatively few of them—we estimate between two and two and a half per one million people—they were far too dangerous. I regret to say that our first plan of action was to take these people out of the equation. Over eight thousand people die every day in the United States— what was a thousand more? Especially for the betterment of society at large?"

I sat up in my chair. "You were killing the Chip Utilizers because they were able to use a technology that they were unknowingly implanted with?"

He smiled sadly. "Barbaric, I know. But it was the case, nonetheless. We, unfortunately, determined that there was no other real alternative."

My mouth dropped open. "You could have removed the chip! Or turned it off. Surely if you could create it, you could find a way to stop it!"

He smiled grimly. "That's the big question, isn't it? I'll admit, at first, we were quite hesitant to do any damage to our technology. It was too good and too useful. When something could do such tremendous things, from curing diseases to saving kidnapped children, millions of lives could be saved. Was the loss of two-millionths of the population a noble cause for that kind of gain? At first the answer was yes."

This gave me pause. His thought process horrified me, but at the same time I could understand it. It was easy to talk about in numbers, much harder to talk about in actual people. It wasn't like the chip would kill 2.5 per million people—the government would have to murder them. One scenario was a rare side effect, a loss that may have been worth the gain. The other was something else entirely. A government tasked with finding and killing its own innocent citizens.

"That said, we ultimately came to the conclusion that there was no other alternative than to find a way to void the chips. Unfortunately, we quickly learned it didn't work. That's the thing about artificial intelligence, isn't it? It can grow in ways the creators didn't see coming. We attempted to turn off the chip of our lab rats, and no matter how many times we tried, we got the same result: the rats went crazy, as in clinically insane. We could only hypothesize that the chip had implanted so far into the brain that it had become a part of it. Turning it off seemed to flip some kind of switch in the brain." He shook his head, as if he really didn't like reliving these memories. "The thing about invention is that it takes engineers, scientists, and philosophers. You need all three. The scientists determine whether a thing *is possible*, the engineers figure out *how to do it*, and the philosophers determine whether we *should* do it. Our philosophers weren't very good." He blew out a breath, as if this were simply a disappointment, rather than an abominable misuse of science and a massive detriment to humankind.

"But you all continued to chip people?"

"There was a lot of debate, of course, but the downsides were so few and the possibilities so great it only made sense to continue on."

"Did you go back to killing the outliers?"

"At that point we were still trying to figure out what to do about the anomalies. The practice of elimination was still in play during this time."

I couldn't fathom that kind of carelessness. They were still chipping people, knowing full well that some of them would have to be murdered. "Please tell me you advanced the technology to a place it can be successfully turned off?"

"Well, not exactly. But we have made adjustments, and the anomalies are fewer than they once were." He waved away my concerns, as if I just didn't understand the full capacity of the upside to the technology. Which admittedly, I didn't. But it was hard to focus on the upside when you were one of the people they deemed so great a threat that your life had to be forfeited. For the anomalies, the downsides of the chip were as big as the Grand Canyon. Before I could ask more questions, Dr. Rucker continued, "Your parents came on the scene right around that time. They were professors at Brown University, and both were well known in academia for their progress in the neurosciences. They were really quite talented. And as fate would have it, they were both found to be Chip Utilizers."

My mouth dropped open. I was completely caught by surprise. "I . . . I didn't know that."

He looked at me sadly. "There are a lot of things you don't know."

I huffed out a breath. "So I've been told."

"Ch . . . anning." He said it like "shhhhanning." "When your parents came on the scene, everything changed. We learned how useful CUs could be. There was no doubt they could be dangerous, but there was a flip side that was exponentially greater in value. Imagine the possibilities—"

Agent Davis cut in again. "Let's save that for later, Dr. Rucker."

Dr. Rucker nodded. "Of course, of course." He turned back to me. "With your parents on board, we learned that finding and gathering the Utilizers was absolutely imperative. We needed them. Not only could they teach us so much about the technology, but their use to our country was unmatched. We created a technology that connected to the chips, and when one was used outside our jurisdiction, that person was flagged. As we began the process of finding Utilizers, we realized that they varied greatly in the way they were able to use their chips. Most had no idea what they were doing. And they couldn't be taught. It was just something that happened when they got overly angry or emotional. They were of no use to us, and they posed very little threat to humanity. The majority of the CUs were people who could upload messages to another's chip at will. They were a threat to humanity at large. They could compel people, erase memories, and generally get them to do anything they wanted. But there were others still who could do more than just use the chip to send messages. There were a few, very few, who had great control over their chips, and it seemed as if their brains had become so connected that they were part computer. Among other things, they could upload and download information."

My breath stilled in my lungs. There really were others like me. Everyone looked at me, gauging my reaction to Rucker's latest revelation. I turned back to Dr. Rucker and said, "Sorry, this is all just really terrifying. Please, go on."

He just kind of smiled. "We needed all the CUs. If we were going to live in harmony with this new technology, then all CUs had to be trained. Those rare CUs were so different from their counterparts that they got a different name. They were Advanced Neurological Gateway Elemental Links. So very few in number, but so unbelievably valuable. We called them ANGELs. That's how the ANGEL Project began."

SEVENTEEN

MY PALMS WENT SWEATY, AND my heart rate increased. My mouth felt like it had been stuffed with cotton. I went to take a sip of the water in front of me, when I noticed an agent, a woman who appeared to be in her early thirties, was looking at me intently, almost without blinking. She was studying me—I could only presume to get my reactions. I tried to school my heartbeat but didn't know how. I managed to withstand the urge to wipe my hands down my pant legs, but I saw her exchange a look with Agent Davis. It was too late; they were both aware of my near panic and continued to watch me closely.

I did my best to keep the tremor out of my voice when I asked, "What exactly do you want with these ANGELs?"

Dr. Rucker's expression brightened when he laughed. "What do we want with the ANGELs? Quite literally, everything."

Davis cut in again." ANGELs are more equipped than you can imagine to help our democracy. They can aid in negotiations and help us facilitate peace in ways unforeseen. CUs are valuable in their own right, but the only way to know what our enemies are planning is through ANGELs."

I cleared my throat. "How many ANGELs have you found?"

The brightness of Dr. Rucker's countenance faded. "Three."

My eyes bugged out of my head. "Three? You've only found three, *ever*?"

"It's a very rare thing, Ms. Walker. And unfortunately, of the three, one died of cancer, one left the FBI, and the other is . . . incapacitated at the moment."

Anton stilled beside me. All of a sudden most of the people around the table were looking at him, myself included. He wouldn't look at me, but I could see the tightness in his jaw and the hardness in his eyes. I wasn't the only one who took note of his distress.

This was obviously sensitive to him. Was it a woman? One he'd had a relationship with? A romantic relationship? And what did they mean by "incapacitated"? I couldn't help but ask the last question.

A dark-skinned woman with a head full of beautifully long, teeny-tiny braids was the one who answered my question. "The individual in question is unable to give us the aid we need. It seems as if the stress of being the only ANGEL has been too much." Everyone at the table shared a look of disappointment about this individual. But none reacted like Anton.

Anton's grip was tight on the arms of his chair—whatever he knew about the incapacitated ANGEL, he didn't want to talk about. My interest was piqued, and not just because I wanted to know what had Anton so upset, but because information about the ANGELs was vital to me. Unfortunately, it would have to wait.

Davis turned to Dr. Rucker. "Let's move on."

Dr. Rucker nodded. "You were just a toddler when your parents started working with us. We were all very curious to see how you would react to the chip. With both of your parents being utilizers, you had all the genetic makeup of a utilizer yourself, and quite possibly an ANGEL. We were all very hopeful. You began showing signs of being a utilizer early on, around the age of three."

I sat up then, shaking my head. "No. That's not possible. I wasn't chipped until I was five. I remember it, clear as day."

Dr. Rucker looked perplexed. "You remember being chipped at the age of five?"

I looked him straight in the eye. "I absolutely remember it. I remember every second of it."

Dr. Rucker exchanged a glance with Agent Davis that I couldn't quite interpret. It was followed by Rucker rubbing his forehead and taking a few notes.

Davis gave me a grim smile before he spoke. "Channing, you're going to find that you have two types of memories. One type is real—those are fuzzy and change over time, the memories becoming less clear as you age. The other type are perfectly clear, almost like it happened yesterday. Those memories are so clear and concise they feel as though you're watching a movie of yourself on the big screen. The memories never change—they're static in their perfection. You can feel the physical sensations of the time and almost smell the room where the memory took place. The latter is an implanted memory. That memory has been downloaded to your chip, and those don't fade with time."

I shook my head vehemently. There is no way the memory was implanted. I've thought of the moment I was chipped thousands of times throughout my life. That was a pivotal moment for me. It's not the type of thing one forgets. "No. No. Memories may fade over time, but it's been scientifically proven that on days where something significant happens to you, you remember that day more clearly, even the little things. The day I was chipped was as significant a day as I can imagine having."

"How about the day your dad was sent to prison for life? That sounds significant. How clear is your memory of that event?"

I paused for a minute, recalling that awful day. I definitely remembered it. I remembered the hard wood bench I was sitting on. I remembered the judge. He was a dark-haired man who seemed to take no pleasure in delivering the sentence. I remembered the absolute relief on my dad's face when he looked back at me after he found out he was serving a life sentence for first-degree murder. Relief he was going to prison? I couldn't understand it then, but I could now. He knew by his going to prison, I would be free from TAP, at least from the worst of the threat. But that was it, really. I couldn't remember what I was wearing, or who was sitting next to me. I couldn't remember what the judge looked like, nor the amount of people in the room. The event—the very significant event—was fuzzy.

The memory of being chipped was so clear I could

touch it. I remembered everything. I could see the individual strands of my mom's hair as she leaned over me and soothed, "Don't be afraid, Channing. It'll just be a little prick." I could feel the softness of her sweater against my arm and smell her floral perfume mixed with the antiseptic odor of the room. I could feel the sting of the needle, and the slide of it underneath my skin. Everything. I could recall it all in perfect clarity. Just like it was a movie being played back to me. I sat back, my mouth open in disbelief. "Why? Why would someone implant me with a memory of being chipped at the age of five?"

Dr. Rucker rubbed his forehead again. "That's the question, isn't it? If we could find the answer to that, we would probably be able to put the puzzle of you together."

They thought I was a puzzle because I hadn't used my chip over the course of my life. But I knew the answer to that puzzle—it was because of abject fear. What I didn't know was why my dad, the only person I could imagine who'd done it, had implanted me with false memories. My head was beginning to hurt, and I knew where the pain was leading—I'd felt it more than enough for one day. I winced at the acute ache. I mentally let the issue of my false memories fade to the back of my mind. Thinking about it wasn't likely to help me unlock blocked memories, but it would certainly cause me considerable pain. There was nothing for it but to mentally move on.

Everyone seated around the table watched me closely. Agent Davis looked particularly surprised when I was able to calm myself down. His eyebrows rose, and his face shone with an expression containing more than surprise. It was surprise combined with deep interest. But in just an instant, he cleared his expression and said, "I know the first realization that you've been implanted with information comes as a shock. Understanding the difference between an implanted memory and a real one is imperative. It will be a large part of your training with us, and it will become second nature to you with practice." He nodded for Dr. Rucker to proceed.

I held up a hand. "I'm sorry. I just need a minute. This is all a lot to take in." I blew out a breath and asked, "Is there a restroom I can use?"

"Of course. Agent Garcia can show you the way." He motioned Anton and me toward the door. I didn't hesitate to jump up from my seat. I needed to get out of there. I needed to be somewhere private so I could freak out. I needed to *breathe*.

Once we were in the hall, Anton grabbed hold of my hand and gave it a squeeze. I turned to him, trying to tell him with my eyes how creeped out I was. He shot me a very small, but also a very resolute, shake of his head. I got the message and walked with him in silence. I wanted to tell him all how unbelievably freaky it was to have false memories. But I was also dying to ask him about the incapacitated ANGEL. Who was this person to him? And if I proved to be an ANGEL, as I was quickly suspecting I was, was it better to try to hide that? I definitely didn't want to become "incapacitated."

When we got close to the bathroom door, he slid in front of me to open it. Just as his body brushed against mine, without moving his mouth, he quietly said, "There is no privacy here, even in the bathroom. Don't do or say anything you don't want them to see or hear." Then he stepped back with the door open and said, "This is a long way from Mike's Punching Bag. Are you hanging in there?"

I let out a breathless chuckle. "We're definitely not in Kansas anymore."

He smiled, and I motioned with my head to the opened bathroom door. "I'll be right back."

One look in the mirror confirmed that I looked as exhausted as I felt. After using the facilities, I splashed some cold water on my face. I dried off, the brown paper towel rough against my skin. I hadn't put any makeup on that morning, and I found myself wishing I had. Not that I wore much, but a little mascara and concealer went a long way toward making a girl feel confident. I was so far from confident in this place, with these people who seemed to know more about me than I did.

I couldn't believe just this morning I'd told Darcy I was moving out. It felt like months had passed. Now, here I was at Quantico, in some underground private part of the Special Agents facility. My life had definitely taken a turn—I just didn't know if it was for better or worse.

I *did* want the FBI training, that much I was sure of. Now that I knew for a certainty I'd been manipulated through the chip, I wanted nothing more than to see the difference. I wanted my life back—my real life. I had an intrinsic need to know what was real. And as far as I could see, only the FBI was offering me that opportunity. However, I'd had about as much information as I could take for one day. My brain was hurting, my body was hurting, I felt like my bones were hurting. I needed a meal and at least twelve hours of sleep. But Dr. Rucker wasn't finished with his story, and I knew I was going to have to power through. I blew out a breath and left the bathroom.

Anton held my arm in his as we walked back to the meeting room. "Feeling better?"

I shrugged. "Marginally, I guess."

He gave a ghost of a smile. "How overwhelmed are you on a scale of one to ten?"

"One hundred."

He laughed. But I wasn't kidding. I'd never known overwhelmed before. The thought that my memories, what I knew of my life, could be wrong was making my stomach turn.

He looked at his watch. "I'd say they'll wrap this up for the day in another half hour or so. We government types don't usually work this late. Especially on a Sunday." He winked. "As soon as we're done here, I'll take you to the dining hall. I think we've all heard your stomach growl no fewer than three times during the meeting."

I smirked. It was true. I'd hit the point of hunger where even liver and onions, a dish one foster family had served on the regular—and I'd hated—sounded good.

Anton opened the door and motioned me in. As soon as we sat down, Dr. Rucker, who clearly liked to hear himself drone on, started in right away.

"Where were we? Oh yes, you showing signs of being a Utilizer. That began around the age of three. Your chip would turn on without any aid from us on occasion. You couldn't do it at will, of course, but we were very hopeful that you would, eventually. This went on for several years, but we were never able to get you to do it at will. We grew concerned that you were another CU who would never gain the capacity to use it. We already knew at that point utilizing the chip wasn't something one could be taught.

"That was when tragedy struck. Your mother was killed, and your father went to prison for life. We got him the best criminal defense attorneys money could buy. But he'd already admitted he was guilty, and he stuck to his story, never wavering. There's only so much an attorney can do at that point. The thing is, we knew your father; he was no killer, and certainly not of those he loved. We don't know what happened that fateful day, but we were one hundred percent certain that your father did not kill your mother." I rifled through the memory of my parents that night. While I could remember the scene, I couldn't remember the specifics, much like the courtroom. That led me to believe the memory was real, and my father did, in fact, kill my mother. But at this point I had very little trust in my memories, and I chose not to comment. For one, I wasn't certain of anything, and secondly, if what I remembered was indeed true, then my dad was trying to hide my abilities from TAP. The fact that he murdered the woman he loved, effectively wasting his life in a prison cell just for my freedom, wasn't something I was going to throw away. "That said, there were many details surrounding your mother's death that we couldn't make sense of. One of the most significant was you ending up in foster care. My wife and I tried to get custody, but your father refused. He wanted you with family only—a thing he knew was hopeless—or the foster care system."

THE ANGEL PROJECT

He shook his head. "That really affected me. I loved you like a daughter. You were homeschooled by your parents, and several TAP staff members. You spent your whole childhood at our facility. I wasn't the only one who fought for your custody—we all wanted you." That hit deep. I was *wanted*? There were people who were willing to take care of me? People who loved me like their own child? I found myself blinking back unexpected tears. "I visited your father in prison, begging him not to allow the state to send you into the system. I tried to appeal to his fatherly side, telling him the atrocities of the foster system. I tried to appeal to his scientific side, telling him that if you went into the system, we may never know your full potential." Dr. Rucker shook his head, sadly. "He wouldn't budge. He wouldn't even give me an explanation."

I, of course, knew why he wouldn't allow a TAP staff member to have custody of me. But, I'd had a really hard life. Moments so difficult that merely remembering them had the power to make me physically ill. My father's attempt to save me had caused me so much pain and suffering. Had it been worth it? Ultimately, I had still been found. Perhaps it would have been better for me to grow up in a loving home and deal with the consequences of being a CU, or an ANGEL—as the case may be. I wonder how my dad would have reacted to the turns my life had taken. Would he have regretted his actions? The truth was that if I had followed his advice, I never would have written the book, and I certainly wouldn't have used the chip on Darcy's dad. Instead, I would be living my very average life with Darcy. One in which I had a job and friends I could count on. The life I'd craved my whole existence and then threw in the trash.

There was a song I liked with the lyrics, "Life's like an hourglass, glued to the table." Those words made more sense now than ever before. There was no going back, not to my simple life with Darcy and Cole, and not to the moment I showed my parents what I could do with my chip. My life was what it was. I only had the present. What would I do from here? That was what mattered.

One thing was certain, I couldn't take any more information.

Fortunately, Agent Davis looked at me and said, "I think you've heard enough for one day." There were both looks of agreement and blatant disagreement from around the table. But no one voiced their opinion. Agent Davis was clearly top dog here. "Anton will show you to the dining hall, and after that, to a place you can sleep tonight. As for everyone else, please stay in your seats. We're not done here."

Anton and I stood and began to walk out of the room when I thought of one more thing I felt they should know. I stopped and everyone looked at me. I cleared my throat. "So, I'm sure you all know this, but I wrote a book. It was picked up for publishing by Walton and Barker. The book is called *Chipped*." I smiled awkwardly. "I'm sure you all can guess what it's about."

Davis chuckled. "Yes, Channing, we know about the book. We've requested Walton and Barker put the publishing on hold. To be sure, it's not the book we're worried about—people have been writing books about computer chips in the human body for decades." Wink.

"No one ever thinks they're real." He smiled. "Our main concern is you will become less of an asset to us as a famous person. The FBI prefers their agents keep low profiles."

I looked around the room. All eyes were on me. I forged ahead anyway. "So, if I choose not to work for the FBI, then I can release the book?"

Davis smiled tightly. "With a few changes, yes."

I stuttered out a shaky, "O . . . okay. Thanks, I guess." Anton laid a hand on my arm, signaling that it was time to go.

We walked out. Just before the door snicked shut, I heard the room explode in noise. Then the hallway was completely silent. It was maddening. I knew they were talking about me, and I really wanted to know what they were saying. I was starving, but I would've given up food to be a fly on the wall in that room, and that was saying something.

Anton looked at me, his eyebrows raised in question. I just sighed. I didn't know what to say, and I simultaneously had too much to say. I didn't forget that the walls here had ears. I opted to stay silent on our walk to the elevator and out of the building.

Once outside in the chilly air of the crisp autumn night, I finally took a deep breath. We stopped walking for a second, and I stepped away from Anton and rubbed my face roughly with my hands. I wanted to cry, maybe even laugh in shock, but mostly I wanted to hide. There was only one way to hide in plain sight, and I'd learned it well in the foster care system. I had to hide my real feelings, thoughts, and emotions—lock them away deep inside.

Then I could display what I wanted those around me to see.

There was one burning question I had that couldn't wait. Well, two burning questions really, but only one that I felt comfortable asking. I dropped my hands and turned to Anton. Being outside, I was comfortable enough to finally ask. "How did Dr. Rucker make the switch from TAP to the FBI?"

"Dr. Rucker never left the FBI. The group that calls themselves TAP split from us back around the time your mother died." He gave me a minute to let that sink in. "I was only a teenager when it happened, but from what I understand, things got crazy here. Your parents were huge assets to TAP; when they left, things went a little wild." He winked at me. "Dr. Rucker's interesting, though, yeah?"

"Ha. 'Interesting' is one way to put it. I might have used the term 'mildly insane.'"

Anton laughed. "He's a genius. Though genius is really only a hop, skip, and a jump to insanity."

"I've never been more grateful to not be a genius."

We started to laugh, when suddenly my thoughts stopped in their tracks. "Why don't I remember him? If what he said is to be believed, shouldn't I recall Dr. Rucker? Even just a little? He doesn't look even mildly familiar to me."

Anton looked at me intently. "I'm quite sure they are asking that same question downstairs. Rucker wasn't the only one there who you knew from your childhood."

I was gobsmacked and reeled with the information. "I knew other people there? Which ones? How well?"

THE ANGEL PROJECT

None of them looked even remotely familiar. How could my mind have been so effectively scrubbed of those memories? How did the chip work like that? Were the changed memories replaced by others? Rucker had said that I'd been homeschooled—that I'd spent all my days with TAP; I didn't remember any of it. But I didn't remember being in school before the foster care system at all either. Somehow all of those memories went missing, but I didn't realize they weren't there until now. My head started to pound, and I growled in frustration. Was there no way to get my past back?

Anton studied my reaction, and it made me bristle. What was he looking for and why? Where did our friendship lie, really? Who was he loyal to? It seemed like he was loyal to me earlier while feeding me information, but how could I be sure it wasn't some big FBI play? Was he going to tell them everything I told him? Was he out here with me to extract information? I figured the FBI was always sending him with me because he was the person I was most comfortable with. We'd become friends—but was our friendship fake or real? Now that we were in FBI territory, were they using him to get to me? Even if our friendship was real, he worked for them, and being in the FBI wasn't a fair-weather thing. Anton knew how to get me to talk. He knew how to make me feel comfortable. I so badly wanted to trust him, but if I did, it could cost me everything.

Anton nudged my upper arm and spun me around to fully face him. "Hey, don't look at me like that. I'm on your side, Channing. I have many issues with the way they do things around here. More issues than you could possibly know. But first and foremost, I am your friend and ally." His words were pretty, but I wouldn't trust anybody here. I couldn't. At least not for now. Just because he didn't approve of all of the FBI's practices, didn't mean he would—or could—choose me over them. But there was no reason to voice my thoughts—no reason to argue when he couldn't convince me otherwise. "Don't worry about the people here you may or may not have known as a child. It's obvious your memory has been wiped. No one is going to try to jog your memory of that time—we all know that's not how the chip works."

"I can never remember?"

He shook his head. "Once a memory has been changed, there's no getting it back. Trying to regain lost memories has proven time and time again to be very dangerous mentally. Part of what you'll learn here is that the practice is futile."

We walked a little farther before I asked my other burning question. "What happened to the ANGEL who's incapacitated, Anton?" I wanted to know both what happened and what the person meant to Anton. I really wanted to know if it was a romantic relationship, which I wouldn't ask, because it was absolutely none of my business. Yet the fact would not stop the growing curiosity in my mind.

He looked away from me then, his jaw ticking, nostrils flared. Then shook his head. "That's a story for another day."

I put my hands on his cheeks and forced his face back to mine. "The time is now. I need to know what happened to that person." I needed to know because I could be next.

THE ANGEL PROJECT

I wanted to be prepared and informed. I had options—they were few, but they existed. For one, I could act like nothing more than the average CU. This I knew for sure: there was no way I would show the FBI what I was really capable of until I knew what had happened to the other ANGEL.

Anton's jaw ticked even tighter, and the vein in his neck bulged to the point I could see the blood pumping through it. "I can't tell you, because I don't know what happened. I have to show you."

My eyes widened, and I gestured ahead of us, even thoughts of food forgotten. "By all means."

He shook his head. "I can't take you there now." I was about to object, but he cut me off. "I will, Channing, but it's too late. I'm not permitted to at the moment, and there are eyes and ears everywhere here."

I felt the bad kind of chills run down my spine. "We're being watched right now?"

He nodded, once. "Without a doubt. You're on FBI property—literally everything you do here will be recorded."

That made me stumble a bit. "Are they listening to us as well?"

"No. As long as we talk softly, the audio can't pick up much out here." He looked casually to the left. "Currently, the camera angle is to the side of us, so the lip readers can't pick up what we're saying. But it's moving directions, to get a better angle. Time to keep moving."

EIGHTEEN

ANTON HANDED ME A BLUE lanyard with white "FBI Academy" embroidered lettering. Attached was an ID complete with my picture and name. They must have pulled the picture from the California Department of Motor Vehicles because I easily recognized my state ID picture. It wasn't a flattering photo—I looked like a half-drunk, drowned rat. Anton donned his own ID; his was black with white lettering and reading "Special Agent." His picture was most definitely flattering, and when he saw me staring at it for a beat too long, he winked.

"Of course your picture is good and mine is crap." I rolled my eyes.

He smiled widely. "I'm not gonna lie, I think the team was surprised by how attractive you are." He nodded down to the ID hanging from my neck and cringed. "They were all expecting you to look a little more like that."

I laughed and punched him hard on his arm. "You're a jerk. And just FYI, I got this photo taken right after one of our workouts at Mike's. This"—I gestured around the ID—"is your fault."

THE ANGEL PROJECT

He smiled like the Cheshire Cat. "That picture is starting to grow on me."

He pulled open the door stating ***No Shorts*** in bold print, and we entered a vestibule where we scanned our IDs to enter the dining hall. A large American flag hung directly above the FBI logo. It was the first thing I noticed, followed by a huge room, from the ceiling of which hung the flags of the different states. It was nicer than a school cafeteria, but still had that industrial feel. The large space was about half-full. Black tables and light wood chairs in all different configurations crowded the area, with a large double-sided drink and soft serve ice cream station in the middle. To the side of the dining hall were the kitchen and the food offerings, which were vast. Just the sight of all the food made my mouth water.

As we made our way over to the food, which smelled even better than it looked, I did my best to hide behind Anton. I was sick of people staring at me, and earlier that morning when I rushed to see Cole at the hospital, I had just thrown on whatever clothes I could find—a white T-shirt and dark skinny jeans with white sneakers. All of which were now dirty. I didn't look at all professional, and I was worried I was going to stick out like a sore thumb.

But when I finally looked up, I was relieved to see that no one seemed to notice me at all. No one was even looking our way. And people were dressed in all kinds of attire. There were very few wearing suits; most were dressed in cargo pants and T-shirts, or other casual attire. Relieved, I stood up a little straighter and stopped crouching behind Anton.

L.A. CLAYTON

When we made it to the front of the line, I asked for the vegetarian chili and a steak. I wanted something that was really going to stick to my ribs. I was so hungry. The worker gave me a look telling me I should know better. Anton gave me an elbow to the side and said, "Only one main dish. Hard rule."

I blew out a breath—I really wanted both. "Steak, please, with potatoes."

The worker nodded and handed me my plate, which to her credit, she overloaded with food. Then we walked down the line to the fruit, muffins, and desserts. I got another plate and loaded it with all of the above. Anton snorted. I shot him a look which immediately shut him up. Then I picked up yet another muffin, and he laughed out loud.

"You gonna need some help getting all that to the table? I could call some guys over."

"I would cut you with this knife if I had another hand."

He laughed all the way to the empty table in the corner of the hall. Anton dropped his tray down and said, "You eat. I'll get us drinks."

I nodded, already ready to shove a huge bite of potatoes into my mouth. "Don't forget the ice cream."

"Wouldn't dream of it."

I had food in my mouth before he got even a few feet away, and I moaned loudly enough that he looked back at me, eyebrows raised questioningly. In response, I just leaned my head back on my chair with my eyes closed in ecstasy. Food had never tasted so good.

THE ANGEL PROJECT

It certainly wasn't the first time I'd gone twenty-four hours without eating. I'd gone a lot longer than that. It had been a long time since those hungry days in foster care, but that kind of thing sticks with you. It was why I hated being truly hungry. There were many days back then that I didn't know if I was going to eat at all. There was one family I stayed with that could hardly be bothered with such trivial things as feeding us. I was with them for six long and hungry months. We were always fed at school, breakfast and lunch, and it took some time before I eventually got used to going to bed hungry. The hardest days were Fridays; we knew we would be lucky to get a meal or two until Monday. On the weekends, I was occasionally able to steal ramen from the pantry and eat it dry, in secret. I sometimes shared my loot with the other foster kids in the house, but sometimes I was just too hungry and ate it all myself. Those selfish moments were followed by deep guilt when kids younger than me were crying in want of food. I hated those days and being hungry like this made me feel as though I was once again that scared little girl.

I never went hungry when I lived on the streets—or at least not too hungry. Food was one thing I always allowed myself. Even if it meant elongating my time on Skid Row. I used my savings to eat if need be. I needed food in a way that was unexplainable. My need for food was more significant to me than a full stomach, more than sustenance for my body. It was a security, an assurance that I could take care of myself, that no one could deny me the necessities of life.

When Anton came back with my water and blueberry ice cream, I'd already eaten most of my steak and mound of potatoes. I grabbed for the ice cream like a starved animal, and I didn't even care what he thought. Though I tried not to, I couldn't help but take a moment to reflect. It was easy enough to see that the stress of my day and the unknown state of my future was making me feel like that scared ten-year-old hiding in a broom closet, shoveling dry ramen down my throat. That girl who didn't have anything to count on the next day, not even a meal. Back then, I'd lived in constant survival mode, and considering what I'd gone through today, I was right back there. No certain future, no idea what tomorrow would bring, no one I knew for absolute certain I could count on.

I stopped eating the ice cream and sat back. I hated this loneliness. I hated the uncertainty. That feeling of insecurity was so intense, it was starting to make me feel nauseated—enough to stop eating, which in my current state of mind, was a big deal. Was this a cycle I was always bound to repeat? I'd done this to myself, after all. If I hadn't been so cavalier that night with Darcy's dad, if I'd let her fight her own battles, I would never have been caught as a CU. I had thought writing my book was such a clever way to find out more about myself, but all it would have done was call attention to two things: one, that I was in fact a CU—possibly an ANGEL—and two, that I was absolutely clueless. I knew so little back then. I was grateful the FBI had put the book's release on hold with the publisher—the last thing I wanted was for it to be released. TAP probably would have been knocking down my door in an instant.

I let out a sigh, suddenly exhausted. Anton looked up from his plate. "Full?"

I shook my head. "No, but full enough to sleep." In that foster house, our bodies had been in survival mode just as much as our minds were, and binge eating, without stopping to feel full, had kept us alive.

He dropped his fork and knife and announced, "Come on. I'll take you to your room."

I shook my head. "No, it's okay. Finish your food; I can wait."

He studied my face for a few seconds and went back to eating. I pulled my feet up onto the edge of my chair and rested my head on my knees.

A couple of hours later, I lay in my bed, not sleeping.

After dinner, Anton had brought me to the George Washington Building. It was basically a high-security coed dormitory. Not that I'd lived in a dorm before, but I'd seen enough television to understand the gist. I was assigned for the night to an apartment-style space with two bedrooms, each equipped with two beds, dressers, and desks. In between the rooms was a small living space with an even smaller kitchen and a decent-size bathroom the four occupants shared.

It was far from fancy, but certainly adequate.

I had three roommates, two of whom I'd seen in the meeting earlier, and Ashti, whom I'd met on the car ride from the airport. The woman who had been studying my reactions in the boardroom was the second roommate, Ginger. The third was the woman with the long, teeny-tiny braids in her hair who'd told me a little bit about the incapacitated ANGEL. Her name was Frida.

Ginger introduced herself to me first. "Hi, Channing. I'm Ginger Skye. My parents were going to name me Candy but decided that Candy Skye sounded too much like a stripper name, so they went with Ginger." She laughed and shrugged.

I smiled and shook her hand. I wasn't sure how to address the whole stripper thing, so I let it drop. "Nice to meet you."

Frida put out her hand next. "Welcome to the FBI. I'm Frida—a CU and a CU trainer. Looking forward to working with you."

I blew out a breath. "Another CU? That's three of us in a single apartment. Before today I didn't know if I'd ever meet another in my life."

Ginger piped in. "Four, actually. I'm a CU and a behavioral scientist."

Frida smiled. "Most of us felt the same way before coming here. Don't worry, you'll get used to it."

Ashti waved at me and said, "You get the privilege of being my roommate. You better not snore."

Again, I wasn't sure what to make of Ashti. Was she teasing me, or was she serious? "I've never been told I snore."

"Good. You'd know by now." Then she spun around and walked into the room on the left.

Ginger sneered at Ashti's back. "Don't mind her.

THE ANGEL PROJECT

She's a total terror when she's tired"—she bit her lip and smiled—"and when she's not tired, for that matter." Frida, Ginger, and Anton, who'd kindly stayed for introductions, all laughed.

I arched an eyebrow.

Anton gave me a placating look. "She's not that bad." Then he paused for effect and said, "On a very rare occasion, she can actually be pretty cool."

Ashti yelled a curse at us from her room.

Anton, Frida, and Ginger laughed again. I didn't; I had no desire to make an enemy of Ashti.

Now, having been so exhausted earlier that I could have slept on a rock, I couldn't seem to fall asleep on this fairly decent bed. My thoughts were running one hundred miles per hour. Being at the FBI Academy was messing with my head. I had no idea what to expect while I was here. Even Anton was tight lipped about what I would be doing. One thing I did know was that he would be my tour guide of the premises in the morning. I was looking forward to that.

I was staying with a behavioral scientist; a CU trainer; and Ashti, whose job, aside from being a CU and an agent, was not apparent to me. There were three other CUs in this apartment. Three more people who could use the chips implanted in their brains to upload information to another's. I knew this was just the tip of the iceberg. I'd never imagined such a place. I'd always thought that all the people who could use their chips would be with TAP. But this was an alternative to TAP, a welcome one.

That said, I wasn't entirely comfortable with the FBI

either. Mostly due to the fact that I had no idea what I was doing here. What did they want with me? If I was, in fact, more than the average CU, what then? Would I be staying here for the foreseeable future? Would I have a choice in the matter? It certainly didn't feel as though I did.

Even with all these unknowns, the elephant in the room of my mind was the pink Post-it in the pocket of my jeans. I couldn't help but think of Pax and his phone number and his strange message. I kind of felt like he was someone I could call on, but only if I was at my wit's end. Honestly, I had no clue when to call him, or who he was, or how he could help me. But if it came down to it and I felt desperate, I would call. It was an option.

Ginger had lent me some pajamas and some clothes for the next day. Before he left, Anton suggested that I call Cole to see if he could send me some of my clothes. Before I could retrieve my phone from my pocket, Anton warned, "Just FYI, every single interaction you have on your phone while on the premises will be recorded and read. That includes anything you search, any social media encounter, every text and phone call. There is no privacy here."

Well, that was certainly a surprise. "That seems like a violation of several constitutional amendments."

He smiled. "It's the FBI, Channing."

The lack of privacy really did feel violating. But for me personally, it didn't matter much. I had no real social media presence to speak of, aside from the accounts Walton & Barker had made for me, which I didn't anticipating using anytime soon, if ever. And I now only had one friend I could call. I'd just have to be cognizant of what I searched.

Cole answered on the first ring. He agreed to send my clothes, but he had about a million questions I couldn't answer. The only things I felt secure in saying was, I was safe and I was with the FBI. I kept trying to tell him there really wasn't much else to talk about, but he was frustrated and told me it wasn't good enough. Which I totally understood, but what else could I do? I certainly wasn't going to break the confidence of the FBI while on the premises.

I finally fell into a fitful sleep which hardly felt like sleep at all. I woke to Anton sitting on the end of my bed at the crack of dawn.

"You *do* snore."

I kicked him and he fell off my bed and onto the floor. If I hadn't been so unbelievably tired, I would have thrown up my hands in glory. As it was, all I could get out was a croaked "That was so satisfying."

He rolled over onto his back, chuckling and rubbing his rear end. "Payback's a—"

I cut him off. "And I do *not* snore."

He groaned as he lifted onto his feet, then risked coming close enough to flick my forehead. He laughed at my expression. "If looks could kill . . ."

I shushed him. "You're going to have to deal with Ashti if you don't quiet down. I don't know her well, but I really don't want to see her tired and angry."

He chuckled. "Yeah, you should avoid a tired and angry Ashti at all costs. Good thing she's already gone." I lifted my head toward her bed and finally fully opened my eyes. Sure enough, her bed was empty and made. She had been so quiet getting up and ready I hadn't realized her absence. That was rather thoughtful—surprisingly so. "Everyone's gone. Frida let me in as she was leaving. The FBI isn't some cushy call center job you can start at ten a.m."

"I had to clock into that job at nine a.m., thank you very much."

"In your pajamas."

"An ideal job, in my opinion." I realized they were probably expecting me clock in soon. I would have to call and tell them that . . . I was quitting? That I needed to take a leave of absence? The right answer was probably the first, but I was hesitant to give up my old life so quickly.

He laughed. "Well, you're not in Kansas anymore, Dorothy." He smacked my behind over the covers. "Get up and get moving; we've got a lot to do." He walked toward my door. "By the way, you do snore. You said last night no one had ever told you that you snore. Well, I'm telling you now. You snore. If it's any consolation, it's kinda cute."

"Snoring is never cute. And I don't snore."

"Keep telling yourself that. Now get dressed. Time's a-wastin'."

I threw a pillow and hit him in the back of the head just before he made it out the door. I threw my head back and laughed, completely missing the pillow coming back at me until it hit me square in the face.

THE ANGEL PROJECT

"This is the gym, which among many other things, houses an Olympic-size pool. They have recently expanded the gym. It's pretty sweet. Quite the step up from Mike's."

After dragging me out of bed, Anton had taken me to the dining hall for breakfast and then on a walking tour of the training academy grounds. It was incredibly impressive. I'd seen tons of diverse classrooms set up for a various types of learning and training situations, firing ranges, a massive library, and the TEVOC—or Tactical and Emergency Vehicle Operations Center, where agents in training learn to drive while being shot at and hit with other cars. Fortunately, I wouldn't be undergoing that particular training anytime soon. I didn't even have a driver's license.

We didn't go into the gym, but I was excited to know there was a place to work out. I hoped there were punching bags. I was so stressed out with the shear number of unknowns in my life I really wanted to hit something. If there weren't any bags, I knew Anton would find a way for me to physically release the frustration I felt building up, even, and especially, if it meant hitting him.

"Now I'm going to show you what is arguably the coolest place in the facility."

"Cooler than what we've already seen?"

He pumped his brows at me obnoxiously. "Just wait."

L.A. CLAYTON

We walked for close to a mile and came upon a sky-blue sign on the side of the road. It said:

Welcome
to
Hogan's Alley
city limits

CAUTION: LAW ENFORCEMENT TRAINING EXERCISES IN PROGRESS. DISPLAY OF WEAPONS, FIRING OF BLANK AMMUNITION, AND ARRESTS MAY OCCUR IF CHALLENGED. PLEASE FOLLOW INSTRUCTIONS.

HAVE A NICE DAY

I looked over at Anton, obviously puzzled.

He smiled widely. "Welcome to Hogan's Alley. The nation's most crime-ridden town." As if on cue, shouting, screaming, and gunshots suddenly rang through the air. He looked at his watch. "Ah, right on schedule. Hogan's bank is being robbed. Makes me miss the good ol' days of agent training." His smile had grown from ear to ear.

"Is this the mock town Vik was telling me about yesterday?"

He waggled his eyebrows. "That it is." He took a deep breath, as if he could smell the happy memories Hogan's Alley brought back. "I love this place. Come on—let's go watch the action."

I didn't move. When he looked back, I pointed to the sign. "I really don't want to get arrested today. I've got enough problems."

THE ANGEL PROJECT

"Trust me, getting arrested would be the least of them." He delivered the words jokingly, but I could see the truth in his eyes. What was he not telling me? Would he always be so evasive? It was like he was trying to tell me something without telling me. I knew attempting to push for a full explanation was a road to nowhere, so I just tried to let it go.

Walking around the grounds was like a breath of fresh air. The combination of being with Anton, the crisp weather, and zero talk of brain chips was like a salve on my fears. Anton tugged me toward him and into a side hug. "Come on. This place is really fun, and I guarantee you won't get arrested. I've been here a thousand times, and I know all the ins and outs."

I blew out a breath and nodded. He grabbed my hand and pulled me forward a few steps until I was keeping pace with him. It was weird to see Anton here, as an FBI agent. Weird to think that just yesterday morning I'd thought he was a personal trainer. I never even suspected he wasn't who he said he was all those years at Mike's. I didn't know if that explained more about my naïveté or his expertise. But he was happy right now, and at least for the moment, I could see it wasn't an act. I wanted to let him have this moment of happiness. I hardly knew anything about the real Antonio Garcia, but I was sure he'd dealt with hard things. Whatever happened with the incapacitated ANGEL had affected him greatly. That person, whomever he or she was, meant a great deal to him. And yet, he managed to go on with his life. He managed to be happy. What I wasn't sure of was whether he was uniquely good at burying his head in the sand or if he was just good at compartmentalizing.

The shouts and gunshots got louder as we got closer to the town center. Once we were within sight of the action, I gasped.

I didn't know what to expect, but it certainly wasn't this. There truly was a whole town. complete with buildings, streets, sidewalks, streetlamps, stores, a bank—which was currently being robbed by an armed gunman—a post office, drugstore, movie theater, hotel, several streets of single-family homes, and more beyond what was within direct view. I craned my neck to see farther down the road, then laughed. "There's a Subway here?"

Anton smiled. "FBI trainees gotta eat."

My mouth dropped open. "It's a *working* Subway?"

"With certified sandwich artists and all."

I shoved him lightly in the chest. "Come on. Seriously?"

He laughed. "I wouldn't joke about my favorite Subway. It really is functioning. And there really are sandwich artists there. They just happen to be sandwich artists with a clean government background check."

I guffawed. "This place is insane!"

"You haven't seen the half of it." He motioned with his head to a bench about ten feet down the road. "Let's watch."

We looked on as police officers and FBI agents surrounded the bank. There were even paramedics on site. The police sirens were blaring, and a man who looked to be the chief of police yelling into a bullhorn at the gunman to drop his weapon and come out with his hands up. The FBI agents were together with a group of police officers; I guess they were devising a plan.

Inside the bank a teller stood with her hands up and several bank patrons were laying on the floor.

The chief yelled into the bullhorn, "You don't want to hurt anybody. Put your gun down and come on out."

Out of the gunman's view, FBI agents donned their gear and lined up against the building to the side of the door. Anton clicked his tongue. I looked at him to gauge his reaction, but he was riveted, watching the scene unfold directly in front of us. The FBI looked ready to move, and Anton chuckled. "Bad idea, guys."

While the chief continued to talk over the bullhorn, another police officer gave the signal to the waiting agents. They went in mid-sentence and shot the assailant. He fell to the ground.

The EMTs immediately went into the bank. A few went directly to the gunman, while the others went to help the hostages. The FBI agents sent the unharmed hostages to the police to give their statements. And both the FBI and the police took pictures of the crime scene. Once the EMTs had all hostages checked out and the gunman in the back of their vehicle, someone yelled, "Cut!" and everyone let out a breath, relaxed, and started talking.

One of the FBI agents, who looked far from happy, called on everyone to be quiet and to gather round. The assailant came to stand by the agent in charge, shaking his head. The agent proceed to correct just about every action they'd taken.

Anton whistled. "This is a new group. They only got about two things right."

"That just proves how little I know about all of this, because it all looked pretty good to me." I shrugged. "I liked the way they went in while the police officer was actively speaking on the bullhorn. I thought it was clever—the assailant's attention was split."

"His attention was split, which actually makes it exponentially more dangerous. When they get spooked, they go to their weapon as a protection and shield. They should have given him much longer to come out on his own. He hadn't hurt anyone, and he exhibited no signs that he would. They should have smoked him out. This would have gone terribly in real life."

Huh. Well, that made sense. "Good thing these guys are here for training, then."

"No doubt." He slapped his knees. "Let's go get some Subway."

The restaurant was packed with lunch goers, many of which were dressed for their roles as criminals in Hogan's Alley. We got our food, free of charge, due to the lanyards hanging around our necks. Everyone was wearing them—there were many different colors, which signaled the entity for which they were training. Even the criminals had tagged lanyards.

"Are these paid actors?"

Anton shook his head. "Nah, most of the criminals are trainers. It's a good vantage point to see how the trainees are doing. The trainers can throw a few curveballs as the group gets more advanced."

After eating and watching a street-gang fight get broken up, we left Hogan's Alley.

We went out of the town through the back, opposite

the way we came and continued to walk farther from the FBI Academy. The farther we walked, the darker Anton's mood became. I couldn't wait any longer to ask, "Where are we going?"

Anton swallowed and took a minute before he answered me. "To a place only known by a few."

I growled. "Anton, I hate it when you're cryptic. That's the bulk of what I've gotten from you lately. Give it to me straight; I can take it."

"There are things I'm permitted to tell you, and things that I'm not. That's why I'm cryptic."

"So this falls under the things you're not supposed to tell me?" He nodded. "You can take me there, but you can't talk about what it is?" How utterly ridiculous.

He nodded. "This is a place we don't speak of, ever, unless we are on the premises or in a soundproof room."

I looked at him; he was facing forward, and his face looked like it was carved from stone. He'd been weird like that lately—one thought or thing could set him off, but he didn't tell me what was upsetting him. "Shouldn't I be vetted before I go there? Don't I need some kind of background check or clearance?" He chuckled, but it wasn't out of humor.

"What's funny about this, Anton?"

He shook his head. "Absolutely nothing is funny about this. But let me assure you the minute you showed you are a CU, you became vetted. This place is where you will spend the bulk of your time while you're here. To the public, Quantico is a place dedicated to the marines and the FBI. The place where we're going is technically part of the base, and not part of the base."

"What?" Nothing he said lately ever made any sense. It had gotten beyond old.

"If you're coming here from inside the marine base, it appears you're leaving." He pointed to the gate up ahead. There was a sign saying, *Marine Corps Base Exit— Not for Public Use. Violators Will Be Arrested and Prosecuted.* "But if you're coming from outside the base, you'll see a gate that's marked, 'Quantico Marine Corps Base. Trespassers Will Be Prosecuted to the Fullest Extent of the Law.' The place we're going is off the books. It's not somewhere you can get to without access. And without access, one—even one who worked in Quantico daily— would have no idea it exists." He practically spit out the last sentence, as if the short explanation had cost him all of his patience.

"What is making you so angry?"

"I'm not angry." He said it before I could even finish my sentence.

I was about to retort with attitude when it finally hit me. This, his face, his stiff posture, the anxiety rolling off him in waves, it was exactly the way he'd looked last night when Dr. Rucker had brought up the incapacitated ANGEL.

I grabbed his hand and tugged. This was what I'd been waiting for. I needed to know what had happened to this person like I needed oxygen, and now that I was so close, nothing was going to stop me. "Let's go." If he was surprised at my change of attitude, he didn't say as much.

We walked through the marine base exit with the push of a button. On the other side was the prettiest, narrow, one-lane road, lined with autumn foliage. The air was crisp and ideal for being outside. The beautiful scenery was juxtaposed with Anton's foul mood. And I couldn't deny the apprehensiveness growing within me the closer we got to our intended destination. It wasn't that I didn't want to know—I *had* to know what had happened to this person. But what if it was something horrifying? And the most important question, the one that weighed on me the most: *Was I next*?

We didn't talk for the rest of the walk. Not until we came to a gate attached to a chain-link fence. The fence was at least twenty feet tall and looped with barbed wire at the top. There was a sign proclaiming: *Quantico Correctional Facility*. I turned to Anton. "Is this a prison?"

He didn't speak; he just stared straight ahead. "Anton, is this a prison?" I asked a second time, more forcefully.

"Is this a prison? Depends on how you look at it."

The dread I was feeling turned to ice in my veins. I took a step back, and Anton finally looked at me, like really *looked* at me. "I spent almost a year in jail, and I'm never going back, Anton."

He debated how he wanted to respond. But I didn't want him to think carefully about his words. I wanted him to blurt them out. I wanted to know what he was thinking. "It's a prison to the outside world. Inside, it's different. For most people anyway."

My body started to tremble. "What does that even mean?"

He looked at the gate. "To some it's a prison, to others it's a freedom."

What was he talking about? I felt like I was a second

grader trying to understand Shakespeare's *Cymbeline*. "Anton, you are making no sense, and I am really freaking out right now. I'm not going in there unless you tell me what this place is."

"Ironically, I can't tell you what it is until you go in there."

"What in the hell, Anton?"

He turned then and grabbed me by the shoulders. "My demons are in there, Channing. *Mine*. It doesn't mean yours will be. It's not what you think, that much I can guarantee. I'm not going to lie to you and tell you I like this place. I don't and it's no secret. For the world, this is a local, privately owned prison." He made a circle with one of his hands. "There's video and audio surveillance here, and if I were to break protocol for you for the sole purpose of reassuring you, then I would lose my privilege to return here. And that is something I refuse to risk." His breaths were coming out harsh and fast.

He wanted to go in. Or rather he didn't *want* to go in—he needed to. Who was in there that he wanted to see so badly? I didn't get a chance to ask before he went on. "So, if you'd rather, you can turn around and walk back the way we came, but I am going inside." He paused for a minute, then smirked, "This is where the magic happens." He looked at me like I was supposed to understand what he was saying. Maybe I should've caught on by now, but I was too scared to see past the prison gates. He rubbed a hand down his face. Softly, he said, "Channing, I wouldn't let anyone hurt you. You can trust me in that."

Trust Anton? I couldn't even trust myself. My memories were a mixture of implanted and real, and I could barely tell the difference. How could I trust the FBI, or anyone who worked for them? They hadn't even told me what they wanted with me. There were the vague talks of me working here, of seeing what I was capable of, but no one had given me any specifics.

I took a deep breath. We were both having our own issues right now, and neither of us seemed capable of helping the other. Anton had given me fair warning, he was fighting his own demons at the moment. Whoever that ANGEL was, they were someone very special to him. I needed to respect that, as well as his extreme feelings surrounding this place. I knew I was going to follow Anton inside. I just hoped I'd come back out. That was my real fear. What if they never let me leave? Anton claimed this place just looked like a prison to keep people out, but prisons were created to keep people in, and I knew from Anton's cryptic words it served both purposes. If I went now, at least I had Anton with me.

I nodded, and Anton let out the breath I didn't know he'd been holding.

Then he walked me up to the side of the gate, directly in front of a box he opened to reveal a keypad. He looked at me and assured me, "You can open the gate."

I blinked at him in disbelief.

He pointed to the keypad. "It's fake. There's no code." He pointed to his head.

"What? I'm supposed to open the gate with my chip?"

He nodded. "All CUs can."

I shook my head. I didn't want to. I felt like my chip

would leave a mark, like a fingerprint. I wasn't sure I wanted them to have it.

He hesitated for a second, then shot me a tight, mirthless smile. Then he turned to look at the keypad. He stared at it for just a few seconds, until it gave a low beep. Then the gate began to slide to the left.

My stomach dropped to my feet, and tears of betrayal stung my eyes. Anton was a Chip Utilizer.

NINETEEN

I DIDN'T SAY A WORD. I couldn't. I didn't trust myself to speak; I just stared straight ahead. For so long, all I'd wanted was to be understood. I wanted to understand *myself.* Anton, whom I'd seen three times a week for the better part of three years, was a CU. He knew how much I'd suffered in my life. He may have not fully understood that the chip was the cause of all of my problems for the bulk of that time, but he'd certainly been aware for the past forty-eight hours.

That thought made me groan in embarrassment. I'd told everyone I'd been dying to meet other CUs, and they'd all known that I'd known one for years. Ashti, on the way to the academy—the way she'd looked at me when I'd said how excited I was to meet another CU. They must have all thought I was such an idiot. Why didn't he tell me? Why wait this long? Why leave me to look and feel so incredibly stupid? "*Why*? Why would you not tell me?"

"Can this wait until we're inside? *Please*?"

His "please" sounded like an actual plea. Like he was

begging me not to make a scene out here. It was hard for me to wrap my brain around the fact that we weren't alone when I couldn't see anyone around us. But a quick look showed there was surveillance equipment everywhere. There were cameras along the fence and the gate, and plenty of them were focused directly on us. It seemed typical of a prison to be loaded with surveillance equipment, but it still felt violating. There was a reason that people valued privacy.

I bit my lip. I wanted to say, *No, we're going to talk about this right now.* But I knew it would only serve to make me look more ignorant and childish than I already did. I felt small and ridiculous. And whether it made sense or not, I felt betrayed. Had I no friends? No one I could trust to just tell me the *truth*? One thing I knew with certainty was I had no friends in the FBI. The people here did not care for me. My value was measured only by what I could do for them. That was as far as it extended. Even with Anton—perhaps especially with Anton. All he'd ever done was lie to me. That broke my heart more than I cared to admit.

I shook my head. "No need to explain." I already got it. He didn't care for me like I cared for him. Maybe that was the problem with having so few friends. It was hard to tell the difference between the real and the fake—you just held on to whatever you could. Anton had been the latter. He had been paid to spend time with me. I was his assignment. No matter how much I longed for it to be more, for me to mean more to him, I just didn't.

I was angry, hurt, and feeling sorry for myself, which in general was not a good place from which I should make decisions. If we talked about this now, I'd say things to Anton I'd regret. But it cut me to the core to know he'd consistently lied to me. And even when he could have, he didn't tell me the truth. What did he want from me? How did keeping the truth from me benefit him? It must have in some way, because he certainly wasn't holding back for *my* sake.

Anton blinked hard at whatever he read in my expression. He looked almost disappointed in me, which was so unbelievably unfair. I would not be the bad guy in this scenario. If I were honest, he wasn't the bad guy either. He was just doing his job. The problem was that *I* was the job. The sooner I understood that, the better it would be for both of us. He didn't deserve my hard feelings. We had been in a one-sided friendship. I made more of it than it was. I was an idiot. End of story.

I nodded that the conversation could wait until later. Later, as in the twelfth of never. I never wanted to revisit this issue. It was too embarrassing. All it would prove was that I was too naïve.

Anton didn't show much relief at my acquiescence; his face was still hard as he motioned me forward through the gate. I only hesitated for a second. The instant we stepped over the threshold, the gate began to slide back into place behind us. The ominous feeling that swirled within me was almost too much. I was officially locked in this place, whatever place this was.

Anton again used his chip when we got to the door, which was charcoal gray and so heavy, I would have guessed it was made of solid iron. The door buzzed, and it slowly creaked open, the hinges sounding ready to buckle under the weight of it.

Through the door was a vestibule and another door, not quite as heavy as the first. The vestibule was dingy, with a concrete floor. Dirt and grime filled the corners. The place could've used a good scrubbing, or three. Anton again used his chip to open the second door.

Inside the building looked nothing like the outside. I was really and truly expecting it to look like a prison: cold and damp, with flickering fluorescent lights. But it looked like an office building. A rather nice one, with marble floors and lots of glass. The woman working in the Special Agents Building last night greeted us in the reception area. That caught me off guard. "Hello, Anton." She smiled at him warmly. Still smiling kindly, she nodded at me. "Ms. Walker, welcome."

I tried my best to smile back, but I couldn't. My feelings of dread were too strong, and I couldn't have forced politeness in that moment for everything in the world. Her phone rang and she put a finger up, asking us to wait. Anton didn't want to wait. I could feel anxiety rolling off him; I was surprised it didn't topple the poor receptionist over.

After a couple of "yeses" and "uh-huhs," she said, "I'll see to it" and hung up the phone. "Agent Davis would like to see you in his office in ninety minutes." She looked at Anton and gave him an understanding smile. "He would like you to give Ms. Walker a tour until that time."

Anton nodded his head and let out a long breath. Then he nodded at me, which I could only assume was a

THE ANGEL PROJECT

signal to follow him, because he started walking away. I had to jog to catch up and continue to take quick strides to keep up.

We passed several halls of offices as well as two places to eat. One resembled the dining hall from the academy—it was large and spacious. No flags, though. The other was a café-style eatery, with a black-and-white checkered floor and cute booths and tables along with a display of sandwiches, salads, and baked goods. The smell of coffee called to me, but we passed everything too quickly for me to get a good look. I just got quick snippets. So much for the tour. The building seemed to go on forever. "How big is this place?"

"The facility sits on more than sixteen thousand acres."

Sixteen thousand? Wow. I lived with a foster family once whose house sat on one acre. That was a ton of land for Southern California. One acre. Sixteen thousand was impossible to wrap my brain around.

We passed a bright, colorful hallway. I craned my neck to see down its entirety, but it simply too long. It looked like an elementary school. Handprints in all the colors of the rainbow lined the walls, along with banners and posters and self-portraits, obviously drawn by children, hanging in a line over a coatrack. I stopped.

Anton grabbed my arm and pulled me forward. "Not yet."

I yanked out of his grasp; I had no desire to be touched by him. "What's down there?"

Hurt crossed his features momentarily. "I'll take you there and show you, but not yet. There's something I need to do first." Every word coming out of his mouth was short and terse, as if he were the one with the reason to be angry.

I didn't ask any more questions.

We finally came to an unmarked hallway. It was all white. White floors, white walls, white door at the end. It made me itchy. Anton's steps slowed, and his breaths became heavier. We walked to the door, and as was typical with this place, his chip was the only means to enter.

One five-second look from Anton and the door clicked open. On the other side, everything was still white, with little pops of color that stood out here and there: a blue folder, a red thermos, a green reusable lunch bag. The people who worked there wore white—some of them in lab coats, some in scrubs. They wore lanyards of a variety of colors. Was this a hospital? A clinic? Everyone who saw us smiled, some of them sadly, at Anton, and openly studied me.

Anton didn't talk to anyone, despite being greeted by several people.

Just past what appeared to be a nurses' station, he took a sharp left, and we went down yet another white hallway, this one with several doors on each side. Each door had a small window. Even though we walked quickly, I could see a person in each room. Most of them were adults, but some appeared to be teenagers. My heart caught in my throat when I remembered Anton's words from the airport. "*We have Chip Utilizers who literally go insane over having to stop.*" That's what this place was. It was an insane asylum for the chip users. A place where they kept the *incapacitated.*

THE ANGEL PROJECT

I peeked in every window we passed, more curious than ever to get a look at the ANGEL who meant so much to Anton. Most of the people looked drugged, which, frankly, was probably a mercy. But more than that, aside from the vacant stares, most of the people looked normal. Regular people, like me. The orange jumpsuits were what I'd imagined people in a place like this would wear, but they were clean and well maintained. I didn't know why that was particularly harrowing, but it was. Could I be locked in one of these rooms and drugged until I was none the wiser? It seemed so wrong. These people were here through no fault of their own. They hadn't asked to be chipped. This was the fault of the people who'd kept them locked up and drugged. A by-product of their dangerous science and technology.

There was a loud banging on one of the doors and I thought my heart was going to jump out of my chest. I audibly yelped when I looked over and saw a man with his face pressed up against the window, trying to get our attention. Anton looked at me, at the blatant fear on my face, and his hand started to reach out toward mine, but he pulled it back quickly, seeming to rethink the move. I looked back at the man in the window, who was still watching us. My hands trembled, and chills ran up and down my spine and limbs, leaving gooseflesh in their wake. I put my hands in my pockets in an attempt to still them, but I took them back out immediately. Having my hands hidden away made me feel even more vulnerable.

Anton stopped at the end of the hallway. There were two doors there. It seemed like he couldn't decide which door he wanted to go in. He looked at me pointedly once, and chose the door on the left. He stared at it for a moment, and then the door opened to a sort of viewing room filled with chairs, desks, and computers, all of which were facing the wall on the right, which wasn't a wall at all. It was a two-way mirror.

There were only a couple of people in the room when Anton and I walked in. One of them was Dr. Rucker, and the other was a woman I hadn't seen before. She was blonde with shoulder-length straight hair. They stood up when they saw Anton. Dr. Rucker smiled and greeted us warmly. "Agent Garcia and Ms. Walker. I thought we might see you here today."

I tried to smile at him, but I was still shaking at the shock of this place, and I couldn't get my mouth to tilt upward. Anton didn't bother with niceties. "How is he?"

He?

I turned to the window, which I knew looked like a mirror to the person on the other side. Instead of the hospital room I was expecting to see, there was a living room equipped with furniture—a contemporary rug covering the stained hardwood floor, a couch, a coffee table, and end tables with lamps and plants. On the other side of the living room was various exercise equipment. Past the living room on one side was a bedroom and on the other, a small kitchen. The only part of the scene that didn't look like an average apartment was the door. It looked like the others in the hospital wing: heavy and white with a rectangular window. Next to the door, a little higher than the handle, was a large red button encased in plastic. It looked like an emergency button, like someone would push if they were in there taking care of the man and needed urgent help. What could have happened to him?

As if merely thinking about him had summoning power, out of the kitchen walked the most attractive man I'd ever laid eyes on.

He had blue eyes framed by dark lashes and deep, heavy brows. His hair was thick and dark, with a loose curl pattern that shone in the lamplight. His skin was deeply golden, and he had a short but dense beard that was so dark it verged on black. He was wearing a black V-neck sweater with the sleeves pulled halfway up his forearms—which were roped with muscle—and medium-wash jeans that frayed where they met his bare feet.

He looked like Anton. But more attractive.

He walked toward the mirror and sat on the couch facing us. His mouth was moving, but his eyes were still. I couldn't look away.

Anton took a deep breath beside me, which pulled me out of my trance.

"Oh, you know; Dom's about the same," Dr. Rucker answered. Anton's shoulders slumped only slightly, but I could sense his disappointment at the news. "I can't seem to pull him out of the mental place he's in, as usual. He's aways been a stubborn one."

At that Anton gave a ghost of a smile. "Runs in the family."

Dr. Rucker chuckled and patted him on the back. "That it does, Anton. That it does." He turned to me and lifted his arms. "Channing, what do you think of our facility?"

He was all smiles and pride. My mind was stuck on

the man who was sitting on the couch, staring at nothing and everything. I blurted out the first thing that came to mind. "I'm not sure what to think, actually."

Dr. Rucker laughed. "That sounds about right. It's a remarkable facility. But I'm sure it will take some time to acclimate. Maybe later I can show you the lab where I used to work with your parents."

I sucked in a breath and finally fully focused on Dr. Rucker. "This was where my parents worked?"

He nodded. "This was where the ANGEL Project was born. You spent the bulk of your childhood here. Doesn't any of it look familiar to you?"

I shook my head. How in the world had I ended up in Los Angeles? The more I learned about my past, the more the questions piled up. I felt like my life was an episode of *Lost*—full of never-ending reveals. And those revelations only served to bring on more confusion. I really hoped I had a better ending than the show.

"Huh." He rubbed his chin. "Well, this place looks very different now than it did back then. It's grown quite a bit. Maybe the lab itself will jog some memories for you."

I nodded, but knew it wouldn't. For reasons I didn't understand, my memory had been wiped clean of this place. I doubted the lab, or any other area, would suddenly bring it all flooding back. That wasn't how the chip worked.

Dr. Rucker picked up the papers strewn across the desk at which he'd been working, put them in a red folder, and tucked it under his arm. He nodded to his companion. "This is Dr. Sara Brandt; she's a neurologist.

THE ANGEL PROJECT

She spends the bulk of her time with Dominic. Sara, you know Anton, of course." She nodded her head, and Anton smiled tightly. Dr. Rucker motioned to me. "This is Channing Walker, our newest CU."

Dr. Brandt held out her hand. "Nice to meet you, Channing. I've heard a lot about you."

I shook her hand and worked hard to offer a feeble smile—it was the best I could do in the moment. "Nice to meet you too."

Dr. Rucker shifted toward the door. "We'll let you have some privacy, Anton."

After they were gone, all that remained was deafening silence.

When I finally looked at Anton, he wasn't looking at me. He was looking at Dom. "That's my brother, Dominic. He's the incapacitated ANGEL."

His brother. I figured as much when Dr. Rucker implied they were related. The resemblance couldn't be denied. But to have it confirmed hit me on a visceral level. It made me so sad. How had this affected Anton? I supposed in every way possible.

I grabbed his hand and pressed it twice with mine. The ill feelings I had toward Anton were quickly set on the back burner. Even if our friendship was one sided, I would uphold my end. He needed someone right now. His brother, whom it was obvious he cared for deeply, was in some strange state of consciousness. It struck me then that maybe Anton was as alone as I was.

When I went to let go of his hand, he grabbed hold of mine tighter. I sighed and stepped closer to him, hand in hand, and we watched his brother together. I don't know how long we stood there, but eventually Anton spoke. "Want to meet him?"

"Yes," I replied without hesitation.

The corners of his mouth just barely tilted upward.

We exited through the door we'd entered in and used the one that was next to it. Anton opened it with his chip, as usual. It appeared that the only way around this place was with the use of the chip. I was going to have to get used to the practice.

Dominic didn't turn at the sound of the door opening. He didn't so much as flinch. My sadness deepened.

The apartment smelled like cleaning products had been used recently. There were also strong hints of a rich, fresh citrus cologne. It must have been Dominic's. It dawned on me then, regardless of his mental state, he seemed to go through the motions of life. His apartment was sparkling. He was clean, fed, dressed in regular clothes—no orange jumpsuit here—he obviously exercised, and he even wore cologne. But he didn't notice when his brother entered the room?

What had happened to this man?

"Hey, Dom." No response. Anton went over to his side of the couch. I followed his lead and sat on Anton's other side, just on the edge of the couch so I could see around Anton to Dominic. His beauty was a thing of wonder. He could've been a model for any product—everyone would buy it. I'd probably buy hemorrhoid ointment if it had his face on it.

What had happened to this man? The question was running through my mind on repeat. Why was he like this? He was conscious, but not. He appeared to be a normal, healthy adult male, until you got closer. Until you saw his concentrated stare and the way his mouth moved so fast, not even an expert could make out the words. I wasn't even sure they *were* words. More like gibberish. Or calculations—numbers, maybe? Dominic may not have been looking at anyone in particular, but his stare wasn't like the drugged people down the hall. It was anything but vacant. He was *thinking*. It was like he was thinking so hard that there was no room for anything that wasn't automatic. No room in his brain to make conversation or acknowledge other people around him. That would've required too much from his already-overloaded brain.

I had an overwhelming urge to sit by Dominic and do things I shouldn't. Things I swore I'd never do again. I wanted to look into his eyes, turn on his chip, and *see*. It was such a dangerous thing to do. Such a dangerous desire. I'd gotten myself in so much trouble before—it had cost me so much heartache. But more than that, it was so completely out of line, so utterly violating. And if I did connect to his chip, I was sure that somehow they—the powers that be, in this place—would know what I'd done, and I didn't want to play that hand yet. But more than anything, Anton was in a fragile state, and I didn't want to offend him, or do anything that would put him over the edge. So I sat there, my body on fire with the need to know what this man had experienced, or was experiencing, but did nothing.

Anton put his arm around his brother. "It's been a while, man. I'm sorry it's been so long since I've been here to see you." No response from Dom. Anton's voice choked on the words when he said, "You look good, bro."

Anton bent his head down and used his free hand to roughly rub his face.

I felt awkward watching this intimate moment. My thoughts were everywhere and nowhere. I burned with the desire to know what was going on with Dom. I literally felt like the fire would consume me. Not able to sit there any longer, I stood and walked a few paces away from the couch. Dominic's face followed my movements.

Anton's eyes shot to me like a bolt of lightning. Then he looked back and forth between me and Dom. Utter shock shone on every corner of his face. His breath was frozen in his lungs.

I moved again and Dom tracked me.

Anton uttered a single word: "How?"

Dominic continued to stare at me, his mouth still moving, but something in his eyes was different. It was like he knew I was there. He wasn't looking into my eyes, more like in my vicinity, like he couldn't see me, but he knew about where I was. Why in the world did he react to me and not his brother? I feared it had something to do with our shared capabilities regarding the chip.

I literally shook with the need to see inside his brain. I averted my eyes. I couldn't look at Dominic for one more second without doing the one thing I swore I'd never do again. The emotions in the room were too high. It felt like electricity was crackling through the space. If I looked in his eyes, I wouldn't be able to stop myself. My chip was already turned on, my head buzzing. But this time the buzz wasn't small or light—it was huge and all consuming. It was overpowering, stealing my breath, stealing my strength to abstain.

THE ANGEL PROJECT

I ran to the door and tried to pull it open. I tugged and it wouldn't budge. The buzzing in my head grew stronger, and I risked a glance back. Dom was standing, his body angled toward mine, ready to follow me. Anton was right on his heels, his eyes shooting between me and Dom at a pace that must have made his head spin. I looked back to the door and stared at it, my chip already on, and willed the door to open. Nothing happened.

I was beginning to panic. I briefly thought about lifting the plastic covering over the red button and slamming my palm against it, but I was afraid it would bring more attention to me and why I was experiencing such a connection to Anton's brother.

I shook my hands out and tried to pull the door open harder. My body was so flooded with adrenaline. I could hear Anton speaking, or yelling maybe, behind me, but I couldn't understand what he was saying. And I didn't care. I mentally screamed at the door to OPEN! And it finally clicked. I pulled on the door, jumped out of the room, and yanked the door closed behind me.

TWENTY

I TOOK A FEW STUMBLING steps and fell to the floor. I crawled to the wall and pulled my knees up to my chest and hid my face against them. Then I concentrated on my breathing, which was easier outside the room. My whole body was trembling, my muscles strung tight. I couldn't think, couldn't process.

The night with Jenna flashed into my mind and I didn't have the strength to push it away. It was raining. I was coming home from work, and Jenna was sitting in the rain on the sidewalk by my tent, high as a kite. Again. She'd been trying so hard to quit, but she was so addicted that no matter how long she went without it, she always seemed to find her way back to the needle. Heroin was just that kind of drug.

Jenna was so beautiful, with her long strawberry-blonde hair, fair skin, smattering of freckles across her nose and upper cheeks, and her perfect teeth. Even living on Skid Row and her on-again, off-again heroin use couldn't dim her beauty. A rare thing, for sure. When she was sober and happy, she was a force to be reckoned with,

THE ANGEL PROJECT

but sadly, it never seemed to last very long. I didn't really consider Jenna a friend—more like an acquaintance. She came and went as she pleased. Or rather, as she was forced. She would sober up and move back in with her mom and dad from time to time, but she'd inevitably get kicked out. Her well-to-do parents had had enough of watching their daughter ruin her life. That's when I'd see her hanging out in Skid Row.

    The first time I saw her, she looked so lost and sad. It was clear she didn't belong, with her flared jeans, black puff-sleeved sweater, and shiny, hot-pink pointed-toe flats. Her hair was long and curled just right, and even though she'd cried off her makeup, she was still just so pretty. Too pretty for that place. Too *rich* for that place. I'd approached her that day and asked if she was okay. She shook her head. "My parents kicked me out and cut me off. My purse and phone were stolen. I have no ID, and nowhere to go, and I'm hungry and kind of freaking out right now."

    The fact that she'd tell me, a perfect stranger on Skid Row, all of that, just showed how truly clueless she was. Aside from what I gathered from her appearance, she'd just confirmed she came from a family with money and she had parents who loved her. They might have kicked her out, but clearly only as a tactic to scare her straight. Anyone there could, and would, use her to get money from her family. The first rule you learn on the streets: never show your hand. You never want people to think you were worth anything to anyone, and you never want anyone to know you have anything valuable—be it in possessions, lifestyle comforts, or food. I ate at work, and the food I ate on the street was meager and cheap. Things like processed day-old bread and donuts—stuff the grocery store either sold incredibly cheap or gave away. If someone broke into my tent looking for food or money, all they would find was half-moldy, months-old hot dog buns, and they'd move on quickly.

I helped her that first time—brought her into my tent and let her use my phone, a thing I didn't do for anyone. But I knew if I left her outside, she'd end up physically assaulted, or worse. She called a friend and was picked up. After that, she come around on occasion, whenever she was without another place to go, and I would help her out when I could. Fortunately, she'd smartened up and didn't look quite so bougie after our first encounter. It was so sad to see someone who'd had all the opportunities in the world handed to her on a silver platter, and the only thing she picked up from the plate was heroin.

This time, as I got closer to her, I could see that things weren't normal. She wasn't just sitting in the rain, strung out. She was passed out, flopped against the lamppost in front of my tent. I'd seen people in all stages of overdose on the street. I took one look at Jenna in her current state, and I rushed over to her, grabbing ahold of her soaked shoulders. "Jenna! Jenna, wake up!" I shook her, but she wasn't responding. Her body was like Silly Putty, completely moldable, with no pushback. I was starting to freak out. I screamed her name until my throat ached and people were sticking their heads out of their tents, telling me to shut up. I crouched down and slapped her in the face. I'd seen it make people come to in movies and television shows, but it didn't seem to work in real life. I felt for her pulse and found a faint one. Relieved, I called 911, and then I sunk down in front of her and sat in the rain, grateful that Jenna wasn't dead.

I then became angry. How could someone who had so much be so stupid? How could she treat her life like this? I looked at her pallid face in the moonlight, rainwater running down it in rivulets, her mascara smudged around her eyes and streaking her cheeks. Her mouth was hanging open and slack. It was the first time I'd seen her look truly ugly.

"Are you trying to kill yourself?" I yelled over the rain. "What were you thinking?" And that's when I saw it. The roll of money I'd had hidden inside a leather belt. It was just as I'd left it, rolled tight and secured with a red, white, and blue rubber band. The belt was expensive and made to hide money. I'd bought it after getting mugged when I'd first moved to Skid Row. At the time, I'd kept all of my money in the same place: on me. I learned quickly that was not the way to do things. I didn't have a bank account because I didn't have an address, so I did some research and found the best thing was to hide money in several places. That way you were sure not to lose it all at once if something bad happened. I normally wore the belt to work, but I had been in a hurry that morning and left it in its hiding spot.

I didn't know how Jenna had found that money, but she'd taken every last dollar of the several hundred I'd secured in the belt. She knew how long I'd struggled to make and save the meager money I earned. She knew I had absolutely no one to turn to. No one in the world was willing to take care of me if I lost everything. She had rich parents who loved her and would always take her back if she were willing to change. But *she* had stolen from *me*—the girl who had nothing and no one. I was so mad I was shaking as I grabbed my money from where it stuck out of her pocket.

Between my shaking anger and the rain, I didn't notice the light buzzing in my head. I didn't see anything but red until I was in her head. Until I was seeing her chip in my mind's eye. But I saw more than that. My chip seemed to connect to hers in a way I didn't know was possible. I knew I could send her a message, so I did. I told her she would never do another illegal drug for as long as she lived. But I instinctively knew I could do other things as well. Things that were wrong. Things I should have said no to but didn't.

I took something from her that night, and it was so much more than her free will. In the moment I didn't even care. I didn't think about how wrong it was, or how much I'd regret it later. In the moment, I saw something I wanted, and I knew I could have it. A thing she threw farther down the toilet every time she got high. It was so easy. It only took moments, and suddenly I was more than I once was. I had something I'd never thought I'd have. It felt amazing and absolutely horrible.

The door to Dominic's room opened and closed with a whoosh of air bringing me out of my dark memory. I didn't look up. I couldn't. Within a moment, I felt Anton's hands grasp my biceps and pull. On my way up, I chanced a glance at his face, and I could see a mixture of emotions playing there, but the greatest was wonder. He was in awe I'd evoked a response from his brother. As if

I'd had something to do with that. I really didn't want him having any positive thoughts about me in that moment. I didn't deserve it.

He pulled me tightly into him and held me for what felt like several minutes, whispering my name over and over. The sound of his voice washed over me. Whether we were real friends or fake friends, I didn't care, and I don't think he did either. We were both alone, and we both needed someone for our own reasons.

In my ear, he quietly asked, "Can you act normal? Like none of that ever happened? Just for a few minutes?"

Could I? I took stock of my body. My breathing had somewhat normalized; my severe shaking had turned into a small tremble. The buzzing in my head was gone, meaning my chip had turned off.

I nodded my head into his chest. He let out a breath and pulled back slightly so he could see my eyes. Whatever he saw there placated him enough that he pulled away from me, grabbed my hand, and began walking us down the hallway and out of the psych ward.

Several minutes and even more hallways later, we reached a door. Anton opened it to reveal an apartment, much like the one Dom lived in. There was a living room, a bedroom, a bathroom, and a small kitchen. Anton gave me a pointed look and held a finger to his lips. Then he said, "This is my room within the facility. I don't stay here much, but we all have them."

I said the first thought that came to mind. "It looks like Dominic's room."

He nodded. "Yeah, that's on purpose. We don't know what's going on with Dom, but we thought it would be a bad idea to throw him in a padded room. We wanted things to look familiar. They built the room to duplicate his room in the facility, with the exception of the two-way mirror. The office space was built simultaneously to study him. When that happened, almost three and a half years ago, he still communicated with us to a small degree. But eventually it stopped, and he's been in the state you just witnessed since."

Three and a half years? Dominic had been like this for *three and a half years?*

Anton held up a finger, went into his room, and came back out with a device. It was a small rectangular box with two antennae. He flipped the switch and set it on the coffee table. "Audio and visual blocking device. Supposedly there isn't any surveillance in our rooms, but I don't trust anyone."

He turned to me, his expression as solemn as I'd ever seen. "Channing, what in the hell happened back there? I need every single detail. Please."

I nodded my head but continued to stand there silent for a minute. I didn't really have any answers, not solid ones. I had a theory, but in order to explain it, I'd have to tell him the story of Jenna. I didn't want to tell him that story for several reasons, but two stood at the forefront of my mind. The first was that the incident would reveal too much information regarding my capabilities with the chip, information I wanted to hold close to the vest, and the other was that it painted me in a terrible light. I ended up blurting out, "I don't know. I couldn't explain it if I tried."

"You're going to have to try, Channing."

THE ANGEL PROJECT

I shook my head, hoping it would settle all of my jumbled thoughts. How could I tell Anton without giving away everything I was? "It was just so strange. One minute I was fine, the next, my chip was on, outside of my will—or at least I don't remember turning it on—and . . ." I shook my head again. "I don't know. I was just out of control."

"It's been over two years since Dom has made any effort to communicate in any form. Since he stopped, he has not acknowledged a single person's existence. Not one single person. Until today. When you ran out of the room, Dom followed you. He stood there at the door—I couldn't pull him away for several minutes. He was looking for you. He wanted to see you. And that is—" He shook his head. "That is inconceivable. So, I'm going to ask you again. What happened back there, Channing?"

I blew out a breath. It wasn't right to hold back from Anton. Not in this situation. It wasn't that I thought he deserved my loyalty—he didn't. But I didn't want to be the same person I had been with Jenna. I didn't want to go back to being the scared girl in foster care who stole food and kept it all for herself. Prior to moving in with Darcy, I'd committed to change, to become a better person, to not let my circumstances define me. And that person, that new person I'd become, she would help Anton, regardless of the associated consequences. This was bigger than me, bigger than my self-preservation. Dominic had been suffering for years, and there was a chance I could help, or at least shed some light on the situation. Intuitively, I knew it was one or the other. I either helped Anton with Dominic, or I helped myself.

There was no doing both. But after reliving those moments with Jenna, there was only one decision I could live with. "In order for this to make sense, I need to start at the beginning. And before you get excited, what I have to tell you may bring up more questions than answers. I do have a few questions of my own first."

Anton's expression was a mixture of relief and suspicion. He nodded his head for me to continue.

"Three years ago, when I accidentally used my chip and you were assigned to me, what did the FBI know about the way I'd used my chip?" Anton looked confused, and rightly so. I wasn't sure how to word my question. "Okay, let me try that again. When someone uses their chip—a CU—what does the FBI see? Only that it was turned on? Do they see that a message was sent? Can they see what that message was? Can they see anything else?"

The confusion didn't leave Anton's expression, but he answered my questions. "We can see that it was turned on at will. Even if it was an accident, the person was able to turn their chip on unassisted. Which means they're a CU, even if they don't realize it."

"Can you see what they did with their chip? Can you see if a message was sent? Can you see what the message is?"

He shook his head. "I'm probably not explaining this well. We can see that a CU has turned on their chip and activated the chip of the person they're with. That's what makes a real CU—not just someone who can turn on their own chip, but a person who can use their chip to activate and connect to another's. The first without the second is useless."

THE ANGEL PROJECT

"Does the first happen often without the second?" The question was off track, but my curiosity was piqued.

"Hardly ever. When it does happen, it's typically believed to be a malfunction of the CU's chip. Though, we honestly aren't one-hundred percent sure, and there are other possibilities, like the person's chip theytried to activate is dead, or is an NU—a Nonutilizer. The chips are programmed to work together. If a person can turn their chip on, then activating the chip of another is almost automatic. The chips speak to each other."

"A Nonutilizer?"

"A person who the chip doesn't work for. It seems their brains don't allow for it. No matter how many chips we feed these particular people, they remain an NU. They're about as rare as CUs."

Cole. "Do these NUs have a place here?"

"Beyond testing?"

I nodded.

"No. We have no real use for them."

"Huh. It makes sense that if there are CUs, there are other various unforeseen exceptions as well." That was something I would have to mull over later. There must have been hundreds of variations and mutations, even if they were minuscule. These chips mixed human DNA with artificial intelligence, and DNA was so wildly varied that there was no way the chip worked the same in every mind. "That's going to have to be a conversation for a different day. What I wanted to know was, When a CU uses their chip to manipulate another, can you *see* what happened? Can you see what message was sent?"

He shook his head. "No. We can't see the exchange,

just that one probably occurred. And we can typically deduce what occurred by the action of the manipulated person afterward. For instance, if a CU walked into a convenient store and turned on their chip and the chip of the attendant, we can see that. In those situations, we would use GPS tracking from the chips and pull up security footage of the event. If we see the attendant voluntarily handed the CU all the cash in their register and seemed completely at ease with the situation, then the answer is pretty clear. To the rest of the world, it might look like the two were working together to steal from the convenience store, but we know better."

That gave me pause. No one had any idea what I'd done to Jenna. They were clueless. This whole time I'd thought we, the FBI and I, had been playing a game of cat and mouse, one where I was the mouse. Maybe I was wrong. Maybe I was the cat.

TWENTY-ONE

Anton's smartwatch buzzed. He looked at it and swore. "We have to meet with Davis. This"—he gestured between us—"is not finished."

I outwardly nodded, but inside I let out a deep breath of relief. Davis had just bought me time to think, something I desperately needed.

Anton hesitated, but eventually he stood. "We'd better not leave him waiting."

"Is Davis, like, top brass here?"

He chuckled. "More or less. Davis is a director for the Science and Technology Branch of the FBI. He answers to plenty of people above him, but no one knows the ins and outs of the neurochip technology like he does. With few exceptions, they let him run this place. It's a strange division, but one that proves incredibly beneficial for our government, particularly with use of the CUs when they need them."

"Why does the government need CUs?" The million-dollar question. Why was I really here?

He clicked his tongue uncomfortably. "You should ask Davis." His watch buzzed again. "We'd better go."

When we got to Davis's office, he gave us a kind of look that was half smile and half reprimand. I wasn't sure how to interpret it. Anton showed no reaction. He just said, "Sorry we're late."

Davis smiled. "It's no problem at all, Garcia. I love waiting." Anton sighed.

Davis turned to me. "So, what do you think of our facility, Channing?"

"It's really overwhelming, actually. It's huge."

Davis nodded and smiled appreciatively. "It's quite something."

I smiled awkwardly. "That it is, sir."

Anton cleared his throat. "Channing has some questions for you."

Davis looked at me, eyebrows raised.

I didn't really want to be put on the spot with Davis, but I did have questions. A lot of them. One in particular I desperately wanted an answered was, "What use does the government have for CUs?"

Davis steepled his hands on his desk. "That's a good question. In order to answer it, I'll have to go back to when the chip was created. The bulk of what we do here at the FBI is federal criminal investigation, as you probably already know. That's part of the reason we, instead of the other bureaus, have jurisdiction of the CUs. CUs were originally criminals—implanting thoughts in others 'minds *is* criminal activity—and we were tasked with finding them."

"Finding them and killing them, you mean."

He gave me a patronizing smile. "In the beginning, yes. The CUs appeared as an obvious and very dangerous threat."

"No due process for the innocent CUs?"

Another smile, this one with a touch of condescension. "No, at the time there was no due process for terrorists." He held up a hand to stave off my response. "That's how CUs were seen then. I wasn't part of the FBI back in those days. I was little more than a confused young man who could upload thoughts into people's minds. I hate this part of our history as much as you do, but we can't go back in time and change it, so you are going to have to live with the fact that it happened." He gave me a pointed look, as if to simultaneously say, *It is what it is* and *Stop being so naïve.*

"The FBI and t the chip's creators were smart enough to study the anomalies before eliminating them, however. They learned, and their opinions evolved, lucky for the three of us." Wink. "Like Dr. Rucker told you last night, the chip can do many things, but it was originally meant to assist the government with criminal investigation. And it absolutely has. For example, with the neurochip, we can use GPS tracking to find whether a suspect was indeed at the place of the crime as well as where their current location, should we need to bring them in. It's helped to eliminate thousands of wrongful arrests and subsequently wrongful guilty pleas and charges. Unfortunately, it can't detect crimes before they happen, but it's certainly second best." Another wink. Good grief, was he that cheesy, or did the man have an eye twitch?

"The neurochip is also a huge asset for studying and relieving the symptoms of neurological diseases. We've gained a ton of ground, medically, in that arena. There is still a long way to go, but most recently, through the study of Brain-Computer Interfaces and with the application of nanoneurochips, we have successfully been able to make new pathways in the brain to work around the brain clouding of MS. That has been huge. The medical capabilities of the chip for things like migraines and Parkinson's and Alzheimer's are absolutely miraculous. Here, at the FBI, the medical interventions are not our area of expertise, but those are undoubtedly some of the most important applications of the chip and a huge focus of the current study. Our facility houses the research labs.

"Those are the main applications of the chip as it stands today. For the FBI, the GPS tracking is by far the most important—we use it multiple times on a daily basis. When the chip was created, it was with tracking and medical interventions in mind. Those goals were met and are ever increasing in their capabilities. There are hundreds, if not thousands, of applications of the chip for the benefit of society, but these are the two areas we have focused on, and really the only two areas we can focus on without people discovering their chips."

That was part of this whole thing still tripping me up. "Did anyone ever think about how wrong it is to implant people with a device without their knowledge or consent? Listen, if I suffered from a neurological disease and there was a neurochip medical device that could help me, I would likely sign up for it. Pets are microchipped all the time, for their safety. These are things I understand and support. But unknowingly putting neurochips into the brains of the entire human race? That's unconscionable."

"Are you okay with a child getting kidnapped and sold into sex slavery? Do you have any idea what they do to those children?" I sputtered, but he didn't give me time to answer. "How about a serial killer roaming the streets, looking for their next victim? Rapists? Drug dealers who focus on minors? Child pornographers? Child abusers?"

"Enough! Of course I'm not okay with those things."

"Do you have any idea how many children are saved with the chip every single day?" He paused for effect. "You cannot imagine the horrors that have been avoided. We can catch a kidnapper in the act. The minute a crime is reported and it goes into the system, we can find the perpetrator and save the victim. No more Jeffrey Epsteins, no more Ted Bundys. The chip obviously comes with some unforeseen side effects, but the truth is, we"—he pointed to the three of us—"are rare—extremely so. We are an exception, but we can benefit society in huge ways as well. By and large the chip works just like it was intended. It's solving crimes and helping the ill. So, to answer your question, do I think it's wrong to chip people without their knowledge? No, not when it's to the benefit of society. The Patriot Act may have been controversial, but when we use that information to stop terrorist attacks, no one complains. We aren't interested in the average citizen's everyday business. If you're not a criminal, then the chip can only serve to benefit you."

I wasn't sure what to think about all that. Certainly, it changed the way I viewed the chip, but I still had issues with it. As I did the Patriot Act or the government gleaning anything they wanted from our phones, right down to our private conversations and pictures. But those things were already happening. I knew that, and I still owned a phone. But it was my decision—I had a choice in the matter. I understood the argument for government spying was that if you weren't committing crimes, you should have nothing to worry about. That may be true, but I deeply appreciated autonomy. Also, the government wasn't inherently altruistic; governments are made of people, and people are fallible.

I had to admit, though, that perhaps in today's world, autonomy was a thing of the past. In that sense, how different was the chip, really? We were already spied on—nothing was private. We could bury our heads in the sand, or we could accept it. And I couldn't deny that if someone asked me point-blank, "Would you give up a bit of your autonomy to save children from sex slavery?" I would say yes in a heartbeat.

Davis was still talking. I pushed my mental deliberations aside for later. "The CUs were something unforeseen, a rare consequence of combining technology and human DNA. An outlier. The chip was never meant to upload information to another chip. It was never meant to embed so deeply into the brain that it became an integral part of it. It was never meant to be used to compel another human being. CUs are able to use their chips to do all of the above, and more. That's a frightening thing. And admittedly, for the dangers alone, CUs had a rough start."

THE ANGEL PROJECT

Rough was far too gentle a word to describe extermination.

He gave me a pointed look. "But, as we now know, CUs, while they have the capability to do so much damage, also have the capability to do so much good. CUs have proven to be one of the most amazing results of the chip.

"The government has been utilizing CUs in a myriad of ways, but none more so than foreign policy. As foreign diplomats, CUs can calm anger, rein in extremism, encourage honesty, and promote tolerance. CUs can stop wars and spread democracy. They can literally be facilitators of world peace."

My eyes widened. The chip had always seemed evil to me, a way to control people. Which, I supposed, in this application, it still was; but maybe it could serve a greater purpose. I'd spent my entire life terrified of the chip, of what could happen to me if TAP or the government found out I could utilize my chip. I never stopped to think of other possibilities.

Davis sat back in his chair. "That's what the top CUs do for us here."

I held up my finger. "If CUs can influence foreign dignitaries, wouldn't we have to be chipping said dignitaries?"

Davis nodded. "We do chip foreign diplomats every chance we get. Chips can go into drinks or meals. So far we've had great success getting chips to those in power." Again, I understood why they were doing it, but regardless of the positives, it felt unethical. Was the goal to be a one-world power, with the United States in charge but no one the wiser?

I moved on. "What makes one a top CU?"

"Like all of the discoveries we've made with the chip, we've found that even in the case of those who can utilize their chips, there are levels in their abilities. All CUs can use their chips to implant—or upload. There are some who can read what is on another's chip. There are some that can download from another's chip. There are some who can not only download, but actually compel—they can make a person behave a certain way, not just suggest by uploading a message. An ANGEL can do all of the above, and more."

He looked at me expectantly, as if I were going to admit what I really was. What my capabilities were. I knew I could download and upload for sure. But I hadn't had enough practice to know much more. I wanted to discover all of my capabilities, but the thought scared me as much as it excited me. There was so much I didn't know, so much I wanted to learn. But there was a huge part of me that just wanted to run away screaming. I had to admit that my deep reaction to all of this information was strange. I didn't know enough to be as deeply scared as I was. I had to wonder if it was due to what my father had told me as a child. I also couldn't help wonder if that fear was so deeply embedded in me because it was implanted. "Can uploads onto one's chip be deleted?"

Davis looked at me thoughtfully for a beat, then said, "Not without consequences. We don't know how deep those consequences go—as in, how damaging the effects are to the brain—but we do know the first and foremost consequence is excruciating pain. We've found it's better to start from where you are, rather than go back. You have been implanted with information. We don't know it all. You are the only person who will be able to tell what's real and what's implanted in your chip, and with training you'll be able to do that pretty well."

"Pretty well?"

"It's not a perfect science. When a thought is uploaded onto the chip, it's foreign—but only for an instant. The brain quickly steps in to make up the difference. For instance, if your name wasn't Channing, but you were implanted with that information, all of your memories would start to align with the new name. People would call you Channing in your real memories. Your brain would adjust to adhere to the new truth." I swallowed. "That's why we really don't recommend the practice of trying to discern every thought or memory. It's futile, and even when you discover what's fake, there's little recourse."

I took a deep breath. "So in this example, if my name wasn't Channing Walker, what might it have been?"

The room was so silent you could hear a pin drop, and Agent Davis searched my eyes so hard I nearly broke contact. But I refused. I wanted to know. He finally answered. "If your name wasn't Channing Walker . . . it would have probably been Charlotte West."

TWENTY-TWO

CHARLOTTE WEST. *CHARLOTTE WEST.* IT meant nothing to me. No déjà vu. No pain in my head. No recognition at all.

I took one of my memories, the one with my parents at the beach, when I was making a sandcastle. My mom encouraged, "That's looking really good, Channing." I tried to plug Charlotte in instead. Only then did the fog start. I tried replacing Channing with Marie. Nothing. I began to rifle through my memories, the real ones—as far as I could tell—and replaced Channing with Charlotte. Over and over again. The fog was so thick I could cut it, and my head began to pound. I could feel the pain begin behind my eyes and to the left. That electric zapping. I couldn't help but wince.

"Channing, stop. It will only get worse."

I shook my head, trying to remember. I remembered my dad kneeling in front of me after killing my mother, before the police came. "You can never, ever use the chip again. Do you understand me, Charlotte?"

The pain reverberated through my head. I yelped and

grabbed it with both hands, bringing it down to my knees. Tears sprang in my eyes as the shooting, electrifying pains played ping-pong through my brain.

"Channing, stop!" I couldn't tell who was yelling at me. The pain was so intense, I could barely breathe. My mouth filled with saliva, and I instinctively knew what was coming. But before the contents of my stomach made their way up, Anton had grabbed my face and pulled it upright. "Channing, you have to stop. Now. You are Channing Walker now. That's your name. Say it. *I am Channing.*" When I didn't respond, he held my face tighter. "Say it."

"I am Channing." Even just saying the words calmed me significantly.

"Good. Repeat it. *Believe it.*"

I verbalized it three more times and then again in my head, reversing the memories from Charlotte back to Channing. The sharp pains had completely abated, and the dull pain was beginning to subside. I crumpled down into my chair and began to open my eyes. The light in the room seemed ten times brighter than it had before. I closed them again. I took a few deep breaths, then attempted again to open my eyes. This time it was easier. I looked straight ahead to Davis.

He was patiently studying me. "That's the pain I was referring to earlier. The first consequence of trying to change your uploaded information. When you get beyond the pain, that's when things get ugly."

That caught my attention. "There's something uglier than the pain?"

He smiled sadly. "We believe the pain is a warning.

We've had some CUs try too hard to get past the pain; they end up in the psych ward. We think that their chip short-circuits, and it messes with their mind. Once they're in that place, we can't get them back."

I nodded and then took a second to breathe. "Is that what happened to Dominic?"

"We don't believe so. Whatever it is Dominic is going through seems different. But it's hard to know. We haven't had enough ANGELs to compare." He looked at me again, like he wanted me to confess to what I really was. Was I an ANGEL? Honestly, I didn't know. I had suspicions, but no clear answers. I knew I could do more with the chip than the average CU, but beyond that, it was all a mystery to me. I'd used the chip a total of eight times in my life. And six of those times had been in the past few days. My experience was nil.

I merely sat there while Agent Davis waited for a response to his blatant implication. He studied me for a minute, then seemed disappointed. "Do you have any other questions for me, Ms. Walker, or is that enough for today?"

I shook my head, relieved. "I've had more than enough for one day."

He smiled sincerely. "There's a room prepared for you here. Anton can take you there."

At the question in my expression, Davis asked, "You want to train, right?"

I did want to train. I needed training desperately. I knew there were potential dangers in the FBI knowing what I could do, but there were definite dangers in me not knowing what I could do. "Yes."

THE ANGEL PROJECT

He nodded once. "Good. Your training will start tomorrow."

After the meeting with Davis, we stopped by Anton's room before he escorted me to mine. He turned on the surveillance blocker.

"Listen, I know that was a lot, and I know you're tired, but we still need to talk about what happened earlier with Dom."

I threw myself down on the hard gray couch and sighed. "I can upload and download information."

His brow furrowed. "How could you know that? You've hardly used the chip at all."

I was quiet for a second, but eventually figured I had little to lose at this point. I pulled my feet up onto his couch and rested my arms on my knees, and I told him the first part of the story of Jenna. I didn't tell him what I took. I was going to, but he cut me off.

His mouth was hanging open. "Is that why . . ."

I cocked my head to the side. "Is that why what?"

He shook his head. "Is that why you were wandering around Skid Row so often, especially around the time we'd first met?"

"You knew I did that?" He nodded. "Huh. I guess I should be more aware of people following me."

He smiled tightly. "I wouldn't be much of an FBI agent if you knew I was following you."

I smiled, but annoyance was right beneath it. The idea of being spied on for all those years still chafed.

He sighed. "I was just doing my job, Channing. For the record, at the time I felt badly about it. I thought it was a huge waste of time."

I wasn't sure why, but that hurt a little. It must have shown in my expression because he quickly course corrected. "My brother was here, at the facility, in a condition that I didn't know how to fix. In hindsight, I think that's why they assigned me the job. I was getting obsessed, staying with Dom twenty-four hours a day. When they sent me, particularly in the early days, I was so angry. For all I knew, you were a one-time CU, completely insignificant. It seemed clear to me they were just trying to get rid of me. It wasn't until later that I learned who you really were. But in the beginning"—he shook his head—"I was in such a bad place. I felt guilty for leaving my brother. But then I started to really enjoy the time that I was with you, and . . . I felt guilty about that too."

Oh. That was an explanation I hadn't realized I needed to hear from Anton. After meeting Dominic, I felt like I understood Anton better, but I hadn't thought about what it would be like to be taken away from your brother—who was not in a good state—and put on a job thousands of miles away. A seemingly pointless job. "Did you ever get to see Dom while you were working with me?"

He nodded. "Those vacation days I took over the years were all spent here. It's been over six months since my last visit; that's the longest I've ever gone without seeing him."

"I'm sorry you had to make that sacrifice."

"That's the hardest part. After a while it didn't feel

like a sacrifice." He smiled wistfully, then tried to shrug it off. "Is that what you were doing back then? Looking for Jenna? To what, see if the message worked? To see if she stayed sober?"

I really didn't want to move on from the conversation about us—I had so many questions about the time he trained me—but I didn't want to push him. "Yeah, I spent a lot of time looking for her." I shook my head, wishing I could dislodge all those memories, make them disappear. "I felt terrible; I wanted to give it all back."

His brow furrowed. "Give what back?"

I chuckled humorlessly. I looked everywhere but at him. I was horrified that I had to tell him, or anyone, this part of the story. "Her education. She was an English major. She loved writing. I stole that from her."

His eyes widened. "What are you talking about, Channing?"

I looked up. "The truth, Anton." I blew out a breath. "That rainy night with Jenna was pivotal for me, in so many ways. When I realized I was in her mind, that my chip had connected to hers, I knew there was no point in backing out. My dad had told me that just turning the chip on would allow TAP to find me. And I was so angry at her, so unbelievably angry. All the times I'd helped her, that I had taken her in for a night or two. The nights I fed her. The nights she cried as she was coming back down, because she'd messed up again. She stole from me. I just couldn't believe it, which I know was my naïveté shining through, because of course Jenna would do whatever she had to do get her next fix. It was just such a slap in the face after all I'd done for her."

Anton was so riveted he barely moved. "So when I was in her mind and I'd realized I was beyond the point of no return, I *looked*. I looked at what was on her chip. It was the strangest thing, because I was looking at computer code and *reading* it. It was so easy and came so naturally that it took a second for me to realize what was happening. My chip was translating the code as fast as I could see it. Before I knew it, there was a whole section, or file—as it were—of Jenna's collegiate studies. She was an English Literature major, and it was all there, all of this *knowledge*. There were books about grammar that she'd read. There were papers she'd written, all the drafts. So many books, classic and modern, and all the class discussions about them. Dissertations, and papers, poems and plays. It was all there. All of this knowledge that I could never attain on my own, knowledge Jenna had just thrown in the garbage.

"My mind salivated for it. I don't know how, but I knew I could take it. I knew that with a single command, all of that knowledge could be mine, and Jenna wasn't using it anyway. Somewhere in my head I knew I shouldn't, that it was wrong, but my desire had surpassed my ability to think clearly."

I swallowed. "With one thought, I did it. I took what wasn't mine."

I stole a glance at Anton. His eyes were so wide, they looked like they were made of fire, like he couldn't blink because his eyelids would burn right through. "After that, I was out of her head in a flash, like a kid who'd stolen candy from the grocery store. I was in such a deep shock when I heard the sirens, I went into my tent and left Jenna on the sidewalk, telling myself I didn't want to implicate myself in her mess, but knowing it was really because I was so freaked out by what I'd just done." I blew out another hard breath. "I didn't know what would happen when she came around. Would she know what she'd lost? Would she know how she'd lost it? I had no idea.

"I was reeling from guilt and so much fear. All I knew in that moment was they were going to come for me. TAP was going to come, and it was my fault. I'd suffered through a life in foster care and on the streets to avoid TAP, and with one bad choice born from an accident, I'd brought it all on myself."

I'd stayed in my tent for three days. The first one, I lay there in fetal position, just waiting. Waiting to be arrested? Killed? Taken and studied for science? I didn't know what TAP would do, but I knew it had to be bad. My dad had killed my mother to save me from it, after all. But no one came the first day.

The second day, I moved out of fetal position and lay flat on my back, this time thinking about more than what would happen when I was caught. I was rifling through the information I'd stolen from Jenna. It was weird. I knew it wasn't mine, but it was all there, and I understood it, just as if I was the one who'd spent four years at CSU instead of Jenna. However, regardless of how distracted I was with Jenna's schooling, I was still waiting for a bullet to come through my tent and straight into my forehead. But no one came the second day either.

The third day, I got out from under my covers. I sat up and thought of all the reasons TAP may never come for me. It had been twelve years since my father had gone to prison. Maybe TAP had been disbanded? Maybe the creators had realized what they'd created was wrong and they'd jumped ship? It was quite possible they didn't know I was out there and still capable of using my chip. I sat there all day and thought of the possibilities. And subsequently, of all the things I could do with the chip. So many things...

"I stole it, Anton. I saw it there, in her chip. Her college education, just sitting there for the taking." I scratched a sudden itch on the back of my neck; I was so uncomfortable talking about this, I felt like I was getting hives. "I wanted to make something of myself, to get off the streets. In that moment of poor judgment, I'd decided that *I* could put her education to good use, because she certainly wasn't." I shrugged. "She stole from me, and I guess I thought it was fair play." I laughed humorlessly. "As if eight hundred dollars for a college education was an even trade. I've regretted it every day; but I also haven't. I'm a horrible person."

Anton cleared his throat, and when I looked at him, he was shaking his head, frantically. "Channing, the chip doesn't work like that. There are a few CUs who can download information, but they can't steal. It's not how computers work. A computer can download from a hard drive, but it doesn't take the information. After the download, both computers have it."

"Not if you delete it from the original hard drive."

His eyes bugged out of his head. "What? I'm not sure that's even possible." He studied me for a minute, and his expression waxed quizzical. "What happened to make you believe you did that?"

THE ANGEL PROJECT

This kept getting worse and worse. I hated that I had to tell Anton what I had done. I hated that I had done it. I thought I'd made peace with it, but the nausea swirling thickly in my gut proved otherwise. "Because, at the end of the download, I had the option to delete the original source. I was so scared that she would find out what I'd done that in a split-second decision, I opted to delete it completely." I could hardly get the words out through my tight throat. I groaned and buried my face in my arms. "I can't tell you how awful I feel about it. Does Jenna even know she went to California State? Does she know she spent four years studying English literature? I stole that from her—a huge chunk of her life. I deleted it. I knew that if I could just find her, I could give it back." **I looked at Anton then, tears streaming down my cheeks.**" I tried to find her for so long. I regularly searched through Skid Row, but she was never there. Ironically, the one good thing I did for her, implanting the message that she would never use another illegal substance again, may have been the one thing that kept me from making amends. A girl like Jenna would have no reason to spend time in Skid Row if she were sober." I wiped a tear traveling down my cheek to my mouth. "I even tried to find her parents. I had no idea where they lived. I searched the whole Los Angeles area online, but to no avail. She just . . . disappeared."

Anton sat back, his eyes wild and blinking uncontrollably. He didn't look at me, probably because he was as ashamed of me as I was. It took a considerable amount of time for him to speak. "That's . . . that's . . ." He looked at me then, but it wasn't in disgust; it was something else. Something I couldn't decipher. It may have been surprise.

Or concern. Or fear. Maybe all three, mixed with a serious helping of disbelief.

I swallowed, and another tear escaped my eye, running down my cheek. I didn't realize how much I wanted Anton to approve of me. How much I wanted anyone to still care for me after hearing what I'd done. I had to admit that even just telling another person about what had happened with Jenna relieved some of my burden. I'd been carrying it so long on my own, I don't think I realized just how much it weighed me down. I was glad I'd told Anton, even if it changed how he saw me. I was who I was, warts and all.

"I'm sorry . . . I'm just . . . just trying to process." He blinked hard and looked at me without the judgment I was so sure I'd see. "The very first time you used the chip as an adult, you were able to upload, download, and delete—the last of which I've never heard of anyone being able to do." He stopped his train of thought and jumped up off the couch to standing. "Channing, what happened with Dom? Why did you freak out in there?"

I was going to get whiplash from the speed of his subject change. I could see he'd gone somewhere mentally, but I had no idea where it was. "Um . . ." It took me a second to rewind my mind back to that moment—a second Anton clearly didn't want to give me. He was staring at me, imploring me to talk. "When I was in there, with you and Dominic, it felt just like it had with Jenna. I wasn't angry like that time, of course, but my senses went crazy, and before I knew it, my chip was on. I knew if I looked at him, I wouldn't be able to stop myself from encroaching on his mind. I wanted to so badly, I can't describe the desire. It was one of the strongest sensations I've ever felt."

Anton was so still, only his eyes moved when he asked, "Why didn't you do it?"

I furrowed my brow. "Because it's a total violation? You were right there with us. I felt like I should have at least had your permission, since I couldn't get your brother's. It seemed wrong to strong-arm my way into his brain."

He shook his head. "Sorry, I asked the wrong question. How did you manage to stop yourself from doing it?"

"You were there. You saw me freak out. I wanted to look so badly, Anton. I can't explain it. I had to literally run out of there to avoid it."

Anton was silently staring at me, his jaw working, for so long that I had to look away. My doing so seemed to pull him out of his thoughts. He came over and crouched down in front of me and placed his hands on my shoulders, the action putting our faces close. "Channing." He looked into my eyes for a few seconds, then dropped one hand off my shoulder and roughly ran his hand though his hair, pulling slightly. "There is so much to tell you, so much you need to understand to make sense of what you went through with Jenna and then with Dom."

I didn't know how to respond, but I didn't need to—he couldn't get to the explanation quick enough. But instead of talking, he pulled his phone out of his pocket. Then he took a minute to pull something up and held out his phone to me.

I gasped.

My mouth dropped open. I could barely make sense of what I was seeing. "What?" I shook my head in disbelief. I looked up at Anton. "How?" It took me a minute to fully process the picture of her. She was in a suit. It was a professional government picture, like the ones I saw lining the walls when we first walked into the Special Agents Building. I sat back, looking anywhere but at Anton. "Jenna was an agent? She was a plant?" I couldn't believe it. All of the suffering over Jenna...

Anton put his phone down and gently took hold of my chin. "Yes. Jenna Freeman was a plant. Her name is actually Jenna Cook, and she's an agent." He looked sad, and a little worried I was going to freak out.

I sputtered, trying to get the words out. "But why? Why would the FBI bother planting Jenna? Why put so much effort into me, a person who'd never used the chip?"

He let go and sat on the couch next to me. "It's a surprisingly common practice. When a person is suspected of being a CU, we send someone in, another CU, to make an assessment."

"How could I have been suspected of being a CU? I hadn't used my chip since I was eight."

"I don't know the details, but the FBI got intel on your name change. They found out who your parents were, and they wanted to see if there was anything there. They were desperate at the time. Dom, the only ANGEL they had to work with, was having some unknown malfunction with his chip. They were looking into any viable source. Living on the streets made it harder to track you down. But we eventually did through your work. You don't remember this, but that's where Jenna first met you." My head started in with the telltale ache. "She broke into your mind there and implanted the relationship between the two of you. When you saw her on the street, it was actually the second time the two of you had met." My head started to really pound then. I grabbed it with my hands, trying to alleviate the pain. I felt Anton's hand on my back. "That's the only part of this explanation that should trigger your chip." I sighed in relief, even though the pain was still very much present. "Jenna is often sent on those jobs. She has some rare strengths. She's what we call a Stealth. She's good at infiltrating even the most sensitive of minds, and she can do it undetected. She is extremely talented. Implanting the relationship is always the first thing that she does. Then she creates a situation she believes will get the subject to use their chip. I remember when she came back from that mission. She seemed different. She—" He cleared his throat, while several emotions played across his face. He was friends with Jenna. Maybe more. "She wasn't herself."

"What do you mean, she wasn't herself?"

He shook his head. "Normally she gets a subject to turn on their chip pretty easily, which she seemed to with you. But she's trained to avoid any infiltration. Not just uploads, but downloads as well. She didn't even realize you had infiltrated her mind. When she was picked up by the ambulance, she didn't flash her FBI badge like she normally would have. She was confused, out of sorts. The EMTs really thought she had a serious drug problem. We had to send someone from the Los Angeles office to pick her up. She flew back here and seemed to come back to herself for the most part after the incident, but she didn't want to do missions anymore. She was freaked out but couldn't explain why. We knew you used your chip, but we had no idea what happened. Davis suspected something more than a simple attempted use from you, but there was no way to verify it. He was regularly checking in with Jenna to see if anything had come back to her about that night. Now it makes sense why he never found anything. He was looking for something that had been added, not something that had been deleted."

"Nothing had been added?"

He shook his head. "No. She remembered you trying to implant the thought about the drugs, and she was able to flag it as an implant—a thing you'll learn to do here—but after that she didn't remember anything until she was sitting on the sidewalk alone and disoriented." He shrugged. "We all thought it was a fluke, because after that incident you didn't use the chip again. That's a big reason why I was so upset a month later when they assigned me to watch you."

"Because I seemed insignificant, and the job was requiring you to leave Dom."

"Right. It seemed like an outrageous waste of time. No one, and I mean *no one*, who has ever been able to use the chip at will has ever *not* used it again. Once they discover what they can do, the influence they can have over people, they don't stop. They do it constantly, several times a day, until we take them into custody. I guess that's what I'm the most confused about: *Why* did you stop? It doesn't make any sense."

"I wasn't planning to stop." I told him about Sherry

THE ANGEL PROJECT

and her disabled son, and the cottage on the beach. "I realized it wasn't right. Even if I wasn't going to get caught, using people wasn't right. I didn't want to be that person. Even if I couldn't give Jenna back what I stole, I could change—I could become a good person from that moment on."

"There's something else you should know."

I shook my head. "Anton, I don't think I can take any more. I'm so tired and so emotionally drained."

"Just one more thing, and then I'll take you to your room." I reluctantly nodded. "Jenna could use her chip in a way that encouraged people to use their chip with her. She could make a person desire for their chip to turn on, making it seem like they'd done it on their own, when really it was her doing all along." I nodded. That made sense. My chip turning on that night felt like an accident. I'd thought it happened because of the intense emotions I was feeling. But in looking back, I could see now I hadn't asked for it to turn on—activating a chip took specific action, action I hadn't taken. "She can make you want to use it. The pull is already naturally there—when two chips are on, they want to connect—but Jenna can up that sensation. With her, they feel like magnets, making it almost impossible to control. And she's not the only one who can do that."

My mouth gaped when the light finally turned on. "Dominic can do that too?"

Anton nodded. "But Dom is far more powerful."

TWENTY-THREE

I LAY IN BED THAT night, tossing and turning. I really needed a good night's sleep, but I knew it wasn't in the cards.

Dominic had manipulated me into turning on my chip. Dominic was trying to get me to see into his mind. *Why?* That was the million-dollar question. An ANGEL, who'd had no communication with anyone for years, tried to communicate with me, albeit in a forceful way. He was trying to show me something. In my mind, it could only be one thing: he was trying to show me what had happened to him. And I couldn't stop thinking about it. Before he'd dropped me off at my room, I'd tried to convince Anton to take me back to Dom instead.

"Believe me, no one wants to see what Dom is trying to tell you more than me. Maybe I can finally hit that red button taunting me every time I'm in that room."

"What is that red button? Is it for an emergency?"

He contemplated his response for a second. "Of sorts. It alerts the most important people in this building that Dom's awake."

THE ANGEL PROJECT

"You think I'll be able to . . . wake Dom up?"

"I don't know, but you're the first person who's been able to get through to him in any capacity in years. It's the first time I've felt hope in a long time."

"So let's go. Let's see what's going on in his brain."

He shook his head. "The psych ward is closed for the night. Unless Davis or Dr. Rucker are with us, there's no getting in there at this hour. And I'm not ready to involve them."

I didn't want to involve them yet either. I was sure my trust issues, particularly with the government, came from my father. He must have uploaded a message to my chip instructing me to fear them and distrust everything, because I was sure my level of dubiety was deeper than the average American's. But what I didn't know was if those trust issues were something I should lean into or distance myself from. The things Davis had talked about, the good that comes from the chip, those things spoke to me. Saving innocents from criminals, healing various neurological diseases, facilitating peace between neighboring countries—those things were unparalleled in the betterment of society. The idea that even as an anomaly—a CU, or an ANGEL, whatever the case may be—I could take part in that kind of work made me want to trust them. I wanted to be good, to have something good come from me. My life had been a series of unfortunate events, but maybe that could all change.

Frustrated that we couldn't go see Dom right then, I let Anton take me to my room. As it happened, mine was only a few doors down from his. We stood in front of the door. Anton finally insisted, "You have to open it. No one can open your door but you."

I scrunched up my face. "How does that work?"

He smiled. "Your chip is connected to the door."

"How?"

"Chips have serial numbers. When a chip implants, it activates and sends a signal. All it takes is a few clicks of a keyboard to find out the serial number of the chip connected to any person."

That was logical, I supposed. "Okay. So how do I open the door with my chip?"

He looked at me with a question in his eyes. "You did it earlier, didn't you?"

I scoffed. "I was under duress. I'm not sure how I did it. My chip was already on, and I just, like, mentally screamed at the door to open."

He laughed loudly. I'd forgotten what he looked like when he was unabashedly happy. His whole face lit up, his perfect teeth on glorious display, his eyes sparkling. I couldn't help but smile. "Try it again; it'll be easier this time."

I rolled my eyes, but my smile remained in place. I looked at the door and turned my chip on. It almost immediately connected, and the door gave a soft click. "Whoa. That was easier, and also a little weird. I've never connected with an inanimate object before."

He laughed again. "Your chip connected to the computer chip in the lock, not the door itself. This isn't Hogwarts."

That made me laugh out loud. "I wish it was. I'm from the Harry Potter generation. You have no idea how badly I wished Hogwarts was a real place when I was a tween."

His smile dimmed. "You probably were living in a cupboard under the stairs with some awful family at the time."

"Yeah. There wasn't a day that went by that I didn't wish for a letter to arrive with the message that I was going to be whisked away to some magical place." I chuckled. "Books were a much-needed escape. But the trip back to reality hit hard."

He walked me into my room, which looked just like his—like a hotel room with an efficiency kitchen. But it was more than sufficient, and I didn't have to share it with anyone. Ashti, in particular. That brought up another question. "So the girls I stayed with last night? Were they just there for the night? Do they stay here sometimes, or do they stay in the George Washington Building full time?"

"The room in the GW Building are meant to be overnight accommodations. It's just a place to stay on the nights federal agents are at the academy. Ginger, Frida, and Ashti are assigned that room any night they need to stay at Quantico. The rooms in this facility are temporary. The only people who stay here are trainees." He paused. "Well, trainees and me. I live here when I'm not on a job to be closer to Dom. The Washington Building is a lot like this one, in the sense that everyone who has a room there is a CU and they all work for the bureau. The girls you stayed with last night, as well as anyone else who stays in that building, are assigned all over the country. They were only here last night for your initial meeting. They come in occasionally for work and when they do, they stay in their assigned room in the GW building. It's easier to have a room over there, then have to come all the way back here."

"You're the only person who lives here full time?"

"There are a lot of people who work here full time, but none of them live here. It's just me, the trainees, and the people in the psych ward." He smiled tightly. "This building is never free of workers, though; we have people here on third shift." Before I could respond, he added, "Oh, and the kids live here too, of course."

I'd forgotten about the hall resembling an elementary school. "Who are the kids living here? The children of the employees? And is everyone in this building a CU? How does that work? Do we each have to take a shift somewhere, like the cafeteria or something?"

He put his hands up. "Too many questions for one night. After we see Dom, I'll give you a full tour. We need to get up early, though; your training starts in the morning." Wink.

I groaned. "No. You can't start up with the winking. Davis does it constantly. It drives me nuts."

Anton full on laughed at that. "Right? It's so annoying, but also strangely contagious." Wink.

I laughed while I shouted, "Stop!"

Wink. Wink. Wink.

I shoved him out the door.

Hours later as I lay awake, the only thing I wanted to do was go to Dominic. I still felt it—the pull. I had all day. I didn't know if it truly existed, or if the knowledge I was allowed to see into his mind magnified the desire, stirring something in me that felt magnetic. But the feeling was there, and it wouldn't be denied, so much so that I couldn't sleep.

I finally gave up and got out of bed. I did some resistance exercise, took a long, hot shower, and threw on the clothes I'd been wearing when I arrived. Anton had had them laundered for me. Nothing felt like a good, clean, pair of jeans. After I was dressed, I brushed my teeth and combed through my long, thick, brown hair with the cheapest brush ever made—I think it may have been a doll brush, in all honesty, but I was grateful they'd offered me some necessities.

I looked at the clock, hoping that it was almost time for Anton to come get me. It was 3:30 a.m. I groaned. It would be hours before he came. I paced the room. I could hardly believe where life had landed me. In a matter of a few days, I'd gone from being a somewhat normal twenty-something to a known Chip Utilizer, with what seemed to be an open-ended job opportunity with the FBI.

My pacing was interrupted by a pull I felt on my mind, on my chip. No matter how hard I tried, I could only keep my mind off Dominic in short spurts. I wanted to see him. I *had* to see him. And I couldn't wait until morning.

I took a deep breath and opened my door.

The hallways were silent. The only sound was the buzzing and whirring of the various machines that kept a building like this running. I was pretty good directionally, but trying to get my bearings here was difficult. I had been so distracted with my anger toward Anton earlier that I hadn't paid enough attention to know how to get to the psych ward. I sighed, wondering if I should go back to my room. But the pull in my mind wouldn't subside.

I looked back the way I came and then forward. I took about ten steps forward and felt the pull in my chip grow fainter. "No way." I turned around and took twenty steps in the other direction, and the feeling, that unexplainable pull, grew stronger. "Unbelievable."

I shook my head and followed the feeling, rather than my instincts. The pull grew as I passed the hallway with all the stuff for kids, and I was sure it was leading me in the right direction. I was reeling from the shock of it, the idea that Dominic was so strong that he could manage to call to my chip from across the building. Was he really doing this? On purpose?

Everything he did seemed to be on autopilot. He did all the things he needed to do to stay alive, and more, really. He was clean, his room was clean, he was obviously fed and dressed. If his muscles were any indication, he exercised. He just didn't communicate. So, that begged the question: Was he cognitively communicating with me, or had his chip taken over?

That was what scared me the most about the chip. Could it become so entrenched in our brains that we were more computer than human? I knew I was more human than computer—I really never used my chip; I lived my life without it. But for someone like Dominic, who used his every day, probably several times a day, could it become more? It seemed logical that he leaned into it a lot and that possibly, eventually his brain became more computer. That's what it had seemed like to me when I saw him. It was like he was a processor. Like the bulk of his mind was processing information—or code—and all that was left was enough room for him to do the things required to live. Those requiring little thought.

I turned down the white hall with the white door at the end. I was somewhat shocked to find following the strength of the pull on my chip had landed me in the right place. But the other half of me wondered what in the world I was thinking. Anton had told me the door was locked, locked to us anyway. I stared at it. I growled under my breath. So close, yet so far from learning what was in Dom's mind. Why had I traveled all the way over here in the first place?

I stood there, feeling the pull as strong as ever, and thought. I could wait for someone to leave and try to sneak in after them, but there was no place to hide in this hallway. It was long, and there were no doorways other than the one at the end. Not to mention it was perfectly white—there was no hiding in plain sight here. I could simply try my chip and see if the door opened. If it flagged something in the system, I could use the excuse that I was new and couldn't sleep so I'd decided to give myself a grand tour.

The second course of action seemed like the best one. I was already here—it seemed such a waste not to at least give it a try.

I walked up to the door, and before I even turned on my chip, it clicked open. I jumped back into the corner thinking someone must be coming out, but I waited for a minute and no one came. That left only two options: the door just happened to open on its own, or someone—

Dominic, knew I was coming and opened it for me. The latter possibility freaked me out, but not enough to look a gift horse in the mouth.

I looked through the small rectangular window and didn't see anyone at the nurses 'station. I walked in as silently as my sneakers allowed. I heard a commotion down one of the hallways. It was the hallway farthest from Dominic's, but I had to pass it on my way. I peeked around the wall to see where all the noise was coming from. At the end of the hallway there were several doctors and nurses trying to get ahold of a screaming and flailing man. They were trying to get him back into his room, but he was putting up a serious fight. They were so preoccupied with him that I was able to cross the hall without being noticed.

From there it was an easy path to Dominic's room.

As I got closer to his door, I saw it was open. Just barely, but enough that all I had to do was push and I'd be in. I paused, my breaths shallow and trembling. My shaky fingers were freezing, my whole body on high alert. I was ready to turn around and bolt when Dom's door was pulled open from the inside, and I saw him, still the most beautiful man I'd ever seen, standing in the doorway. I jumped and let out a quiet yelp. He may have been stunning, but this whole situation unhinged me on a level I'd never known. He was looking at me, but not entirely. His eyes were on me, but his stare was concentrated on something else—something inside his mind. His mouth still moved at a grueling pace.

He didn't beckon me in with his words—he beckoned me in with his mind. I felt it then, the strength of his power over my chip. My chip buzzed, and there was nowhere else to look but into his eyes. Before I knew it, I was in Dom's room with the door shut behind me. I felt like I was in a trance, but I knew that wasn't it exactly. I didn't know how to explain it: I was in my own mind, I could feel and move my limbs the way I wanted to, but he was there also, not commanding, but *requesting* I do certain things, like come in and sit on his couch. He put the idea there, and I did what he suggested, but I knew I had the option to refuse.

Once I was seated, Dom sat next to me. He was angled toward me, our knees touching. My body buzzed where it touched his—the kind of buzzing completely unrelated to the chip in my brain. He took my hand in his and intertwined our fingers, holding our hands up between us. I felt electricity course through my arm. I swallowed, so overwhelmed with feelings and emotions. The buzzing in my head and body were so strong that I didn't have a place for it all. I felt like electric shocks needed to shoot out of my fingertips and toes to alleviate the power of it, to avoid sudden combustion.

I looked from our joined hands to Dominic's eyes. This time his stare actually seemed to be on me, like he was looking at me with purpose. And then he opened his mind to me, and I *saw*.

TWENTY-FOUR

I GASPED. AT FIRST, ALL I could see was code. Code upon code. File upon file. Too much. Too much for any one mind.

Then I went deeper and started to see more. My heart stuttered. I felt like time and the air around me stood still. Like the very dust floating around us had frozen in place.

Dominic didn't have just one chip. He had *thousands*. His brain looked like a city the size of Hong Kong, all lit up in lights. Each light was a chip. And each chip was activated.

I shook my head. I couldn't take it—the noise, the confusion. I was in every one of those chips at the same time. They were all processing code, different code. My chip translated at breakneck speed, code upon code upon code. None of it made any sense. I felt like I was getting a piece of everything but all of nothing. My mind was a jumbled mess, and my chip couldn't take the onslaught; it was going to fry and turn to ash. I could feel the heat of it—a spot in the upper left of my head, getting hotter by the second. I shook my head harder, trying to get him to let me go, to set my mind loose. I couldn't handle any more. I felt like I couldn't breathe, like I was going to suffocate in that city of lights.

I tried to pull myself out—out of his brain, away from all of his chips. There were just so *many* of them. I needed air. I needed out of this room. I wanted to run and never come back. I'd leave this whole facility. But as if he knew what I was thinking, the connection to our minds strengthened.

Stop fighting it.

I heard the words as if he'd said them, but I knew instinctively that I hadn't heard them with my ears. I couldn't really compute the fact that Dominic and I were communicating—this was huge. All I could focus on was the burning in my head.

I shook my head and spoke aloud. "I can't, Dominic. My chip is burning—it's hot and it's hurting my head." My panic escalated. I was going to end up in the psych ward. My brain was going to fry, and I would be lost. I'd be that guy with his face pressed against the window, scaring all the passersby. "Please. You have to let me go." My voice was choked, and I could taste the salt in my tears as they began to course from my eyes to my mouth and chin. I'd never get to tell Anton that his brother was capable of communication because I'd be a vegetable.

Stop trying to see, Channing. Let me show you.

"I don't know how to do that."

Suddenly one chip was lighter than the others. I knew instinctively it was the one he wanted me to look at. The one he wanted to show me.

Let go of the others.

With a deep breath, I honed in on the brightest chip.

It opened up to me, and the rest of the chaos fell away in blissful relief. My chip began to cool, and I let out a breath I hadn't realized I'd been holding. I sunk back into the couch, and Dom did as well, but he didn't let go of my hand.

Thank goodness that worked. I could hear him breathing hard.

I lifted my head off the couch and looked at him. "You didn't *know* that would work?"

All I knew was that you were about to leave and never come back.

While I was in his mind, connected to his chip, my vision of the outside world had been muted, like I was trying to look through foggy glass. I couldn't see his face exactly.

He tugged on my hand and pulled me back up to sitting. Then I heard his voice, or rather his mind. Despite coming through the chip, I could still hear what he sounded like—his cadence. It was a phenomenon I would have to investigate later.

How are you here? In this facility?

"Um . . . How do you know who I am?"

Let's make a deal. Question for a question?

"Okay . . ."

I asked the first question.

I almost laughed. He was so normal under all the chaos. "Okay, well, it's kind of a long story, but I'll try to give you the *Reader's Digest* version. I was unknowingly set up by the FBI over three years ago to see if I was a CU.

THE ANGEL PROJECT

I am. But I didn't use my chip after the set up until recently. The FBI put your brother on the case anyway, and he became my trainer to keep an eye on me, I guess. I began to use my chip just a couple of days ago, and then I got picked up by TAP, then rescued by the FBI. So now I'm here. Your turn."

I have a lot of questions about what you just told me, but a deal's a deal. How do I know you? Look at the chip you're currently connected to.

I furrowed my brow and looked at what was on the chip. I sat straight up, suddenly on high alert. "How . . . ?" I was aware of the hand I was holding, the breaths flowing in and out of my lungs, the beat of my heart, and this file. That's it. That's all that existed. "How do you have this? How did you get this?"

That information's on a different chip . . . Wanna see it? I heard the teasing in his question. It was so strange and weirdly familiar to communicate like this.

It took me a second to respond—I was too busy filing through the chip I was currently in. It was me. It was *my* file. It held video and pictures; I could see myself as a child, a toddler. I could see my parents, and the facility, a younger Dr. Rucker. There were files containing information about my chip, its serial number, its size. I could see paperwork written in my parents' hands, information they were reporting about me. This whole chip, it was all about me. Mine was just one of the files in Dom's head. What else was here? Why did he have this information? How did he get it? Why did he have so many chips? I finally explained, "I want to see everything. Just not all at the same time."

He chuckled, and I could feel him smile. His mind turned from serious and desperate to something warm and bright—happy. He felt so full of joy and excitement, like a kid on Christmas morning. Was I the first person he'd communicated with in all this time? That must have felt amazing to him, indescribably so. But if he was capable of communication with me, then he could probably communicate with anyone in the same manner. He must have been choosing not to.

That's not the case, actually.

He could hear my thoughts?

I can when our chips are connected.

That was disturbing. That meant he knew I thought he was the most beautiful man I'd ever seen.

The happiness I'd felt in him warmed into something glorious.

Ugh. "Don't let it go to your head. Looks are meaningless."

Good thing I'm more than just good looks.

His happiness was so overwhelming, it was like looking at the sun. Too much glory.

"Tone down your happy. I can't concentrate."

Can't stop, won't stop.

I laughed. "You sound just like your brother."

Anton says that? He got that from me.

"Dominic. Stop. I need to concentrate. I need everything on this file."

In all seriousness, it will help if you see the other file first. I wasn't thinking straight in bringing you to this one. I was just trying to keep your attention.

I shook my head fractionally and spoke out loud,

even though I knew it wasn't necessary. "Too late. You opened this one, and I can't move on until I know it all."

He sighed.

I allowed my chip to begin uploading. But before I got very far, I realized that the file was too big. I knew from my experience with Jenna that I could filter information through my chip and into my memory, then delete it from my chip to create more space, but that was a process, and this was too much. I had to stop, but I desperately wanted to continue. This was about me; I couldn't just leave without it.

If you want to download the file, you're going to need another chip.

I reared my head back. "Uh ... no. No offense, but the last thing I want is to be stuck in a padded room for the next three and a half years."

I admittedly went too far, which you would've seen if you'd looked at the other chip first. Also, my room is hardly padded.

"Well, mine would be. I'm not the all-powerful ANGEL that you are. They wouldn't create a new wing of the facility just for me."

You have no idea what you are.

"And you do?"

I do. I know all about you. I knew you before we met yesterday. I recognized your chip serial number the minute you walked in the room. If you saw your real history, you would know what you're capable of too. You could do that, if you got another chip and downloaded the file.

"I was told by Davis that if I worked too hard to

remember my past, I'd fry my brain and end up in the psych ward."

That's not exactly true. For the average chipped person, their brains live in harmony with the chip; they work together seamlessly. But in the rare case of a CU, the brain recognizes the chip and its capabilities, and they can work separately from each other. Because our brains are separate from our chips, we're able to flag and even block incoming uploads. Unfortunately, it's the same separation that makes it difficult to override or change information once it has successfully uploaded. When the information we're trying to recall is different from the information on our chip, things become dangerous. The brain and the chip cannot work against each other—that causes irreparable damage. But if we download new information onto our chips, we can see the world as it really is, without the dangers of trying to override. It's all in how you go about it.

I was quiet for a moment, pondering what he'd said. It felt right to me. I'd already seen things on the file that didn't coincide with the memories I had of my childhood. It was obvious from what I'd already seen that I had begun using my chip much earlier than age eight. And yet, seeing it there and understanding something different didn't seem to bother me. "So I can download old information like it's new information, and that flows in harmony with the chip?"

Exactly. Old memories become new again. What had been uploaded to your chip, things your dad may have uploaded, for example, cannot be overridden, not by your brain. But old memories can be uploaded as new information, and it's accepted by both your brain and your chip. You will have both the old and the new. But if you want your old memories, the truth about yourself, you're going to need another chip.

I desperately wanted that file. But the last thing in the world I wanted was to have another chip. The one already had ruined my life—I had no intention of doubling down. Why was my file so big? I had downloaded four years of Jenna's education in what felt like an instant.

Your file is more complicated—the most complicated I've come across. So much of it was deleted, and then added to, and deleted again. The chip detects all digital footprints. I was able to recover things meant to remain permanently buried. Because of that, your file is like the difference between downloading a movie in 360p and 4K. Also, that chip contains not just your file, but your parents', as well as others pertinent to you. It's massive.

"How do you have all of this information? How did you get it? And why is there so much about me? I was only here until I was eight."

Now, those are the right questions to ask. As for how I got this information, that's what I've been trying to show you. As for why there is so much about you? I assure you that the answer will shock you. You are not who you think you are.

"What does that even mean?" Such a convoluted and obnoxious thing to say. Which obviously made me want to get another chip in order to download my file, the exact thing Dominic wanted me to do. But why? Why did me knowing my past matter to him?

My thoughts suddenly changed. I needed to see what had happened to him. I had to know why he had all of those chips. Who'd done that to him? That pull that I'd become so familiar with in Dominic's presence was back, dragging me out of my file and enticing me to look at another chip he'd now made shine the brightest. "Stop it." I recognized his handiwork now. He was influencing me, and the call was almost too much to deny.

He smiled. *You're learning so fast. Don't you want to know why this is so easy for you?*

I huffed. "Yes! Of course I do."

Well, then, you're just going to need one more teeny-tiny little nanochip.

"It sounds like you're pushing heroin."

I'd be lying if I said the information I can collect with all these chips isn't addictive.

That wasn't hard to believe. Being able to take in so much, to *know* so much . . . it could definitely be a drug.

I wanted my file, but not enough to take in an extra chip. Not that I even knew how to acquire one. I could process this file without the use of another chip, but it would take me coming here every night for months. I didn't even know how long I'd be in this facility for training. The only way I was guaranteed to get it all was if I got another chip. Which, right now, I was neither willing nor able to do. I was just going to have to keep the knowledge that Dominic had my file and delete the rest. Without converting it to memory, I wouldn't be able to look back on it. To read the notes my parents wrote about me, to learn who my parents really were. To learn who I really was. Letting go of it all felt like ripping off a limb. I couldn't delete it. But the feeling to delete it came on so strong I almost did. I huffed. "Stop trying to control me."

Your chip is full. I can teach you how to store more information.

"I don't want more information." Lie. "I want *this* information." Truth.

Channing, please be reasonable.

"Don't tell me I'm being unreasonable. That's as bad as asking a girl if she's on her period. It's not unreasonable for me to want to see my past. Especially because I know so little about it. So much of what I know of my early years has been implanted. I need to know what's real. That is not unreasonable."

Huh. Whether or not you are on your period was going to be my next question. Guess I'll skip that one.

I tried not to smile.

You're right, it's not unreasonable for you to want to see your past, but I know you won't be able to. It's too much to go through in a month, let alone the hour we have left until you're going to have to go back to your room. There is something I need to show you, and it will help you understand what happened to me.

I closed my eyes. I knew I would have to let my file go. I saw the option to delete right there in the front of my mind, and I chose it.

And just like that, the file was gone. But I knew Dom still had it, which was better than it being gone entirely, and so much more comforting. I would have to come back here every night and access it piece by piece.

I looked back into Dom's city of lights for the information he wanted me to see. A picture of me as a three-year-old with my parents suddenly popped up on my chip. "Thank you."

You're welcome. I went back to access the chip he'd highlighted earlier, but it was no longer bright.

I thought this might be easier.

In an instant, a file of Dominic's personal memories flooded my mind.

I saw Dom on jobs, speaking with foreign diplomats from different countries all across the globe. He used his chip and his stealth to penetrate their minds and their chips. He would implant information, information that would make the dignitary see things the way we, the United States, wanted them seen. Dom's work did so much good, it was amazing. He created fair trade agreements and negotiated treaties and international accords encouraging other countries to acknowledge human rights as well as value the environment. I saw Dominic literally stop wars and contentions among neighboring nations. But not everything was rainbows. Through his work, he'd seen many things that gave him pause, and that pause over time grew to serious concern. That concern led him to research, and that research led him down the rabbit hole of the century.

The scene switched, and I saw Dom in a lab with Anton. They were joking and laughing together. Anton's facial hair was thick and a little more grown out than he usually wore it; Dominic's face was shaved clean. They looked so similar with their wide smiles and perfect teeth. Handsome. Both of them had blue eyes that just wouldn't quit, but Dom's were a shade brighter than Anton's—almost turquoise. They looked so normal and happy. In all the time I'd known Anton, he'd never looked that content. It made me feel more than a little guilty. Here I was communicating with his brother, probably his dream come true, without him.

I couldn't hear what they were talking about, but I knew they were content just to spend time together. Anton stepped out of the room for a minute, and as soon as he was gone, Dominic grew serious and shifty. He moved to a locked cupboard, and after opening it with his chip, he pulled out a syringe with a short needle. With one more peek at the door, he stabbed himself in the bicep and emptied the contents of the syringe into his arm.

The memory switched to another scene. It was a second one with Anton and Dom; they were wearing different clothes but otherwise doing the same thing, laughing and joking around while doing a little work. As soon as Anton was out of the picture, Dom gave himself another shot.

There were countless versions of this same thing. It was always in the lab, and it was always Dom with someone else. Most often it was Anton, but sometimes it was Dr. Rucker, or Davis, and even Ashti on one occurrence. As soon as whoever he was with walked away, he would administer a shot to himself.

The memory switched to one with Dom alone, at the door of the lab. He was looking around for other people, but to his relief, he was alone. He opened the door, though not with his chip. He use a different one. One he'd implanted himself. That's what was in the shot—chips. He had a lot by this point, and he could access them all. He walked into the lab and sat down in front of the computer. Then he connected with it. He looked just like he did now—his eyes were vacant, and his mouth was moving as fast as it could go. He was downloading from the computer. All the information he could get. It wasn't long before he hit the capacity of one chip, and then he'd move on to another and then another.

He could download quickly, but he couldn't process it nearly as fast. The human brain is magnificent, but it's no match for that kind of computer. He didn't want to sort through it—at least not then. He wanted to get the information and look at it later. I saw similar scenes, followed by him administering another shot to himself, and then him downloading from the lab computer over and over.

He gave himself *hundreds* of chips and took in information at a speed I'd never thought possible. But he was downloading too much, and not processing enough of it. Regardless, he continued to gather intel from all over the world. So much information. Too much.

It would take years to process all of that . . .

I looked up at him. "That's so reckless. So unbelievably dangerous. Why would you do that?"

In hindsight, I can see it was too much. But the stuff I was learning . . . the stuff I have been learning, it's worth it, Channing. It's how I have your full file, I have everyone's file in this place. I know more about the science behind the chip than even Dr. Rucker.

"How can you say the information is worth it? Dominic, you've been processing for *three and a half years!*" I threw up my arms. "You may have all this information, but you have no way to use it. You're stuck in this room and with the way things are looking in your brain, you're never going to get out of here!"

I am, because you're going to help me.

TWENTY-FIVE

"You're insane."

I closed everything down, turned my chip off, and jumped off the couch. His eyes tracked me, but his mouth was still moving. He was processing, and he would be for only heaven knew how long. One thing I knew was that I wasn't falling down that rabbit hole with him, not for anything, not even for my own file. I'd lived without that information my whole life, and I could live without it now.

I felt the telltale buzzing in my head and shut it right down. Then I went to the door and tried to open it. Nothing. I looked at my watch. It was 5:20 a.m.

I closed my eyes. I was so angry at Dom. Why would he be so utterly irresponsible? His brother, whom he clearly loved, had been sick with worry about him for *three and a half years*. Terrible things had happened in this world in that time, things he could have stopped as an ANGEL had he not been so stupid. It was all his own doing, and it all just made me so angry. Now he wanted to drag me into his mess? No. Just no. I wanted no part of this nightmare he'd created.

I stood there at the door I couldn't open due to the early hour, so angry that I refused to connect to him and ask him to open the door and let me out.

What was he thinking? How could he do this to himself? How could he do this to his brother? How dare he tempt me with my file? A growl shot out of my mouth.

The buzzing in my head started up again. I didn't shut him out this time. There was only one way I was getting out of here, and it required his help.

Channing, I'm not asking you to do anything dangerous.

"Yes, you are."

I understand the limits now, and the solution is as clear as day to me.

I didn't say anything. After a minute, he went on.

I wasn't the first person to implant more than one chip. There's one person who has many more than me.

I didn't want to ask, I didn't care, but I knew he wasn't going to open the door for me without telling me. "Who?"

Your father.

The door clicked open, but I stood there for a moment because all the air had left my lungs. What did I say to that? There was nothing I could say. As soon as I felt I could walk on steady legs, I left as fast as my feet would carry me.

I got back to my room, and it was only minutes before Anton knocked on my door. Those were the shortest and longest minutes of my life. What would I say to Anton? He was expecting me to go and see his brother with him this morning. A thing I *could not* do. He was anxiously awaiting the moment I would connect with Dom and see what was going on with him. He'd probably hardly slept in anticipation. I didn't have any siblings, but I knew that if a person I'd loved that much had been all but comatose for three and a half years, I'd move heaven and earth if helping them were a possibility.

I paced around my room. It'd been so long since I'd had a good night's sleep, but I felt wide awake. My heart was beating so fast I knew I was running on pure adrenaline. I couldn't keep up this pace forever. My life had gone in a direction in the last several days that I never could have foreseen, and I didn't know if I had the grit to handle it all.

Part of me wanted to tell Anton everything, every word—or thought, as it were—that Dom and I had exchanged. But the larger part of me felt like I shouldn't. I couldn't determine exactly why I felt that way, but I did. Why hadn't Dom ever tried to talk to Anton? Or *had* he? He'd implied that he couldn't talk to just anyone, but why was that? What was special about me that made communication between us possible? What did he know that I didn't? But the answer to that question was easy. Everything. He knew *everything* that I didn't. And he'd taunted me with that information. He'd shown me my file, my past, with all the deleted scenes, knowing full well I wasn't going to be able to download it, and then he'd told me to "add another chip" as if it were as easy as breathing. He may have known what had happened in my life before it turned upside down, but he had no idea the suffering I'd endured since. He may have known that I had been in foster care, but he didn't know the abuse and rejection I'd suffered. That was something a report couldn't tell you. He probably knew I went to jail for selling meth, but he didn't know what I'd gone through to end up there—that I'd been stuck in that living situation through no real fault of my own. He may have learned that I'd squatted in someone else's apartment, but he didn't know that I'd been swindled into believing it was my own. You might think you know someone by knowing their history. That you understand a person because you know what they've been through. But you can never understand a person from reading a file; a report could never convey the depth of affliction that kind of life thrust on the soul. It made me angry that he felt like he *knew* me.

In fairness, I was aware that when Dominic said that *he knew me*, he was referring to my history with the chip. I knew that he was talking about all of those things I couldn't remember about my life prior to the age of eight. He knew what thoughts I'd been implanted with, what my life really looked like before my mom died. I knew he wasn't saying that he understood my life after that time. But that was the life that had shaped me; my life after the age of eight was the only life I really knew. The chip had caused a series of events in my life that cascaded downward like a thousand-foot waterfall. I despised the chip. I despised what it had done to my life. When I'd seen the hundreds of chips Dominic had, I thought I was going to be physically ill. The thought of doing that to myself— of adding to the thing that had caused the greatest miseries in my life—I just couldn't imagine doing that of my own free will.

I wasn't stupid, though. I knew that my childhood, the part of my life that was spotty, was instrumental to understanding myself, the chip, and possibly, hopefully my parents. And that information would only come through downloading the file. I deserved to know who I really was. I deserved to know why my life had taken the hard turns it had. I had memories from before my mom had been killed, but I didn't know what was real or fake. And without another chip to download the information, I never would.

I couldn't live with that.

So, when Anton knocked on my door, I opened it and said, "Let's go."

He seemed surprised to see me up and dressed. "I was about to apologize for being here earlier than we'd agreed on"—he looked me up and down—"but it appears you're as anxious as I am to get started." He smiled, and there was so much hope in it.

I looked down at my watch. It was 5:45 a.m. He was supposed to get me at 6:00 a.m. "Yeah, I'm definitely anxious to see Dominic."

He looked so earnest. "Thank you so much for doing this, Channing. Dom's been like this for so long"—he shook his head—"I just want to know what's going on with him." He blew out a breath, and his eyes flicked to the floor for a second. "Even if it's not possible to help him. I just need to know."

I felt like I was mocking him, knowing what I knew. It wasn't at all fair to Anton, who, if I was being honest

THE ANGEL PROJECT

with myself, was the brother to whom I should have been loyal. But who was loyal to me? Anton cared for me, of that I was sure, but he was loyal to Dominic. I didn't blame him for that—Dom was his family. Dom, for all I knew of him, seemed loyal only to himself. He was willing to use me. He was willing to risk whatever he needed to, including my mind, to get what he wanted. I was here because everyone—Davis, Dr. Rucker, and all the people in power here—thought I could be of use. Who was worried about me? No one, as usual.

As much as I wanted to help Anton, as much as I cared for him, I had to put myself first. This place, the people and practices, were still foreign to me. I knew if I stepped wrong, I could get myself in too deep, and I'd never get out. I'd never have a normal life. That—a normal life—was what I wanted more than anything else. The one thing I'd never had. I didn't know how to get it, but I did know that if I showed them all what I was capable of, which was more than I even knew, if Dominic was to be believed, they'd never let me leave.

Anton and I arrived at Dom's door, and he looked over at me. "You ready?"

I nodded, and Anton used his chip to open it. Dominic was standing there staring but not at the doorway. His face was as blank of recognition as always, but I could feel him there at my chip. Not in it really, but almost rubbing against it, coaxing it to open to him. It was so soft, I wouldn't have noticed it if I hadn't been on high alert. In that soft connection I could sense his surprise and his relief. He hadn't been expecting me to come back. That made two of us.

I felt the buzzing in my head, and I wasn't sure if I'd turned on my chip or if he had. He was good. Was Jenna that good? Is that how they got people to turn on their chips? It was almost automatic.

When I allowed my chip to connect to Dom's, the noise from earlier started up. Bits and pieces of information from thousands of files all at once filled my mind, quickly overwhelming my senses.

Channing.

I shook my head, trying to clear it. How had I escaped this nightmare the last time? My chip started to heat. I couldn't tell it to only pick up on Dom. My chip was picking up on everything—it was an onslaught of epic proportions.

Channing. Focus.

There was a chip shining brighter than the others, and I almost sagged in relief. I grabbed hold of it and the noise fell away. Once I was attached to one chip, my chip automatically began to translate code. It wasn't a full file, just bits and pieces of one. The file was downloading but taking its sweet time because there was too much happening in Dom's brain all at once. I didn't bother to see what was on the chip; I didn't care, and it probably wouldn't make sense to me anyway. I would delete it as soon as we were done here. It was such a relief to be out of the commotion, it felt like a cooling balm on burning skin. With my chip not on fire, I was able to hear Dom.

You came back.

I responded in my mind. It still weirded me out how familiar this—talking between minds—felt. Still angry, I gave a terse response. *What do you want me to tell your brother?*

Pause. *It's better for him if he doesn't know we can communicate.*

That made me mad. I wanted to be mad on Anton's behalf, but it's possible I was just looking for reasons to be mad at Dominic. *Your brother is dying to communicate with you. He's my friend, and I don't like deceiving him.*

Channing, he's my brother. Of course I want to tell him everything, but it will put him in danger. It's better for him if he doesn't know.

Anton was there, and it seemed like he was looking between Dom and me. I could hear him talking but couldn't understand him. His voice was distant. I had to really focus on him to try and hear what he was saying, and even then, it was hard to comprehend. I felt like my brain was trying to reach for it, the outside world, but it was so far away. Reading his lips and body language at the same time helped. I finally understood the gist of his question. "Are you in his chip?"

I turned back to Dominic. *What do you want me to tell Anton?*

Tell him that I'm processing. That you can see that I have too many files for my chip and that it's going to take some time.

I took a deep, irritated breath. That may have been the truth, but it was far from the whole truth. Anton would go on being as clueless as he currently was. He would continue to believe that his brother would come around someday.

Dom's voice came into my mind again. *I will come*

around someday. *I don't want my brother to give up on me.*

Frustrated, I said, *Don't respond to my thoughts unless I'm using them to talk to you.*

His inner voice rose in volume. *Well, you're practically yelling them, so it's hard to tell whether they're directed at me or not.*

I growled. It might have been out loud—I wasn't sure.

"Channing?" I knew Anton was talking to me—I could see him looking at me with his mouth moving, but it was just so hard to focus on it.

Dom's voice again came into my mind. *That's how I've felt for three and a half years. I can hear what's going around me, to an extent, but it's really hard for me to focus on it. It feels like it's all background noise, and it mixes with the noise already in my head. I have to concentrate so hard and then swim through the mayhem just to make sense of it. Forget about responding. It's virtually impossible when you're connected to the chip. The brain just doesn't have the capacity to focus on both at the same time. About a year in, I just stopped trying.*

That had to have been awful. He was living in that noisy confusion. To be bombarded nonstop with all of those downloading files. I couldn't imagine it.

Am I allowed to respond to that . . . ? When I didn't answer, he asked, *Are you on your period?*

I began coughing to cover the laugh I knew was more physical than mental. *Don't do that! If you don't want Anton to know we're communicating, then don't make it look like we are.*

THE ANGEL PROJECT

Anton was still trying to get my attention. *I have to talk to him.*

Tell me what happens.

I disconnected from Dom's chip and turned mine off. I took a minute to get my thoughts together. I cleared my throat. "Sorry, I can't really hear you when my chip is connected to someone else's."

His eyes were huge. "You were able to see?"

I nodded, and he blinked in disbelief and then smiled brilliantly. He grabbed ahold of my shoulders and said, "Channing, no one has been able to connect with Dom since this happened. Not a single person." I could feel my brow furrow. That must have been Dominic's doing. He didn't let them in. He didn't want them to know what he'd done. There was so much hope in Anton's expression it made me feel deeply guilty. I couldn't imagine the relief he'd feel to know that his brother was fine. Dom was still there and his mind was firmly intact. "What did you find? What's going on?"

I nodded. "He's processing, Anton. So much information. He bit off more than he could chew, and it's taking a long time to get through it."

"I don't understand."

I bit my lip. "I'm not sure how to explain what I saw. All I know is that his chip is processing something massive."

"From what I understand of the chip, if a CU who has the ability to download tries to take something too big, it doesn't allow for it."

Right. That was exactly what had happened to me when I'd tried to take my entire file. It can't be done.

What was I supposed to tell him? I couldn't exactly say, *Your brother stupidly loaded his brain with way too many chips, then proceeded to take in thousands upon thousands of files, and now he's so backed up he's getting pieces of thousands of files at the same time, and it's all slowed to the speed of molasses.*

My mouth dropped open. I knew what Dominic wanted me to do. And it just might work.

"What? What is it?"

My mind was running a mile a minute, but I had to respond to Anton. There was a time that I was a master liar. I'd left that Channing back on Skid Row, but I channeled her now. I shrugged. "Sorry, I thought I'd stumbled on a possible reason but almost immediately realized it couldn't be it. I'm just thinking through ideas of why Dominic could be stuck in this state. But honestly, your guess is as good as mine. Better, really—I'm so new to this." Apologetic smile. "I assume he managed to do something extraordinary and that's why his chip is stuck in this mode."

Anton sighed and nodded. He was disappointed. I wished I could tell him the truth. There was one truth I could share and I didn't think would go against Dom's wishes. I grabbed ahold of his hand and held it tightly. "He's there, though, Anton. Behind all the noise and confusion in his head. Dom's still there."

Anton became emotional, and I wished that Dom could see it. I wished that Dom knew how much his brother loved him. Dom knew Anton loved him. But with Dom's brain solely dealing with processing, he couldn't really understand what was going on in the outside world.

He couldn't really understand the suffering Anton had endured from having to see his brother in this state for so long.

Anton pulled me in for a hug. "Thank you."

I felt bad for Anton because I wanted to be there for him, but I didn't have the time or the capacity for it. It took a lot of work to formulate constant lies that didn't contradict the lies you'd already told. With everything already going on, my mind had hit max capacity.

I had to think about Dom. His configuration was too small for his needs. I needed Anton out of here so I could talk to Dom alone. I had an idea formulating.

To my great disappointment, Dr. Rucker and Dr. Sara Brandt walked in the room. Dr. Rucker looked surprised to see us at first. But the surprise quickly turned to understanding. "Have you all been here since yesterday?" He laughed. I smiled and attempted to laugh at his dumb joke, not wanting to let on that I had in fact been with Dom for far more of the last twenty-four hours than anyone knew.

Dr. Rucker looked at Anton. "It's good to see Dominic have visitors." A momentary sadness washed over his face. "Visitors seem to have dropped off over time."

Anton's shoulders drooped a touch.

"How's our favorite patient doing this morning?" Dr. Rucker turned to Dominic and patted him on the shoulder.

To no one's surprise, Dom gave no response.

Dr. Brandt smiled at Dominic and said, "I'm going to check your vitals, Dom." She then proceeded to check his blood pressure and temperature. He showed no sign he even knew it was happening. It was strange, the comparison between the person he was now and the person I saw when we were connected through our chips. He had so much personality underneath all the computing, but no one could see it. Last night he'd said he recognized my chip, that he could see my chip serial number, and that was how he knew who I was when I entered his room for the first time with Anton. Could he see that now? Did he know Dr. Brandt and Dr. Rucker were here, and touching him? He wasn't even reacting to being touched. I wondered if he could feel it? I made a mental note to ask him about that later.

Anton pulled lightly at the hand that I hadn't realized I was still holding. I let go and looked at him. He nodded toward the door. I didn't want to leave—I wanted to talk to Dom—but I could see time alone with Dominic would have to wait until the wee hours of the morning. I was frustrated, but there was nothing for it. I followed Anton out of Dom's room.

TWENTY-SIX

ANTON LOOKED AT HIS WATCH. "You've got one hour until class starts. Let's get some breakfast and I'll show you around."

I could hardly concentrate on his words. My mind was back in that room with Dom. I needed to talk to him, and I was frustrated that I had to wait. Absently, I murmured, "Yeah, sure. That sounds good."

He looked at me quizzically.

I smiled but knew I still wasn't connecting with the here and now. "Sorry. My mind's back with Dominic. I just can't stop thinking about what's going on in his head." I realized I was a few paces back from Anton and quickened my steps to catch up. "Speaking of which, why didn't you say anything about what I'd seen to Rucker or Brandt?"

"Oh, right." I'd known him for long enough to recognize that his eyes looked ever so slightly shifty. "I probably should have. I'm still letting it ruminate. I wonder how he managed to download too much. As far as I know, it's impossible"—he chuckled—"but Dom was never one for limits. He was always surprising people with his ANGEL capacity. He could do things the rest of us could only dream of. I was always covering for him when he'd get himself into trouble." He smiled wryly. "Which was pretty much all the time." That made me laugh. I'd seen Dom in action in his memories, and the guy was straight up reckless. Anton's smile dimmed. "This is the first time that I don't know how to help him. But I still want to try, and I guess I'm not ready to tell the powers that be what I'm up to." Then under his breath he muttered, "Dom, what have you gotten yourself into?"

I let that question hang in the air as we walked into the café I'd seen the previous day. It was really cute and homey. It was set up with a fireplace in one corner, booths along one wall, and tables filling the remainder of the room. It smelled amazing, like fresh cinnamon rolls. It was about half-full of people dressed in all kinds of attire, but mostly casual. I felt at ease in my white T-shirt and jeans. A small comfort. Ginger's clothes didn't fit me as well as I would have liked. I looked forward to getting more of my own clothes.

We walked up to the counter and were greeted by a smiling and enthusiastic employee. "Anton! Long time, no see, brother! Where you been, man?" The employee looked over at me. "Who's this pretty lady with terrible taste in men?"

Anton's smile was wide. "Hey, Reggie. What's up, man?" He clapped Reggie's hand over the top of the display and shook it, ending the slap-handshake in a fist bump. "They're still letting you work here?"

He laughed heartily. "They better. I run the place."

THE ANGEL PROJECT

Anton turned to me. "This is Channing Walker. She's new here."

I waved awkwardly. "Hi, Reggie. Nice to meet you."

He nodded at me. "Nice to meet you too, young lady." He pointed to Anton. "You be careful with this one. Years back, he used to come in here with a new lady every week."

Anton rolled his eyes on a laugh. "It's called working, Reggie."

Reggie's expression turned positively sardonic. "Is that what you call it these days?" They both laughed. "What can I get you two today?"

They both turned to me, but I was still studying the menu on the chalkboard behind the counter. "You go ahead, Anton. I'm still trying to decide." To Reggie I said, "Everything looks amazing."

He smiled. "Then get one of everything."

Laughing, I patted my stomach and said, "Don't tempt me."

Reggie winked at me and turned to Anton for his order. "Um . . . Can I get an egg-white omelet with all the veggies, no cheese? Aaaaaand . . . a side of fruit and one piece of avocado toast?"

"Coming right up."

They both looked at me expectantly, and I gave Anton a face. "Ugh. So healthy. You're annoying."

I turned back to a laughing Reggie, who said, "I like her."

I smiled and gave my order. "Can I get what he's having with a few exceptions? I want cheese on my omelet, and I definitely want one of those gigantic cinnamon rolls."

"My kind of girl." We paid with a tap of our badges. Eating for free was a pretty awesome perk. "You two find a seat and we'll bring your food out to ya."

We thanked him and made our way over toward the booths.

Anton looked back at me. "You're going to share that cinnamon roll, right?"

"Do I need to remind you what happens to people who touch my food?" His eyebrows rose in question. "I cut them," I deadpanned.

He laughed. "How could I have forgotten? So violent."

We found a booth by the fireplace. It was so nice and relaxing and normal I almost forgot I had a computer chip in my brain that I could use to connect to chips in other people's brains. That and the fact that I was in a building doubling as a prison, about to be taught how to use the aforementioned chip. And that there was a man who was currently being studied in a room about a quarter of a mile away who was absolutely fine except for the fact that his brain was so backed up with downloads that he was stuck in processing mode and had been for over three years. A man who expected me to help him out of his otherworldly situation. And just like that I was right back in reality. Sigh.

Our food arrived; it was steaming hot and tasted just as good as it smelled. "Wow, this place is awesome. How cool is it that it's right here in the building? I feel like we're at a café in Santa Monica."

Anton smiled. "There are two other restaurants here. One is Italian and the other is Mexican. They all work from the same kitchen. So everything you can order here, you can also get in the cafeteria. But sometimes it's just nice to feel like you're somewhere else."

"That's funny, in a weird way. It's a bit of a letdown, if I'm honest."

He smiled. "Sorry, I didn't mean to ruin the magic."

"Too late." I took a couple bites while listening to the hum of conversation around me. "So who's Reggie? Aside from the cool guy working here?" I scrunched up my forehead. "He said he runs the place? Is he a CU? It seems like all the people I've met so far are CUs. This is strictly a CU facility, right? Will I have to take a turn as a café counter girl? Because, I've got to be honest, I'm not likely to be as enthusiastic as he is." I used my fork to point to the man behind the counter. "Reggie's fantastic at this job."

Anton laughed. "That he is, and I, for one, would be shocked if you were half as friendly." I smirked. "Fortunately for the rest of us, we're not going to have to find out just how unfriendly you'd be behind the counter. Reggie's not a CU. He works full time for the facility."

That piqued my interest. "Really?" Anton nodded. "How do you explain all the weird things that happen here? I mean, I assume the training in this place isn't your average training."

He looked a little uncomfortable when he said, "Yeah, uh ... this is probably going to sound kind of strange, actually. The employees here don't exactly realize where they work."

I tilted my head closer to Anton. "Come again?"

He cleared his throat. "There are about five hundred CUs in here at any given time. It takes over fifteen hundred full-time employees to run this facility. The CUs could never train, run missions, and keep this place running at the same time. Our time is too valuable, and there aren't enough of us."

"I'm still not following."

"The people who work here don't fully understand what this place is." He scratched his head. "They've been . . . led to believe they work in a different place than this." He cleared his throat. "Through the chip." He let that sink in for a few seconds. "Reggie really does run the café, he just doesn't know exactly where he works or what we do here."

My fork was frozen halfway to my mouth. It took me a minute to respond. "You have to be kidding me." Anton looked uncomfortable but didn't say anything. "Please tell me you're kidding."

"Trust me, none of us particularly like it. But it's the only way. We have to have employees; this facility can't run itself, and it's not safe for the employees to know what we do here."

"Anton—" I tried to find the right words for what I felt, but I didn't know where to start. "These people are *mind controlled* to work here? What do they think they do? If Reggie thinks he runs this café, where does his family think he's working? Don't they ever want to come visit him?" I was flabbergasted.

"Reggie knows he works for the FBI. He believes he runs a café within the academy. That's why his family doesn't come to see him in action. They don't have clearance."

I sat back. That actually wasn't as bad as I thought. I was imagining that Reggie thought he ran a café off a main thoroughfare in DC or something. Him thinking he worked for the FBI was much better. Technically, he did work for the FBI—a super high security section of it. A section he could know nothing about. I could understand the need for discretion. It was still gross that he was controlled through the chip on a day-to-day basis, but it wasn't that big of a stretch. "Okay, I kind of understand that. What about the rest of the employees here? Do they all think they work for the academy?"

"More or less."

That was an evasion if I'd ever heard one, but I wasn't going to call him on it. I'd heard enough for one morning.

We finished eating and said our goodbyes to Reggie.

Anton and I walked around the corner, and he turned us down the hallway that looked like an elementary school. I ran my fingers along the wall of painted handprints. "What is this place? I've been meaning to ask since we passed it yesterday."

Anton smiled wistfully. "This"—he motioned around us—"is where Dom and I grew up."

Confused, I asked, "You didn't grow up with your parents?"

He shook his head. "Most CUs are found as children, early teens at the latest. They can cause a lot of trouble when they're young and realize they can have and do whatever they want." He smiled like the Cheshire Cat.

I laughed. "I can only imagine the mayhem you and Dom managed to create before you guys were brought here." We walked farther down the hall and saw several classrooms. They were full of kids. There must have been at least a hundred children of all ages. "I understand why they can't be out there in the world, but what about their families?" I looked at him sadly. "Did you and Dom have to leave your parents? How old were you?"

He nodded. "I was eleven and Dom was nine. Our parents were influenced to believe they were sending us to boarding school. Thanks to the chip, they wanted to send us to boarding school."

My mouth gaped. "Seriously?"

He smiled sadly. "It a mercy, really. We couldn't stay at home; it would have been too dangerous for everyone involved. Through the chip, they were led to believe that they were doing what was best for us. And because they believed we were at boarding school, we could call and otherwise communicate regularly. It was better than the FBI taking the memory of us away from our parents, like TAP did when they first started acquiring child CUs." I gasped, but he just shrugged, used to the dark history of TAP. "And technically speaking, this is a boarding school. Our parents just didn't realize the type of things we were learning."

"Ha. I guess that's true. But how sad." I looked at all the kids that had been taken from their families. There was a little redheaded girl working at a desk. She had fair skin and freckles, and she was just beautiful. She couldn't have been over the age of six. It made my heart hurt. These kids weren't in foster care, and this wasn't an orphanage, but it felt like one, because none of these kids had their parents. I knew what it felt like to grow up without parents who checked on you at night, without their hugs and kisses. And those poor parents who'd had their children ripped away from them. Even if they believed that it was the right thing to do, they had to give up those late-night quiet moments watching their children sleep. They had to give up those hugs and kisses. Even though they were influenced to believe it was the right thing to do, their arms and hearts must have felt so empty. It just seemed barbaric.

Anton was looking into a classroom when he said, "It is sad, if I'm being honest. I like to spend a lot of time here with these kids. Almost all the CUs do. We know what it felt like to be here as children. I feel a level of love for these kids that I think could only be surpassed by what I'll feel for my own children someday." He looked at me, his face a mixture of emotions. "I was one of the lucky ones. I had my brother here. Because the ability to use the chip has a genetic component, there are a handful of siblings here. There are also CUs who met here and married and had families. Those kids are the luckiest of all. They get to be raised by their parents."

"How does the genetic component work? How often do CU parents produce children who are CUs?"

He shrugged. "Genetics are weird. Sometimes two redheaded parents have a child that's a blond. And sometimes two dark-haired parents produce a child with red hair. If you're a CU, you have the recessive gene making compatibility with the chip impossible, requiring your brain to work separately from your chip. That gene has to be on both sides of your family, but it may only show up in one child, or none at all, or it could show up in all of your children, as is the case with my family."

My eyes bugged out. "Are there more Garcia children here?"

He laughed and put his hands up. "No, no. My parents stopped at two. I don't think the world could handle any more than that."

I let out a breath. "I know I couldn't."

We walked into a classroom. I was a bad judge of children's ages, but the kids looked to be around eight to ten. "Mr. Anton!" As soon as we walked into the room, Anton was bombarded with shouts and hugs. The kids were so excited to see him, and he them, tears started to prick my eyes.

We stayed for just a few minutes so as not to upset their classroom for too long. As we were leaving, I had a thought. "Are the teachers mind controlled to think they're in a regular classroom?"

He shook his head. "The teachers are CUs. Well-trained CUs."

I laughed at my stupid question. "Oh, right. Of course. I can't imagine the trouble a classroom full of little CUs could get into with a civilian teacher."

"I'm sure they'd love to find out." Anton's phone pinged with a text. He took a look at it and gestured toward the exit." Looks like it's time to go learn some stuff."

Anton escorted me out of the school hall and back to the main hallway connected to every location. We walked a little way and then knocked on a solid white door with a black plate that said *LAB*. "I can't get into this room with my chip. It's only programmed for the chips of people who regularly work here. Fully trained CUs can go almost anywhere else."

The door buzzed and Anton opened it, letting me enter first. There were only two people inside: Agent Davis and Dr. Rucker. I thought I'd be meeting with other new CUs, learning how to coax a person into letting me into their mind. Instead, it was just the four of us, in the lab, which was the size of a house. I recognized it immediately from Dom's memories.

Agent Davis smiled at me and Anton as soon as we walked in, but Dr. Rucker was the first to speak. "Channing, welcome to the lab. Or should I say, welcome back to the lab?" He looked at me expectantly. "Well? Does any of this look familiar? This was where you were practically raised. Not much has changed, really. We've had a few upgrades over the years, of course, but overall, it should look a lot like it did the last time you were here."

I gave him a pained smile. "Not really, no. Unfortunately, none of this looks familiar."

He looked at me searchingly. Then harrumphed. "I don't understand. You seem to have been wiped clean. But why?" That was the question of the century.

Davis interjected. "It's no use trying to remember something that's been manipulated through your chip. We've been down that road already." He looked at me pointedly, and my head ached at just the thought.

"Yes, yes. That's all true, but it's quite the mystery, is it not?" Anton and I both nodded. "Come over here,

Channing. Agent Davis and I were just looking at the latest batch of nanochips."

I walked over to where the two were peering into a rather small container. I joined on Rucker's side, and when I looked over, it was hard to tell what we were looking at. Confused, I asked, "Are these nanochips?"

"About one billion of them." Dr. Rucker pulled out a small scooper, like one you'd find next to a bulk candy bin and picked up just the tiniest amount. In that small little pile, there must have been tens of thousands.

"The chips are that small?" It looked like a container of very finely milled black powder.

Dr. Rucker smiled. "They are just seventy nanometers wide and seventy point five nanometers high. Or in other words, they are seventy billionths of a meter wide and seventy point five billionths of a meter high. The diameter of a single red blood cell is seventy-five hundred nanometers."

"That's unreal." I was floored. "How can something that small have such large capabilities?"

Dr. Rucker was all smiles now. He was in his element, and it was clear he was proud of his work. "It has everything to do with their programing and placement. They sit in just the right spot in the brain to connect to it. They have no batteries and power themselves from their environment. They have a one-hundred-year lifespan. Nerve cells grow into and meld with the chip, making it essentially part of the body."

"What I don't understand is why you have so many. This is a billion chips, and the population of the United

States is only about three hundred and fifty million. Didn't you say this was just the latest batch?"

Dr. Rucker waved away my question. "So few of them meet their mark that we need a fair amount more than the population."

"Let's move on, shall we?" Davis asked. I didn't want to leave the nanochips; I couldn't believe how small they were. I could have looked at them all day. Unfortunately, Agent Davis had other plans. He went over to the computer and sat in front of it.

On my way over, I went to the locked cupboard from Dom's memories. "What's in here?" I asked Dr. Rucker.

"Oh, those are some test chips." He came over and opened up the cupboard. "We use these to test on already chipped rats to see how they react to having more than one chip, just for research's sake."

I looked at the syringes that I'd seen in Dom's memories and said, "Huh. Any interesting findings?"

Dr. Rucker lifted his brows and smiled. "Always." Then he went to close the cupboard and I slipped a finger under the hinge to keep it from closing all the way. Then I distracted the older man with a benign question about the chips, a thing he could talk endlessly about.

Agent Davis cleared his throat and motioned me to a chair next to the computer and facing him. I sat and then, over his shoulder, he dismissed Anton, "Agent Garcia, that will be all for now. You can get back to your work."

Anton smiled tightly. "Channing is my work, sir."

Davis laughed. "Right, we'll keep it that way until Ms. Walker gets acclimated to our facility. But for now, at least the next couple of hours, you can get caught up on other things, or go visit your brother."

Anton looked uncomfortable leaving me there, but he was given no other choice. With one quick glance to see if I was okay—I most definitely wasn't—he left. As much as I didn't like being assigned to someone, I really did feel more comfortable with Anton around. I didn't especially want him to leave, but I knew neither of us had a choice in the matter. He gave me a look that was half sympathy and half worry for me and then let himself out the door.

I decided the easiest way to interact with Agent Davis and Dr. Rucker was to act like they were the smartest people in the world and that I was super grateful to be under their tutelage.

Davis smiled at me. "Channing, if it's okay, we'd like to run some tests. You're missing so much of your childhood. And while we don't know who would have done this to you, or why—a thing that will likely stay a mystery—we would like to see how your brain and chip react to different questions."

I swallowed. "Like a lie detector?"

He shook his head. "Not at all. We are going to ask you questions about your past, and all we need you to do is answer honestly." He paused and chuckled. "I just realized how much that sounds like a polygraph. It's not. We can't tell if you're lying. What we're looking for is how your chip and brain respond to the questions. Your chip is separate from your brain. They process things differently, and when your chip overrides your brain, which it will in the case of implanted information, it should show up on the screen."

Dr. Rucker piped in. "It might help us discover what you know, and don't know, as the case may be, so I can stop asking you inane questions about things you don't remember."

"That would be nice, actually." They both laughed. "Honestly, I *would* like to know what you know about me. I want to know what my parents were like when they worked here, and what I was like. I want to know where I sat to do my homework, and who I regularly interacted with. But I don't want to go through what I did yesterday in Davis's office." I motioned to my head. "And I certainly don't want to go beyond the pain and end up in a straitjacket." I sighed. "There are a lot of holes in my history, and I'm worried they'll never be filled."

They both looked at me sympathetically, which meant my plan to play as innocent as possible was working. They wanted me clueless, and I had no problem letting them believe it was the case.

They spent the next several minutes hooking me up to the computer. I had so many wires attached to my head and chest I looked like I was about to undergo a sleep study. As soon as they were finished, Dr. Rucker looked at me excitedly. "Ready?"

I nodded. I was nervous about what the computer would show. But it seemed to me they were *hoping* to glean information from this, not that they were certain they would. That meant I still had wiggle room.

Dr. Rucker asked the first question. "Channing, how old are you?"

"Twenty-five." An easy question that made me think they must have been trying to find a baseline. Oddly enough, my age had been at the very forefront of my mind since Anton had taken me to see the kids. I knew that Anton was thirty-one—I used to tease him that he was old back at the gym—which meant Dom was twenty-nine. If Anton and Dom came here when they were respectively eleven and nine, that meant that I was four when they'd arrived at the facility. We would have spent four years together here.

Dr. Rucker had mentioned that I "homeschooled." Maybe that meant my parents kept me with them instead of leaving me with the other kids.

But I had another theory, and it had to do with the reason speaking with Dominic through our chips felt so natural.

"What is your birthday?" Dr. Rucker asked.

"July twenty-fourth." Dr. Rucker and Agent Davis exchanged a glance. The way they looked at each other confirmed one thing for certain: I did not, in fact, know my real birthday. I couldn't help but think back to several conversations I'd had with Darcy, who was always into astrological signs. I was a Leo, or at least I thought I was. But Darcy was always saying that there was no way I was a Leo because I didn't fit the profile in the slightest. I would just laugh and tell her it was because astrological signs were garbage, but it turned out she was right, after all. I wasn't a Leo.

Dr. Rucker turned his gaze toward me. "Channing, I'm going to say a list of names, and I want you to tell me if you recognize them, and who they are. Okay?"

I nodded.

"Evelyn West."

"Um, my mother? I know her as Evelyn Walker, but I was told my last name used to be West." I was trying to phrase it in such a way that it didn't trigger my brain and chip to go to war with each other.

"Very good, Channing."

"Steve Bellinger."

Not even a little familiar. I shook my head.

"Ms. Hanrahan."

"Sorry. I don't remember that name."

Dr. Rucker smiled tightly. "No need to apologize, Channing." He paused for a second. "How about the name Johnny?"

I shook my head. Rucker sighed.

Davis asked the next question. "Channing, I'm sorry for the sensitive subject matter, but do you remember the day your mom was killed?"

"Yes." It really wasn't all that sensitive of a question to me anymore. It was an awful day, a pivotal one for me, certainly, but it didn't make me nearly as emotional as it once had. My dad killed my mom while I watched. It was a fact. I'd already spent time examining that particular memory to see if it was perfect like when I was five and implanted with the chip. It wasn't. It was blurry and changed a little bit every time I recalled it. It was a real memory.

"Can you tell us what happened?"

I used every bit of my acting skills. I allowed my lip to quiver, and I bit it hard enough to cause me a little pain, hard enough for my eyes to water. I sniffed, and Dr.

Rucker put his hand on my back. "We're sorry to be so invasive, Channing, but we'd like to know what you know about that day. We need to see if it matches up with our record of that day."

I nodded and let my eyes blur, like I was back there in the memory of the moment. "My parents were fighting." Davis and Rucker were on the edge of their seats. "I can't remember what they were fighting about."

"Try, Channing. Try to remember what the fight was about," Davis coaxed.

I let out a breath and acted like I was trying to remember harder. "I don't know. It was about things I couldn't understand. Adult stuff. I do remember the name TAP coming up, but that's all I can recall." Davis nodded for me to continue. "The fighting escalated, to yelling and then screaming. I'd never heard my parents like that before. My mom brought me into it; she said she was going to take me away from here. She threatened to take me away from my dad and TAP. Then my dad's hands were wrapped around her throat. She was trying to breathe, but she was making these awful noises, choking ones." I stopped to take a breath. This part of the story was true, and the details were still disturbing to me. "I was so young. I should have called the police, but I didn't. I just watched. I watched my dad choke the life out of my mom, even after her body sagged and he was holding her up by her throat, he continued to strangle her. And I just stood there." It was easy enough to allow the tears to flow. "I don't remember much after that. I remember the police coming and my dad being arrested."

Rucker asked, "Who called the police?"

"It wasn't me. I think my dad called them. He seemed shocked by what he'd done, like he couldn't believe he'd killed her. He kept looking at her lifeless body in confused horror. Like he was surprised he was the one who made her that way."

I don't know why I decided to tell them my mom was the one who wanted to take me away from TAP. It was a lie, obviously, but it felt right in the moment, to change it up and keep my dad out of it. I wasn't loyal to him, or at least I didn't think I was. But he was my only living parent. I didn't want Davis and the FBI to hunt him down.

The more I was learning about my history, the more I questioned *everything*. I needed that file. I needed to know who I really was. And more than that, I needed to know who had changed my memories and *why*. Maybe it was indeed my dad, but why change so much? How had I ended up in Los Angeles when I was raised in Quantico, Virginia? Where was I actually born?

"I need a break." I began to pull the sticky tabs from my chest. Dr. Rucker and Agent Davis exchanged worried glances. They got up and began to help me take the tabs off. Once I was free, I covered my face with my hands, breathing hard. With my voice choked, I asked, "Can I just have a minute?"

Davis answered, "Of course, Channing. We have some things to discuss, but we'll just step outside for a minute and give you some privacy."

As soon as I heard the click of the door, I jumped up from my seat and went to the cupboard I'd covertly stopped Rucker from closing all the way earlier.

I pulled out a syringe, the same type I'd seen

Dominic use in his memory. I didn't hesitate. I pulled up my sleeve, used my teeth to pull the cap off the needle, and emptied the contents of the syringe into my bicep.

TWENTY-SEVEN

THAT NIGHT BEFORE I CLIMBED into bed, I set the old-fashioned alarm clock on my nightstand for 3:00 a.m. It was a little after ten o'clock now, and I desperately needed those five hours of sleep. I lay back in bed and tried to clear my mind.

There was a part of me that couldn't believe what I'd done. And another part that was thrilled I'd finally taken some action. I had no idea why so many of my childhood memories had been manipulated. I felt like I was a shadow of the person I was really meant to be.

There was no question in my mind that it was my father who'd done this to me. And, for the record, I did believe that he'd done it to protect me. But foresight was not 20/20, and what he'd done, stripping me of everything I knew and putting me in foster care across the country, had not had the outcome he'd hoped.

There was a piece of me that thought I would have been better off had I minded my own business and stayed with Darcy. But there was part of me that was missing, a large part, and I knew it. I'd known my memory was spotty, that my mind wasn't whole, even before I got here and had it confirmed. I knew it when I was younger. It affected everything.

What I'd told Darcy the last night that I was with her, about me not being normal, was all true. I couldn't have normal relationships; I could barely have normal friendships. I thought of Jenna, how Anton had said when she'd returned after the altercation with me, she wasn't herself exactly. That was so utterly relatable. That's how I'd felt my whole life. Like I was missing something. Something big. Now I had the power to get it back.

And even if it hurt me, even if it meant more trouble in my life, I wanted it. It was time I was a whole person, regardless of the consequences.

The alarm woke me up, and I was surprisingly groggy. I thought I would jump out of bed when it was time to go see Dominic. But a body could only go so long on adrenaline. I almost lay back down, but if I didn't see Dom now, then I'd have to wait another twenty-four hours. I got up, but I'd be lying if I said my sheets weren't calling my name.

I felt his pull on my chip as soon as I was up. I quickly threw my clothes back on and quietly left my room.

I knew my way better this time, but the pull on my chip still helped to guide me to the psych ward. The door clicked open for me just as it had the night before. The only difference was I now knew it was Dominic opening it. All of the nurses were again trying to calm some patient who was down one of the long halls opposite Dominic. I knew now this was his doing as well. I didn't know how he did it all, but I was done being ignorant. I was going to start to learn.

I got to Dominic's door, and I didn't even check to see if it was open—I already knew it would be.

He was there waiting for me. The feeling against my chip, the soft knock, coaxing me to turn it on—the feeling was remarkable in its subtleness. I *had* to learn how to do that. I turned on my chip and it all but automatically connected with Dominic.

The noise began, but it wasn't as bad this time. It was quieter and not as confusing.

I felt Dom's shock. *You did it.*

"I did." I showed him the memory of me in the lab meeting with Davis and Rucker. The whole thing, from seeing the nanochips, to the computer, to me giving myself the shot.

Channing. You gave yourself the whole thing?

"I did."

Do you know how many chips that is?

"No." Alarm began to creep in. It was a stark contrast to my earlier confidence.

Each one of those syringes has one hundred nanochips.

My eyes practically bugged out of my head. I took in one hundred chips? "I figured there was more than one in there—I just thought it was more like ten."

Definitely more than ten. Ten times more, to be exact.

"Yes. As it turns out, I can do simple math." I refused to freak out. The damage was done.

It's okay, Channing.

"Well, of course it's okay for you."

He smiled. *It's great for me, actually. Don't worry, you can handle a hundred chips, no problem. All of the new chips are made to connect and network with the first. It'll be so seamless you won't even realize it's happening.*

I took stock of myself. Everything felt normal. The only difference was the ease with which I connected with Dominic's chip, which may have been worth the extra chips in and of itself. "I don't feel any different. Not really."

You won't feel any different—take it from an expert. Most people can't get more than one. The chips, the nanochips they currently give the public, are programmed to recognize if there's another chip already implanted. If there's already a chip present, the extras self-destruct and work their way back out of the body. The chips in the cupboard are different. They're made without the programming to self-destruct and allow for more than one implantation.

"Why would they put one hundred in a single syringe?"

They're used in animal testing. Having more than one chip is still in the testing phases. Though I suspect Rucker and Davis have tried it on themselves.

"Why do you say that?"

Just a suspicion.

"I want my file."

He smiled. *I want you to have your file.*

THE ANGEL PROJECT

"You do?"

I do. Very much.

"Because you're in it, aren't you?"

I am. But that's all I'm going to say about it. It's only safe to relearn the information through your chip. It's right here.

I could see the brighter chip and was about to download it when he stopped me.

Can we try one thing first? Because once you get into your file, you'll be lost in there for a long time, and I don't know how you'll feel when you're done.

"That sounds ominous."

I wish I could say it's all rainbows and unicorns, but it's not.

"Rainbows and unicorns?" I laughed, but he just smiled wistfully. "Don't worry, Dominic, I know that, and I'm not changing my mind. I'm all in. But yes, I'll help you first. I think I know what you need me to do. You're bottlenecked. I can take files that you've downloaded and delete them from your chips, allowing for more room and speed. When you've finished processing what you already have, I can give you the files back one by one."

The relief in his mind was so acute I felt like I could touch it. *Yes. Yes, Channing. That's exactly what I need.*

"Where do you want me to start?"

With the files that haven't even started to download.

When I looked harder, I saw chips that were blinking, twinkling almost. I went to those and found files still waiting to be processed. The chips worked a lot like random access memory. They were never meant for long-term storage—the information they collected was meant to be processed into the brain and become part of it immediately. The brain works like the hard drive for long-term storage. But Dominic, in taking in so many chips and so many files in such a short period of time, had gotten himself into a jam of epic proportions. Seeing all of his chips was still a shock to my system. He was practically half robot at this point.

He laughed. *We're all part robot. You and I just happen to be aware of it.*

"That's actually true. On a side note, I thought I told you not to listen to my thoughts unless they were directed at you. It's really unnerving."

All of your thoughts are coming through your chip. You can stop that, you know.

"I can control how my thoughts are processed?"

Your brain and your chip—or chips, as the case may be—work together seamlessly almost all the time. In the case of CUs and ANGELs, we are able to separate our chips from our brains at will.

"Yes, I remember that from before."

It's the same thing with your thoughts.

"I'm not following."

Our thoughts automatically run through our chips—it's part of how the brain and the chip work together. But when you use the chip to connect to other chips, you're using your brain and your chip as separate entities. You can disconnect your thoughts from your chip in the same way.

"How do I do that?"

The way you showed me that memory earlier? You did it through your thoughts. Memories aren't stored in the chip. You managed to purposefully run a specific memory through the chip to mine. You can do that with your thoughts too. You just separate them.

"Huh. That makes sense. It's something I'll have to work on later. I know I have a lot to learn, but at the moment I don't have the capacity. Let's get you out of artificial intelligence mode and back to your human side before we get into all the things I can do."

Deal.

I got to work downloading and deleting. It was faster and much easier than I'd thought it would be. With all the available space I had, things processed in a blink. The weird part was when I downloaded a file, I knew what was on it. But it wasn't just that I knew what was on it—I owned the information, just like I had with Jenna and her degree. It was mine to use. The main difference here was that the files were random. They didn't make much sense to me because they were out of order. It would be like trying to learn calculus without ever having learned multiplication.

I worked for hours downloading and deleting. The more space he had, the faster he could process.

We went on like this for almost two weeks. I would "train" with Rucker and Davis during the day and meet with Dom at night. In the evenings I would usually have dinner with Anton. Anton was always trying to get me to go see Dom in the mornings to try to work with him, and I typically would, but at Dom's persistence, I never told Anton about the progress we were making.

Every night I took and deleted files from his chips, Dom's processing speed would improve, and he would process faster, getting through more of the brain/chip traffic jam exponentially with each passing day.

Training with Rucker and Davis mostly consisted of them hooking me up to their computer and asking me prodding questions I had no answers for.

On the thirteenth night with Dom, I asked him what they were trying to learn from asking me this random stuff.

"They're trying to gauge what information you've been implanted with. Every time they hit on a question or piece of information that lights up your chip faster than your brain, it shows you've been manipulated. When it works the other way, it shows natural thought process. It's far from a perfect science, and Rucker and Davis have small minds with small capacity. What they really want is to know who did this to you and why. The question they really should be asking is: What are you capable of? That answer would solve the puzzle in one."

"How can they possibly find the answer to that question? I don't even know what I'm capable—"

I sucked in a sharp breath. I stopped talking, stopped downloading. I stopped everything. "Dominic."

I pulled out of his chip and shut mine off.

We were looking at each other in real life. He was looking at me, *really* looking at me. His mouth was no longer moving at a heart-stopping pace. "Dominic."

"Channing." His voice was scratchy from disuse, but he was there. He was fully conscious. He blinked several times.

We stared at each other for an immeasurable amount of time. And then in one quick motion, Dominic put his arms around me and pulled me to his side so fast that I was half on his lap, enveloping me in the tightest hug I'd ever had.

I could feel the wetness of his tears on my shoulder, and I knew my own tears were wetting his shirt as well. Two weeks. It had taken less than two weeks to get Dom out of the mess he'd gotten himself into, the mess he'd been trapped in for three and a half years. Even though I knew I couldn't possibly understand what he was really feeling, I'd been in the hell that was his head. He'd been suffering for so long, and I almost couldn't believe it had worked. We'd pulled him out of it. It felt like a miracle.

I pulled back. "It's unreal." I shook my head in wonder. "You were just talking to me out loud. I heard your voice with my ears. It was so unexpected it took me a minute to realize. You're back."

He roughly wiped the tears from his face. He looked so different. If I thought he was attractive before, it was nothing on what he looked like now. He was so animated, so *human*. I started laughing. I didn't know how to handle the onslaught of emotions I was feeling. "Dominic, I can't believe it!" I laughed some more and threw my hands up in the air. "We did it!"

He joined me in laughing and cheering, and his face shone like the sun when he smiled. His utter happiness was so poignant tears began to well up in my eyes again. It was the most beautiful and authentic moment I'd ever experienced. He held my face in his hands and wiped the wetness from my eyes with his thumbs. "Channing, there are no words to express my gratitude." I immediately began to shake my head. He held it still and looked deeply into my eyes. "Let me try." He only got out the word "Thank—" before his chin began to quiver.

"Dominic, I feel like *I* should be thanking *you*. This was an experience unlike any other. It was like seeing the sight restored to a blind man. I'm just glad I got to be a part of it."

With his hands still cradling my face, he pulled me forward. His expression was earnest while he studied my eyes, and then my lips. I swallowed. I may have been a novice to romance, but I'd seen enough television and read enough books to understand what was going on here. My heart sped up as his face ducked closer to mine and when his lips were just a hair's breadth away from mine, he stilled. I didn't move a muscle, I couldn't. Maybe I was supposed to close the gap, I didn't really know. Fortunately, when I didn't move back or stop him, he closed it himself.

The first touch of his soft lips on mine was so feathery I almost couldn't feel it with all the sparks that were flying in my body. He pulled back again, just slightly and when I didn't scare away, his hands moved from cupping my cheeks to cradling my neck. He used his thumbs to tilt my head slightly and with one second of eye contact, his lips were on mine again. This time his lips were fitted snugly to my own. He began to move his mouth over mine in the sweetest and most gratifying way. All I could think was that I never wanted him to stop. In that moment I felt like I could very literally kiss Dominic for the rest of forever. Doubts crept in eventually though. I worried this was a thank you kiss. That it meant infinitely more to me than it did him. Dom's childhood and adult life, while far from normal, hadn't been stilted like mine. He'd probably kissed tons of girls. I'd had very little in the way of experience, and none nearly as meaningful to me as this. I'd been inside his head, talked to him mind to mind. There was an intimacy there that I couldn't set aside. I didn't know if he felt the same, and the uncertainty was making it difficult for me to stay in the moment. Then he suddenly pulled me fully into his lap and deepened the kiss and all my thoughts went blessedly silent.

We went on like this for a few more amazing moments, and when he eventually pulled back, I wished he would close the distance between us one more time. He didn't though, instead he just looked at me. He studied my eyes, rubbed his thumbs across my cheekbones and the pads of my lips. He ran his fingers through my long hair, and every once in a while he would huff out a shocked breath. Then he said something I definitely didn't expect. "It's really you. I can't believe it's really you. Channing, you have no idea how long I hoped to see you again."

My head began to hurt. That telltale fog and pounding returned. I'd already surmised that Dominic and I had a history, but to hear it confirmed started the war between my chip and my brain, because I wanted to remember. He must have seen the pain cross my features, because he switched the line of conversation to something that pulled me out of whatever shared history we had in a flash. "I want to kiss you again."

I nodded my head rapidly. He smiled and right before his lips touched mine, the thought that Anton was the last person I'd kissed blared to the forefront of my mind. It was like a bucket of cold water poured over my head. The kiss probably meant nothing to Anton. I knew he was just trying to hide me from TAP, but it was still as awkward as all get out that Dominic's brother was the last person I'd kissed.

Which brought on another thought. I pulled back in a hurry and I put my hands over his and insisted, "Dominic, we should go wake up Anton. He's going to have a heart attack." I pulled back further and slid off his lap. "As much as I could spend the rest of the night kissing you," he smiled, and I shyly returned his grin, "I feel terrible that I'm here spending time with you by myself, and he has no idea that you're awake." I grabbed Dom's arms excitedly, "He's going to freak out. I want to witness the moment when he first sees you." I thought for a second. "That's how you can thank me. You can let me watch when Anton first sees you're back." I rubbed my hands together excitedly.

He smiled flirtatiously. "I was under the impression that I was just thanking you. And I would really like to get back to thanking you some more."

I finally understood the phrase "my insides turned to mush." But I shoved all the desire down and focused. "Dominic, get your head out of the clouds. This is important. Anton deserves to know."

Sadness crossed his features momentarily, but it was gone as fast as it came. It was replaced with determination. "Channing, Anton can't know. Not yet."

I pulled my face back, out of his hands. "Dominic, no. You can't do that to him. He loves you. You don't understand how this will affect him. He's been waiting three and a half long years for this. He hasn't been able to help you, and the guilt, Dom—it's eating him up."

"I love him too, Channing. And that's why he can't know. The less he knows, the safer he is."

I shook my head. "I don't understand."

"But you're about to." His chip rubbed against my own, beckoning me to turn it on. I did and was immediately immersed in my own file. Dominic had all but begged me not to take my file before I helped him. I'd agreed, reluctantly at first, but I was so excited about the progress we were making with him that I'd let it fall by the wayside. Now here I was. Dominic had already straightened the file out, adding back the deleted pieces in the order in which they had happened in real life. Suddenly, my mind was flooded with images, both video and still that my chip read instantaneously. All of it flowed so seamlessly together, it was like I was watching a movie of my childhood.

And it changed *everything*.

TWENTY-EIGHT

THE FIRST THING THAT CAME up was the paperwork that my parents, Charles and Evelyn West, had filled out when they'd been recruited by the FBI to assist with the neurochip technology.

The scene switched to the lab. My parents were there with me in tow. I was a child of maybe one and a half. I toddled around the lab, my dark hair in short pigtails on the top of my head, while my parents worked with the group. There were several people there, all experts in their own field, but the only one I recognized was Dr. Rucker.

My parents proved to be a huge asset in the realm of neuroscience and brain chipping. They were fascinated with the science of it and amazed by the capabilities. For as much study as had been done on the brain, there remained so many unknowns. But the chip allowed them to be inside a person's brain in a whole new way. They were both first and foremost academics, and this was a new world of neurological study.

They were shocked to find out they were not only chipped, but they were anomalies of their own kind. My

THE ANGEL PROJECT

mother was a CU, with the ability to turn on her chip and connect to another to send messages—messages with the power to infiltrate the neocortex and land themselves in one's permanent memory. They discovered the mind would shift to make room for the message and build around it, making the individual's reality fit that new understanding.

My father was something else entirely. At the time, he still fell under the CU umbrella, but it wasn't long before they all realized he was something much more.

He could not only turn on his own chip and connect to another's, but he could *see* inside a person's chip, inside their mind. For him it was not just a miracle of science, but hope that the oldest and most frustrating questions in neuroscience could possibly, finally, be answered. My dad began to experiment with his chip. He discovered he had the ability to not only upload messages, like my mother, but also download. He could download information from people's minds and use it as if it was his own. He could learn languages, sciences, how to perform open heart surgery, and the like, all instantaneously.

He was the first to have more than one chip. He gave them to himself in secret and ran his own tests. He found that the extra room created not only space but also speed. It was only a matter of time before he found that he could use his chip to connect to computers and download information that way. He was unstoppable, and so different from the average Chip Utilizer that they had to label him differently. He was the first human to show the Advanced Neurological Gateway Elemental Link. The acronym "ANGEL" was quickly adapted, and the team thought it was a fitting name, because in a technological age such as ours, the link between human and computer theoretically made one capable of just about anything.

They firmly believed that if my father just happened to be an ANGEL, then there had to be more. And so the search began. ANGELs and CUs had power to affect the world in remarkable ways. The work of the chip had always been about neuroscience progress and advanced criminal investigation. But now something new had been born, and the team was determined to find and utilize all the ANGELs.

Though the original goals of the chip were still valid and researched on a consistent basis, the idea of ANGELs was so powerful the group named their sect of the FBI the ANGEL Project.

The scientists and engineers first tried to create these ANGELs from typical CUs. When they couldn't be trained, they tried adjusting their chips, but every attempt failed and created a slew of brain-damaged CUs. Through barbaric methods of testing and study, it was found that neither CUs nor ANGELs could be made.

It wasn't long before testing indicated those who could utilize their chips shared some similar genetic components. Testing me for the gene was an obvious choice, as both my parents were anomalies. That testing indicated those genetic components had been passed on to me. Everyone in the group, my parents especially, anxiously awaited the time that I would show signs of being a Chip Utilizer, and more hopefully, an ANGEL.

The FBI and the CIA began to use my parents on all sorts of jobs. They were proud citizens of the United

THE ANGEL PROJECT

States and more than willing to do whatever work it took to soothe angered nations, influence treaties, and deeply plant the benefits of democracy into the minds of leaders worldwide.

My parents traveled to far-off countries to speak with, and manipulate the minds of, foreign leaders and dignitaries. Individually my parents were assets, but together it seemed there was nothing they couldn't accomplish.

While my parents were away on missions, I was watched by various members of the group. Dr. Rucker and his wife, Carmen, kept me most often. My parents didn't want me with anyone who wouldn't recognize it if I used my chip. I was on watch twenty-four hours a day from the moment I showed the genetic capability to be an ANGEL.

With more and more CUs coming onto the scene, my parents were relieved of their jobs as foreign diplomats and were allowed to have the job they really wanted: working at the facility full time to research neuroscience in regard to the chip—and parenting me.

It wasn't long before CUs began being identified at younger and younger ages. With most of the population being chipped at birth, mere children were discovering they could influence the people around them by just willing it to be so.

TAP made a program, a school, where they could teach the Chip Utilizers what they were capable of and eventually train them to serve their country.

It was around the age of three that I began to show signs of being an ANGEL. When we were alone, my father worked with me to coax me into turning on my chip, which I could do. I could hear him talk to me in my mind, and I would respond back aloud. He eventually taught me to respond back internally.

My dad kept the fact that he believed me to be an ANGEL to himself; he wanted time to see how I was going to develop without the added pressure from the group. He told them all that I was showing signs of being a CU.

Things had grown difficult within the group for my father. His capabilities were growing by the day, and it was starting to make things uncomfortable. Some of his colleagues were fearful, and others were deeply envious. Even my mother wasn't immune to feelings of envy.

The trouble in the group solidified his desire to keep my growing capabilities a secret. He didn't want me in the school with the other kids, opting instead to keep me with him and my mom in the lab. He and I often had mental conversations during the day, to train, just the two of us. He taught me how to implant messages and download information from other people's chips by the time I was four.

Something stuck out to me then, as I watched myself interact with my parents as a child just shy of five. And it struck me to my core. My mother's belly was round. She was pregnant.

The school within the facility had grown in size to have more than one classroom, and child CUs were being added to the ranks weekly. I used to sneak over to the school to watch the other kids and wish that I could be with them. My mother thought I should be, and my father finally allowed me to attend class with the other kids one day a week.

I sat next to Dominic Garcia. I was five at the time and he was nine, but I could tell he was different than the other kids. Dominic was the first person, besides my father, who I could communicate with through the chip. Because of this, we often migrated toward each other in class. He'd help me draw rainbows and unicorns, my two favorite things, and I'd teach him the lessons my dad was teaching me about how to use the chip. I told him what my father told me about the need for secrecy. We couldn't tell anyone about our capabilities.

As I got older and the threat grew of other people in the group finding out what I could do, my father implanted a message within me that I was never to tell anyone about my capabilities, including my mother.

But that message didn't stop me from talking to Dom between chips. I wasn't telling him about my capabilities; I was showing him. And we were the same, him and I. He stuck up for me when the other kids thought I was weird. He would draw with me when I was sad and needed a break from all the fighting at home.

My home life was difficult. My parents were always on edge. I was often charged with watching my little brother, Johnny, while my parents fought in their room. I would read him books and tell him grand stories about faraway places I'd make up on the spot. He was sweet and snuggly and almost always smelled like maple syrup because toaster waffles were one of the few things I could make.

Relations between my parents continued to deteriorate. And it was becoming increasingly difficult for my dad to manage my mother's mind. She didn't like that my dad was an ANGEL. She didn't want him to have an advantage over her. But my father couldn't change what he was any more than she could.

One day when I was sad in class, Dom asked me if I wanted him to draw me a picture of Una. Una was a unicorn Dom had imagined up. She was mischievous and had extra special capabilities and was always getting herself into different kinds of trouble. He used to make me books about Una. He wasn't the best artist, so he would author them and let me draw the pictures. We'd been writing stories about Una for two years.

Even as an eight-year-old, I knew Dom was just humoring me with the stories, but I loved them, and they never failed to make me smile. He knew when I was sad, and he would coax me to open up about it through the chip, but never out loud. I'd tell him about my baby brother, Johnny, and my parents, and about what I was learning in the lab. He asked me a lot of questions about the things I was learning with my father in particular, and in a matter of time, he was able to do a lot of the things we discussed.

I laughed when Dom asked me if I wanted him to draw a picture of Una for me, because his pictures were so bad, they were more likely to sour a child's mood than brighten it. My dad walked into the classroom to get me while Dom and I had this conversation between our chips. His mouth gaped open.

THE ANGEL PROJECT

My father had been going into my file on the lab computer and deleting or adjusting anything pointing to my extra special capabilities. He knew Dominic and I were friends, and that we sat next to each other in class. If he'd ever questioned why I'd gravitated toward someone of the opposite gender who was significantly older than I was, it probably, in that moment, made perfect sense. Constantly deleting things from his and my files was hard enough—there was no way he could add Dom to the list.

TAP had not yet successfully located any more ANGELs. They'd found hundreds of CUs with a wide range of capabilities, but none of them had shown the skills my dad had. He infiltrated their chips often enough to know that some in TAP were beginning to think that ANGELs were capable of too much and that they were a threat that might have to be eliminated. It seemed for the moment that the ANGEL Project would be about eliminating ANGELs rather than utilizing them. He well knew the history of TAP in regard to CUs, and they were very much capable of eliminating whomever they wanted.

When he saw Dom and me communicating through the chip, he was faced with the fact that there was another ANGEL—one who wasn't related to him, and that meant there had to be more. Dom was a child of thirteen at the time and clearly a good friend to me. My father began to change tactics. He thought maybe he ought to try and persuade TAP that ANGELs were more of an asset than they were a threat—a thing he wasn't even entirely convinced was true.

It was only six months later that my not-quite-three-year-old brother, Johnny, began showing signs that he was like me and my dad. The only problem was he showed our mother instead of our father.

When Johnny showed my mom what he could do, she went directly to my father. He was horrified that both of his children could be hunted down for how the chip interacted with their brains. He used her chip to adjust her memories of Johnny. He wanted as few people to know about his son's burgeoning capabilities as possible. That was when things really went south.

My mother had begun to suspect that my dad had been manipulating her through her chip. My mother knew my father was what TAP called a Stealth. Any CU could turn one someone else's chip, but the action would be flagged in the system. Stealths could use their chips to delicately coax a person into being the one who turned on their own chip, flagging nothing. Stealths showed up seemingly randomly in all levels of CUs. My mom grew concerned he was manipulating her without her knowledge, and so she, clever woman that she was, devised a work-around. She'd worked with a few of the engineers within TAP, and together they'd created a device that was worn on one's head and connected to their chip. They called it a transmitter. The goal of the device was to make it so any CU could use their chip like an ANGEL. ANGELs had too much power, and there were too few of them. When worn on the head, the transmitter could upload messages, read what was on a on an individual's chip, and download information from another's chip. They could block a CU from opening the wearer's chip, and they could force a chip open. In testing, even the strongest CUs weren't able to deflect it.

THE ANGEL PROJECT

When my father infiltrated my mother's mind to adjust her memories regarding Johnny's capabilities, she was wearing the transmitter. It was hidden by her hair. She knew for sure then that she was being manipulated, and she lost it. She started to become paranoid and bitter. Bitter at my father, bitter at TAP, at all of it. Even the transmitter, the ability to be an ANGEL, couldn't quell her fury.

She made a plan to out TAP to the public. She was going to go to media outlets and tell her story. She would tell the public what the FBI had been up to, about how they had all been chipped, and the consequences the chip could have. It wasn't that she'd never had moral issues with the chip—she had. But she'd always been convinced that the good outweighed the bad. The power the chip had to save lives through neurological advancements, and for public safety through advanced crime investigation, had always been worth the downside in her mind. That was until the chip was used against her. Then all bets were off. The chip could take everything away from a person, everything they'd worked for, everything they *knew*. It was too powerful when used for nefarious purposes, and she was ready to tell the world about it, hopefully to end the practice of chipping the public altogether. My mother was a well-credentialed woman, and there was every reason for the public to believe her, particularly with all the proof she'd gathered.

The fateful night of her death was different than I'd remembered it. I was with my brother, and my parents were fighting again. My dad had infiltrated her mind and seen what she was planning to do. He didn't bother trying to manipulate her through her chip because she always wore the transmitter. Instead, he tried to make her see reason.

He told her it would have dire consequences, that if the public found out there were nanochips in their brains that couldn't be removed, people would go insane. There would be a revolution the likes the world had never known, with no end in sight. He agreed the practice should be stopped, but the people who were already chipped, it was over for them. There was no recourse. His own experiments had yielded the same results as prior groups had found. Turning off the chip did something irreparable to the brain.

That wasn't the only problem. It would have dire consequences for our family. He told her I was an ANGEL too—not just Johnny. And that we weren't the only ones. There were others too.

She went slack jawed for a moment as several emotions crossed her features. The first was anger, then overwhelming sorrow, but in seconds it turned to acceptance. "I knew you were manipulating me. I caught you in the act, but to hide things about our *children*? This is madness. The chip is madness. Can't you see that?"

With his eyes imploring her to see reason, he begged, "I was trying to protect them, and you. It is madness, Evelyn. And I agree that it has to end, but they will come after us. They will come after our children. They will be hunted."

She started blankly into the distance, then turned back to my father and smiled sadly. "It still has to end, Charles. Even if we all go down with the ship." She turned to look at us, a single tear running down her cheek. "Even if my babies go down with the ship."

My father tried to coax her chip open, and when it didn't work, he went in with force. But she'd trained for this very moment, and she shut him out.

My father put his hands over my mother's cheeks, and in a voice that was thick, plead, "Don't do this, Evelyn. Give me a chance to find another way. We can do it together."

My mom started shaking her head. "The plan is already in place." Her expression was resolute, even with regretful tears streaming down her face. Her eyes were imploring my dad to understand. "You'll see it's the right thing to do."

My father dropped his hands to her shoulders and said, "Is there nothing I can do to convince you otherwise, Evelyn?"

She shook her head. "No." Silently weeping, my father moved his large hands from her shoulders to her neck and began to squeeze. My mom didn't stand a chance against my father's strength. Her eyes bulged when she realized what was happening. The only noise she could manage was a choking sound. She couldn't scream, so I did it for her—I screamed at the top of my lungs. Johnny, who couldn't fully grasp what was happening, cried loudly, yelling for his mom.

My dad looked at Johnny and me, recognition dawning that we were there, in the room, watching him choke the life out of our mother. The look he gave us was pure sorrow. But he didn't stop until my mother quit the fight, until her lips were blue and her hands fell lifelessly at her sides, her body still.

He looked at me then, sobbing quietly, and said, "Charlotte, you and Johnny go to your room. Don't leave there until I get back."

He went to the lab and adjusted our files to reflect that Johnny and I had never shown capacity to be CUs. And he added a delayed change to our chip serial numbers so once we were in foster care, the numbers would change and TAP wouldn't know how to track us. We would be officially lost to them. Then he went to each member of TAP and made his final manipulations to their minds. It was the end for him, and all he wanted was for his children to be able to leave this place and just maybe live their lives in the real world.

When my dad came back, he sat Johnny and me down and manipulated us into believing a different story than the one we'd witnessed. He then erased Johnny from me and me from Johnny. Then he called the police.

TWENTY-NINE

"I HAVE A BROTHER." I breathed out the words, more breath than sound.

The seat next to me on the couch sunk in with Dom's weight. He must have gotten up during the time I was swallowed up in the information in my file. "You have a brother." He took my hand, trying to get my attention, but I couldn't look at him. I was wrapped up in the revelation. So many things I thought I'd known had been turned on their heads. And knowing the truth made me feel more lost when I should have felt found. All I was left with were more questions.

Unaware of my mental state, Dom continued speaking," I don't know much, but I know that Johnny left here at the same time as you. Your dad had so thoroughly adjusted or deleted all the files here that no one was aware you or Johnny had any capabilities at all, including me. I remembered you, but not that you were an ANGEL. I didn't learn about what really happened until I connected with the lab computer and started downloading deleted files. Everything made more sense when I pieced together what was there with what had been changed and deleted. It was the same with Johnny's file. He was younger and there was less there, but he had your and your dad's capabilities. After your dad's guilty plea, when the two of you were sent into state custody, you were sent to two different places. I can only assume your father was the one to ensure it happened—he was the only one powerful enough to make it happen. He changed your memories, names, birthdays and birthplaces, then sent you to opposite parts of the country in hopes that you would never be found."

I turned to look at Dom. "Do you know where Johnny was sent?"

He nodded. "Florida."

Florida. I was sent to California, and my brother went to Florida. I wondered if that was an ode to our mother. She loved the beach.

Dom went on. "I won't pretend to know your father's mind, but I assume he thought that the two of you would be safer if you were separated." I nodded, sure that was true, but still completely dumbfounded. "It would have been almost impossible for the two of you not to learn about your real capabilities if you were together."

It was strange, having been manipulated through the chip and then having snippets of your life downloaded back in. I still couldn't *remember* that I had a brother—I just knew I did. I could see the love I had for him in those files, but I couldn't *feel* it, because all of that had been erased. How could I not feel that?

Had he gone to foster care? Did he ever go hungry while an older girl stole food and ate it alone, refusing to share? Was he ever hurt by the people who claimed to be caring for him? Was his heart broken by a family who refused to love him? Was he ever homeless? The horrible questions just kept on coming, and I cried. "Do you know anything else about him?"

Dom pulled me in close while he shook his head. "Not much. I was only thirteen when you all left. TAP was a mess, that was easy enough to see, but I wasn't privy to much information back in those days. All I know about Johnny is that he was here until just after his third birthday, he was an ANGEL, his memories were adjusted, and he was sent to foster care in Florida." My heart sank at the thought of a three-year-old in foster care. Too young to really understand what was happening to him. "Your father insisted on foster care for both of you." He looked at me sadly. "I'm so sorry, Channing. I love my brother—having him taken away would have been unspeakable."

The saddest part was that my memories had been so thoroughly adjusted that I didn't feel that loss, the loss of being separated from one's sibling. Not the way that I should have. Now that the knowledge of Johnny was there, I felt something for him, something akin to worry and definitely curiosity. But in reality, he was a stranger to me.

It made me so mad at my father. How could he take us away from each other? In foster care, they worked hard to keep siblings together. We could have had each other; instead, we'd had to live through the experience alone. I wondered if I felt so much more alone through that time because somewhere in my bones, I knew I had a brother, that I had someone who loved me and who I loved, and I'd lost him too. Taken from me in the most complete way, taken from my very memories.

Dominic cleared his throat. "Even though my memories were adjusted, I missed you. I know you don't remember it, but we spent a lot of time together. I loved you like a little sister. Aside from Anton, you were the only person here that I clicked with." He chuckled humorlessly. "After you left, I couldn't figure out why I missed an eight-year-old girl so much. Not until years later, when I finally saw my own deleted files and learned that we had a much stronger connection than I'd remembered. We were both ANGELs. You were the only other one I knew, the only one I could talk to, that I could learn from. You were so advanced at such a young age, far more than I was. There are a lot of my own memories that I want to share with you from that time, but it's going to have to wait." Dominic turned toward me and became serious. "Channing, there's something else I need to show you, and it's going to be really hard to see."

I felt chills prick my spine. "You're making me nervous."

"I hate this for you—I hate that this is reality—but you deserve to know. Not only that, but you *need* to know. What you saw was a portion of your file and your father's. Now you need to see your portion of your mother's file."

The chills pricking my spine now ran across all of my skin. Before I could say anything, a file slammed into my mind and onto my chip. It was my mother's. But it was only the end, after the time that she'd helped to create the transmitter.

THE ANGEL PROJECT

She'd seen the power of the chip. She'd seen what it could do to the minds of all human beings and in particular, leaders of other countries. The way a simple upload could change the course of a nation. With the transmitter, she could have the power my father refused to take. He was a coward, and small minded. They'd spent years fighting over how my father should be using his ANGEL power and status, that he should be the president of TAP, of the FBI, of the United States. He was a smart man, and with all the power the Brain Computer Interface gave him, the world could literally be his oyster. His and hers. Together they could have it all.

But my father was having none of it. He only wanted what was best for his family and for neuroscience. He'd never wanted the burden of being an ANGEL. He biggest dream in life was to go back in time to when they were professors and had a quiet life. But that quiet life was never coming back, and he simply refused to accept it.

Things came to a head when he tried to manipulate her about Johnny's capabilities. She used the transmitter to see inside his chip, to see what he was thinking. He didn't want her to know what their children could do because he was afraid that she was going to use them like she tried to use him. *Children.* Both of her children were ANGELs.

She devised a plan.

A few nights later, she told my father that she was going public with the information about the chip. The news produced the desired outcome. My father panicked. He was terrified and began to tell her all the reasons it would ruin them. That their children would be hunted down. Was that what she wanted?

The scene was the same as the one I'd seen in the earlier file. My parents were fighting, and Johnny and I were watching.

My father put his hands over my mother's cheeks, and in a voice that was thick, said, "Don't do this, Evelyn. Give me a chance to find another way. We can do it together."

My mom started shaking her head. "The plan is already in place." Her expression was resolute, regardless of her tears. Her eyes were imploring my dad to understand. "You'll see that it's the right thing to do."

But instead of my father encircling his hands around my mother's neck, my mother discreetly tapped on her transmitter and looked deeply into my father's eyes.

To my absolute horror, she implanted the image of him putting his hands around her throat and choking her to death. She implanted the image of him killing her, right in front of their children.

He dropped to the floor over what he thought was her dead body, but in actuality was only empty space, and let out a cry from deep in his chest.

My mother came over to me and Johnny and uploaded the same message to us. All of a sudden, our mother wasn't standing in front of us—she was on the floor, our father hovering over her, his hands wrapped around her neck. I began to scream, and Johnny began to cry.

My mother then came back and provided a body. A woman with fair skin and a dark chin-length bob. The woman had been choked to death. We were all so entrenched in our belief and shock and grief that we didn't even see my mom moving about the room. It was like she, the real her, wasn't even there. To us she was dead, and anything defying that understanding couldn't penetrate.

With the use of her transmitter, my mother adjusted the minds of everyone at TAP to believe she looked like the dead woman who was lying on the floor of our house.

The file ended abruptly.

Dominic was talking, but I couldn't understand him. My ears were ringing, and I felt like I was having some kind of out-of-body experience. *How*? How could she do this? How could *anyone* do this? Was my mother alive? Where was she? Where could she possibly disappear to? Had she simply forgotten about her children? Not that I would have wanted to live with her after what I'd just witnessed, but was she so ambitious that she didn't care about the human beings she'd created?

I felt Dom's hand on my shoulder. It managed to somehow ground me in reality, in the here and now. "That's all I have on her. I'm so sorry, Channing."

I shook my head, and I could taste my salty tears. Dr. Rucker's words from when I first got here rang in my mind. "The thing is, we knew your father; he was no killer, and certainly not of those he loved. We don't know what happened that fateful day, but we were one hundred percent certain that your father did not kill your mother." I bent over and groaned out a sob. I wished that I had been so certain. He was lost to everyone he loved, and he actually loved me and Johnny. He wanted a better life for us. I'd known from my memories that he was trying to save me from having a life he didn't want for me, but I had always, without a doubt, believed he'd killed my mother. I had no idea who he really was. "My poor dad."

Dominic rubbed my back. "Everything that happened after was in the file you already saw. All the rest is still true. Your dad believed he murdered his wife. He pled guilty and separated the two of you. He was in a rush and made rash decisions regarding you both, but I believe he was trying to protect you."

I sat up. The hurt in my soul for both my brother and my father made my bones ache. I honestly didn't know how I was going to go on in that moment. My brain had been so thoroughly adjusted so many times. Why was I even here? Who was I? Why would my mother bother to leave me alive? If she was never going to look for me, what was the point of it all?

I gasped and sat straight up.

When you're questioning your existence, call me.

With his fair skin and dark hair, he was an older version of the little boy I cared for as a child; he looked like a perfect mixture of our parents. *He looked like me.*

I pulled out the pink Post-it Note I always kept in my pocket, let out a deep breath of shock, and rubbed a finger gently over the lettering. Over his handwriting. "My brother's name is Pax."

THIRTY

"Johnny?" Shock sounded in Dominic's voice.

I looked over at him still next to me on the couch, and I nudged his chip. A thing only days ago I'd wished I could do but now was suddenly natural to me. It seemed that some parts of me were returning. I felt like the history I now had access to had cracked open a part of me that had been locked up tight. I was suddenly positive I was a Stealth like my dad.

Dom turned on his chip, and I showed him my interactions with Pax. When the memory I shared with him was complete, he sat back into the couch, eyes wide, and said, "Whoa."

I took a deep breath. "My thoughts exactly."

He turned his head to me. "We have to find him."

I held up the Post-it. "I've got his number." Then I smiled. I had my brother's number. I'd seen him and he was grown and healthy and smart. I remembered the look on his face—he was worried about me. He wanted to help me. I had a brother and he'd found me. A little too late, but he'd found me. I reeled in astonishment.

Thoughts of my mother dragged me back down, but not as deeply as I would have imagined. I had something more than her: I had a brother who'd found me. I did have one question. "Why didn't my mother ever look for us?"

Dominic's expression turned contemplative. "It seems clear enough from her file that she would have wanted your and your brother's ANGEL status. She wanted power, and as children you would have been hers to manipulate and exploit as she pleased. It seems logical that she would've looked for you both. On the other hand, she wasn't a great parent, and was more married to science than her family. Perhaps she didn't want to raise the two of you, but rather find you later when you would have been of more use to her? Either way, I don't think she was prepared for the action your dad took. He changed your names, birthdays, even your chip serial numbers. Then separated you and Johnny, with no knowledge of the other. I don't know that she could have found you if she'd tried."

I mulled that over. For the first time in my life, I saw my time in foster care as a blessing instead of a curse. I would rather be homeless and living on the streets of Skid Row than with her. "That might be true. I doubt she looked very hard for us if she did at all. She wasn't the best mother when she was with us. Add the small fact she made us believe she was dead at the hands of our father." Something dawned on me then. "The TAP people who tried to take me, they were wearing transmitters."

Dom sucked in a breath. "Yeah, we learned that the hard way. We've lost several people to TAP's manipulation. After you all left, the main group who made up TAP fractured. This facility and all we do here was absorbed by the FBI—we're now fully a government entity. But we learned, about a year after that time, that TAP still exists." He took a deep breath. "We believe your mother is the head of TAP."

And the hits just kept on coming. I scrubbed my face with my hands, then nodded. "That's the only thing that makes sense. After all she did, she wouldn't have just gone into hiding and given up on the chip. She created the transmitter to enhance her power. She wouldn't have stopped there." I paused. "You keep saying 'we.' Who had you been working with?"

"Agent Baldric and I had been working together, along with a couple of other agents, one of whom was taken by TAP and, we can only assume, brainwashed. That's a big part of the reason I don't want Anton to know that I'm awake. I need to finish the work Baldric and I started, and it's too dangerous for a regular CU. I refuse to risk his safety. After the incident with TAP, it was just Baldric, a brilliant agent named Vik, and me—who's been unavailable for a long time. I don't know what the team has been up to, but I sure hope they're still fighting the good fight."

"Baldric?" I must have said his name with too much of the distaste I had for him in my tone.

Because Dom said, "You've met him? He's a great guy and one of the few around here with his head on straight. In addition to being a CU, Baldric's also an Impenetrable, a person whose chip cannot be turned on by anyone but him."

"That would be extremely useful. I didn't know

Impenetrables existed, but I sure wish I was one. I've met Baldric; he was one of the agents who rescued me from TAP. It was Baldric, Vik, and Anton. Baldric's fine, I guess. He wasn't all that nice to me."

Dom arched an eyebrow. "He was probably worried you'd be more like your mom than your dad."

I reared my head back. "Ouch."

"It wasn't long after I recovered the deleted files from your mother and father and we pieced together what had really happened that I ended up overloading my brain. Before that time, I was trying to get Baldric to look for you. We knew that you were an ANGEL, and our team could have really used another. But he was against it. He thought if you were still alive, you would have already been using your chip. He must have changed his mind and decided to look for you when I landed myself in here." He looked at me and shook his head. "I still can't believe that they found you. Granted, I wish they would have brought you in sooner—maybe I wouldn't have been stuck for so long." He smiled. "Little Charlotte, all grown up." He looked me in the eye. "I would have found you, Channing. I would have looked for you with or without Baldric's permission. After I got your file and knew what really happened, I would have looked for you, and I would have never given up." The way he was looking at me, the depth of intensity, I wasn't sure what to do with it, so I changed the subject.

"Dominic, what are we going to do? I need—"

But my sentence was cut short when I noticed that we weren't alone. My mouth gaped, and I sucked in a quick breath. Dominic turned around just in time to see Anton in the mouth of the doorway.

He was looking at us, his eyes searching one face and then the other. He stepped in the door and let it close behind him. His shock was so full that he was standing there just inside the room as still as a statue. I wasn't even sure he was breathing.

Dominic said, "Anton."

And then the spell was broken. Anton blinked, and in his expression I saw confusion, hurt, disbelief, and utter shock. Then almost as fast as a tick of the clock, Anton swerved to the wall beside the door and lifted the plastic case over the red emergency button.

I saw his hand up, poised to strike it, and I heard Dominic say, "Anton, no!" at the same time that I yelled, "Stop!" The command reverberated through my mouth and brain in a way I couldn't describe. And then the craziest thing happened. Anton froze. His hand hovered over the button, but hadn't gotten quite far enough to press it.

Dom and I looked at each other. His eyes were wide when he questioned, "How did you do that?"

Only then did I feel the buzzing in my head. I hadn't even realized I'd turned on my chip. I shook my head slowly and shut my chip down. "I have no idea." And I really didn't, but the action of freezing someone felt familiar to me, kind of like talking to Dom through our chips. "I think I've done it before; I just don't remember."

Dom walked out from behind the couch and toward Anton. He walked around him, waved a hand in front of his face. Even touched his arm. When there was no reaction, he pulled Anton's arm away from the red button. Then he placed himself between Anton and the button.

He turned to me. "Can you unfreeze him?"

"I . . . I don't know." I walked closer to Anton and looked into his eyes. They were still open and showing all the emotion of the moment. The shock he must have been feeling. I wasn't sure how I had gotten him into this situation, but I hoped I could just open his chip and, I don't know, unfreeze him?

I turned my chip on, and to my surprise, his was already on. He wasn't frozen, exactly—his chip was in a struggle with his body. The chip kept sending messages to his brain not to move, and his brain sent the message to his body. But Anton was a CU, and his brain and chip were separate, so his brain was trying to override the message, but the chip kept giving it and freezing him again every time he'd make even the slightest of movements. I sent the message to his chip to stop fighting his brain, to allow Anton to have his will back, and then I pulled out. Nothing. He was still stuck there. I looked at Dominic, and I knew the worry I was feeling must have shown on my face, but all he said was, "Try again."

I went into Anton's chip a second time, and I tried to relax my mind. It had to be a message—maybe one with as much force as the first. Out loud and through my chip, I yelled, "GO!" I felt the message upload, and to my utter relief, Anton began to move his hand forward with force right into Dom's abdomen.

Dom let out a grunt. That had to hurt; Anton was ripped. Anton exhaled a shocked breath. "You're awake."

THE ANGEL PROJECT

Dom smiled through the pain and grunted out, "I was never asleep, brother."

Anton's eyes began to fill, and he pulled Dom forward into a hug. There was a lot of hard back slapping involved. Both of them were overcome with emotion but stepped back and shook it off. Anton then cocked his head. "Was I frozen?" Dom smiled and pointed at me. Anton's eyes widened to the size of saucers. "*You* did that?"

I shrugged and smiled awkwardly.

Dominic smiled widely." You have no idea the things she can do, brother." Anton's head whipped to me again. I shrugged. "She doesn't either, for the record."

Anton, unsure what to make of the new information, shook his head a few times as if to let it all sink in. Then he looked at both of us and said, "Listen, there's a lot that the two of you don't know. But to make it short and sweet"—he turned to Dominic—"Dom, I've been working with Baldric. When you went haywire, he approached me and told me that the two of you had been working together and that he needed me to help him. I wasn't as useful as you were, as I'm not an ANGEL, but I did my best. We've added a few people to the group since then." He turned to me. "Channing, you're now part of the team."

That was a shock. "I'm part of the team?" Why would anyone want me on their team? I was all but worthless. What Dominic had said about me not knowing all the things I could do was true. I didn't know hardly anything, and I didn't know how long it would take me to learn.

Anton nodded. "Yep. Baldric wants you. This is your official welcome. I was actually looking for you this morning to bring you in, and you weren't in your room. This was the tenth place I checked." He looked at both of us and said, "Guys, we gotta go."

Then in a flash, Anton pushed Dom out of the way of the red button and pressed it.

"Anton! What are you thinking?" Dom's face was white with panic.

"Hang on. It's not what you think. Frida switched the signals on this button. The only people who will be alerted that you're back are me, Frida, Vik, Ashti, Ginger, and Baldric."

Dom stepped back, calmer now. "The group did grow."

"There's no time to chat. We have a job and everyone's on it." He looked at Dom, "Well, everyone but you. **The powers that be don't know you're back yet, and if they did, they'd never let us take you so soon after waking up.** They're going to want to study you for months. So, to avoid that drama, we've got to go now."

Dom snickered. "Still believe it's easier to ask for forgiveness than permission?"

Anton smiled. "Old habits, man." They both laughed.

Anton turned for the door. I hesitated. Dom grabbed my hand and looked me in the eye. "Channing, I've got you. I know who you are, and I'm going to make sure that you do too. You are far more valuable than you think. Beyond that, you're valuable to me, for more than your capabilities." My heart glowed both from the way he was looking at me and the words he said. I wasn't alone, and perhaps I never would be again. I blinked a few times and then nodded.

I got my wits about me and asked, "Where are we going?"

Anton smiled back at me. "We're going to infiltrate TAP."

Those words, words that would have terrified me to death just days ago, now felt empowering. They felt right. I had a lot to learn about who I was and my capabilities. But my goals in life had changed. I no longer wished for a normal, quiet existence. I wanted two things in life: to find my brother, and stop my mother. From this moment on, I would no longer see myself as a victim, and I knew deep in my soul that success would be inevitable.

So, when Anton opened the door and he and Dom walked into the white hallway of the psych ward, I didn't hesitate to follow.

THE END

THE TRANSMITTER

Chapter One

PAX HOVERED OVER THE KEYBOARD; his fingers poised to make the necessary adjustments to the manuscript he'd stolen from Channing's computer. He was stressed out and under the gun, and if he kept biting the inside of his cheek the way he was, he was going to gnaw a hole right through it. Pax wasn't a writer, and he could never be as eloquent as his sister, but there was an opportunity here, and he wasn't about to let it pass. The FBI may have thought they'd put a hold on Channing's book release, but Pax and his crew had a different plan, and the wherewithal to carry it out.

"How close are you, Pax?" Harper asked for at least the thousandth time. He didn't respond—he just bit into his cheek harder and kept typing. She pulled the phone away from her ear and whisper yelled, "When will it be done?" She huffed out an angry breath when he refused to answer. "You can be so irritating, you know that?" He again withheld his response.

She sighed loudly and pressed the phone back to her ear. "He's still working on it, Harris. He said he'll be done *on time*. You'll have it by midnight." Harper hung up the phone and pointed to him and said, "You better not make a liar out of me, Pax." Then she proceeded to pace the large executive office. It was a corner office, on the top floor of a gorgeous building, just a block off the Magnificent Mile. The cavernous space was filled with top-of-the-line custom furniture, authentic rugs from all corners of the earth—the value of which could feed a small country—shelves full of books no one ever read, and a stunning crystal chandelier. To top it off, the whole space smelled like roses, thanks to the oil diffuser Greta had insisted on. Pax hated the smell of roses, but he tried his best not to complain about the musky scent, as it was Greta's office, after all.

Harris Green was Channing's editor within Walton & Barker. Pax and Harlow had used their considerable talents to lead the publisher to believe they were FBI agents and that, with a few adjustments to the original text, the release of Channing's book, *Chipped,* could go on as scheduled. They were instructed to make those changes and to have the revised manuscript to Harris by Monday. It was Tuesday. They'd been given a twenty-four hour extension but were told the whole project would have to be put on hold if Pax and Harlow couldn't get it to them by today.

Harlow was all but stomping on the faded Persian rug as she walked back and forth in front of the massive desk Pax was sitting behind, her long red ponytail swinging from side to side as she went. She was wearing kelly green pants and a Rolling Stones T-shirt that had a multi-logo graphic of an open mouth with the tongue sticking out, in a variety of colors. The shirt was knotted, and a sliver of the fair skin of her abdomen shown through. He knew they both looked out of place in the elegant office space in their casual clothes. Greta was constantly reminding them that no one wore jeans to work at Brink Technology. But they never listened to anything, and Greta well knew it. Pax didn't have time for a break, but he couldn't help spending one precious moment checking out Harlow's creamy skin, icy-blue eyes, and the light smattering of freckles across her nose. She was beautiful and stylish in a way that left an imprint on one's soul. At just nineteen—one year his junior—Harlow was impossible not to take notice of. "Your pacing is distracting."

She looked at him in mock surprise. "Oh! He speaks!"

He would have rolled his eyes, but he didn't have the time or the energy for the action. Instead, he just looked at her and deadpanned," I'm doing the best I can here, Sash. But you need to leave. Go get a Coke or something." He looked at his watch and swore. "Give me an hour."

She blew out a breath. "That's probably a good idea. I could use some air. Maybe—"

A phone rang. It took him a second to realize that *the* phone rang. The phone that Pax always carried, even slept with. The phone that he brought with him in the shower, and carefully sat on the ledge to make sure it didn't get wet. The phone that never, ever left his sight. The phone that only one person had the number to.

Harlow gasped. Pax froze.

It rang for the third time. "It's her," Harlow said.

Pax looked at the phone and finally was able to move his limbs. He picked it up, pressed accept, and said, "Channing?"

ABOUT THE AUTHOR

L.A. Clayton has been an avid reader her entire life, devouring books at an alarming rate. Her husband often jokes that if she didn't buy so many books they could retire. She went to bed one night a reader and woke up with a fresh memory of a dream she'd had the night before, sat down and became a writer.

L.A. Clayton lives in St. Louis, MO with her husband and their four young children. She makes time for writing in between wiping noses and packing lunches.

Follow L.A. Clayton on her Facebook page:
https://www.facebook.com/authorlaclayton/

Made in United States
North Haven, CT
16 September 2023